PRAISE FOR

SETUP

"Collins combines personal tragedy, international intrigue, and vicious assassins to create a rousing thriller in *Setup*. With his marriage on the edge of failure and his law enforcement career in tatters, Booker takes a job in rural Virginia. There he meets the patriarch of an influential family, who heads a corporation targeted for a Senate investigation led by Booker's wife. As the story unfolds, Booker discovers connections between efforts to silence him, attacks on his family and friends, and the horrific event that started his downward spiral. Throughout the story, Collins skillfully weaves in historical references that add to the story's authenticity. The characters are engaging and believable. The crisp dialogue and fast pace keep the story moving relentlessly to the ending that is both unexpected and satisfying."

—C. V. Alba, award-winning author of *e-llegal commerce*

"Ray Collins delivers a gripping, high-stakes thriller in Setup. With vivid characters, international intrigue, and heart-pounding action from DC to rural Virginia to Geneva, this page-turner will keep you guessing until the very end. A masterful tale of corruption, conspiracy, and redemption."

—Jeffrey K. Schmoll, award-winning author of *The Treasure of Tundavala Gap*

"*Setup* is an engaging page-turner from Ray Collins, taking readers on a fast-paced journey through the nation's capital, rural Virginia, Switzerland, Germany, and Afghanistan. A disgraced Fairfax County detective, Andrew Booker, struggles to reconstruct his life after an unintended killing leaves his career and personal life in shambles. Plot twists will keep readers riveted through the final chapter."

—Karen Hughes, former White House communications director

Also by Ray Collins:

The General's Briefcase *Motive for Murder*

Setup
by Ray Collins
© Copyright 2024 Ray Collins

ISBN 979-8-88824-566-8

All rights reserved. No part of this publication may be reproduced, stored in a retrieval system, or transmitted in any form or by any means—electronic, mechanical, photocopy, recording, or any other—except for brief quotations in printed reviews, without the prior written permission of the author.

This is a work of fiction. All the characters in this book are fictitious, and any resemblance to actual persons, living or dead, is purely coincidental. The names, incidents, dialogue, and opinions expressed are products of the author's imagination and are not to be construed as real.

Published by

3705 Shore Drive
Virginia Beach, VA 23455
800-435-4811
www.koehlerbooks.com

SETUP

RAY COLLINS

VIRGINIA BEACH
CAPE CHARLES

This book is dedicated to my wife, Betty Ann,
who inspired my writing and made life meaningful.

CHAPTER 1

WASHINGTON, DC
2023

This was where the manhunt was destined to end, after endless sleepless nights, countless cups of black coffee, and one dead cop.

The street was unnaturally quiet, late on a baking-hot July night, in the cloistered neighborhood of mansions near the intersection of Massachusetts and Wisconsin Avenues in the District of Columbia. Only a few blocks from Embassy Row and the Washington National Cathedral, the neighborhood was rife with diplomats, government officials, politicians of all stripes, and wealthy entrepreneurs.

The mansions were hidden from the street, although their presence was showcased by twenty-foot fences of Colorado blue spruce. No cars were visible in either direction. Had any motorist been brazen enough to park by the sidewalk-barren road, a Metropolitan Police Department cruiser would have been certain to check out the vehicle.

After stashing their unmarked a discreet distance away, MPDC Detectives Andrew Booker and Louella Bernstein hurried quietly toward the recently vacated residence of Franco Moretti. The detectives were checking out a report from a neighbor who was walking his German Shepherd just before midnight when he claimed he'd spotted the fugitive sneaking into his former residence.

Moretti had gained notoriety as a criminal on the FBI's Most Wanted list. Book and Lou had squandered half of July attempting to track down the fugitive. They took over after the FBI and the US Marshals Service abandoned the search in the Washington area based upon reports the killer had fled overseas, probably to Sicily where his relatives were high-ranking mafia. Moretti—wanted for murdering his wife, business partner, and a police detective, as well as the brutal killing of a mother and toddler during a carjacking—had disappeared in June.

"Someone's flashing a light in a second-floor window," Lou said, pointing at the right side of the residence.

"That's the master bedroom," Book said. "There's an intruder. Based on the neighbor's report, it's Moretti. Call for backup."

"Done," she said, nimbly keying the 10-33 *officer needs assistance* transmission. Her iPhone's GPS would pinpoint their location.

"We'll wait for backup to arrive . . . hold on . . . the light's moving. He's headed for the stairs. The son of a bitch must've found whatever he was looking for."

"We need to go in *now*," Lou said. "We've never been this close. Let's get the bastard."

"I'll keep him pinned down inside," he said. "You wait here and alert backup to what's going down."

"Like hell I will," she said, giving Book an angry look. "I'm going in. We can't lose him when we're this close."

He was neither surprised, nor particularly upset, by her attitude. Lou had never taken to the role of junior partner in their partnership. Book had learned from his training officer the value of compromise to preserve a strong team.

The daughter of Rosa Bernstein, a Black mother who was a lieutenant in MPD's Internal Affairs Bureau, and Abram Bernstein, a Jewish civil rights attorney, Lou had inherited her parents' independence of spirit. Her attitude was not humbled by experience as a guard on the Maryland Terrapins winning basketball team.

Tightening the Velcro on the Kevlar vest that protected her torso, Lou sprinted flat out toward the front entrance of the residence.

Fast as he was, Booker struggled to keep up. Not only was she a decade younger than his forty years, she'd narrowly missed being selected for the Olympic basketball team the year before joining the MPD.

Undaunted, he turned on the afterburners and almost closed the gap, just as Lou came to a halt before a massive walnut door. She grabbed the handle, soundlessly opened the unlocked door, drew her Glock, and slipped inside. He entered on her heels. He paused in the foyer to give his eyes a few seconds to adjust in the dim light filtering through the windows from a murky sky.

Book leaned close to Lou and whispered in her ear, "Remember, there are two ways down from the second floor—the main staircase that leads to the foyer where we are and the back stairs that exit to the kitchen, garage, and the pool patio."

She nodded impatiently. "I memorized the layout when we investigated the murders of the wife and his partner."

Book whispered, "Cover the back staircase. I'll go up the main staircase. We'll box Moretti in. If he tries to get past you, don't hesitate; shoot to kill."

"Not to worry. I'll waste him, and I won't lose any sleep over it."

Lou pivoted and walked swiftly toward the rear of the residence.

Book stood stock-still and stared at the steps leading to the second floor. He was getting concerned because the glare from the flashlight was no longer visible. The quick arrival of the detectives would not have allowed time for Moretti to reach the stairs, descend, and flee. Logic demanded he was still on the second floor.

Why'd he kill the flashlight? Does he know we're here? Did a lookout alert him? Lou may be in danger.

He took a half-step in the direction of his partner, halted, and paused to reflect. Common sense told him to stick to the agreed plan.

Lou was a big girl, capable of taking care of herself.

Moreover, if he followed her to the back staircase, there was a risk she'd perceive him as a threat and open fire without warning. She was famous for a hair-trigger reaction, honed through endless hours at the range. Even if she recognized her partner in the dark, he'd be leaving the front of the mansion wide open for Moretti to flee. Shrugging, he edged toward the main staircase and began to climb, slowly and quietly, pistol at the ready. The richly carpeted, squeak-free stairs posed minimal risk Moretti would hear his approach.

● ● ●

Lou stalked through the opulent dining room, glanced at a mahogany table designed to seat an even dozen and a glass cabinet that showed off sets of fancy dinnerware, and entered the spacious kitchen. A night light above the sink illuminated a rack of gourmet copper bottom pans dangling from a fixture over a massive granite worktable. A Wolf gas range and a Sub-Zero French door refrigerator completed the image of a kitchen fit for a master chef. She couldn't resist a hasty comparison with the cramped kitchen in her Chinatown condo, whose marginal condition was more than made up for by a fast commute to MPD homicide's offices.

Get your head out of your ass, Bernstein. Concentrate on finding Moretti. She halted midstride, cocked her head, and strained for any sound that would provide a clue about the fugitive's movements. All she could make out was a subtle murmur from the forest of ornamental Japanese maple trees, just outside the pool patio, swaying in the breeze.

Satisfied with the quiet, she took a step forward, only to be blinded by the beam of a high intensity tactical flashlight. Simultaneous with the light, the silence was shattered by gunfire.

The impact of bullets slamming her protective vest dead center between her breasts drove the breath from her lungs. Gasping, she reminded herself this was no worse than being struck by a basketball thrown with maximum velocity. A flash of pain in her left shoulder was a grim indication the Kevlar hadn't stopped all the incoming fire.

Instinctively, she blinked her eyes in reaction to the sudden brilliant light. Guessing she was taking fire from one or more confederates of Moretti, she fired and kept firing in the direction of the light beam.

A guttural scream told her she'd scored a hit on her attacker. Her eyes, now wide open, caught a glimpse of a figure kneeling by the outside doorway, attempting to raise his weapon. Calmly centering the Tritium illuminated sights on his head, she shot him three times. In combat, there's no such thing as too dead.

Before she could assess any remaining threats, another attacker stepped into the kitchen from the direction of the backstairs and started shooting. He was a better marksman than his partner. One of the bullets entered below her jawbone. She fell to the tile, blood trickling down the right side of her neck. She struggled to raise her Glock to return fire, but her system was in shock. Muscles failed to respond. The Glock slid to the floor. Looking up, she watched in despair as her attacker walked toward her, pistol raised to deliver the coup de grâce.

• • •

Book heard the volley of gunshots emanating from the kitchen area. His gut alerted him a worst-case scenario was unfolding. *Lou is under attack.* He spun and began rushing back down the front staircase, taking the steps two at a time. Reaching the foyer, he caught movement out of his peripheral vision.

Moretti stood like a statue at the head of the stairs, holding a bulky object in his hands. Book faced a choice between two bad outcomes. If he pursued Moretti, Lou would be unprotected. If he hurried to aid his partner, the fugitive they'd pursued for the past month would escape.

Realizing there was no choice, he raced toward the rear of the residence. As he reached the dining room, he heard Moretti's mocking laughter coming from the foyer.

CHAPTER 2

A tactical flashlight lying on the kitchen floor illuminated the scene. The first thing Book saw was Lou sprawled on the tile. Towering over her was a tall raw-boned man sighting a pistol.

"Drop your weapon, scumbag," he shouted, more to distract his partner's assailant than out of any expectation the command would be obeyed.

The gun barrel swiveled from Lou to aim at the detective. Both men fired simultaneously.

The bullet from Book's Glock impacted dead center in the attacker's face.

The attacker's bullet sailed into the otherwise pristine dining room. The sound of shattered glass echoed in the kitchen.

Book knelt by Lou, cradling her in his arms. Blood oozed from a shoulder wound and pulsated from a neck wound. He pulled out his handkerchief and used it in a futile effort to stanch the bleeding from her carotid artery.

Her eyes blinked and she gave Book a questioning look.

"Did we nail the bastard?"

Choked up, emotion blocked an immediate reply. Book had seen enough of the dead and dying, both in the military and as a police officer, to realize it was unlikely Lou would survive her vicious wounds. Comfort, not honesty, was called for.

He nodded solemnly. "We nailed him. Moretti's killing days are over."

"I knew we'd get him," she said, closed her eyes, and sank into a stupor.

Easing her body onto the tile floor, he whipped out his cell phone.

"Officer down. We need a bus ASAP. Alert backup Moretti has escaped. He's in the neighborhood, but he fled his residence a couple of minutes ago."

Book set his cell phone on the tile and redoubled efforts to stem the blood flow from Lou's neck. Desperate to find a more effective bandage, he grabbed a towel hanging on the stove's door, placed it on top of the handkerchief, and pressed firmly against the jagged bullet wound. Despite a fair knowledge of battlefield first aid, he had no idea whether his ministrations were helping.

Approaching sirens died, signaling the arrival of backup.

He was relieved to recognize a couple of former SWAT buddies when they ran into the kitchen, one of whom was Zach Waterman, his old SWAT commander.

Close on the heels of SWAT were a couple of paramedics, bold and impatient enough not to wait for the residence to be cleared. Barely giving Book time to get out of the way, a husky young Black woman and a beefy fortyish White man knelt beside Lou and began to check her vital signs. A slight frown on the woman's face was the solitary hint she shared his view concerning the seriousness of Lou's condition.

Without delay, Book briefed Zach on the situation.

"My guess is these two"—he gestured to the pair of dead attackers—"were the only bad guys in the residence, apart from Moretti himself. To be safe, the house and grounds need to be cleared. That said, tracking down Moretti is the top priority. He couldn't have gone far. He fled out the front door three or four minutes ago."

● ● ●

Book—frustrated he couldn't participate in the investigation of the residence or the search for the fugitive due to officer-involved rules—spent an anxious time at the Moretti mansion in response to orders of the SWAT commander. He prowled the halls, upstairs and down, observing his colleagues carrying out duties he usually performed at crime scenes. As time passed, more and more police showed up—detectives, forensics, and patrolmen who had their hands full keeping back nosy neighbors and the omnipresent media.

The SWAT commander confiscated the Glocks carried by Lou and Book as evidence. In return, he slipped Book a pistol for protection on a temporary basis.

Zach said, "Once we got word you and Lou had a serious lead on the fugitive's presence in his old residence, I organized the SWAT team to serve as backup."

"Thank God you did," Book said.

"My guys are canvassing the neighborhood. So far, nothing on Moretti. He might have gotten away on foot, but that's unlikely, since you saw him at the top of the main staircase carrying something bulky. He probably had a driver waiting after he fled the residence. If so, they escaped. MPD put out a BOLO."

Book shrugged. "Moretti's long gone. This time he's probably really headed out of the country."

Zach said, "Forensics found a safe hidden in the floorboards under the Persian rug in the master bedroom. The safe was empty, but there was an indentation at the bottom of the safe suggesting a sizable box had been concealed there for a long period of time."

Once he'd completed due diligence at Moretti's residence, Book retrieved his unmarked and pointed it toward George Washington University Hospital. GW had been the hospital to which the Secret Service rushed President Ronald Reagan after he was shot by John Hinckley. Book recalled Reagan's famous quip to his wife Nancy, "Honey, I forgot to duck." A line that will live in the gunshot Hall of Fame.

A level-one trauma center, with a full array of surgeons in-house twenty-four hours a day, the hospital was the best facility for treating Lou's gunshot wounds. Moreover, the paramedics would have gotten her from Moretti's place to the hospital in record time, taking advantage of the sparse northwest traffic in the wee hours.

He left his vehicle in the emergency room parking lot, entered the bustling, noisy waiting room, and waved down a nurse who looked vaguely familiar. He eyeballed her name tag to refresh his memory.

"Nurse Knightley, paramedics brought in a female detective shortly after midnight. She's a gunshot victim. Any idea where they took her?"

"I remember you, Detective Booker. Is she your partner?"

"Yes."

"Detective Bernstein was taken directly to the operating room, SOP for serious gunshot wounds."

"Could you fill me in on her condition?"

She waved her hand dismissively, a sign she couldn't or wouldn't give him a full response. "I wish I could tell you more. The only thing I can say is she was alive when she came through Emergency."

"Thanks," he yelled over his shoulder as he ran for the elevators leading to the OR.

Once at the nurses' station outside the operating room, Book deliberated how to proceed. He knew the doctors and nurses in this wing walked a life-or-death tightrope twenty-four-seven. Heavy-handed questioning would be counterproductive. He searched the staff but saw no one he recognized.

Finally, he bit the bullet and approached an attractive Asian nurse who seemed to be directing the flow of traffic.

"Excuse me Nurse Tran, I'm Detective Booker. My partner, Lou Bernstein, was brought here with a serious gunshot wound to the neck. Do you have any information about her condition?"

The nurse looked up at Book with large almond-tinted eyes, seemed satisfied with what she saw, and raised a finger in a wait-a-moment gesture. She consulted coding on the colorfully lit status board hanging on the nearest wall.

"Detective Bernstein is still in surgery . . . wait a second. Doctor Kennan is coming out now." The nurse pointed with a silver pen at a tired-looking surgeon exiting the OR.

The doctor appeared to Book to be in his late thirties, but he had that I've-seen-it-all-and-most-of-it's-awful attitude trauma surgeons develop early in their careers. He was a short man, mostly bald on top, with a fringe of hair fighting a losing battle with gray.

"Doctor Kennan," Nurse Tran said, waving to the surgeon who trudged over. "Detective Booker is Bernstein's partner. He's asking how she's doing."

The doctor sized Book up for several seconds, stood up straighter, and placed a friendly hand on the detective's rumpled and bloodied sport coat.

"Let's step into a waiting room away from this commotion where we can talk."

Fearing from the doctor's tone he knew what was coming, Book trailed behind.

Once seated in the recovery waiting room, Doctor Kennan said, "I'm sorry. She didn't make it. Her right carotid artery was punctured. The detective lost more than a liter of blood before she arrived at the hospital. My team worked on her for over an hour attempting to repair the damage. She was in outstanding physical condition, but there was too much trauma and blood loss from gunshots to her neck and shoulder. She died during the operation."

Book sat in stunned silence, trying to contain his shock. He resisted the idea that someone as full of vitality and joie de vivre as Lou could simply die. He couldn't avoid thinking the gunfight wouldn't have happened had he insisted on waiting for backup.

The surgeon sat quietly, giving the detective time to take in the devastating news.

At length, Book mumbled, "Please thank the operating room team for their efforts on Detective Bernstein's behalf," which he knew Lou would want him to say, if she were still able to call the shots.

Book trudged through a dimly lit parking lot, vowing he would move heaven and earth to track down Moretti and make the fugitive pay for Lou's death.

CHAPTER 3

Accompanied by Marlene, Book walked inside the Wright Funeral Home a few minutes before Lou Bernstein's service was scheduled to begin. His wife had given him a heads-up that the service would be conducted by relatives, since the facility was owned by Lou's uncle Curtis Wright. He guessed Curtis was the distinguished Black man standing next to Lou's parents Rosa and Abram Bernstein.

Pointing out the trio to Marlene, he said, "Lou told me she got her height from her dad and her athleticism from her mom. Looking at the two of them, you can see how that's the case."

Upon spotting Lou's partner, the Bernsteins headed over to greet the Bookers. Rosa gave Marlene a welcoming hug, even though the two women had barely connected in the past.

Abram vigorously shook Book's hand. The attorney seemed to tower over the detective's strapping six foot two.

Rosa turned to Book and said, "Come with me. We need to talk."

Puzzled, he followed as Lou's mom led him into what appeared to be Curtis Wright's private office. She closed and locked the door. Pointing to a leather settee, Rosa took the place nearest the window and gestured for him to sit next to her.

"Just listen to what I have to say before you react. I'm not going to beat around the bush. People tell me you're agonizing over Lou's killing as though it's your fault."

Taken aback, Book blurted, "It was my fault."

Rosa shook her head, commenting, "What part of 'just listen' didn't you understand?" in the tone of a lieutenant in Internal Affairs chewing out a subordinate.

Properly chastised, the detective mimed zipping his lip.

"Lou said you asserted your seniority, and most of the time she acquiesced. What happened that night at Moretti's residence was wholly predictable. You decided on waiting to enter until backup arrived. Lou insisted on charging in to ensure the fugitive had no chance to escape."

She paused to assess Book's reaction.

He nodded glumly.

"You went along to avoid a time-consuming argument."

He nodded again.

"Having Lou cover the back stairs while you watched the front ensured Moretti had no way to escape with whatever he'd come to the mansion to recover. Any partner would have done it like that. There was no way to predict Moretti's confederates would ambush and kill Lou. You did nothing wrong. The fugitive's escape was unavoidable."

She seized Book, her fingernails digging into his shoulders like talons of steel, and shook him with a ferocity comparable to what Lou herself might have done.

"Lou's killing was not your fault."

Book slumped forward, tears leaking down his cheeks.

Rosa pulled him into her arms and held him close. "Abram and I know what happened and why. We don't blame you. We love you for being a good partner to Lou."

The two sat on the settee in silence for several minutes.

Rosa stood and held out a hand to Book.

"Let's join Marlene and Abram for the service."

CHAPTER 4

MCLEAN, VIRGINIA

"Dad, are you and Mom getting a divorce?"

"No. Of course not. What makes you ask?" The response was a reflex, out of his mouth, without engaging his brain.

Book gazed in surprise at his daughter Rebecca, who stood in the study's doorway. The fourteen-year-old had one hand parked on her hip, signaling her impatience for this uncomfortable encounter to be over.

Like mother, like daughter was Book's next thought. Every day, Rebecca inherited more of Marlene—tall for her age, with the ponytail hanging down behind her back a brighter red than her mom's, complete with a Germanic nose that never hesitated to poke into where it didn't belong.

"I heard Mom talking on the phone with Ellen. Mom said she couldn't take on new clients and she'd have to cut back on her workload. Told her you're so obsessed with tracking Moretti it takes all of her energy to hold the family together."

Book gestured for his daughter to come into the room. He knew his drive to catch Moretti had become an obsession in the three months since Lou's killing. He'd grown increasingly guilty at the adverse impact the search was having on his family. Despite the reassurances from Lou's mother, he still felt responsible for allowing his partner to enter the fugitive's mansion rather than waiting for backup.

When Rebecca turned to close the door, he peered into the hall to see if her brother Jonathan was behind her. The twins often teamed up for serious conversations with their parents. No sign of Jonathan. He heaved a quiet sigh of relief. Rebecca could be a handful all by herself.

Rebecca settled into her dad's Stressless recliner, kicked off her ballet flats, and tucked one leg under the other.

Book rolled his black leather desk chair next to the recliner. "I know things have been rough the last couple of months. Mom understands I have a job to do as lead detective on the task force searching for Moretti."

Rebecca's look gave skepticism a new dimension.

He said, "No way I'll let the manhunt destroy our family."

Rebecca shook her head, the red ponytail swaying. "Sorry Dad. I've heard that before."

Stunned at his daughter's outspoken criticism, Book kept silent.

"I know all about Moretti," Rebecca said. "He murdered his wife and business partner. And he was responsible for Lou getting killed. Before Lou, he killed Detective Shanahan. I met Detective Shanahan when he came to one of our soccer games to watch Eden. He was nice. He never shouted at the girls like a lot of parents."

Book took the comment to mean his and Marlene's occasional cheers at an outstanding play by Rebecca or one of the other girls didn't cross the invisible line of a teenager's idea of good sportsmanship.

She leaned forward, eyes brimming with tears.

Book struggled to keep his face expressionless.

Rebecca brushed away the tears and shrugged, as though trying to distance herself from her own words. "You're the detective in charge of catching the monster. I get that. But arresting him won't bring Lou back. Sending him to prison won't make up for hurting Mom. Don't worry about Jonathan and me. We can tough it out, even though I've had some harassment, but you've got to look after Mom. The other day, I heard her crying in her study. Mom never cries."

Book pulled his chair even closer and reached out to touch his daughter's shoulder.

"I promise you, Rebecca, I'm going to find ways to spend more time with Mom. I'm also going to do better at showing up for soccer games. The new era starts tonight. I've made reservations for our wedding anniversary at the 1789 restaurant in Georgetown. We're all going."

Rebecca's expression brightened. "Isn't that where you proposed to Mom?"

"It is."

"Mom told me you ordered the meal, but, when she said yes, you got so excited you hustled her outside and you guys left without eating."

"True. Romantic, if I do say so myself."

"Extremely romantic. In a birds-and-bees discussion, Mom said that was the night Jonathan and I were conceived."

Flabbergasted his daughter was aware of her parents' intimate history, Book was struck dumb.

• • •

Book counted on putting some points on the board for the good guys as he drove his family from their McLean home in suburban Fairfax County, Virginia into the heart of nightlife in downtown Washington, DC.

On the drive along the George Washington Parkway, he steered cautiously through the thick fog hanging low from the roadway to the Potomac River. The temperature was mild for late October. Rain held off, despite ominous black clouds hiding the moon and stars.

Rebecca said, "Look at the lights of the ghosts flying on the far shore."

Jonathan scoffed. "Those aren't ghosts. They're just tired commuters straggling home along Canal Road after a long day in government offices."

"You have no soul, Jonathan."

Book couldn't believe his good fortune as he whipped into a parking place in historic Georgetown a mere block from the restaurant.

He watched as Marlene stepped out of the Sequoia onto the sidewalk. Already statuesque at five-ten, the four-inch Manolo Blahniks that complemented a black silk Armani pantsuit added to her intimidating elegance. Auburn hair in a flared cut framed her oval face.

Fierce lawyer's eyes telegraphed "don't fuck with this redhead or my family" as she stared down a rambunctious group of college kids sporting Georgetown Hoyas Bulldogs on their sweatshirts and crowding out others on the sidewalk. Book suppressed a smile, watching the ringleader of the group edge away, giving his wife a wide berth.

Rebecca and Jonathan bounded out of the back seat of the SUV. Hints of the heartbreaker Rebecca was turning into shone through a coltish shyness. Jonathan stretched to his full height, standing next to his sister. With black hair, square jaw, and wide shoulders, a preview of the man he would become was beginning to show.

Book's attention was drawn to the shadowy image of a stocky man smoking a cigar who walked briskly to the corner of 36th Street and leaned against a lamppost. Book recognized him instantly. Moretti.

Book squeezed Marlene's arm.

"Take the kids inside and order. You know what I like. I'll be back in a few minutes. There's something I've got to do."

Marlene gave him a puzzled look but herded the youngsters into the restaurant. Book counted on her to realize he wouldn't make such a request without a good reason.

He whirled, drawing his Glock. Holding the weapon at his side so as not to alarm passersby, he raced toward the shadow. He believed fate had given him a chance to avenge Lou's killing.

Moretti threw away the cigar and took off running south toward the Potomac, glancing back to check whether his pursuer was following. Book caught a glimpse of his nemesis when he dashed across the street and into an alley.

Sprinting to the alleyway, Book paused by a brick town house to peer around the corner. The gloomy sky was a major hindrance. Heavy fog from the nearby Potomac River obscured his vision. The alley was a black hole with an imaginary DO NOT ENTER sign.

The detective stood stock-still, senses heightened to catch any movement or sound. He could hear a barely discernible shuffling and chalked it up to rats scurrying through garbage.

Backlit from the hazy twinkle of distant streetlights, Book knew he would be an easy target if he stepped into the alley.

He was nervous Moretti could see him. Try as he might, he couldn't catch a glimpse of the fugitive. The alley posed a simple gamble—let a killer escape or risk his life. He resolved not to let Moretti get away again, no matter how high the stakes.

"Now or never," he muttered as he crept into the alley. The Tritium illuminated sights on the Glock glowed. No target was visible. He inched forward in a shooter's stance.

Without warning, a vague form shambled toward him like a disembodied specter, a dark form barely discernible against the gloom.

"FREEZE. POLICE."

Ignoring the warning, the specter continued to stagger forward.

Book ducked instinctively when he heard the telltale crack of bullets, coming from the direction of the advancing figure. They whistled over his head.

His Glock exploded. Three rounds aimed at center body mass struck the specter. The figure jerked, lurched a few steps, and fell face down on the brick pavement.

Out of nowhere, the shrill whine of a siren pierced the night.

The flashing light bars of a police cruiser illuminated the alley. Two cops jumped out.

"What the . . ." Book puzzled how they'd gotten here so soon.

"POLICE. Drop your weapon. On your knees. Hands behind your head."

Blinded by a Maglite, Book obeyed immediately. He was humiliated to be on the receiving end of commands he'd often uttered.

"Hold it. I'm a cop. Detective Booker."

A stout Black woman, about five-eight, with a veteran's tough stare, held her weapon at her side. Book pegged her partner as a nervous rookie who pointed his pistol and looked as though he was about to fire.

"Let's see some ID." The senior officer took charge. Blinking, he could read her name tag, Mattie Jackson. He saw the sergeant's stripes on her sleeve. Her air of command indicated she'd been through this routine before.

"I'll show my shield."

After Book verified his identity as a detective with the Metropolitan Police Department, Sergeant Jackson holstered her pistol.

He picked up his Glock, rose to his feet, and explained to Jackson, "I spotted Franco Moretti on 36th Street. Gave chase. Pursued him into this alley. Shot in self-defense when fired upon."

From her nod, he could tell she recognized the name of the number one person on the FBI's Most Wanted.

Jackson approached the prone figure. Shone her flashlight on the motionless body. Leaned over to check for vital signs. Jumped back in alarm.

"What the hell are you trying to pull, detective?" The baleful glare of an outraged cop nailed Book.

In the flare of her flashlight, he got a clear look at the face of the person he'd shot. He was flabbergasted to see it was a Black teenager that lay spread-eagle in the alley's debris—not Moretti. Then he looked closer. It was Scooter.

Book was stunned. The situation baffled him. How had Moretti rigged the scene to create the illusion he was in the alley, but managed to push the kid into the line of fire?

Horrified to have accidentally killed the youth, but befuddled by the scenario, he turned to Jackson.

He realized the veteran cop was not believing a word he said as she listened, for the second time, to the detective's allegations about the pursuit of Moretti.

"Stop bullshitting. You're under arrest."

With a "don't try anything" look, Jackson leveled her pistol at Book, confiscated his Glock, and cuffed him. For the first time in his life, he experienced the debasing routine of being locked into the rear of a police cruiser.

CHAPTER 5

WASHINGTON, DC

The administrative hearing to determine the culpability of Detective Andrew "Book" Booker in the shooting death of Julian "Scooter" Thomas, age fifteen, convened three weeks later on a blustery November morning.

Looking wise and judicial, Jeremiah Birmingham, whose bald head sloped into an immense forehead, was the presiding officer. An impressive six-six giant, who topped the scales just shy of three hundred pounds, he had a "take no prisoners" reputation.

The good news was Book had heard Birmingham treated almost everyone as equal, irrespective of gender, race, or ethnicity. On the bad news side of the ledger, he was reputed to hate *all* cops who had the misfortune to become the target of an administrative hearing.

"Detective Booker, you knew the victim, Julian 'Scooter' Thomas?" he asked in a tone that allowed for one possible answer.

"Yes, I did." Book struggled to keep his features neutral, determined to win this battle of wits and will.

"Testimony from your fellow detectives indicates you were on the lookout for Thomas. According to reports, he harassed your daughter, Rebecca Booker, near her school."

Following the advice of his police union lawyer, who had cautioned him to speak only when essential, Book kept silent. Sitting quietly, he couldn't avoid a heart spasm while he conjured up the image of Rebecca's tears when she'd related the incident with Thomas.

"Your daughter was tracked down by Thomas after a drug deal gone bad," Birmingham pressed.

Book said, "No," his voice guarded. "I searched for the teenager to set him straight about a case of mistaken identity. Rebecca was never involved. Another girl confided to my daughter that she bought the drugs from Thomas."

Birmingham said, "When you found Thomas, did you 'set him straight?' Did you drug the victim, lure him into that alley, and kill him in revenge for the threat you believed he posed to your child?"

Book fought to remain calm. Advised by Marlene that any reference to his anguish at shooting the Black teen would be interpreted as contrived and self-serving, he stuck to the bare facts.

"I didn't *find Thomas* anywhere. I chased Franco Moretti, a fugitive on the FBI's Most Wanted list—a murderer who was armed and dangerous. He ran into that alley. Someone fired at me. In the dark, I returned fire at an obscure figure, thinking it was Moretti who was shooting at me. I had no way of knowing the youngster was there. I feel terrible it happened, but Thomas's killing was a tragic, unavoidable accident."

Birmingham raised his eyebrows.

"Crime scene investigators found no evidence anyone was in the alley, other than you and Thomas. No firearm was found. No shell casings were recovered, except those ejected from your Glock. We only have your unsupported word you were fired upon."

"I was set up. No shell casings were recovered because the shooter fired a revolver. Whoever shot at me escaped through the other end of the alley, while the police were arresting me."

"Detective, you were in the Army in Iraq and Afghanistan after 9/11, correct?"

"Yes."

"You were a sergeant in Special Forces upon discharge?"

"Yes."

"Three years before becoming a detective, you joined DC's SWAT unit, the Emergency Response Team. The SWAT commander said you were the 'best of the best.'"

"The SWAT commander was always generous in his evaluations."

"With such an outstanding record in the military and in the police, do you expect us to believe you would miss your target and shoot an unarmed Black teenager. Someone you've admitted you had been searching for?" Birmingham never raised his voice, but his questions reverberated against the walls of the hearing room.

"I was in close pursuit of a dangerous fugitive. The alley was pitch dark. A figure came toward me, ignoring the command to freeze, even though I'd identified myself as a cop. Shot at twice, I followed protocol and returned fire. I now realize the shots came from someone lurking in the alley behind Thomas. There was no way of knowing Thomas or anyone other than Moretti was even in the alley."

"Let's return to your tour in Afghanistan for a moment. The soldiers in your unit said you had a nickname, 'Mad Dog.' What did that mean?"

"You'll have to ask them." Book's stomach cramped. He knew what was coming.

"We did," Birmingham said, unable to keep a note of triumph from his voice. "They testified you would kill as many of the enemy as possible in combat. Your buddies said you did this in retaliation for Americans slain. Why were you so aggressive?"

Sweat trickled down the back of the detective's neck. His shirt was soaked under both arms.

"Afghanistan was war. The Taliban was the enemy. 9/11 started there. Our troops were being gunned down and blown up. Insurgent warfare at its ugliest. We had to stop the Taliban with force. Fight terror with fear of reprisal. Raise the stakes."

"Become a Mad Dog," the presiding officer said.

"I was a soldier, doing my duty."

"Were you doing your duty or seeking vengeance when you killed a defenseless sixteen-year-old?"

"The alley was a setup, staged by Moretti." He clenched his fists in frustration. The system was grinding him down. He knew his life was heading for a train wreck, and there was no way to get off the tracks.

• • •

The administrative hearing dragged on. Book was saved by the unwillingness of the DC police to hang one of their own out to dry and incur even worse publicity.

The media crucified the detective and derided the DC government for refusing to mete out punishment. Book's resignation was accepted but was a product of unofficial blackmail. A court trial ended with acquittal by a hung jury, thanks to a brilliant defense by Lou's attorney dad Abram Bernstein. The prosecutor refused to retry the case. Book's career in the District was finished.

Months of stress destroyed his personal life. In the spring, Marlene hinted at divorce if he couldn't pull out of the paralysis that gripped him from morning to night. Rebecca and Jonathan spoke to their dad, when at all, in monosyllables.

Book was on the brink of turning into the cliché of an ex-cop—a bitter, self-pitying drunk. He sat in a bar on M Street, near the location where his career had been destroyed, nursed a bourbon, and agonized over who set him up and why.

CHAPTER 6

JEFFERSON COUNTY, VIRGINIA
2024

Carmen Garcia bounded down the staircase from her apartment above the garage at Stephanie Wilkerson's hundred-acre farm. She glanced with mixed feelings at her green, piece-of-shit Honda Civic. Even used, the car had given her good service for four years at the University of Virginia. Striding past her personal car, she climbed into an almost-brand-new Ford Police Interceptor—SHERIFF emblazoned on the door—and drove it out of the garage. On the ride to Courthouse Square, she wondered if this Friday morning would bring more surprises from the sheriff.

Slipping into one of the assigned spaces in front of a multistory brick building on Main Street, she looked with pride at the bronze plaque beside the front entrance, "Sheriff's Office, Jefferson County, Virginia." Radiating a feeling of belonging, the rookie deputy sheriff strode across the scarred wooden floor in the heart of county law enforcement. She waved a cheerful good morning to Shirley Ralston.

Shirley smiled and waved back. "Morning. The sheriff wants to see you."

Shirley was a vivacious woman with brown hair, pushing forty, with a Nationals sweatshirt hanging over her blue jeans.

Administrative assistant to Sheriff Pat Garrett for over ten years, her good humor tended to smooth relations with colleagues in the office. Carmen had heard she knew by sight damn near every person who lived in Jefferson County.

Gazing through the blinds in the wall, Carmen noticed a tall stick of a woman in dark clothing standing in a corner of the sheriff's office. "Who's in with Pat?"

"Horsewoman Mary."

Pondering the cryptic reference, Carmen was distracted by laughter from the nearby office occupants—Sam Headley and George Lyman. The pair were as different as Laurel and Hardy.

Overweight and out of shape, George did nothing to improve the look of an unpressed uniform. His gut hung over his belt like an inner tube ready for a ride in the river. Misogynist and racist, the roly-poly deputy never met anyone he couldn't belittle. Carmen's gender and Hispanic heritage were prime targets for George's so-called humor.

Sam was rail thin, with stringy hair hanging over his forehead and a nose hooked like a hawk's beak. Not the sharpest knife in the drawer, the skinny cop was affable, but prone to go along with his chubby buddy.

"Crazy Mary, you mean," George said.

"Mind your mouth, George." Shirley shot a sharp look at the deputy, annoyed, which was as close to angry as she allowed herself on most occasions. The sheriff's staff knew to steer clear when she gave *the look.*

She turned to Carmen. "Mary's a friend of Sheriff Garrett. Years ago, she was a champion horsewoman. Wealthy. Lived in a big house on the outskirts of town. A string of thoroughbreds in a grand stable provided ample testimony she was an expert equestrian."

Carmen looked back at the statuesque figure in the sheriff's office, as if to match that image with what she was hearing.

"Her husband and two children were killed in a tragic auto accident. She went through a rough patch. Lost everything. Now, she's homeless. Her behavior's a bit strange at times. Mary never lost her love of horseflesh, especially quarter horses. She used to ride them in the rodeo. Some folks"—she glared at George and Sam—"call her 'Crazy Mary' 'cause she looks after horses."

"Whaddya mean, 'looks after horses'?" Carmen asked.

"At night, she goes into stables and checks to see if the animals are properly cared for. When there's a problem, she comes by the station and complains to the sheriff. He follows up, much to the annoyance of some of our so-called leading citizens."

Carmen saw Pat glance into the outer office.

With a talk-to-you-later gesture to Shirley, she hurried to the sheriff's door, gave a courtesy knock, and walked in.

Every time she saw Patrick Floyd Garrett, Carmen was reminded how much he was the spitting image of his namesake and distant relative, Pat Garrett, renowned for killing William H. Bonney, better known as Billy the Kid. He stood tall, a drooping black mustache prominent on a gaunt face. She'd heard scuttlebutt around the office that he dyed his hair, including the bristles on his upper lip, but everyone was careful to keep this speculation out of earshot of the boss. Pat was known as a brutally straightforward lawman, with few other affectations.

Sheriff Garrett rose from behind his desk. He got right to introductions.

"Mary, this is Deputy Sheriff Carmen Garcia. Carmen, meet my good friend, Mary Connolly."

Horsewoman Mary was a striking presence, albeit shy. Almost as tall as the sheriff, she stood ramrod straight, not budging from her chosen place in the corner of the office nearest the window overlooking Courthouse Square.

Sensing from the visitor's rigid posture her reluctance to endure the intimacy of a handshake, Carmen gave a polite smile.

Mary's skin was bronzed and cratered from too many years in the sun and saddle. Her snowy white hair hung down her back in a ponytail, caressing the silver belt cinched around an ankle length black denim skirt. A western style blue shirt with pearl buttons was topped by a buckskin jacket with leather fringe dangling from the sleeves. A Lady Stetson lay on the chair beside her. Black Ostrich cowboy boots completed the horsewoman ensemble. With her delicate bone structure and willowy looks, she could have been a stand-in for Katherine Hepburn as spinster Eula Goodnight teaming up with John Wayne as Rooster Cogburn.

Carmen pondered the incongruity—Shirley called Mary "homeless," but she dressed like cowgirl royalty.

Mary fixed the deputy with a piercing gaze. "Do you ride?"

Flustered by the abrupt question, Carmen hesitated. "I'm just a beginner. I moved here four months ago to take this job. I'm staying at Stephanie Wilkerson's farm. In return for taking care of the stable, she's letting me live in the apartment above the garage. Stephanie's kind enough to give me riding lessons; she says the horses need the exercise. Now that it's so nice and warm, I ride every morning before coming to work."

"Stephanie keeps a clean stable," the horsewoman pronounced. She gave Carmen a searching look.

The young woman began to feel anxious at the scrutiny, wondering if she should say something to break the silence. Taking her cue from the sheriff, she kept quiet.

After a few moments, Mary said, "Stephanie is good at taking care of horses, but she's never been much of a rider. After this is over, I'll give you lessons myself."

After what *is over?* Carmen pondered.

CHAPTER 7

Interpreting Carmen's bafflement as acceptance of riding lessons, the sheriff tilted back the antique oak swivel chair behind his desk and said, "Now that that's settled, I'd like Mary to tell you what she just told me. Please sit down."

Prepared to hear another scandal of a stable with neglected horses, Carmen sat. She wasn't sure what she'd expected when she accepted Pat's offer of the deputy sheriff position, but she had a feeling her goal in life wasn't to check out mismanaged stables.

The veteran horsewoman remained standing. After several beats, Mary broke the silence.

"Last night, I saw a man murdered."

Although shocked by what she'd just heard, Carmen resolved to appear calm. The deputy sensed from Pat's stillness that doing nothing was the proper response.

Mary continued speaking in the same modulated voice she'd used when talking about riding lessons. "Last night, around midnight, I went to inspect the stable at the Bronson place. While there, I saw a man murdered." She stopped talking and stared at Carmen.

Carmen now understood why the sheriff asked her to join the meeting with Horsewoman Mary. She anticipated an assignment to follow up on the alleged murder.

Mary continued, her hands tightly grasped together. "When I got to the stable, I heard two men arguing. Their yelling was upsetting the horses, causing them to stomp around in their stalls. I was about to tell the men to knock it off when they began fighting. I couldn't see them very well, but one man was taller and stronger. He kept striking the smaller man. The big guy pulled a knife and stabbed the other guy. I could hear the other guy begging him to stop. But the knife kept rising and falling. From the light outside the stable, I could see red on the smaller man's white shirt and suit jacket."

Mary trembled, hands shaking, and moved to the chair. She didn't sit but clung to the back for support.

"What did you do?" Carmen said.

"Not a thing. I was too frightened. The killer leaned over the body and felt the pulse in the neck of the smaller man. Leaving the body by the stable, he walked toward the main house. I couldn't believe my eyes. How could anyone be so cold blooded?"

Carmen kept silent, wondering what was coming next.

"Once the killer was out of sight, I sneaked up to the stable and took a closer look at the dead guy. His throat was cut, and his chest stabbed several times. The poor fellow looked like a salesman, wearing a cheap suit and tie. His white shirt was blood red. I was too scared to call 911. Anyway, it was too late to help him. I wandered around for hours, driven by feelings of guilt for having done nothing for him. I was scared, but I forced myself to go back. Would you believe there was no body? No blood? No trace of a struggle?"

She stared fixedly at Carmen. "I know what they call me behind my back—'Crazy Mary.' Last night, I feared for my sanity. Had I seen a murder? Had I imagined it? *Am I crazy?* In the harsh light of morning, I knew what happened was real. That's why I decided to notify the sheriff."

CHAPTER 8

After Mary Connolly left, Pat asked Carmen to remain to discuss the case.

"I'd like you to handle this alleged homicide for the time being. I've filled the position of detective-lead investigator. Today's Friday. The new man starts Monday. He's an experienced big city detective. He'll take charge of the case when he arrives. You'll work with him."

"Why me? I've limited police experience. I know nothing about homicide—assuming that's what's going on here. And I'm just getting to know the county."

"Being an outsider makes you ideal for this assignment," Pat said. "You won't hesitate to knock on doors a local might avoid. Everyone wonders about the goings on at Bronson Stables, where Mary said she witnessed the crime. Maybe you can find out. Besides, since you grew up in a rural county, you can understand the significance that the supposed murder took place at stables owned by the chair of the county board of supervisors in ways that the new detective might not. You can ask anyone about anything. Everyone will assume you're just being naive 'cause you're a newcomer."

"Christ, Pat, I *am* naive."

"Yeah, but you're smart and I know you picked up a lot from watching your dad operate as sheriff in a county very much like Jefferson."

"Is that why you hired me? That and the fact you served with my dad in the war? It sure as hell couldn't have been because I'm a woman and Hispanic to boot." Despite the hint of bitterness in her voice, Carmen refrained from mentioning she'd taken crap from George and Sam on both scores.

"My ties with your dad go way beyond fighting in Bosnia together. He saved my life." Reacting to the surprise in her expression, he added, "You heard right."

Pat leaned forward in his chair. "We got separated from our Special Forces unit. I'd been wounded in an explosion. Your dad had been shot, although I didn't find out until later. We hid in the woods for two days. He made sure I had water, even though at the end he must have gone without. He carried me most of the way until we could rejoin our unit. If it weren't for him, I'd be buried in the Balkans. He was awarded the Silver Star."

Carmen listened with amazement. She never knew. "The award was displayed on the mantel in our living room, but he never said a word about what he'd done. The politicians in our county somehow found out he was a hero. They talked him into running for sheriff. He was elected in a landslide. Dad's still the only Hispanic sheriff in Virginia."

She stared at Pat.

"I get it. Dad told me to apply for this job because he saved your life."

The sheriff shook his head.

"I'd give any offspring of Jose Garcia serious consideration. But that's not why you were hired. You were far and away the strongest candidate. You finished first in your training class at the Virginia State Police Academy. And I'll admit, your gender and ethnicity were a plus, since I'm trying to create a more diverse group of deputies. Prove I was right in picking you. Get out of here and start investigating."

CHAPTER 9

Carmen headed out to the Bronson place. She decided to keep Horsewoman Mary out of the investigation. If there'd been a murder, minimizing risk to the eccentric informant was crucial. If the incident were the ravings of an overactive imagination, little would be gained by feeding the woman's hallucinations.

The deputy spotted the sign BRONSON STABLES, with its colorful wooden painting of racehorses charging around a track and through the open gate.

The stable was an imposing structure, constructed of multicolored stone, with a slate roof and overhung steel doors leading to an outside training area.

Carmen walked into the stable, admiring the twelve stall doors and glossy shellacked oak walls. Eight stalls were arrayed along the west side of the building, four on the east. Each stall opened onto a spacious interior. She was surprised to see horses in just three of the stalls. The others were empty, their wooden floors swept clean. The smell of horseflesh, hay, and manure was the same as at Stephanie Wilkerson's stable—the same, yet subtly different.

The center of the stable floor was paved with small red tiles. The high ceiling was lit with a modernistic light network.

The tack room was at one end, with pristine saddles, bridles, and other gear hung along three walls. The wall facing the door displayed pictures of championship horses, along with the trophies won by Bronson Stables. An adjacent storage room held feed and other supplies.

Even new to horse country, she could tell this was a high-class operation. She wondered why a proud history was entering a period of decline. According to county gossip, related by Shirley Ralston, at one time the Bronson family was at the apex of Virginia horse society. Today, the stable looked barely used.

● ● ●

"Who the hell are you? What the fuck you doin' in my stable without permission?"

Startled by the gruff voice, Carmen turned and saw a wizened old man with wisps of gray hair. He held a riding crop in one hand, half raised, which made her wonder if he was about to strike. Her hand drifted to her holster, but she hesitated before drawing her pistol.

Taking a second look, she realized he was not a serious threat, even though he was younger than he first seemed, perhaps fifty. He was half a head shorter than Carmen, and so cadaverously skinny he resembled a scarecrow in a cornfield. His countenance was worn by the outdoors and pitted from adolescent acne.

"I'm Deputy Sheriff Garcia. Sheriff Garrett sent me here to check out a report of suspicious activity in the stable. I take it you're in charge?"

"Damn straight. I used to race these horses until I became head trainer. Now, I'm in charge of the whole shootin' match."

Pausing, his face wrinkled when the import of what she'd just said registered.

"What 'activity'? I know ever' fuckin' thing goes on 'round here. Ain't nothin' suspicious."

She watched with silent amusement, giving the crotchety old jockey time to look her over from head to toe, noting the uniform, badge, and weapon holstered on her hip—all signs consistent with her claim of being part of the sheriff's office.

"You're not from around here. I know everdambody in these parts. I ain't never seen you."

"I joined the sheriff's office four months ago, but I was born and grew up in Southwest Virginia."

She amazed herself with the last comment, a blatant attempt to curry favor with the cantankerous stable supervisor.

Even more amazing, it worked. His hostility appeared to ebb a bit.

"Oh, I thought you was one of them immigrants. Ain't too many of 'em 'round these parts."

"What's your name?" she asked, deciding the easing of his mood argued for getting down to business.

"Fix. Fix Magruder."

"What kind of a name is Fix?"

"When I was a jockey, I won most of the time. The other jocks always said, 'The Fix is in.' The name stuck. They didn' mean nothin' by it. Jist their way of feelin' better 'bout losin'."

"Well, Fix, does anyone work the stable with you?"

"Nope. I do it all myself since things have quieted down, jist three horses. Course there's this nig—" Fix coughed. "There's this Black kid who comes once a day to muck out the stalls. But I do all the real work."

"Fix, you keep a clean stable," Carmen said, ignoring his slip and echoing Horsewoman Mary's praise.

The ex-jockey said nothing, but slowly bobbed his head in acknowledgment. A bit more acrimony chipped off his crusty demeanor.

The deputy decided the time was ripe to cut to the chase. "Could we have a look around outside the stable?"

He looked puzzled. "What's there to see outside?"

Shrugging his shoulders resignedly, he trekked out into the sunshine.

A red-tailed hawk, wings widespread on the prowl for small mammals, flew across the azure sky.

Carmen walked around the perimeter of the structure, eyeing the ground with care, not sure what she was looking for, but confident any anomaly would jump out.

The ground outside was well packed, with the marks of a rake and push broom etched in the dirt. She noted hoof prints where Fix or another rider had led horses for their morning exercise.

The mysterious thing was that nothing was mysterious. Everything appeared in order. If there had been a murder the night before, as Mary reported, it was not apparent in the light of day.

With Fix walking in step beside her, she almost completed circling the stable, when, without warning, she halted. She struggled to figure out what had caught her attention.

Fix stood beside her, fascinated as he watched her stare at the dirt.

"Wait a damn minute," he said. "Now I know what's *suspicious*. This dirt right here." He pointed to the spot on the path where she was staring. "See how soft the ground is. Not stomped down hard from fifty years of horses walkin' over it." He kicked at the path for emphasis; his boot removed a clod of soil.

"Wait here," he said.

The deputy watched him scurry toward the storage room. He came back brandishing a rake and began scratching with the tool, soon scraping out a circle about four feet in diameter and three inches deep.

She now realized why the different textures of this part of the path had caught her subconscious eye. She mentally reconstructed events as they must have transpired.

After the knifing, the big man removed the corpse of the small victim. The killer returned with a shovel and scraped away any sign of a murder. He removed blood and other evidence, filled the hole with fresh dirt, and tamped it down.

In the dim light, Mary hadn't been able to see any evidence of the struggle and knifing, because every sign had been obliterated. No wonder Mary doubted her sanity.

Confident she'd accurately reimagined events of the previous night, Carmen was baffled about her next move. Unless the body turned up, there was no way to confirm a killing occurred. The evidentiary dirt and implements used to sanitize the crime scene were doubtless long gone. She looked up at the mansion on the hill and shook her head, deciding it was premature to raise questions with the owners. Monday, when the new detective arrived, would be time to take the inquiry to the next level.

She turned to Fix, who was staring at her quizzically. "I'd like you to do me one more favor. Check the storage room and let me know if there's a shovel or any other tool out of place."

He hurried inside. He returned at a slow pace, a frown deepening the creases on his forehead.

"My shovel's missing. How'd you know?"

"Just a good guess," she said. "Fix, I've got to go now. I'll be sure to tell Sheriff Garrett you've been a big help."

An unaccustomed grin cracked the old boy's face. His chest popped out like a proud rooster.

Driving out past the Bronson Stables sign, she wondered what the hell she should do until Monday.

CHAPTER 10

Carmen was running on fumes all morning. She was overdue to have a late lunch at the Jefferson Café.

The restaurant occupied a place of honor on one corner of Courthouse Square and was a favorite hangout for those with official county business—lawyers, clerks, and court visitors. Sheriff Garrett and his staff often stopped by to eat lunch or pick up carryout.

She'd dedicated her day to hunting for clues that would shed light on the stabbing victim. If he were a resident of the community, he'd be reported missing, sooner rather than later.

Carmen had a hunch the victim was an outsider. If so, the café was a prime spot to begin the search. Soon after her arrival in the county, she'd learned this popular watering hole was the news center for the community. The best source was the café's owner, now bearing down on her with a steaming mug of black coffee.

"Hey, Alice," she said to the fiftysomething smiling at her. She accepted the proffered drink with an appreciative tilt of her head.

Alice Higenbotham multitasked as waitress, chef, cashier, or whatever else needed doing. She opened the place first thing in the morning, locked up late at night, seven days a week. The restaurant had never closed except for half a day one Sunday when Alice had buried her late spouse, Gerald.

"Gerald was a sorry excuse for a husband," she'd confided to Carmen over apple pie à la mode, late one evening, soon after the newcomer's arrival in town. "He had a wandering eye for any gal with a short skirt, but he showed up every day, worked his ass off, and gained a reputation as the best cook in Jefferson County. With me handling the business end of things, we kept this place going for well on thirty years. I miss the old bastard. Most of all on cold winter nights. Gerald had a warm ass."

Carmen thought at the time: *Too much information.*

"Have you had lunch?" Alice asked. "I've got venison stew that's to die for."

The deputy, prone to accept any menu recommendation from the owner, ordered the stew. With no children or close family of her own, Alice had taken on the role of honorary aunt for the new arrival, soon after she became aware Carmen was taking grief from those, like her fellow deputies, George and Sam, who resented her as a woman, and even more for her Hispanic heritage.

During the afternoon lull, Annabel Lee and Lulu, the two waitresses, were occupied with busy work, wiping off and filling sugar containers and salt-and-pepper shakers. With a gesture of dismissal from Alice, they slipped outside for a smoke break.

"There's something I need to ask you in confidence," Carmen said, taking advantage of the interlude when she and Alice had the restaurant to themselves.

"Ask away, darlin'. If I know it, the information's yours."

"I believe someone new in town may be missing. I don't know what he looks like, but he's a small man, probably White, wearing a suit. Does that ring any bells?"

Alice's shrewd eyes lit up. "When you say 'missing,' what you mean is 'dead.'"

"You didn't hear that from me. But let's suppose someone came to town within the last week, ate here a few times, then disappeared. How would I find out?"

The proprietor turned thoughtful. She spoke as though thinking aloud. "People come through town often. Most times, they stop here to eat. Let's face it, you get tired of Mickey D's after a while. I'm guessing this guy comes in by himself. He's not a trucker or a farmer . . . best bet is a salesman, lawyer, or some other white-collar type. We get a few of those, usually en route to or from the courthouse. Most eat here once, maybe twice, if they're passing through."

While she talked, Alice kept a close eye on Carmen to see if she was getting "hot" or "cold" in her remarks. "Three guys who showed up over the last week fit the profile—White, middle class, suit-and-tie types, soft around the middle, not on the big side."

"Suppose I wanted to learn more about these men, how would I go about it?"

"Such men are as predictable as rain in the springtime. They come here, do their business, then leave. Since we don't know what their business is, that's a dead end. They need to eat someplace, and odds are it's here. If so, I've seen 'em, and it's one of those three men."

Alice proceeded to describe the candidates matching the profile of the man for whom Carmen was searching.

"In the majority of cases, they stay overnight, almost never at a private home. That leaves Bea's B&B or the Silverado Motel. Most men prefer the informality and convenience of a motel. At night, there's nothing for an outsider to do, except watch TV or go out for a drink, or maybe a little hoped-for romance at a bar. There's Jake's Bar out on the interstate. Or, if they feel like living it up, they might travel the twenty miles to the Old Virginny Bar and Billiards, just off Route 7, east of here."

"That's it?" Carmen asked, half disappointed there were so few clues and half relieved the task was more manageable than she'd imagined.

Carmen spent the rest of the weekend tracking down the leads she'd been given. Late Sunday night, she crawled into bed exhausted, disappointed she hadn't discovered one frigging thing.

She mentally summed up her efforts, concluding the sheriff's goddamn detective better hurry up and get here, because she was stumped.

CHAPTER 11

JACKSON COUNTY, VIRGINIA

Book pulled off Route 11 outside the Old Virginny Bar and Billiards and nestled the Toyota Sequoia between a rusty red F-150 Ford truck and a 2005 green Chevrolet Silverado. He was bone-tired and thirsty for a cold beer after the two-hour drive from the Booker residence. In his mind, cutting back from getting high and sometimes drunk on whiskey to settle for one beer called for self-congratulations.

The muddied gravel lot was Saturday-night-full of pickups and an assortment of vehicles of all ages and styles. A blue Jaguar XJ Sedan was parked near the entrance, angled to take up two spaces. He would not have been surprised to see the British blueblood in his neighborhood in McLean, but the luxury car seemed out of place here in the boondocks.

He shut off the Sequoia's engine and sat for several minutes. The melodramatic goodbyes of Rebecca, Jonathan, and Marlene had left him emotionally drained. He'd accepted Marlene's offer to keep the sixty-thousand-dollar sport utility vehicle, on the grounds the SUV would get more use in the rural area around Jefferson County than in the Virginia suburbs where mud was nonexistent, and snow and ice seldom impeded the roads more than a day or two.

Though loath to agree to a one-year trial separation, Book saw no alternative in the face of Marlene's insistence. He was shaken by the seemingly casual acceptance by his wife and children of the decision to get along without him, maybe forever.

Ever the lawyer, Marlene had dictated the terms of the separation: "Book, get your shit together." Whatever the hell that meant.

She would look after the twins, who were finishing their freshman year at Langley High School. Langley was a public high school, but it sported a student body from affluent and influential families—senators, congressmen, and cabinet secretaries—with bragging rights to one of the highest SAT scores in Fairfax County.

Marlene would commute four days a week to a prestigious law firm in DC. Doubtless working at home nights and weekends, following a grueling routine to put in her customary eighty-hour week. Small wonder she'd earned a partnership before she was forty.

During the sixteen years of their marriage, Book was never bothered by the fact his glamorous wife was the primary breadwinner. Neither of them came from families with real money. Book's dad was a printer with the Government Printing Office in DC and his mom taught English at the high school in Bethesda, Maryland from which he graduated. Marlene's dad was a county judge and her mom a nurse, both DC residents for several decades. Both sets of parents were now deceased.

They'd met when Marlene was a public defender in the District of Columbia trying a difficult case of a Black teen charged with the murder of a White woman. Book was a patrolman who'd witnessed the incident. After the trial, she'd asked him out to lunch, saying she'd been impressed with the candor of his testimony which exonerated the youth and enabled her to score a rare win in court. She confided the batting average for public defenders was worse than for rookies in the major leagues.

Everyone knew cops—at least not the honest ones—didn't make a fortune. Since the incident in Georgetown where he'd shot and killed Scooter Thomas and lost his job, he had a new awareness of the importance of money.

He was earning bupkis. His pension had vanished in the deal that led to his resignation. Marlene was bankrolling a multi-million-dollar McMansion in Fairfax, one of the richest counties in the US. A three-car garage housed a Mercedes S600 Sedan and a BMW 650i Coupe, with a vacancy for the Sequoia.

His pride had led him to insist on earning his own livelihood. Remembering the far from affluent countryside he'd just driven through, he was starting to second-guess his impulsive declaration of independence.

The more he reflected, the more desperate Book became for a drink. He fervently believed no grown man should have to stay on the wagon for three weeks.

Still, he delayed going into the Old Virginny. Thirst frustrated his determination to keep a low profile. With the bar only one county over from his future stomping grounds, he knew he was tempting fate if he walked into the establishment. He'd vowed to stay off booze and get back in shape before starting the detective job for Sheriff Pat Garrett. So far, he'd kept the pledge. He intended to quit drinking cold turkey after crossing the border into Jefferson County.

He stopped reflecting on recent struggles with sobriety. Thirst battled common sense as he stared at the sign that beckoned those trying to forget their problems, find a sexual partner, seek companionship, hang out, look for trouble, get stoned, spend some quiet time over a cool glass, or try their hand with a pool cue. Thirst won.

So much for brooding over why he needed a drink. He got out of the car. And became another guy who walked into a bar.

When he pushed through the swinging doors, the first thing to catch his eye was a sign hanging behind the bar. Carved in light pine were the first two verses of "Carry Me Back to Old Virginny," the tune that, in varying versions, had been Virginia's state song, until retired more than a decade earlier on the grounds it was offensive to Black people.

Strolling toward the bar, trying not to look desperate for a drink, he scanned the boisterous crowd of mainly young, male, and IvorySnow–White patrons. The bartender looked up through hooded eyes and continued to polish a beer glass with a not-exactly-clean towel. Hanging on the wall, below a rack of beer glasses, a plaque read: "Joe Ferguson, Barkeep."

Corded muscles in thick arms and broad shoulders, offset by a full belly under a stained white apron, told a tale of a one-time star athlete gone soft.

"You a cop?" Joe asked, in a tone that hinted at dislike of the whole breed of law enforcement.

"Not today. Not here. Monday morning I join the sheriff's office in Jefferson County. Tonight, I'm just thirsty."

The barkeep frowned at the unexpected dilemma, forehead creased in thought. At last, he bobbed his head. "What'll you have?"

"Draft beer. Whatever's on tap."

Book felt virtuous for choosing a brew over the bourbon that was his drink of choice. Deep in the honesty of his soul, he knew the challenge of stopping at one drink.

The polished glass disappeared, and, as if by magic, a foam-topped beer appeared on the counter. The first swallow drenched Book's parched throat with a near orgasmic sensation. He resisted the temptation to moan with pleasure.

He thought back, trying to recall when drinking became so important.

In the Army, all soldiers drank a lot. Just something to do with your buddies. Together with fellow cops, from time to time, he stopped by the corner tavern to hoist a few, most often in the wake of a disastrous incident. At no time did drinking impair his performance on the job.

The turning point came after the administrative hearing, when his career was ruined in the aftermath of the tragic Georgetown killing of Scooter Thomas. He'd drifted toward an alcoholic's dependence on booze. Drinking helped to iron out the kinks during the day. To bear the guilt of being suckered into shooting Thomas. To bear the shame of facing Marlene and the twins at night.

Shouts coming from the billiard area interrupted his maudlin introspection and drowned out Kenny Rogers singing "The Gambler." He spotted two figures struggling in the back of the room. Acting on instinct, he slid off the bar stool and headed toward the scene at the establishment's rear.

A gorgeous Amazon, with flowing blond hair, confronted a hulk who towered over her holding a switchblade. The pearl studs on her western style shirt had been ripped away and the blue garment was stained red. Book guessed she'd been slashed in her breast.

She held a long neck Budweiser in her left hand, the jagged bottom dripping. The hulk's right ear leaked scarlet.

"You son of a bitch. I don't fuck for money. If you touch me again, this Bud's for your balls."

"All night you've been playing your cock teaser game," the hulk said. "Now's time to put out or pay the piper."

He reached up and touched the blood dripping from his ear.

"Times up. You lost your chance. I'm going to stick this blade where the sun don't shine."

Book stepped into their field of vision. "Enough."

The battling duo stared at him in disbelief.

He moved to the right, forcing the hulk to turn to face him. Another step and the Amazon saw the opening and slid to her attacker's rear. She hefted the bottle, ready to go on the offensive, but paused in response to Book's raised hand. The woman made a face that telegraphed she could take care of herself but obeyed the unspoken command to stay back.

With his shaggy reddish-brown hair hanging over protruding jug ears and a craggy forehead, the guy was a real colossus. His coveralls were stained with heavy black grease. The sleeves on his T-shirt were cut off, displaying massive shoulders. He had fifty pounds on the detective and towered over Book's six foot two. Even a little drunk, his movements were quick and controlled. This one was no stranger to barroom brawls.

"Drop the knife," Book said, moving into a defensive stance. He considered arming himself but decided to ignore the Emerson Commander combat knife in his pocket and the .357 revolver tucked in a paddle holster at his spine.

Adrenaline was surging. Months of frustration and anger were channeled into the coming confrontation. The chance opportunity to allow his pent-up rage to boil over trumped his determination to keep a low profile.

The hulk's mouth twisted into a menacing grimace. The hand holding the weapon was low in a classic knife fighter's stance. He'd done this before.

A serpent striking without warning, the blade shot forward. Book reacted fast, but the hulk's knife was faster and sliced open his sweatshirt. The cut on his arm stung. Not a serious wound, but a warning he might be taking this guy too lightly.

Book pivoted, driving his right boot into his opponent's left leg. The kneecap shattered with an ear-splitting pop, causing the man to stagger. Not allowing the hulk time to recover, he struck with a foot to the head. Bafflement showed through glazing eyes.

The monster began to slump, and Book gripped his wrist, giving it a hard wrench. He applied leverage by turning his torso, bending the vulnerable body part over his braced forearm. The arm holding the weapon was twisted at an impossible angle and broke. The knife flew under the pool table.

Pulling free, the hulk raised his good hand over his head and let out a scream, his face contorted. "You nosy bastard! I'll kill you!"

Despite his bum leg, he launched a bull charge, catching Book in the midsection and driving him into the wall. Pool cues stacked in a wall rack sprayed in all directions, littering the floor.

Book seized the hulk by the shoulders and shoved him away, bracing for the next onslaught. He sidestepped the predictable lunge, clutched greasy overalls, and smashed the hulk headfirst into the side of the billiard table.

Anger cascading, Book struck a vicious blow to the back of the hulk's neck. He jerked the mangy mane, spun him around, and followed up by slamming a fist into the man's solar plexus.

Just as Book raised his right hand to administer another blow, he was seized from behind in the iron grip of a full nelson by Joe.

"Easy, boy. I think you convinced him he lost the fight. Don't make me call the sheriff. Last thing you want is Pat Garrett unhappy when you start your new job on Monday."

Book shook his head and realized he'd lost control of the situation. A lifetime of police experience kicked in, reminding him how a situation like this should be handled.

"You're right. Maybe it's time for you to call the local sheriff's office and report what happened here."

Joe laughed. "Glad to see you've come to your senses. However, let me explain why calling Sheriff Clanton won't work. You see he doesn't operate quite like Sheriff Pat, treating everybody the same. He happens to have a long-time hate for the Bronson family, and the lady you saved is Lenore Bronson. Besides that, this no-good ruffian is one of our sheriff's many cousins."

The barkeep nodded toward the blond Amazon. "Likely as not, he'd throw Lenore's pretty ass in a jail cell, rather than take her to the hospital in Jefferson."

Oh, Christ, Book thought, *All the women in all the bars in Virginia; why did I have to rescue Jeb's sister?*

CHAPTER 12

Book relaxed in the bartender's grip, knowing he was in the hands of an expert wrestler who'd mastered the full nelson. He was trying to absorb what Joe just said about the local law.

The blond slumped against the billiard table and dropped the jagged beer bottle from her limp hand. Natural fairness was accentuated; her pallor was eggshell white. She began to tremble, like a statue about to topple.

In two strides, Book reached her just before she collapsed.

Lenore groaned. "What's happening to me?"

"You've lost some blood from the knife wound." With conscious effort, he refrained from staring at the tattered blouse. Despite the strains in his marriage, he was determined to resist the attractions of other women.

The red river pouring from her wound had slowed to a stream, but Book knew she would be in trouble if the flow were not quickly stanched.

"Do you have a first aid kit?" he asked Joe, who was busy attempting to revive the woman's assailant.

"This ain't the Red Cross," was the barkeep's terse reply. "You best take her to the hospital in Jefferson County, just twenty minutes up the road. I'll look after her Jaguar. Tomorrow, the car will get collected. This ain't the first time she couldn't drive home." Joe seemed to hesitate, then his jaw tightened.

"Something you should know. This 'uns name is Seymour Clanton. He's meaner 'n a snake. He's got two brothers worse 'n he is. Pa Clanton's the worst of the lot. Would you believe Seymour's the runt of the litter? Some dark night, they're gonna come for you with axe handles."

Book absentmindedly acknowledged the warning, thinking the Clanton clan was the least of his worries.

He quickly made a compress from a clean handkerchief. The reminder of the failed attempt to save Lou clenched his throat.

With the combat knife, he cut the sleeve off one arm of his sweatshirt. Slicing strips from the cotton material, he fashioned a makeshift bandage over the wounded breast, tying it around the woman's well-proportioned back.

She looked up, disoriented. "If you want to feel me up, you should at least be gentleman enough to wait till we're alone."

He resisted the impulse to protest that he was just administering a crude form of first aid.

"Christ, I'm going to be sick," she said. Leaning over the pool table, she proceeded to vomit on the green felt, burying the eight ball under the remains of that night's supper, with an overlay of too much beer.

"You're coming with me," Book said, when she'd finished puking.

"Where we goin'? Your place?"

"No. The Jefferson County Hospital."

He put his arm around her, and they began weaving toward the exit.

"Why do I feel so rotten? I can't even walk." Showing signs of panic, she gasped, "I'm dying."

"No. You're not. You're in shock. The adrenaline from the fight is wearing off. What you're feeling is a normal reaction after what you've been through."

"You sure?"

"Trust me, I know these things."

Book knew far too much about the horrible aftermath of being stabbed.

When he eased her into the vehicle, she looked him full in the face.

"You're a nice guy, aren't you? Why the hell am I never attracted to nice guys? You're even handsome, in a scary sort of way. What's your name, honey?"

"Andrew Booker. Call me Book. What's yours?"

"Lenore Bronson. You can call me Monday through Sunday."

Book's memory quickly recapped his relationship with Jeb Bronson, who'd been Book's commanding officer in Afghanistan, and as much of a friend as a superior officer could be with a noncom. After retiring from the service, Jeb returned to the old homestead to run the family business—whatever the hell that was—following his daddy as chair of the Jefferson County Board of Supervisors. Jeb's phone call had led to the job offer from Pat Garrett, which brought Book to these parts. He felt he owed Jeb big time for pulling him out of the quicksand his life had been slipping into.

He intended to share none of these thoughts with Lenore. Shrugging at acceptance of the hand fate dealt him, he steered the Sequoia onto the highway.

"Sit back and try to rest." He calculated he could shave a few minutes off the customary time to the hospital.

Once over the Jefferson County line, Book put the hammer down and kept on the lookout for the local cops.

He speculated about the irony of getting an escort with flashing lights. A half-smile formed on his lips, marking the first time in months a humorous notion crossed his mind.

In seventeen minutes flat, the Sequoia squealed up to the emergency room entrance. Lenore had fallen into a half-sleep, moaning now and again. Book lifted her out of the SUV and carried her inside.

Spotting the red blotch soaking through the makeshift bandage, a triage nurse yelled, "Looks like a serious wound. Right breast."

Book joined in. "About a half hour ago. She's lost a fair amount of blood."

Emergency staff, scrambling with practiced assurance, placed the patient on a gurney and wheeled her toward the operating area. The nurses called her "Lenore." Book could tell from their body language and comments she was well known in the area.

One nurse patted Lenore on the arm and said, "You're safe now, darlin.'"

No stranger to emergency rooms, Book still felt somewhat at sixes and sevens. He'd escorted numerous felons with knife and gunshot wounds to hospitals around Washington, DC. On those occasions, he knew the drill. He was the one who called the plays, before he turned the bad guys over to hospital attendants. He had no role in the care of those he apprehended. To be honest, in most cases, he had little concern for what happened to the patients in the aftermath of treatment, except for the drudgery of filling out the paperwork.

Not so Lenore. Book felt responsible for her. If nothing else, he'd have to answer to Jeb.

He took stock of Lenore's situation. A ride like the Jaguar signaled she had money. The cost of hospital treatment wouldn't pose a problem. The staff recognized her, so her records would be on file.

Lost in these ramblings, he didn't notice the hospital staffer until she tapped him on the shoulder. "I need you to complete some paperwork on Miss Bronson."

Book registered the "Miss" with relief. That resolved his lingering concern, even though she wore no wedding ring, whether there was a husband in the picture to complicate the situation.

Over the next half hour, he learned more than he wanted to know about the Jefferson County Hospital bureaucracy. He supplied information on the stabbing, shading the story somewhat to jibe with the tale Joe and bar patrons might tell in case the matter ever got to court.

He soon confirmed Lenore lived with her family at the Bronson place. The clerk gave directions, which Book copied in the event he would have to take her home. He was not confident the GPS in the Sequoia's navigation system could guide him to a home address in a rural area in the middle of nowhere Virginia.

After a long and boring period in an uncomfortable chair in the waiting room, a nurse came to usher him into a visitors' lounge near the recovery area. The wait dragged on past midnight. Book grew more and more apprehensive with each tick of the clock. He gave an audible sigh when he saw a physician striding toward him.

"I'm Dr. Warshawski. I operated on Ms. Bronson."

The doctor was a striking Black woman of noble bearing. The way she carried herself made her seem taller than the five-nine he estimated with a cop's eye. More as a man than an officer of the law, he gave her the once over even though he rejected the thought that he might be attracted. Brownish green eyes revealed the smile her lips hid in evident humor at his scrutiny.

"Are you a friend of hers?"

"Not really." After an awkward pause, he continued. "She was injured tonight at the Old Virginny Bar. I offered to help. The bartender suggested I bring her to this hospital. By the way, my name's Andrew Booker. Call me Book. How's she doing?"

Book was aware the surgeon's curiosity about the nature of his relationship with Lenore was not satisfied by the glib description of a chance meeting in a bar. Insufficient reason to transport an injured party to a hospital. That's what ambulances are for.

"The good news is, she's going to be fine," Dr. Warshawski said. "With the proper plastic surgery, in time, her wound should be invisible. I did the necessary repair work for the short term. After she rests for a couple of hours, you can take her home."

Book began to relax.

"Right now, I need to patch up the cut on your arm."

After she finished ministering to the wound, Dr. Warshawski asked, "How about joining me for a cup of coffee in the cafeteria?"

"I never pass up a cup. Thanks."

She confided her first name was "Althea—like Althea Gibson, the historic tennis champion. My dad was convinced I was destined to be a tennis star. He taught biology at William and Mary. He had me out on their courts trying to swing a racket before I was five."

"Did you become a champion?"

She laughed. "Not even close. But Dad attended all of my matches when I captained the William and Mary tennis team."

"What about your mom?"

"She died when I was five." Cutting short condolences, she asked, "How about you? You look athletic. What was your sport?"

"In high school, I played everything—football, basketball, baseball. But that was it. I worked my way through college. No time for sports. Then DC police, the Army, and back to the Metropolitan Police Department."

"What brings you to Jefferson County?"

Book gave her an abridged version of his police career, omitting any mention of the Georgetown killing. "Monday morning, I'll be working for Sheriff Garrett as his lead detective, or maybe they call them 'investigators' down here. I can never get my mind around terminology in a sheriff's office."

He figured Althea sensed the story was incomplete. No one moves from being a big city detective to a rural county in Virginia without some baggage.

Althea's break was interrupted when a nurse stuck her head in the lounge to alert her to the arrival of an ambulance carrying teenage car crash victims.

"Saturday night. You know what it's like." Hurrying out the door, she added, "I hope we can continue this conversation sometime soon, Book."

He gazed at Althea's retreating figure as she left the lounge, denying any intent to take her up on the obvious invitation. He was not ready for an affair, even if the possibility existed. He shrugged, returned to the waiting room, and fell asleep in a lumpy lounge chair.

A nurse nudged him awake and asked, "Are you Miss Bronson's ride?"

Book helped a groggy Lenore into the SUV. She dozed as he followed the written directions to the Bronson place.

Pulling up to the mansion on top of a hill at the end of a winding road past an impressive stone stable, he left Lenore in the vehicle, walked up the stairs, and rang the bell. After several rings and a long wait, a sleepy-eyed Jeb opened the imposing door.

"What the hell are you doing here at four on a Sunday morning, Book old buddy?"

"Your sister was injured at the Old Virginny Bar and Billiards. By chance, I was there. I took her to the hospital. She'll be fine. She's in the car. Help me bring her in."

CHAPTER 13

The spittle of tobacco juice flew in a gentle curve, landing dead center in the brass spittoon. Sheriff Pat Garrett slumped back comfortably in his swivel chair, boots propped on the desk on an overcast Monday morning. He crushed the chaw of Beech-Nut in his molars, relished the tang of smokeless tobacco and molasses, and let out a sigh. His wife's lectures about the health risks of cancer of the mouth from chewing, to say nothing of what the filthy habit could do to his pancreas, were sorely missed.

In a cruel twist of fate, she, who was scrupulous about health habits, was the one who had succumbed to a malignant carcinoma a decade ago.

Chewing, he rationalized, helped him quit smoking cigarettes. He was pleased he could chew in the privacy of his office without violating the almost universal ban against smoking in public buildings, or damn near anyplace else. Glad no one else on the staff was addicted to smokeless tobacco, he imagined it freed him to ignore his own transgressions. He tipped the janitor twenty dollars each month for the thankless task of cleaning and polishing the spittoon.

Chewing helped him think, or so he believed. Today, he was trying to figure out what to do about Andrew Booker. At the urging of Jeb Bronson, he'd hired Book. Mindful of Jeb's clout as chair of the board of supervisors, there was no doubt the scion of the area's most powerful family could get him fired as sheriff, despite his popularity with county voters.

An astute judge of just how far he needed to go to keep their support, the sheriff worked hard to maintain a delicate balancing act vis-à-vis the Good Ole Boys club the Bronsons headed. He had a clear sense of the line he was not prepared to cross. To date, Jeb and Robert Lee before him had sensed there was a line and were careful not to push him too far.

The unspoken agreement was Pat would keep the peace and protect the vital interests of the Bronsons. In return, he had free rein to conduct his duties as sheriff. The Bronsons put up no overt interference in the way he did his job or ran his office. To be sure, there were occasional compromises. Hiring Sam Headley and George Lyman (better known, behind their backs, as Laurel and Hardy) were recent additions to the list, a concession to appease powerful relatives who were allied with the Bronsons. But Pat believed he'd solved that problem by assigning them office chores they were able to carry out with a modest level of competence under Shirley Ralston's close supervision.

Andrew Booker was another matter. The job of lead investigator—the sheriff decided to use the designation *detective* common in several other Virginia jurisdictions—was central to the sheriff's role. The sheriff needed someone in that position he could trust. Was Book that man?

Book's resume was impressive. He'd distinguished himself in the military, with service in Iraq and Afghanistan, rising to the rank of sergeant in Special Forces. His career in the District of Columbia's Metropolitan Police Department was exemplary, gaining high marks in SWAT, and earning promotion to detective in record time. He'd handled high-profile cases and solved more than most of his colleagues, but all this ended abruptly with the incident in Georgetown. Pat had investigated the incident and kept what he'd learned to himself.

Either Book murdered a sixteen-year-old for personal reasons, or he was set up by persons unknown while pursuing Franco Moretti, a dangerous fugitive on the FBI's Most Wanted list.

No matter how long he thought about it, he couldn't figure out which story was true.

The sheriff was embarrassed to admit he'd been influenced by Jeb's recommendation, coupled with the downside of butting heads with the powers that be. The bottom line was he liked Book as a man and admired the stand-up fashion in which he discussed his disgrace. The detective even owned up to his marital problems and heavy drinking. Pat believed him when he said he was struggling to turn back the drift toward alcoholic dependency.

The stakes in taking on the problem-plagued detective would be high, even if there weren't a murder to investigate at, of all places, Bronson Stables. If anyone but Mary Connolly reported the incident, he'd have been tempted to ignore the report. But, he'd had a crush on her since they were students in elementary school, and he couldn't ignore *her*.

With Carmen's confirmation, there remained little doubt a murder had taken place—and been covered up. The sheriff approved the rookie's handling of the situation based on her telephone reports on Friday and throughout the weekend. He knew how difficult Fix Magruder could be. But Carmen had captivated the cantankerous old jockey.

Pat concluded he had no choice but to turn the murder investigation over to Book when he reported for duty later that morning. Coming to the office at the crack of dawn to agonize over different courses of action was a waste of time. Investigating homicide clearly fell in Detective Booker's bailiwick. The sheriff's only room to maneuver was to keep Carmen involved in the inquiry, enabling him to have a direct pipeline on key developments. She was an effective counterweight in the event Book sold out to the Bronsons.

He glanced up as Shirley stuck her head in the door.

"He's here," she said.

CHAPTER 14

"Welcome aboard, Book. Did you get settled over the weekend?" Pat waved his new employee to a chair.

"For now. I'm staying at the Silverado Motel. I don't need anything fancy, but the motel doesn't work for me."

"Shirley can point you in the right direction for house hunting. She knows all the realtors. Most of them owe her a favor."

The detective nodded and sat motionless, signaling he was waiting for the sheriff to take the initiative in outlining his duties.

He didn't have long to wait.

"We had a murder here Thursday night. Occurred about midnight at the Bronson place." Knowing Jeb Bronson had orchestrated the detective's recruitment, Pat searched Book's face for a reaction and saw none, apart from a tightening around the eyes. His new hire was a master of the "cop face."

The sheriff outlined the chain of events. Horsewoman Mary observing the knifing. Reporting the crime first thing Friday morning. Deputy Sheriff Carmen Garcia visiting Bronson Stables later Friday. "Suspicious dirt" confirmation of the crime. Local missing person reports lacking. Unsuccessful efforts to track down anyone from out of town matching the victim's bare-bones description.

"So far, we've got nothing. Not a body. No idea who might have been killed. Our best guess is he's an outsider who's a small man. No description of the suspect, except for a vague notion he might be bigger than the victim. No motive or reason why the incident occurred at the Bronson place. We don't even know if the family's involved."

The detective sensed the sheriff's unspoken reservations. "You're worried about assigning me to the case because of my relationship to Jeb."

"Should I be?" A poker player's expression revealed nothing of what Pat was thinking. A twitch in his handlebar mustache might have hidden the hint of a smile.

"I understand the concern." Book proceeded to outline the situation from his boss's perspective. "Jeb recommended me. He was my commanding officer in Afghanistan. Given his position as chair of the board of supervisors, his endorsement would weigh heavily. If I were in your shoes, I'd be worried too."

"Should I be?" Pat repeated.

"I won't bullshit you. I need this job. My professional and personal life's been in the shitter for months. The chance to be a detective again is a life preserver to a drowning man. If I can't investigate a high-profile murder, I'm no good to you. Rest assured my ties to Jeb won't get in the way."

"Your word's good enough for me." Pat leaned across the desk. The two men shook hands.

"Later I'll introduce you to Carmen Garcia, your new partner."

"There's just one thing," Book said, reflecting on the tragedy that befell his last partner, Lou Bernstein. No way he wanted a partner. *Never again.*

"I like to work alone. When I interviewed for the job, you talked about each of the deputies. Carmen sounds sharp for a rookie, but I can't break her in while trying to solve a sensitive murder with political overtones."

"Get used to the idea of a partner. Jefferson County's different from the big city. Carmen knows rural communities like this one, even though she's from another part of the state. She's well trained and has a good head on her shoulders. I know her dad. He's one of the best sheriffs around. I can tell she picked up a lot from watching him over the years."

Book leaned forward. Pat kept talking to head off any objections.

"Her stepmom was one of the richest and most influential women in Virginia before she was shot and killed during Carmen's senior year at the University of Virginia. Carmen won't be intimidated by either the wealth or political clout of the Bronson family. I'd like you to partner with her for a month. If you don't think it's working out, I'm willing to reconsider."

Book sensed the deputy was being assigned so the sheriff could hedge his bets, just in case the detective proved to be less objective than he claimed. The issue wasn't worth resigning over.

CHAPTER 15

Carmen Garcia suggested Detective Booker join her at the Jefferson Café, where they could get acquainted over breakfast while discussing strategy for the visit to Bronson Stables. Still hungry despite the donut and coffee he'd grabbed at the motel, Book welcomed the idea. His appetite was coming back in response to country living. He ordered blueberry pancakes, crisp bacon, two eggs over easy, orange juice, and black coffee.

"Tell me about yourself," he said.

She filled him in on her background growing up in Southeast Virginia, life as the daughter of the local sheriff, graduating from the University of Virginia, serving the fourteen-week stint at Virginia State Police Academy, and being hired by Pat Garrett four months ago.

"Once I was interviewed by Pat, I decided to accept a job in Jefferson County rather than continue with the state police."

Book had been a detective for enough years to sense major omissions in a personal narrative. He was puzzled by her failure to allude to her stepmom or the horrific murder at UVA. He debated with himself whether to let it go for now or probe, mindful to sublimate his lingering resentment at being forced to accept Carmen as a partner.

"Why'd you decide to become a cop? That's an unusual career choice for UVA grads."

● ● ●

Carmen knew her partner must have his own secrets. How else to explain the transition from DC's Metropolitan Police Department to a county sheriff's office. Pat had given no hint of the detective's background or reasons for taking the job in Jefferson. His omission spoke volumes. She took her cue from the sheriff and decided to finesse the sensitive topic.

Pondering how to respond to his question of why she'd become a cop, she assessed her impressions of Book. While appearing calm, he communicated an aura of controlled aggression. She noted he'd picked a table in the far corner of the restaurant and sat with his back to the wall. From there, he could watch the entrance and the swinging door into the kitchen—central casting for a Western gunfighter. His black hair was tousled, with a strand hanging over his forehead, almost into his eyes, the grayest eyes she'd ever seen.

Book wasn't young, but he had too much restless energy to be conventionally middle aged. The saying, "the new forty is yesterday's thirty," popped into her mind. Shaking herself out of her reverie, she decided to respond to what, after all, was a common question cop to cop.

"My last year at UVA, my stepmom, Katherine, invited me to lunch. Her goal was to make peace; help me get past what started as teenage jealousy over her close relationship with my dad. The clincher was when she told me she was pregnant. An only child, I was astounded, but genuinely pleased to learn I could expect a baby brother."

She was encouraged by Book's apparent interest.

"We were walking back across campus when a sniper shot and killed Katherine and her unborn baby. She bled out in my arms. The assassin was never apprehended, despite the best efforts of the Charlottesville police. My dad even hired the Wellerton agency to join in the search, but they failed to track down the killer. To this day, we have no idea why she was murdered or by whom. My dad was devastated. I sleepwalked through the rest of my senior year. Gave up plans to attend law school. I decided to follow in my dad's footsteps and become a cop."

● ● ●

Book remained silent, moved by the young woman's tragic story. Like most people, there were depths to her character not apparent on the surface. She remained composed while relating dramatic developments that had occurred less than a year ago, hinting at a maturity far beyond her years.

But the nagging suspicion remained she might have sought out this assignment, whether she was aware or not, because homicide had taken on new meaning for her with her stepmom's killing and loss of the brother she was never to know. He decided to downplay his reaction to the tragic tale.

"My condolences for your loss."

They grew silent while Annabel Lee served their breakfast.

● ● ●

Pert and sassy in a time-honored Southern waitress's traditional role, this was Annabel Lee's first chance to flirt with the detective. Not every day a handsome stranger—a newcomer on the sheriff's staff—was a customer at the Jefferson Café. However, Carmen's presence inhibited her overtures, and she settled for watching from across the café as Book tucked into pancakes and eggs.

● ● ●

Eating with gusto, the deputy briefed the detective on her investigation to date, highlighting the visit to Bronson Stables and the discovery with Fix Magruder of the "suspicious dirt"—presumed confirmation of Horsewoman Mary's report of a killing outside the stable. She concluded by summarizing the conversation with Alice about possible candidates for the victim, and her efforts to locate any males matching Alice's description.

"Summing up," she said, "I got nowhere in trying to track down leads about the victim. Needless to add, we have only the vaguest notions about the killer."

The partners agreed the next step was for them to visit the Bronsons.

CHAPTER 16

Robert Lee Bronson stood in front of the giant stone fireplace in the center of the mansion's living room wall. Hanging above the mantle was an oil portrait of a uniformed ancestor—General Robert E. Lee—who'd commanded troops during the South's notable victory at Fredericksburg. Since the surrender at Appomattox, every son in the Bronson lineage had been named after a famous Confederate general. J. E. B. Stuart was Jeb's namesake. Robert Lee scoffed at the mainstream interpretation of historians who argued Stuart had failed at Gettysburg to alert General Lee to the deployment of Union troops, thereby marking the turning point of the Civil War, ensuring the South's defeat.

Jeb Bronson watched as his father went through the familiar ritual of lighting a Cuban cigar. The sixtysomething lord of the manor took care with the cut, slicing off the tip with a razor-sharp blade in a guillotine cutter. He took his time warming the Cohiba cigar—made famous by Fidel Castro—above the flame of a butane lighter, rotating and puffing to ensure an even burn.

All his life, Jeb had done his utmost to honor the family's traditions, first becoming a champion horseman in his teens (like Stuart, his cavalry general namesake), graduating in the top quarter of his class at West Point, serving with distinction in Afghanistan, and retiring from Special Forces a decorated hero at age forty-two. Now, having succeeded Robert Lee as chair of the board of supervisors, he held sway as the political leader of Jefferson County. Above all, in the past year, he succeeded Robert Lee as the CEO of Ares Worldwide, one of the largest, and most influential, of the military contractors that had risen to prominence in the United States and throughout the world after the Korean War.

Jeb was in his teens when his mother left home following a nasty divorce. His father became the dominant influence in his life. There were times when he cursed his father's heavy hand; other times—more frequent in recent years—when he welcomed the power and influence of the elder Bronson.

Robert Lee sank into a blue leather club chair, a signal to Jeb the cigar ritual was complete, having served the purposes of focusing the old man's mind and relaxing his spirit. It was time to get down to business.

Jeb said, "Andrew Booker is coming here soon with Carmen Garcia, the rookie deputy who recently joined the force. Book didn't say what they wanted to discuss, but Fix filled me in on Garcia's inspection of the stable Friday. She was investigating an alleged incident out by the stable Thursday night."

He paused to give weight to his next question. "What the hell went on at the stable?"

Robert Lee ignored the question. "What did you expect to accomplish by pressuring Garrett to bring Booker here? As a detective, for God's sake. You told me his life was a shambles after leaving the DC police in disgrace. His marriage fell apart. Without his wife's support, he has no money of his own. He was on the verge of becoming a drunk. Why rescue him?"

Jeb sighed. "You've always preached to me: 'Keep your friends close and your enemies closer.' Book is both friend and enemy. I got to know him when we served together in combat. He hit rock bottom after the killing in Georgetown. But he's not the type to give up. In time, left to his own devices, he would have fought his way back and begun to investigate circumstances leading to his ouster from the police department."

Trying to head off his dad's expected reaction, he added: "He would have been outside our ability to control. When he's on the payroll in Jefferson County, we can influence events. Moreover, he has none of the resources he would have had in DC."

Robert Lee grimaced, showing his customary limited tolerance for arguments with which he disagreed and which he stood to lose. "We'll play it your way for now. But if Book gets close to the truth, we'll have to deal with him."

CHAPTER 17

HELMAND PROVINCE, AFGHANISTAN
2006

Captain Jeb Bronson crouched behind a rock formation high on a hill and surveyed Helmand Valley, which extended all the way to the river. Out of habit, he checked to ensure the sun was shining on his left shoulder, guarding against any risk of his position being betrayed by light reflecting off the binoculars. He frowned, not liking what he saw.

He spotted a unit of the British 16th Air Assault Brigade in danger of being overrun. An FV107 Scimitar was lying on its side, like an upended turtle. From the angle at which the Scimitar was tilted, the light tank's 30 mm high velocity cannon was useless. The armored reconnaissance vehicle had been damaged by an IED in a roadside blast.

Several of the airborne infantry were tending to crew members wounded by the improvised explosive device. Others were grouped in defensive positions near three Land Rover Wolf vehicles in a convoy with the Scimitar. The British commander was talking on a radio, doubtless calling for reinforcements and air support.

Two platoons of Taliban insurgents were maneuvering to surround the stalled convoy.

Knowing there was no way the British commander could be aware of his observations, Jeb cursed to himself, mindful of the dilemma he would soon be facing.

Jeb beckoned for Sergeant Booker to join him at the forward observation post. "Book, take a look at ten o'clock in the valley."

He handed his subordinate the binoculars and pointed in the direction of the soon-to-be trapped Brits.

Book glanced through the glasses and quickly recognized the threat. "Those boys need our help."

"Not gonna happen," Jeb replied. "The responsibility of our Special Forces Group is to play a lead role in Provincial Reconstruction Teams, building the Afghan economy, and strengthening the society."

Book scoffed. "Sure it is. Yesterday, I spent all day trying to persuade Abdul to stop growing poppies, insisting he shift to another cash crop. After my interpreter cleaned up the farmer's remarks, he raved on for five minutes about how his grandfather grew the best poppies in the valley, his father grew the best poppies in Helmand Province, and he, Abdul, was determined to grow the best poppies in Afghanistan. In summary, we could go fuck ourselves."

"You don't need an interpreter. You speak the local lingo better than any of us."

"Keeping Mohammad guessing how much I understand is a good way to ensure an interpreter stays honest. The point is we're wasting our time on the PRT if we expect to change Pashtun society by changing the local farm economy. I've heard this province produces half the opium in the entire world. The white ends up as heroin in Washington, DC and throughout the rest of the US. We need to focus on fighting the war, killing Taliban insurgents, and, above all, stabilizing things so this country doesn't continue to fall apart like it has since 2002."

Jeb said, "When we turned over military leadership to NATO earlier this year, it became the responsibility of a British general, not ours, to lead the fight in Helmand. They have over three thousand British troops in the province."

"Yeah, but those troops aren't on the scene. We are. Those sons of bitches in the valley are up shit creek without a paddle. Reinforcements will arrive too late to save them."

"Dammit, Book. You think the answer to everything is to gear up for battle. We can't kill our way to victory."

After a pause to let his frustrations simmer, Jeb said, "What's your take on the best course of action?"

Book said, "I'll round up a dozen men and launch a diversionary strike on the nearest platoon. You direct mortar fire from here. Call in artillery. Bring in Apache helicopters, A-10 Warthogs, whatever you can get over target in time. Our forces can react quicker than the British can mobilize Harriers or other air-ground support. If our guys know US Special Forces are at risk, they'll haul ass to help."

"Do it," Jeb said resignedly. "Speaking of ass, my ass is grass when Colonel Owens finds out what we're doing."

"Sweet-talk the bird like you always do." Book started running toward the bullish form of Curt Hartmann, who was charging up the hill in an effort to discover what was going on. The sergeant had a knack for sensing when a crisis was brewing.

The two men jogged toward their forward operating base. Curt listened, while Book issued orders.

"Curt, saddle up. Jeb spotted a British convoy with four vehicles trapped in the valley. Their Scimitar's crippled from an IED. Brits are about to be ambushed by two platoons of Taliban fighters. Round up a dozen guys. Tell them to carry as much extra ammo as possible. We're going to surprise the bandits from the rear. We deploy in five minutes."

Once his men were in position, Book radioed Jeb to open up with mortars and any firepower he could target on the assembled Taliban fighters. When the bombardment began, Curt commenced throwing grenades.

Fred Leonidis was using a M249 squad automatic weapon to lay down a field of fire. The linked belt feeding the machine gun held one tracer mixed with every four rounds of ball cartridges, providing a visual cue for the Americans to direct their fire.

The devastating mortar explosions and incoming fire demoralized the insurgents, who had been about to launch their own surprise attack on the unsuspecting Brits. Book watched the Taliban fighters mill around in confusion. Dead and dying were everywhere.

He fired at one insurgent. The instant the round left his weapon, he realized the target was a young teenager whom he'd just killed. Not for the first time, he swore at war that sacrificed every nation's youth. On the heels of that thought, the thousands who died in the Twin Towers came to mind, together with the memory of who was responsible for that tragedy.

Afghanistan couldn't escape responsibility for being the birthplace of the 9/11 terrorists.

Book watched the Taliban platoon leader looking back to observe the Special Forces unit. The insurgent commander raced from one end of the platoon to the other, shouting at his men, beating several to command their attention.

Book aimed his M-4 rifle and shot the platoon leader, further disrupting the Taliban militants. In the distance, he heard gunfire coming from the direction of the British convoy.

He yelled to Curt. "The Brits have figured out what they're up against. By now, they must be taking fire from the Taliban platoon on the other side."

A second Taliban leader realized the threat posed from the Special Forces unit attacking from the rear. He mobilized a couple dozen militants. They charged, screaming, and shooting AK-47s. Two insurgents were firing rocket-propelled grenades, intended for use against vehicles in the British convoy.

A stinging blow to his helmet knocked Book to his knees. Curt ran over to check him out.

Disoriented, Book said, "What happened? My ears are ringing; I felt dizzy for a second."

"You got shot in the helmet. Nothing penetrated. At worst, you'll have a mild concussion. Relax, you got hit harder on the football field in high school. That goddamned Kevlar's really something, isn't it? In any other war you'd be dead."

"Thanks for the pep talk," Book muttered.

"Get up."

Obeying the order, Book staggered to his feet. He twisted his head, tried to stand straight to test his balance, and glanced around at the unfolding combat.

"You're not seriously hurt. I've got to tend to business." Curt turned to shoot four times, dropping two insurgents in their tracks before they could fire their AK-47s at the Americans.

Recovering, Book spotted Fred Leonidis collapsing. The squad leader grasped his bleeding shoulder. A Taliban fighter was running hard to seize the M249 SAW. Book winged him in the right leg. Watching the insurgent fall, Book's headache eased, enabling him to make the kill shot to the enemy's face.

Curt ran over, picked up the twenty-two-pound machine gun like it was a toy, and trained it on the insurgents. He fired with devastating effect.

Book yelled, "Medic." He pointed to Fred on the ground.

Drawing his pistol, he crawled toward cover. He keyed his radio and shouted to Jeb. "We're getting hammered down here. Rain some hell on that Taliban platoon attacking us."

In response to his appeal, the mortar barrage intensified, knocking the heart out of the Taliban offensive.

Book ducked when shrapnel shredded trees near his position, remembering the soldier's adage, "Be careful what you wish for."

Lifting his head, he realized the bombardment was having the desired effect. The militants sandwiched between the Special Forces and the British convoy were starting to withdraw. Ignoring the shouted commands of their leaders, the insurgents were fleeing in disarray.

He keyed his radio again to reach Jeb. "Whatever you're doing, it's working. The bandits on this side are pulling out. Have you been able to reach the British commander?"

"Roger. We've made contact. You were right. Their Harriers are twenty minutes away. Three of our Apaches accompanied by two Warthogs are less than five minutes out."

Book said, "Tell the convoy we're going to join them from the south side of their position. Ask them, in the spirit of NATO unity, not to shoot us."

"Roger. Let me know when you link up."

Book assembled his troops. In addition to Fred Leonidis's shoulder, two members of the Special Forces unit were wounded.

When Americans joined the embattled convoy, the British commander grasped Book's hand. His handshake conveyed the gratitude he felt and awareness that he and his men had been spared from being exterminated.

"Your Apaches and Warthogs are creating havoc with the Taliban platoon. The militants are retreating. The Apache's 30 mm chain guns and Hellfire missiles are fearsome weapons. And the close air support of the Warthog's guns and missiles are just as scary. Thank Captain Bronson for quick action in coming to our rescue. When the IED blew up the Scimitar, we knew the valley could be the stage for a trap. But we had no idea how many insurgents had surrounded us until you Yanks brought in the cavalry."

Book nodded. "Glad we could help."

He gathered his unit and headed back to the FOB, wondering whether Jeb had been serious about not coming to the aid of the convoy, or whether he was setting up his second-in-command to argue for the rescue, which would have given him grounds to tell Colonel Owens he'd acted in response to the sentiment of his troops.

Jeb may be a friend, but he can be a two-faced bastard.

CHAPTER 18

JEFFERSON COUNTY, VIRGINIA
2024

Book rang the doorbell, while Carmen admired the impressive black-walnut double doors of the Bronson's mansion. A man—taller than Carmen, but shorter than Book, with immense shoulders bracketing a chest like an old steamer trunk—answered the ring. Close-mouthed, he motioned for them to follow.

Walking with a pronounced limp, he guided them into the living room, where the Bronsons rose in unison to welcome the detective and deputy. Book's eyes followed the limping man as he hobbled from the room.

Noting Book's interest, Jeb said, "Adams was wounded by an IED in Iraq. In the explosion, he lost the ability to speak. His leg was injured beyond repair. But he's a useful man to have around and a faithful servant. We couldn't run the house without him."

Expressionless, Book wondered if Adams had anything to do with the murder out by the stable, aware he would fit Mary Connolly's description of a "big man."

After Jeb completed the introductions, Robert Lee said, "Thank you for coming to Lenore's rescue on Saturday. She's prone to find herself in bizarre situations."

Book gave Carmen a look that communicated he would fill her in later on the details of his involvement in Lenore's *bizarre situation*.

The detective said, "Thanks for meeting with us on such short notice. There was a report of a disturbance around midnight out by your stable last Thursday. Two men were seen fighting."

Jeb waved his hand dismissively. "I have no idea what you're talking about. What disturbance? Fix Magruder, the stable hand in charge of the horses, did say Carmen came by Friday morning to look around outside the stable. But he couldn't figure out what she was searching for." He glanced over at his father, eyebrows raised.

Robert Lee sat still, his face a mask.

Book realized open-ended questions were a waste of time. He took a different tack. "Did you have any visitors at Bronson Stables?"

Jeb said, "No visitors; we seldom entertain, and we meet with business visitors out at the Farm. There's no one on the property at night except Lenore, whom you met on Saturday, Adams, who let you in, Fix, who Carmen talked with down by the stable, my father, and me."

Book looked quizzical, waiting to see if more information was forthcoming.

Jeb continued, "There's also a small staff who do the cooking, housekeeping, secretarial work, and take care of the gardens and grounds. But none of them are ever here after nightfall."

Book said, "By the Farm, I assume you mean the complex in the southwest corner of Jefferson County surrounded by a military style fence and marked No Trespassing. Violators Will Be Shot. Am I correct in assuming the Farm borders the Shenandoah River?"

Jeb chuckled. "Yes. The river's there, although a steep cliff makes access to anywhere in Jefferson County impossible. You've been busy since you showed up at our place Sunday morning. I take it you've been out to the Farm."

"On Sunday, I drove all over Jefferson County to get acquainted with the territory."

"I shouldn't be surprised," Jeb said. "I'd forgotten how serious you've always been about doing reconnaissance of any new terrain. The Farm has the warning posted because it's a military installation covered by our contract with the Pentagon."

"What goes on out there? From the perimeter, it appears to be an impressive installation, almost a self-contained community." The detective shifted in his seat to get a better view of his hosts as they hesitated before responding to the question.

"I'm afraid that's classified," Robert Lee said. "Our contract with the military goes back several years, dating before Jeb returned from Afghanistan. The Feds require total secrecy about what takes place at the Farm."

Book reflected on what he'd learned on Sunday in an internet search to explore the Bronson family's business. Thanks to an in-depth analysis the GAO submitted to Congress, he'd begun to put together a picture of the impressive scope of Ares Worldwide's web of contracts with the government.

He decided it was premature to reveal what he knew and suspected at this time. Moreover, he predicted the Bronsons would stonewall any probes to link their military contract activities with the murder.

Today's meeting had confirmed Mary Connolly's report of the killing was accurate. Book was certain the Bronsons knew about the killing . . . at least the old man did.

"Well, we wouldn't want to go beyond our *need to know*," Book said. "The next step is for us to talk with everyone who was here Thursday."

Jeb said, "Anything we can do to help clear up the mystery. I'll give you a list and instruct everyone to speak with you."

CHAPTER 19

Book divided up the list of people known to be on the Bronson's property at any time the previous Thursday. He gave Carmen her assignments, starting with Fix, whom she already knew from their investigation of the suspicious dirt at the stable. His first interview would be with Lenore, hoping she would remember him from the incident at the Old Virginny Bar and Billiards.

He found her in a magnificent sunroom sitting in a wicker chair, cosseted amid multicolored flowered pillows and reading a book. Lenore enjoyed an unobstructed view of the stable. Morning sunshine bathed floor-to-ceiling windows in golden light. From that side of the room, a wooded lake was visible. Book spotted a great blue heron standing at the edge of the water about to swallow a fish it had just caught.

The shimmering glow on Lenore's blond hair called to mind a halo. Thinking of her as an angel, even for an instant, clashed with his image of the vixen in action Saturday night. She continued reading, oblivious to his presence. Embarrassed, he began to feel like an intruder. He coughed.

Startled, she turned to look, closing the book in her lap. He noticed the title: *Team of Rivals*, a popular history by Doris Kearns Godwin he'd seen Marlene reading a few years ago. The book had provided the foundation for the award-winning movie, *Lincoln*.

To break the ice, he said, "I see you're boning up on Civil War history."

Quick on the uptake, she said, "Not the way you may think. When anyone says 'Civil War history'—about which Daddy and Jeb will be happy to regale you—they refer to the military conflict. Godwin focused on the political history. The book is about Lincoln's managerial genius and mastery of human nature in forging a winning team from the foremost politicians of his day. Several members of his cabinet, including Seward and Chase, ran against him for president. All of them thought they were better qualified to lead the Union than Honest Abe. But he kept them together—a true 'team of rivals'—and won the war to preserve the Union."

Book tried, but failed, to mask his shock at this succinct analysis of a topic he was certain historians had struggled with over the past century and a half. He couldn't square the image of this woman with the firebrand he'd seen fighting at the billiard table.

Lenore smiled sardonically. "What's the matter, detective? Surprised the country bimbos around here can read?"

Suppressing a stammer, he said, "Of course not, I just thought—"

"I don't need to hear what you thought, detective. It's written all over your face."

She rose to her feet in one flowing motion, moving close to Book. Her hand reached out and touched his cheek. "And what a face. I misjudged your face last Saturday. I said you were a 'nice guy.' I can see you're not. Deep down, under that hard exterior, you're hard as a rock. But I was right about the handsome part, in a scary sort of way."

By now having regained his composure, but sensing he was losing control of the situation, Book said, "Do you always try to deflect attention from yourself, controlling men by making fun of them? I'm impressed you have perfect recall of a situation when you were under extreme stress. A moment ago, I was about to compliment you on your astute analysis of a period of history. A period about which I'm ignorant."

"Okay detective, you've got me." Extending her wrists, she said, "Put on the cuffs. I'm a closet intellectual. Which in this family is a capital crime."

"Stop hiding behind mockery. I'm tired of you calling me 'detective.' My friends call me Book; I hope we can be friends."

"All right, detective. One click, and I'll friend you on my Facebook page. Or I would if I had a Facebook page."

"Enough fun and games. This is not a social call. We need to have a serious conversation." He gave her a look, deciding there was one sure way to turn off the trite sarcasm. "I'm here to investigate a murder."

She stood for a moment, stunned, then slumped into the wicker chair.

Today's Lenore was the antithesis of the woman about to pass out from her injuries in the Old Virginny Bar and Billiards. Book thought, *She's the personification of a chameleon.*

"Who was murdered?"

"We don't know the victim's identity," Book said. "But we have a reliable report someone was stabbed to death Thursday around midnight on the south side of the stable. A man—we believe a small man—was murdered during a struggle with a much larger man. All signs of the incident were erased by removing the body, scraping up the bloody dirt, and replacing it with other dirt."

Lenore's expression morphed from stunned to amazed.

"With the help of Fix Magruder, Deputy Sheriff Carmen Garcia found the spot where it happened, although Fix is unaware of the significance of the evidence, such as it is."

"What does Jeb say about this?"

"I told your brother and father there was a report of a 'disturbance' involving 'two men fighting.'" Book made air quotes as he spoke. "I didn't mention a murder. They're acting as though nothing happened. They claim there were no visitors."

She shrugged her shoulders. "It's a rare day at Bronson Stables when there are no visitors."

Book continued. "Apart from Adams, they've reported no one on the property who fits the description of a 'big man,' and we have no reason to believe the killer limps. What do you say?"

Lenore turned thoughtful. "There may have been visitors. I wouldn't know. I went riding at the break of dawn Thursday morning. I ride almost every morning. Then I read for a while here in this delightful room, where I come when I want to relax. The rest of the day, I visited a friend in town—Abner Wallace, editor and owner of the local paper, the *Jefferson Weekly*. He's asked me to write a column for the paper. We discussed the offer and agreed on an approach. In the evening, I worked on the column in my study, then went to bed, where I read. I fell asleep around eleven o'clock."

She smiled coquettishly. "Does that account for my whereabouts . . . Book?"

He couldn't help grinning. She'd caught him with the pause. He was pleased she'd called him by name, rather than parodying his title one more time. His visceral response was another reminder of his intention to devote his time in Jefferson County to repairing his marriage.

"*Your* whereabouts are not what concern me, but I appreciate the report. What I need is your help to identify the victim and the killer."

"Why should I help, even if I could?"

"For starters, in return for saving your life at the Old Virginny."

She laughed. "According to Dr. Warshawski, you didn't save my life. But it might have been a problem at the hospital if I'd bled out much more before getting treatment. By the way, Althea was quite taken with you. You should give her a call when this case quiets down."

He pretended to ignore the extent to which he'd registered on the attractive physician's scorecard. "I'm asking for your help because you seem to be in a position to give it when no one else can or is willing to."

"I'll help on one condition."

"Which is?"

"Don't tell Jeb or Daddy I've shared information with you. They're very territorial when anything affects their business."

Book looked puzzled. "Why do you think the killing might relate to their business and not their personal life?"

She frowned, obviously annoyed he wasn't quicker on the uptake. "You don't get it. At Bronson Stables, everything relates to business, and business is Ares Worldwide. There is *no personal life*. At Bronson Stables there's nothing and no one that's 'unrelated.' Except me, that is."

"You talk as if you don't get along with your family."

She guffawed. "You're not from around here. That's for sure. You must be ignorant of how things work in rich old Southern families. Let me spell it out for you. I hate Daddy. I hate Jeb even more. To top it off, they've no use for me. Like many families, we coexist, occupying the same space."

"If you feel that way, why don't you leave?"

"This is my home. I was born here. Grew up here. I love Bronson Stables. I love Jefferson County and the people who live here. Not that I haven't been other places. After my mom divorced Daddy and later died, during my rebellious teens, there was ample reason to leave."

"What happened?"

She sighed. "Maybe someday I'll tell you the root cause of my life getting fucked up. Suffice it to say, I went to live with my Aunt Rosemary in Richmond and stayed there for several years. With my aunt's home as a base, I attended William and Mary, where my major was . . . you guessed it . . . history. Anxious to spread my wings—anything to irritate Daddy—William and Mary was followed by a master's degree at Harvard and a year traveling around the world."

She shook her head.

"After twelve months of aimless wandering, I decided, no matter what I was running away from or running toward, it wasn't out there, in the world. I was going to have to find it here. How pathetic is that? A dysfunctional family is better than no family at all. So, I came home."

Book said, "There's no reason to let on you're helping."

"Enough about that," she said. "One thing is certain—the 'big man' in your midnight scenario is someone from the Farm . . ." She glanced at him to confirm Book knew what she meant. ". . . or someone from the Ares Worldwide site down in North Carolina."

Book gestured to indicate he was following her, knew of those locations and, in general, was aware of what went on in each one.

"Any of dozens of Ares staff could have been here on Thursday. Any of them could have committed the murder. Although I have no reason to think they did or theories about why they would have. The usual liaison with the Farm is Bear Lansky. He's former Special Forces—as are many Ares employees. Come to think of it, you could have been Special Forces."

"I was. Iraq and Afghanistan."

"You've got the look, even though you're bigger than most of them. You're about the same size as Bear. Most guys in Special Forces are more compact, middleweight, or light heavyweight, like Jeb. I've observed their training. Stamina is valued over size or brute strength. The system favors wiry guys who can run forever and hang in there when the going gets tough."

"How would I go about finding out who might have been here?" Book asked, bringing the conversation back on point.

"Not going to happen. If Daddy or Jeb is involved, they won't give you an opening to learn anything. They'll keep Bear or anyone else who might have been at the stable away from here until things quiet down. If there's a record pointing to an official visitor, they'll block your access. The Pentagon will back them because you've no probable cause. Even if you had probable cause, the government doesn't want anyone investigating military contractors."

Book was inclined to believe her, but he had to ask. "Not even law enforcement?"

She hooted. "Least of all law enforcement. Last year, there was a hit-and-run in front of the courthouse. Dorothy Wintergreen, a young clerk who was working late, was struck by a vehicle. Dragged almost one hundred feet before she broke free of the bumper. She died in the ambulance on the way to the hospital. Before she lapsed into a coma, she gave one of the paramedics a description of the SUV she saw just before impact—a black or dark blue Ford Expedition."

Book listened attentively.

Lenore continued. "Everyone in town had seen staff from the Farm driving black Expeditions. Sheriff Garrett tried to get access to search for a damaged vehicle with evidence of a hit-and-run on the bumper. Wintergreen's DNA would have provided positive identification. Daddy stonewalled him. Backing Daddy, the Pentagon supported a no search policy. For a while, it was touch and go whether Pat would resign over the issue, but, when the chips were down, he decided to stay. Wintergreen's death was a much stronger case than yours. You don't have a body. Not even clear evidence anything happened out by the stable. The Bronsons'll laugh in your face."

Book reached out to touch Lenore's arm. He felt a frisson at the soft feel of her skin on his hands.

"I can't solve this alone. You know more about what goes on inside Ares than anyone who's not part of this conspiracy. Will you show me how to look inside the black box?"

Tears came to her eyes, and she wrenched her arm free. She wiped her face. "Damn you, Book. Why did you have to show up to complicate my life just when I was starting to settle for the status quo?"

She turned to look out the windows toward the stable. In a hushed voice, she said, "Yes. I'll help."

CHAPTER 20

Carmen's interrogation of Fix Magruder uncovered no new leads. She came away, however, feeling she'd further ingratiated herself with the irascible ex-jockey who, for some inexplicable reason, seemed to like her.

No one on her list of those who were present that fateful Thursday provided information of obvious face value. The one person left to interview was Adams. Carmen waited in the library for him to show up.

The library walls were covered from floor to ceiling with books of every genre. Several tiers of bookcases were lined with tomes dealing with all aspects of the military history of the Civil War. Other American wars were shelved in chronological order: American Revolution, War of 1812, Mexican War, Spanish-American War, World Wars I and II, Korea, Vietnam, war in the Balkans, the two Iraq wars, and Afghanistan.

Carmen was starting to examine shelves focused on the role of mercenaries in warfare when she heard Adams shuffle through the doorway.

The sheer dimensions of the man were formidable, threatening, even clothed in a somber gray suit. He was taller than she remembered, and his shoulders and chest were gargantuan. She had no doubt the limp was genuine.

The temptation to touch the pistol holstered on her right hip was followed by a muffled laugh for even thinking there was anything to fear in this austere library. Carmen resolved not to be intimidated by the former soldier turned butler. She'd hit upon a method to interview him.

Smiling at Adams, she indicated he should take a seat in one of the matched upholstered chairs facing the small fireplace in the center of an inner wall. From that vantage point, there was a minimum of distractions.

"Mr. Adams, I'm Deputy Carmen Garcia. Detective Booker and I are investigating a reported disturbance out by the stable last Thursday night. Two men were seen fighting. Robert Lee and Jeb Bronson agreed to Detective Booker's request to interview people who were at Bronson Stables on Thursday."

With no more expression than any other statuary scattered around the library, Adams's countenance might have been carved in marble.

"I thought the best way for us to communicate would be to ask you questions and for you to write your answers in this notebook. Will that work for you?" She passed Adams a steno pad and a Sharpie black marker.

Yes, he wrote.

"For openers, please tell me your first name."

Adams shrugged and wrote, *Adams is my name.*

"I see, known by one name—like Pele, Shaq, or Mr. T."

No. Like Adams.

Chastised, she resolved to keep the dialogue focused on the business at hand. "Can you confirm you were here all day Thursday?"

I was here.

"Were there any visitors or houseguests?"

No.

"Did you see anyone who was here on business during the day or evening?"

No.

Carmen could see this line of inquiry was going to prove barren, but she pressed ahead, determined to complete her assignment.

"At any time on Thursday, did you go out to the stable?"

No. Adams no longer bothered to write on the steno pad. He flashed the page with the negative rejoinder.

Determined to break the rhythm of the fruitless interrogation, she shifted gears. No more questions that could be answered with a brusque "no."

"How often do you leave Bronson Stables to go into town or elsewhere?"

Adams faltered, unsure how to respond. Looking frustrated, he wrote, *Several times a week.*

"Where do you go?"

Town, the Farm. He hesitated. *Sometimes into the DC area.*

The deputy was sure each destination was a location Adams was certain she could verify if she bothered to check. What other locations were not mentioned?

"When was the last time you went to any of those places?"

Thursday.

At last, something useful—and a contradiction of a previous answer. "Where did you go?"

Town.

"How long were you gone?"

2 or 3 hours, in the evening.

"Could someone have come to Bronson Stables while you were away?"

For the first time, a crack in Adams's marble countenance was discernible. Anger peeked through.

Again, the compulsion to reach for the comfort of the Glock surfaced, and this time it was harder to resist. No longer humorous, the threat from the big man felt palpable.

How the hell should I know?

The statement clashed with his earlier claim no one had come to the mansion last Thursday.

"During the past two weeks, who has come to Bronson Stables, and when?"

After recording his answers, she concluded the interview. Shoulders tense, Adams limped from the library.

Carmen continued to sit before the fire, staring at the flames, lost in thought.

She reflected on what she'd learned and where it might lead the investigation. Horsewoman Mary's description of the fight and ensuing murder in the sheriff's office was accurate in every detail. Fix Magruder had helped Carmen find evidence of how the crime was covered up. The inescapable conclusion: the two additions to the Bronson household last Thursday—a murderer and a victim—had disappeared. And no one would admit having seen them.

They're either ignorant of what transpired or they're part of the cover-up.

CHAPTER 21

Annabel Lee left the Jefferson Café at eleven o'clock. She'd volunteered to stay later than usual to help her boss Alice close up. This allowed her fellow waitress Lulu to leave early, enabling her to tuck in her nine-year-old and spend time with her husband Jake.

Twice a week, rain or shine, Annabel Lee performed this good deed. She was sure Alice approved, although she never let on, not prone to step over the line of an even-handed proprietress.

This practice was adopted to fulfill a New Year's resolution Annabel Lee had made to honor the state of matrimony, believing it might help her snare a husband. Going to church every Sunday to pray, which was the resolution she'd fulfilled throughout the previous year, was a nonstarter. Besides, the frigging pews hurt her tender butt.

Halfway through the four-block walk from Courthouse Square to her home, Annabel Lee opened her purse, pulled out an unfiltered Camel, and lit up. She thought, *Maybe if I play my cards right, I might wrangle a date with the new detective.*

The exhaustion of a long day at the restaurant dissipated with each puff of the cigarette. Never one to smoke in the house, she ground out the Camel on the sidewalk and stepped onto the porch, noticing both the porch light and the streetlight were dark. Her porch was blacker than a witch's cat.

The squeak of the porch swing transformed her budding

nervousness into full-blown panic. She twirled, with the aim of dashing back to the street. The fastest sprinter on her high school track team, Annabel Lee was confident no one could catch her in a foot race to Courthouse Square and the sheriff's office.

The second she attempted to leap off the steps, she felt arms seizing her around the waist. A scream was choked off by a hand over her mouth. A thumb and finger pinched her nostrils. She couldn't breathe.

Whoever was holding her was a foot taller than she was and unbelievably powerful. She struggled futilely, kicking hard at her attacker's shins.

"Whoa, girl. Those kicks sting like hell. Cut it out or I'll have to hurt you."

Another attacker said, "Quit kicking. Just keep quiet if you want us to let you breathe."

Annabel Lee recognized the men's voices. There was no point trying to fight these hulks. She ceased struggling.

"I'm gonna take my hand off your mouth and nose. You yell, we'll mess you up real good."

Still shaken as her face came free, the young woman was no longer in fear of her life.

"Bubba, is that you? Does your Pa know what you're up to?"

Pa Clanton spoke up. "I'm here, Annabel Lee. So are Bubba's brothers."

Trying to sound calm, but belatedly realizing the seriousness of her situation, she said, "Whaddya want with me? I never did you a bad turn. I never run you down, no matter what other folks said. Live and let live, that's what I say."

"This ain't about you," Pa said. "We jist need you to do us a favor."

"A favor? Hell of a way to ask for a favor."

"If'n you do what we say, you won't get hurt," a new voice chimed in.

"That you Seymour?"

"Yeah, it's Seymour," Pa said. "Now, shut your piehole. Open your door. We're goin' inside."

Recognizing the four dark shapes surrounding her, Annabel Lee knew there was no escape. She reached into her purse, pulled out the key, and unlocked the front door.

"Close the blinds. Turn on the lights you use at this time of night. If'n any neighbors get nosy, it'll go hard on you."

"Whaddya want with me?" she repeated.

"Gimme your cell." Pa took her portable phone and stuck it in a pocket of his coveralls.

"Sit on the couch over there," he said, pointing to a spot next to a Mickey Mouse telephone.

"You're gonna make a call. Here's the number." Pa handed her a piece of paper. "Read what's writ on there."

Reading the instructions, the significance of the axe handles the men were carrying became crystal clear. Her rational mind told her the crude weapons weren't for her, but a lingering fear whispered, "What if?"

Hands shaking, she picked up Mickey, punched in the number for the Silverado Motel, and tried to calm her fears. She mumbled apologies for two wrong numbers before connecting with a groggy Detective Booker.

CHAPTER 22

Barely awake after answering the phone, Book wished for those days when he was quicker on the uptake. He tuned in when the caller identified herself as the waitress at the Jefferson Café who'd served him breakfast. She insisted he come to her home at once. The emergency involved some threat to Lenore Bronson, too complicated to explain over the phone.

Annabel Lee claimed to be frightened for her own safety. The detective picked up on the tremor in her voice, which added credibility to her fear. His suggestion they meet at the sheriff's office was rebuffed; he sensed her reaction to the idea verged on panic.

"Are you sure about this, Annabel Lee?"

"As sure as you eat grits for breakfast," she said.

He hadn't ordered grits. The morning's serving had consisted of pancakes, bacon, eggs, orange juice, and coffee. He wondered if she was being literal or if this was just a saying common to Southern waitresses?

Whether it was her intent or not, the discrepancy put him on guard. He got directions, dressed, collected his weapons, and bolted out the door to his SUV. During the short drive to Annabel Lee's, he contemplated calling for backup but decided not to. He'd rather face a possible threat than be the butt of jokes if the waitress's cockamamie story were to prove to be a scam.

He drove to her address, killed the engine, and turned off the lights. Playing it safe—or maybe just procrastinating—he sized up the neighborhood. Most vehicles were parked in driveways, or perhaps in garages at the back of the property. The few lights in houses seemed about what one would expect near the midnight hour. Annabel Lee's windows were lit, with the blinds pulled, but he could detect no sign of her or anyone else. The yard appeared to be empty. A barking dog almost drowned out the muted sound of a TV playing a late-night comedy show.

Everything seemed ordinary, yet somehow wasn't. Despite outward appearances, something was amiss. He felt the same tingling in the back of his neck he used to get in Afghanistan when he was being watched. He'd learned to rely on such instincts to survive.

He considered calling for backup and again rejected the move. *Time to bite the bullet.*

He unholstered the SIG Sauer 9 mm, his weapon of choice when not on official duty. He kept a round in the chamber. Since the pistol had no conventional safety, it was ready to fire at all times with just a squeeze on the trigger.

He moved onto the porch in a combat stance, silent and ready for action.

Responding to his knock, Annabel Lee opened the door part way. "Run, Book. It's a trap."

Footsteps, coming up on his left and right flanks, converged. He moved to defend himself when a terrible pain convulsed his back, propelling him through the now open door.

He staggered into Annabel Lee. A sharp blow knocked the SIG from his grasp. He remembered Joe the barkeep's warning—the Clanton clan had arrived, with axe handles.

Figuring his best bet was to put some distance between himself and his attackers, Book powered forward into the center of the room, conscious of a grazing blow on his right shoulder. As he moved, he took stock of his injuries—painful, but not yet crippling. His legs had not been touched. His left side was unharmed. With his left hand, he drew the Colt .357 MAG from the paddle holster at the small of his back. When he tried to level the revolver, one of the Clantons pounced and knocked it away. A glancing blow to the head sent Book to the floor.

BAM BAM.

The thought that the bastards had guns gave him a cold chill.

Seymour raised the axe handle over his head and prepared to swing. He wielded it with one hand. The blue cast on the other arm didn't appear to slow him down, nor did the brace on his knee. Book cringed in a futile attempt to evade the blow.

BAM.

Seymour's shoulder erupted in a fountain of red. The axe handle flew across the room and slammed against the wall.

Book looked up in astonishment to see Sheriff Garrett standing in the doorway, drawing down on an older man who had to be Pa Clanton.

Pat said, "Your move, Pa. Put down the axe handle so you can tend to your sons. Your boys all have life-threatening wounds. Bubba's right hip is blown away. Bobby Ray's going to need a left knee replacement. Seymour looks like his shoulder's done for. They'll live if we get them to the hospital right away. Fuck up and I'll kill you. Your boys will bleed to death while I watch. What's it gonna be?"

Hatred flamed on Pa Clanton's face. Clenching the axe handle, he took a half-step toward the sheriff, hesitated, then threw the weapon against the far wall.

"Pat, you son of a bitch, I'll see you in hell someday."

"Maybe, old man," the sheriff said. "But not today."

CHAPTER 23

"Pat, how'd you happen to be near the house?" Book asked, when things had calmed down after deputies and ambulances arrived to cart off the Clanton clan.

"Well, you can thank Homeland Security money. A few years back, the county got some 'no strings attached' funding from DHS as part of the so-called war on terror. I used part of those dollars to buy some fancy GPS tracking devices. I put a GPS beacon in each of the Clanton's trucks. Those damn gadgets pinpoint a vehicle's location within a hundred feet. The techies have invented a computer program that enables me to plot on a map whenever the vehicle with the beacon crosses the Jefferson County line. An app on my cell phone alerts me if any of the Clantons drive anywhere in the county. When I got the alert last night, I jumped into my cruiser and hustled to where they parked their truck. Not much doubt they were after you, Book."

"So, you heard about the incident at the Old Virginny," Book said.

"All my life, I've lived in Jefferson County. I'd be a piss poor excuse for a sheriff if I didn't know what goes on in an adjoining county. Joe Ferguson is the son of an old friend. I remember watching Joe wrestling in the state tournament; he came in first, crowned as heavyweight champ. He told me he'd warned you about the Clanton clan's tendency to settle scores with axe handles."

Book realized he should have leveled with Pat from the outset. "Listen, let me set the record straight..."

"Forget it," Pat interrupted. "You told me you were going to lay off the booze and get back in shape. Does that still hold?"

"Yes, more than ever."

"That's good enough for me. You're not the first guy to be tempted by an open bar. You won't be the last."

Annabel Lee, who'd been listening to the exchange, asked, "What happened after you found the Clanton's truck?"

"The Clantons parked their truck a couple of blocks away. There was no way of knowing where they'd gone. Searching in the dark got me nowhere. I was about to call Book to warn him, but then I realized what Pa Clanton would do, namely lure Book into a trap. You lived around here, so your house was the logical place for a trap. I ran like hell to get here. Some damn dog raised a ruckus at me cutting through its yard. I was worried the barking might alert Pa, who's a lot smarter than his boys. Just as you yelled a warning to Book, I caught a glimpse of him charging through your front door."

"Lucky you came along," Book said. "Seymour was about to plant an axe handle in my head."

CHAPTER 24

Book staggered into his motel room. He halved the strength of the painkillers and muscle relaxants prescribed by Dr. Warshawski, downing the pills before getting ready for bed. After setting the alarm, he removed his weapons and, still clothed, crawled under the covers. Despite his injuries, he was determined to wake by dawn and continue the ritual of running five miles, honoring his commitment to the sheriff to get back in shape.

Drifting off to sleep, he couldn't help smiling at Althea's comments as the comely physician had reviewed his x-ray results. "Since you've come to town, Book, business is booming. You've given our emergency room staff a lot of practice on knife cuts, beatings, and gunshot wounds."

He felt like his eyes had just closed when he was awakened by a loud ringing. He groped for the alarm, pushing the off button while knocking the clock radio to the floor. The annoying ringing continued unabated. His cell phone was the culprit.

He puzzled over who the hell could be calling at five-thirty.

Still half-asleep, he picked up the phone.

"Book. Good morning."

"Marlene. Is everything all right? How are the kids?"

"Everything's fine. I called because I wanted to catch you before your morning run. Sunrise is due soon. How are *you*? You sound a little strange."

"I'm doing great. We had a little incident here last night. I'll tell you all about it when we get together."

Marlene replied, a lilt to her voice, "That'll be sooner than we planned. I'm coming down there this weekend."

"Great," Book said. He'd missed her more than he was willing to admit, even to himself. Living alone in motels sucked. "What's the occasion?"

"I've taken a new job. The firm gave me a partner sabbatical for a year to work on the Hill with Thaddeus Green. The senator asked me to spearhead an investigative task force for the Armed Services Committee, looking into the controversy surrounding the use of military contractors."

Unlike Marlene, Book didn't follow politics. But he knew Green was a US senator from Virginia. Green was one of fewer than a dozen members of Congress with sons or daughters on active duty. He remembered Green's son was a Marine who'd served in Afghanistan.

"Green's a good man. But why you? I know you're a crackerjack investigator, but you've no background with the military."

"Believe it or not, having no background is a plus. Everyone who's connected with the military in any way is suspect on this issue. Green showed me a long list of people he'd considered for this job—retired military officers, congressional staff, lobbyists, leading contractors, and other lawyers—and explained the reason each candidate was ruled out."

Book puzzled briefly over the mysteries of politics in the nation's capital before deciding he'd never figure it out.

Marlene said, "Paradoxically, I'm the best qualified because I have no qualifications at all on the issue. What I do have is a deep resume investigating corporations for financial and other shenanigans. Green said my resume is just what he was looking for."

"Why else did you take the job?"

"You know I've always been interested in politics. Green is one of the few politicians I admire. He's honest. Even better, he's proven his independence from special interests. A big factor in my decision to accept his offer—he was willing to let me write my own ticket for the job. I've been given a free hand to pick my staff. Of course, the senator retains a veto power if either the Democrats or Republicans object on the grounds the staff overall is tilting in one direction or the other. Since I have no preconceptions about how the inquiry should turn out, it's a plus to have the support of both parties."

Marlene cleared her throat. "Best of all, he agreed I could work half-time. That'll free me up to spend more time with Rebecca and Jonathan."

"Sounds like you've covered all the bases. When do you start?"

"I've already started. Most of the staff have been selected. We've begun outlining a strategy for the investigation."

"You always did get out of the gate fast." Book hid his disappointment. She'd made a major life change without finding it necessary to discuss it with him in advance, breaking a pattern they'd followed for sixteen years of marriage.

He could hear Marlene exhale, an unfailing "tell" signaling a major surprise was coming.

"I've already made a significant discovery. Ares Worldwide is the largest and most influential of the military contractors. Ares's CEO is—"

"Jeb Bronson," Book finished for her. "My friend and former company commander, who just happens to live in Jefferson County, and—"

"Who's responsible for you taking the job down there," she finished.

"That's right," he said. "What you may also have learned is that the operational headquarters of Ares Worldwide is located in the county."

"I know. That's why I'm coming—to look things over. What you call 'a reconnaissance.'"

Book said, "What you don't know is I have reason to believe a murder was committed on Bronson's property last Thursday night. We're in the middle of a sensitive investigation with damn few clues. This may not be the best time for you to show up. For all I know, it may not even be safe."

There was a long silence. Even Book's quick-witted wife had the wind taken out of her sails at the unexpected piece of information.

"I'm coming anyway," Marlene said. "For one thing, I want to see you. There'll be time when I get there to talk about how best to handle anything related to the Senate inquiry. Maybe we won't even mention it. Let me think on that. I assume you're keeping the murder investigation confidential."

"Right. No one in Washington has a need to know."

"All right, darling."

Book's pulse ran faster to hear his wife calling him darling, thinking *Maybe our marriage can be saved, after all.*

CHAPTER 25

In the aftermath of the beating he'd taken the previous night, Book was amazed his run went as well as it did. Once he got limbered up, his body responded, although he was still sore. Returning to the motel room, he cleaned up and headed for the Jefferson Café.

Carmen was already there, having staked out his favorite table for their scheduled meeting. She was tucking into a full stack of hotcakes.

Annabel Lee walked in, carrying a tray load of breakfasts out of the kitchen. Book was impressed she seemed to have bounced back from the previous night's incident.

She served the food at another table, then came over to Book. Not saying anything, she reached for his hand and held it for a few seconds. Tears ran down her cheeks. She wiped them off with her apron. Still silent, she bent down, kissed him on the cheek, turned, and scurried back into the kitchen.

Alice watched the drama from behind the counter, came over to the table, leaned over, and kissed Book on the other cheek. Saying nothing, she headed off to wait on some customers who had just come in.

A bemused Carmen asked, "What was that all about?"

"I'll tell you later," Book said.

"Like hell you will," she said. "You promised you'd tell me later about the incident with Lenore at the Old Virginny Bar and Billiards.

But you never said a word. Now you're promising to tell me later about Annabel Lee. Later is now, Detective. No more secrets between partners. What gives?"

"You're right. We're partners." In a quiet voice, he explained how the fight with Seymour at the pool table to protect Lenore had provoked retaliation by the Clanton clan at Annabel Lee's house. He emphasized that Pat Garrett had saved the day by shooting the three Clanton boys. His principal omission in telling the story was neglecting to make explicit the sheriff's threat to kill Pa Clanton and let his sons bleed to death if the old timer didn't put down the axe handle. He wondered if Pat would have carried out the warning, but he doubted his new boss made empty threats.

Carmen listened without interrupting, a troubled look on her face. "Book, you arrived in the area Saturday night. Today's Tuesday. So far, you've been cut with a knife, beaten with axe handles, watched a shooting, investigated a murder—and God knows what else I'm not aware of. What are you going to do for an encore the rest of the week?"

"With your help, Carmen, we'll solve the murder. Anyway, we're here this morning to share ideas. You first. What did you learn yesterday at the Bronson place?"

Reluctantly pushing away the unfinished plate of hotcakes, she pulled out a paper from her purse and laid it on the table. "Based more on intuition than hard facts, I'm convinced Jeb Bronson and his dad are orchestrating a mind-boggling cover-up."

She paused to assess Book's reaction. Apparently satisfied, she continued.

"In interviews with everyone on the list, the stories were virtual carbon copies: 'saw nothing; know nothing.' The scraps of useful information I discovered are summarized on this sheet."

She picked up the paper and showed it to Book. It was a standard matrix. Along the top row were arrayed the names of people she'd interviewed. Down the side of the first column were names (headed by the title "Visitors"), most of whom Book didn't recognize, although

Bear Lansky's name jumped out. In the intersecting cells for each row were days and dates. The matrix showed the time each visitor was at the Bronson property, according to each of the witnesses.

Book tapped the paper, waiting for a further explanation.

Carmen said, "This is the only 'hard' data I collected. Now, we have reports about everyone who was allegedly on the property and when. We can follow up and confirm each report."

"Good job. A clever approach."

Carmen smiled at the praise.

The matrix indicated that Lansky was the most frequent visitor, showing up at Bronson Stables every couple of days.

"Bear Lansky's activity squares with what I learned from Lenore Bronson," Book said. "She reported Lansky was the primary liaison with the Farm. Your matrix details a pattern of a visit every two days over a bimonthly period, suggesting he should have been there Thursday. But no one reported seeing him. Moreover, he didn't show up Saturday or Monday when we were there. I can quiz Jeb Bronson and see if he has an explanation and ask him to elaborate on other visitors."

He slipped the matrix into his jacket pocket.

"By the way, Lenore agreed to assist in our investigation. With her connections, we may be able to get a more in-depth look inside Ares Worldwide. She insisted we keep her involvement secret, especially from Jeb and Robert Lee. Turns out relations with her family are a long-standing train wreck."

CHAPTER 26

After chatting with Alice, Carmen was lost in thought as she wandered toward the sheriff's Office from the Jefferson Café. She wondered if it was time to touch base with Horsewoman Mary. She planned to reassure Mary that the sheriff's office believed her report of the murder was credible. In fact, it was the touchstone for the investigation.

The distinctive ring of her cell phone brought her back to reality. She fished it out of her purse and grinned at caller ID.

"Hi Dad. This is a pleasant surprise. How are things back home?"

"I just called to wish you Happy Birthday."

Carmen blinked. She'd been so caught up in the murder investigation, she'd forgotten her birthday was coming up.

"Thanks Dad, but my birthday's not till tomorrow. Let's hope you're not experiencing early-onset Alzheimer's."

"No way I'd forget the date of the happiest day of my life. I was hoping you could come home a couple of days for a birthday celebration. Without a doubt Pat Garrett will give you a little time off. I bet you haven't taken a day's leave since showing up for work in Jefferson County."

Carmen realized he was right. Four straight months without a break. Even on weekends, she'd focused on the job—doing research on the computer, shooting at a range out on the interstate, or just trying to get better acquainted with the community.

"You'd win that bet. But now's not a good time to be away." She sat on a bench in Courthouse Square and briefed him about the suspected murder at Bronson Stables. "As much as I'd love to see you, it's just not possible."

Her dad's apparent willingness to accept the situation astonished Carmen. They talked a few more minutes about inconsequential events, and he signed off. She sauntered into the office, musing. It wasn't like Sheriff Jose Garcia to give up without an argument.

"Morning, Shirley."

"Good morning, Carmen. Pat wants to see you."

Locking her purse in her lower left desk drawer, Carmen walked across the office. She waved a greeting to George and Sam, both of whom ignored her.

She gave a perfunctory knock and entered the sheriff's office.

"Pull up a chair, Carmen. Book showed me the spreadsheet you put together with names and times of people coming and going at the Bronson place. The chart will be useful in the investigation. Good work."

She tried to hide her pride at the unexpected compliment from Pat, not known for doling out unearned praise.

"I called you in because I'm having a party at my home tomorrow night. You're invited. So is Book."

Heading off any protest about being too busy investigating a crime to take time for a celebration, he continued, "The party's a command performance. Seven o'clock. See you there."

CHAPTER 27

Carmen sat at her desk, wondering why Pat would invite her to a party.

Since his wife died several years ago, the word around the office was Pat never socialized. According to Shirley, the closest the sheriff came to a social life was participating in Cowboy Action competitions sponsored by the NRA.

One incident still perturbed her. When George and Sam thought she was out of the office, she'd overheard them gossiping about the sheriff's periodic visits to a woman in a neighboring county "to get his ashes hauled." She looked up the phrase on Google and confirmed it meant exactly what she expected.

Feeling uncomfortable about prying, but wanting to know more about her reserved boss, she'd finally worked up her courage and asked Alice. The restaurateur related how, after his wife's death from cancer, Pat began a discreet affair with a vet from a neighboring county. Tragically, the vet also contracted cancer and died several months ago. She'd left two chocolate labs, Jake and Boomer, in his care.

Carmen imagined she'd see the dogs at the party.

Forcing herself to stop chewing on the mystery of the party invitation, Carmen reaffirmed her decision to contact Mary Connolly. The woman deserved a briefing about the murder case. She hoped the experience would prompt Mary to recall something else that would help move the investigation forward.

"Hey, Shirley, do you have a minute?" In response to the affirmative nod, she said, "How about joining me for a cup of coffee across the square?"

They walked together, enjoying the pleasant spring weather. Propelled by brisk winds, white cirrus clouds flickered across a sapphire sky. Just a few feet ahead of Shirley and Carmen, pigeons pecked their way across the sidewalk, bobbing their heads as they searched for food.

Shirley said, "You know . . . this is the first time since we met you've asked me to join you at the café."

"You're right. We should do this more often."

The administrative assistant laughed. "Never con a con. Pleasant as you are, you're not just being buddy-buddy. I've watched you. You're all business—one hundred percent cop. What's going on?"

Carmen held up her hands in surrender, an embarrassed grin on her face.

"There *is* an ulterior motive. I need to contact Horsewoman Mary. But I don't know how to track down a woman who's homeless. Pointless to hang around random stables at night hoping she'll show up to 'look after' the horses. You must have a hunch about how to find her. I didn't want to ask you in the office where George or Sam might listen in. Besides, even if you knew, they're the last people you'd want to overhear such a conversation."

Shirley stopped midstride. "Let's sit here." She pointed to the bench where Carmen had sat earlier while talking with her dad.

"Give me a minute . . ." Shirley sat stock-still, deep in thought, staring at the drifting clouds, tumbling one upon the other.

"Sorry, I didn't mean to upset you," Carmen said. "Forget I asked. Let's just go have some coffee."

"Shut up and let me think." After several moments, Shirley signaled she'd decided how to respond.

"There are only three people in the county who know how to find Mary. We each gave her our word we'd never tell anyone.

You wouldn't ask unless it was important. Promise me never to say anything about this, not even to Book. The sheriff already knows, and he'll never tell."

"I promise."

Shirley pulled out a piece of paper and sketched a brief map.

CHAPTER 28

The sound of gravel crunching caused Mary Connolly to jump up and hurry to the front window of the cabin she'd called home the past several years. Much to her surprise, a Ford Police Interceptor bearing the unmistakable markings of a sheriff's cruiser was coming up the driveway.

In her confusion, she wondered if Pat Garrett was coming for a visit. Although the sheriff knew where she lived, he'd never been to her home. *Why now?*

Shirley also knew where she lived, but Mary was certain her friend would never come for a visit. The vehicle was further confirmation; Shirley drove a red Jeep Grand Cherokee, not an official police cruiser.

She watched it creep up the winding gravel road and pull to a stop near the cabin's front door. At that point, she realized the driver was the rookie deputy, Carmen Garcia.

Mary had observed the novice rider from afar the past few mornings, approving the way she mucked out the stable and groomed the horses. But the horsewoman was critical of Carmen's riding skills, although she admitted they weren't bad for a beginner.

Mary blamed Carmen's shortcomings on Stephanie Wilkerson, who didn't know how to coach riding. Mary was certain she could teach Carmen a few tricks in a couple of weeks.

The real question was what had brought the sheriff's deputy

here. Mary assumed Pat or Shirley must have told her where she lived, even though they swore they wouldn't. She agonized over which one had betrayed her.

Mary, panic stricken, thought about bolting out the back door, but took a deep breath and strove to remain calm.

The polite knock on the door heightened her nervousness and triggered the thought, *No one comes here. No one. Ever.*

She opened the door cautiously. "Come in," she said, with a low shaky voice, almost a whisper.

Seeing the deputy's hesitation, Mary screwed up her courage. "Please come in," she repeated in a normal voice, with a hint of genuine welcome, and swung the door open all the way.

"Sorry for showing up unannounced. There's no cause for concern. We just need to talk."

Relaxing somewhat at the reassuring tone, Mary waved her visitor into the cozy kitchen.

Glancing around the room, Carmen noted it was built like a stateroom on a small schooner. Although the exterior of the building was made up of rough-hewn logs, the interior showed the hand of a fine cabinetmaker. The walls and ceiling were mahogany. The floor planks were oak, with tongue and groove construction. Each piece of furniture was meticulously built and perfect for its function. One side of the room was a kitchen, with a table, four chairs, and a well-stocked cupboard. The other side was designed for relaxing, with a couch, rocker, small desk and matching chair, a bookcase filled with books of all types, and lamps placed to maximum effect. The quiet hum of a generator explained the lighting that gave the living quarters a warm and bright feel.

"Forgive me. Where are my manners?" Mary pulled out one of the four chairs with contoured seats that bracketed the kitchen table.

Upon reflection, she realized Carmen must be scared too, probably having heard outlandish stories about "Crazy Mary."

"How about a cup of tea? Or perhaps you prefer coffee."

"A cup of tea would be wonderful."

Mary filled the tea kettle and set it to boil on the gas range. Delicate China cups and saucers were placed on the table. An open pot of honey was laid out. Packets of Earl Grey tea were arrayed in a small silver cup.

"Is that a Jefferson Cup?" Carmen asked. Without waiting for an answer, she added, "My dad bought me one of those on a visit to Williamsburg when I was a little girl."

"The same way I got mine," Mary said, smiling at the recollection.

Tea was poured. The two women sat, reluctant to break the mood of companionable silence.

Mary could stand the suspense no longer. "I must know how you found me. No one comes here. Ever."

"Please don't be upset," Carmen said. "Shirley drew me a map, because I told her it was urgent we talk about the murder investigation. She made me promise not to tell anyone of your location, not even my partner Detective Booker. I swear to you I'll keep your secret."

Twisting her hands, Mary stood up and walked into the living area. She stopped before the window, agonizing whether her sacred privacy would be violated and whether Carmen could be trusted.

Not knowing how to react, Carmen sat immobile on the kitchen chair.

Mary heaved a sigh, came back to the table, and sat down, taking a sip of tea. "I'm not upset. Shirley trusted you because she could tell you're a good person, and it was important you find me. I trust you, just as I do Shirley and Pat. Just as I do Lawrence Ronstadt, my landlord and friend who gave me sanctuary when my family was killed and I lost everything. Several times a week, Lawrence comes by to bring provisions and to make sure everything is okay."

Mary sipped her tea.

"You've heard I'm homeless—crazy too, I imagine. Indeed, I would be crazy if it weren't for Lawrence's generosity. You know, he built this cabin. He also designed and made the furnishings. His ambition was to be a sailor, and his inspiration came from sailing magazines. His father was a carpenter. He learned a lot about building things from him, but he's a self-taught cabinetmaker. Because his wife wouldn't let him smoke in the house, he claims he built the cabin so he would have a quiet refuge to smoke his pipe. I'm not sure that's the whole story. After his wife died, he gave up the pipe and stopped coming to the cabin."

Going along with the tale of how Mary came to be in the cabin, Carmen asked, "How'd Lawrence come to invite you to live here?"

Horsewoman Mary's countenance glowed with the memory. "He said he'd always admired my riding, even when I was 'a little girl sitting atop those giant stallions,' as he put it. I'd been scared of him, like all the other kids and most of the adults. He had the reputation for being an angry man with a vicious temper who'd hurt several men in fights and shot at trespassers foolish enough to cross his fences. Even winged a couple of teenagers with birdshot."

Mary paused and both women focused on drinking tea.

"When problems arose I couldn't handle, Lawrence came to me and suggested I live here. The place had been vacant for some time, and was a bit run down. We cleaned it out and fixed things up. I brought my clothes and a few belongings and moved in. He agreed to help perpetuate the myth of homelessness and to keep my whereabouts secret. Up till today, that's worked."

Mary's countenance eased after telling the story.

"And it will continue to work in the future," Carmen said. "Your secret's safe. Let me tell you the reason for my visit."

Mary looked with intense interest at her visitor and moved to pick up the kettle on the stove. She refilled the cups.

Carmen briefed her on the investigation, starting with heartfelt appreciation and admiration for her courageous visit to the sheriff's office to report the murder. Hearing how the deputy and Fix Magruder had found the strangely packed dirt, the best evidence of the crime, Mary's face lit up and she relaxed completely for the first time since Carmen arrived.

The deputy recapped her fruitless search to identify the victim, highlighting Alice's speculation he might have been one of three recent nonlocal patrons at the Jefferson Café. She gave an abbreviated version of the inquiries at the Bronson's place, naming Bear Lansky as the liaison with the Farm.

"Wait," Mary said, holding up a hand. "You've just reminded me of something. I've seen the murderer before. I'm almost sure of it. You know how you can recognize someone by a distinctive walk or other mannerism, even when you don't see their face?"

Growing excited, she stood and began pacing around the room.

"That's it. I saw him across from the courthouse last Thursday. He climbed out of a black Ford Expedition, the kind they use out at the Farm. No markings. But you can't mistake those SUVs. Always clean and polished, in perfect shape. I'm positive. I didn't see his face, but his movements were distinctive. The way he moved when he killed the man at the stable was the same as the way he moved around the car."

CHAPTER 29

"Shirley, I need some advice," Book said, thinking of Marlene's upcoming arrival. He was determined to avoid having his wife stay at the Silverado Motel.

"What about?"

"My wife Marlene will be visiting this weekend. I've got to find a decent place to live—a furnished rental house or cottage we can occupy at once."

Shirley nodded.

"Your best bet is to see Homer Smedley. Tell him I sent you. Don't say you used to live in Fairfax County, because he hates Northern Virginia. Homer's a rare bird who takes a lot of getting used to. I should know because I dated him off and on in high school. But he's as honest as anybody in that line of work. And he's the biggest realtor in the tricounty area."

The detective thanked Shirley and headed out of the office. As he was leaving, he realized he hadn't briefed the sheriff on Marlene's key role in investigating Ares Worldwide. Her work would intersect with the murder investigation.

He knew there was no possibility of dissuading his strong-minded spouse to cancel or postpone her visit, which provided a golden opportunity for her to see the Bronsons firsthand.

There was no doubt Pat must be briefed, and quickly, on what

Marlene was up to with the Senate investigation and its potential for targeting Ares Worldwide. Book resolved to fill the sheriff in the next day.

Book took advantage of the May sunshine and walked to Smedley Realty, which was located on a side street a couple of blocks from Courthouse Square.

He entered the modest office, glancing at the walls covered with paintings of horse races and pictures of beautiful horseflesh. The same man was showcased in many of the pictures, aging not too gracefully over time.

Book introduced himself to a perky young woman sitting behind a burl walnut antique desk just inside the front door. She asked him to wait while Mr. Smedley finished his current appointment.

Soon, a short, chubby man sporting a full beard and wearing coveralls, emerged from Smedley's inner sanctum, followed by a man in a blue pinstripe wool suit. The two men were laughing.

Bidding his visitor goodbye, the realtor walked over to Book, a broad smile on his face, and extended a hand. Knowing the type, Book was braced for the bone-crushing handshake the realtor attempted.

"Quite a grip you've got there, Mr. Booker."

"Call me Book, or, if it's official business, call me Detective Booker. I joined the sheriff's office on Monday. Shirley said you might be able to help me find a rental."

Book followed Smedley into the realtor's inner office, which carried forward the themes of expensive antiques, mingled with paintings of hunts held in Jefferson County. Once he settled down to business, the facade of phony camaraderie evaporated. Smedley seemed to know what he was doing. He listened to the detective's requirements, including the challenge posed by Marlene's impending visit, and the resulting imperative to settle into a furnished abode in short order.

"I've got just the place for you. Rupert Jensen and his wife are on a round-the-world excursion and will be traveling the better part of a year. Their house sitter—it's a damn mansion really—was a schoolteacher. The young woman got herself pregnant and headed back home to West Virginia. Left last week. The Jensen place is vacant. I had to hire a watchman to look after the place, which is a blamed nuisance. You could move in Friday. Entertain your missus in style."

"Sounds great. What's the monthly rent?"

"*Rent.*" Smedley gave a hearty guffaw. "The rent's free. You're doing the Jensens a favor. Reliable people are hard to come by. No one's more reliable than a cop, above all a bone-a-fee-day detective. Over and above there being no rent, they pay you a hundred dollars a month stipend for your 'trouble' in looking after the place."

Knowing from bitter experience that things appearing to be too good to be true seldom are, Book reserved judgment, but he decided to look the "mansion" over.

To Book's amazement, the property far exceeded his expectations. At the rear of the mansion was a giant pool surrounded by a magnificent tiled patio. The diving area alone, sporting a high dive as well as a standard low board, was larger than most home pools. Book checked the safety of the high dive, noting the markings on the side of the pool showed the depth ranged to nine feet in the diving area and five feet in the shallow end.

He concluded the Jensens were real swimmers. He knew Marlene would love the pool. A champion swimmer in California where she'd grown up, Marlene first qualified for Olympic trials at age fifteen. From freshman through senior years at Princeton, she helped power the Tiger swim and dive team to the heights of Ivy League Championships.

The magnificent Blue Ridge Mountains could be seen in the distance. He was relieved to discover the stable was empty, confirming Smedley's assurances the horses were boarded with a neighbor. He hurried back to the realtor's office and signed a contract.

CHAPTER 30

Pat was in his office, alternating between shuffling the routine paperwork of a rural sheriff in a county with an unbalanced mix of rich and poor and thinking about the killing at Bronson Stables. Growing tired of the mental seesaw, he leaned back in his swivel chair, propped his boots on the desk, and devoted full attention to the murder investigation.

He was gratified Book and Carmen seemed to click. He recalled seeing in Book's face that the detective had toyed with resigning at the prospect of being forced to accept a partner. Pat's motivation for insisting on Carmen's assignment was a transparent lack of full trust in Book's ties with Jeb Bronson.

He glanced up and saw Carmen making a beeline for his door. Boots hit the floor with a thump, and he sat up straight.

Anxious to hear her report, he yelled "Come in" before she had time to knock.

"Sheriff, I've got some good news and some bad news."

He frowned at the flippant opening.

"I'll get the bad news out of the way first. I drove out to visit Mary Connolly today."

"You what . . ." The sheriff was so upset, he jumped to his feet. "How'd you find the place?"

"I'll tell you in a minute. But you should know the visit went well. We had tea. We talked about the murder investigation. She told me the story of how she came to live in the cabin, and she invited me to come back any time. Most importantly, she gave me new information that helps our case." Out of breath at the hurried summary, the deputy awaited the sheriff's reaction.

His face a mask of confusion, Pat sank back into his swivel chair, holding the oak armrests as though afraid he might fall to the floor.

"Shirley gave you a map, didn't she?"

"Yes, sir," Carmen replied. "I promised Shirley and Mary I'd never tell anyone about her living arrangements, not even Book."

"Now four people know," the sheriff sighed.

"They say if you want to keep a secret in Jefferson County, you tell one other person. As soon as you tell them, you kill them. That's the only way to keep a secret. Lawrence Ronstadt should shoot us all—and the old bastard would if he knew the news was spreading."

"But sheriff—"

"Don't you 'but sheriff' me. Give me a minute to get over being mad."

Carmen clamped her lips shut. She squeezed her fingers together so hard her hands hurt. This was one of the few times she'd seen Pat Garrett this angry, and the first time his anger was directed at her. He was a scary guy. Now she understood how he could have shot down the three Clanton boys without losing any sleep.

For the first time she realized the sheriff and Book had the same violence gene—the ability to kill and not appear to be affected. She wondered how she would react in a similar life-threatening situation.

Pat walked to the window and stood there, staring into space. Without realizing it, he'd echoed the pose of Horsewoman Mary when she stood tall on the same spot.

"The damage is done. You can't unbreak a dropped cup. Let's hear the news you think might help our murder investigation."

Carmen gave an abbreviated account of her visit to the cabin, highlighting the moment Mary had remembered glimpsing a silhouette whose movements suggested Lansky was the one getting out of a black Ford Expedition last Thursday—the day the Bronsons claimed he'd not been in town or at Bronson Stables.

Pat made a dismissive gesture when she clarified Mary had not actually seen Lansky's face.

"Just what we need. A report confirming our suspect's whereabouts."

Carmen relaxed a bit, but said, "You don't think the evidence is a bit thin?"

"Doesn't matter how thin it is, it's how credible we can make it seem."

They heard a quick knock. Book walked in.

Without delay, Pat told him Mary Connolly spotted Bear Lansky at Courthouse Square the past Thursday. He didn't elaborate on the circumstances leading up to the report or qualify it by citing Mary's acknowledgment that her eyewitness account was based on a silhouette's movements.

"We need to swear out an arrest warrant for Bear Lansky," the sheriff said.

"Our probable cause is a bit thin," Book said.

Pat said, "In a Virginia county, it takes two things for an arrest warrant: one, the sheriff has to sign there's probable cause; and two, the magistrate has to sign issuing the warrant. I'm prepared to sign. Judge Newsome will too. Your job, Book and Carmen, is to find the fugitive and apprehend him."

Carmen coughed. "I've heard, sir, Judge Newsome doesn't sneeze unless he has permission from Robert Lee Bronson."

"I don't know where you heard that, deputy," Pat began, "but it's dead accurate."

Carmen looked perplexed at the incongruity.

"None of that matters. Believe me. The judge will sign, but not before he calls Robert Lee to ask for approval. He'll get permission in advance, because the Bronsons know I wouldn't force the issue unless we had evidence. They won't risk the type of stink I could raise if push came to shove. They'd rather deal with our little band than face a confrontation with the state police."

"So we'll be able to arrest Lansky," Book said.

"One of two things will happen," Pat said. "You'll arrest Bear—that means he's innocent. Or you won't—that means he's guilty of murder."

CHAPTER 31

Robert Lee Bronson was in his study chomping on a Cohiba cigar and fiddling with papers on his desk when the call came through from Judge Newsome. He detected the nervousness in the justice's account. He had no doubt Pat Garrett had phoned the judge before sending Detective Booker over with the paperwork for the arrest warrant.

In a honeyed voice, Robert Lee said, "Of course, you should sign the warrant. No reason Jeb or I would be upset with you. Purely routine. Detective Booker was out here and spent most of Monday talking with everyone at Bronson Stables. There's no proof a murder was committed. Bear Lansky wasn't on the premises last Thursday. It's all a big misunderstanding. The sheriff is going through the motions. He's covering his ass."

He listened, without interrupting, to the judge's nervous ramblings. "Please, Franklin, don't upset yourself. Just sign the document. If it turns out there was insufficient probable cause, the onus is on the sheriff. Detective Booker's job is to execute the warrant and arrest Lansky. Cooperate. Jeb and I will back you all the way."

Hanging up the phone, he mopped his forehead with a white handkerchief, thinking they'd have to get rid of the judge before the next election.

He punched a button on his desk intercom. "Jeb, get in here on the double. There's a fire we gotta put out."

Jeb paid close attention as Robert Lee filled him in on the conversation with Judge Newsome. He shot an angry look at his father. "Level with me. What happened at the stable Thursday night?"

"The man who was stabbed and killed by Bear Lansky installed a bug in Abner Wallace's office so we could track anything said about Ares Worldwide. He would have been well rewarded, but he threatened to talk if we didn't pay him an extra hundred thousand dollars. Lansky shut him up. Blackmailers can't be trusted with important secrets."

Jeb said, "We're now faced with the reality that Pat Garrett's gone off the reservation. He intends to challenge us on the murder. There's no hard evidence. He's bluffing. He can't win."

"Son, you and I can't afford to show the sheriff's team our cards and call their bluff. We don't know how far Pat will push it. Up until now, he's been willing to go along with us. Even giving in when Dorothy Wintergreen was run over by one of Ares's SUVs. Now, he's resisting. My guess is the arrival of Andrew Booker tipped the balance. More and more, it's looking like bringing Booker here was a mistake."

"Book's here now," Jeb said. "We need to resolve the immediate crisis."

"There's no question what we have to do," Robert Lee said.

Jeb nodded. "Crystal clear. Bear Lansky is leaving North Carolina on the next flight to Doha, Qatar. Records will show his plane departed last Wednesday."

CHAPTER 32

Wednesday night Carmen was getting ready for the party at Pat Garrett's, wondering what to wear. She couldn't wear her uniform. None of her clothes from UVA were suitable. She stared at her closet, uncommonly paralyzed with indecision.

Several false starts later, she settled on the navy-blue pantsuit and white ruffled silk blouse she'd worn to the lunch at the Boar's Head Inn the day her stepmom was gunned down by the sniper. Many times, she'd come to the brink of throwing out the ensemble, but instead she'd sought out a pricey cleaner who'd saved the day.

Driving out to Pat's farm, she recalled the heartbreaking shock of holding Katherine Harriman Garcia in her arms on the lawn of the UVA campus while her stepmom's lifeblood seeped through the outfit. Tonight, on her birthday, these clothes were chosen to honor the elegant woman's memory.

She knocked once and walked into Pat's home. After all, she was an invited guest, and it seemed pretentious to expect someone to answer the door. Two chocolate labs met her in the entryway, wagging tails their credentials as the welcoming committee.

Carmen dropped to one knee and began caressing the frisky animals. "You must be the famous Jake and Boomer Alice was telling me about. You're the perfect hosts to greet guests at the door."

Pat, Book, and Shirley were chatting in front of a massive stone fireplace where a cheerful fire crackled. Carmen noted with interest the display of a Silver Star on the mantel, identical to her dad's award back home. When Pat praised her dad for heroism, he'd never hinted at having received the same honor.

Pat, Book, and Shirley yelled, "Surprise!"

Carmen spied helium-filled Happy Birthday balloons bouncing along the ceiling, carried hither and yon by crosscurrents of ventilation. It dawned on her that this was *her* birthday celebration. She beamed with delight.

Alice bustled out of the kitchen carrying an immense platter of roast beef. She placed the mouth-watering presentation on the dining room table, almost danced over to the young woman, and hugged her.

Carmen said, "I hadn't expected to see you here. What a neat surprise."

"I'm double-tasking. Pat asked me to come as both caterer and guest. A lot of your favorites are on the menu: smoked salmon, shrimp in angel hair pasta, and fruit salad."

Carmen spotted her dad standing at the back of the room with his arms held out in welcome.

She ran to him with a cry of joy, leaning into his embrace.

"Happy birthday, Carmen. Since you couldn't come home, Pat was kind enough to host your surprise party."

"Dad, this is the best birthday ever. I'm flabbergasted." She looked over at her boss. "I had no idea the party was for me. Bringing my dad here was the greatest gift imaginable. Thank you."

Pat, contrary to his usual stoicism, gave her a hug. Book and Shirley followed suit.

The birthday dinner was topped off by a carrot cake, ablaze with candles, vanilla cream cheese frosting, with Swiss chocolate almond ice cream on the side. Carmen received token birthday presents from everyone but her dad. She wondered what he had up his sleeve.

Jose Garcia looked at Pat and said, "It's time."

"Use my study," Pat said, pointing down the hall.

The baffled young woman was escorted to the study.

Jose gestured for his daughter to sit in one of the comfortable wooden chairs in front of the desk. "I should warn you," he said, "your birthday present is going to come as a bit of a shock."

Carmen, who'd been bubbling with energy throughout the enjoyable evening, turned quiet. She grew uneasy at her dad's warning.

"You remember when Katherine was killed, you refused to come for the reading of the will. You claimed you had to return to the university to study for an exam or some such nonsense."

The feeling of guilt she'd experienced at the time returned like a physical weight pressing on her chest. Her sense of loss at her stepmom's death was devastating. She couldn't relive the horror of the murder at UVA while sitting through a reading of the will.

"Believing it would upset you at the time, I kept information from you about Katherine's bequest."

She said in a hushed voice, "I assumed everything was left to you. That's the way it's supposed to work when a spouse dies."

"Katherine made out the will five years ago. Neither of us had any expectation she might die young. You were aware she was a very wealthy woman?"

"I knew she was rich, but I didn't know the details. Both of you agreed to live a simple life. You stayed on as sheriff after the marriage. Our home saw a lot of improvements, but our lifestyle was never extravagant. She bought me a used Honda and funded my attendance at the University of Virginia. A fine education and a couple of trips abroad were the ways I agreed to share the wealth."

Carmen looked grief-stricken.

"I realized too late I'd been an ungrateful bitch. She sensed my feelings of unwillingness to accept her as a stepmom, but she never gave up on me. That last day, at lunch, I realized how much I liked her and how lucky you were to be married to her."

Jose sat quiet for a moment.

"Katherine left me ten million dollars in her will. One of many compromises we made during our married life, as far as money was concerned. I refused to accept more. She refused to leave me any less. She argued that interest on that amount, invested with care, would give me the freedom to do anything I wanted. After I die, the money goes to you."

"Great. My dad's a multimillionaire," Carmen responded dryly.

"The rest of her estate was left to you. The bequest was in the form of a trust I was charged to administer. The present-day value is over one hundred million dollars. I'm proud to say the trust's earned a sizable profit during the past year. In addition, there are substantial stock holdings, a major part of which are in coal and other energy companies, some based in Virginia. I'm not up-to-date on their worth, perhaps as much or more than the liquid assets."

Dazed, Carmen stopped listening when she heard the staggering sum.

"Pumpkin," he said, prodding her awareness with the pet name he'd given Carmen when she was a toddler, "this is real. The bequest is in trust until you reach the age of twenty-five, at which point you inherit it all."

Carmen's eyes flew to her father's.

Jose grinned. "Happy twenty-fifth birthday, Pumpkin."

CHAPTER 33

MCLEAN, VIRGINIA

Saturday morning Marlene Booker luxuriated in the spacious shower at her McLean home, the most relaxing part of her day. After a final rinse, she turned the handle to halt the flow.

A classic Type A personality, her days began at dawn and continued long into the night. She brought the same earnest application and intelligence to her work that had led to academic excellence at Princeton, capitalizing on brains coupled with athletic prowess.

Princeton's achievements had propelled her to Yale Law School, where she capped brilliant success in the classroom with service on the prestigious law review. Her stellar record, spurred by contacts forged at two leading universities, enabled her to join Brown, Chiang, and Shamir, specializing in corporate law. The legal profession proved remunerative, professionally satisfying, and the route to fame. She was celebrated in the pages of the *Washington Post* and in the halls of Congress. Senator Thaddeus Green was not the only politician who tempted her with a position on the Hill, but the only one she respected enough to say yes to his offer.

If asked a year ago, she would have said life was near perfect. A great job, a handsome, loving husband who made her proud of his career—earlier in the military and later as a decorated detective—

teenage twins who provided joys and challenges in equal measure, and a beautiful home in one of the wealthiest parts of the second wealthiest county in America.

That was then, this was now.

Their family life, rocky a few months before, became a shambles with the frenzied pursuit of Moretti in the wake of Lou's killing.

Georgetown abruptly brought an end to a hitherto idyllic life. She'd never doubted Book's account of what happened after he chased Franco Moretti from 36th Street into that dark alley near the Potomac River. But she was shaken by her husband's reaction to the tragedies of Lou's death, followed by the death of Scooter Thomas. Book became withdrawn and spent more and more time alone, often drinking at a bar in Georgetown close to where he lost sight of the fugitive. Their sex life withered, and she could no longer force herself to take the initiative. Book spent less and less time with Rebecca and Jonathan. The twins' resentment and hurt at their dad's neglect was painful to watch.

Her feelings about Book taking the detective position in Jefferson County vacillated. On the one hand, it was a relief the drinking had stopped. On the other, he was now located two hours away in a career move with DEAD END written over the door.

In desperation, she'd insisted on a one-year trial separation. He'd been gone barely a week, and, the truth was, she already missed him. Even when he'd been serving in Iraq and Afghanistan, the bed never felt this empty.

Marlene toweled off in the shower, thinking about what she would wear on the trip to Jefferson County. Something attractive, but not too sexy. She didn't want to give Book the wrong idea. An outfit comfortable and informal—Jefferson was a rural community—but with a relaxed businesslike air in case she decided a meeting with the Bronsons was advisable.

Various ensembles were tried on. All failed to pass the full-length mirror test. One looked like she was trying too hard to attract an estranged spouse. Another had a "fish out of water" look for a rural area. She settled on an outfit she'd grown to like during a short-lived enthusiasm for horseback riding—dark brown tailored slacks, a tan cashmere sweater, brown herringbone tweed jacket, and midcalf boots. That should do it. A Woman for All Seasons.

During the trip, she deliberated how to handle the investigation of Ares Worldwide. *To meet or not to meet with Jeb and Robert Lee Bronson?*

She decided to forgo the decision and trust her instincts as events unfolded on the ground. She puzzled over Book's warning about a murder on the Bronson property. How much truth was there in her husband's caution that she could be in mortal danger?

Was he worried? Or was the story a clumsy effort to discourage her from coming to Jefferson County?

CHAPTER 34

JEFFERSON COUNTY, VIRGINIA

Moving into the Jensen's place and getting things ready for his wife's arrival had caused Book to get to bed late. Nervous about Marlene's reaction to his new abode, he slept restlessly and awoke exhausted.

The mansion was spotless, courtesy of a cleaning crew who came in once a week. He'd laid in groceries enough to last a few days, and even thought to brighten the place with a vase of roses. From force of habit, he'd checked all the rooms, including attic and basement, to familiarize himself with the layout.

He was certain Marlene would appreciate the Olympic-sized pool and diving area. Belatedly, it dawned on him he should have told her to bring a swimsuit.

Having given the king bed in the master bedroom a tryout, he wondered if his wife would want to sleep in the same bed, or whether that was out of bounds. Should he have settled next door in the guest room? *How is this trial separation supposed to work, anyway?*

He reached across the bed and answered his ringing cell phone.

"Book. Hope I didn't wake you. You said you get up before dawn every morning to run, and I wanted to be sure to catch you before you hit the trail."

Feigning alertness, he said, "Lenore, I didn't expect to hear from you." He felt guilty talking with her while lying nude in bed, on a day he expected to see his wife. Book refused to face up to the attraction he'd felt for the enigmatic blond from the first glimpse of her wounded breast at the Old Virginny Bar and Billiards.

"You asked for my help with the murder investigation. I agreed, even though it destroys what little equilibrium I've achieved in my life. The murder, like everything else at Bronson Stables, must somehow relate to Ares Worldwide. Abner Wallace—you remember he's the editor of the *Jefferson Weekly* I told you about—has been researching Ares for several years. He knows more about what goes on at the Farm and in the North Carolina complex than anyone outside the military contract family. He's agreed to talk with you. I've set up an appointment for us to see him at eight o'clock. Will that work for you?"

Unfamiliar with country newspapers—and not too knowledgeable even about the venerable *Washington Post*, even though he'd been featured in several articles during his trial for the killing of Scooter Thomas—Book was unsure what to expect when he walked into the offices of the *Jefferson Weekly*.

Sitting behind a battered ancient oak desk, a teenager just a bit older than his twins was talking—or rather listening—on an old-fashioned phone. Jeans-clad legs propped on the desk, she sat in a swivel chair tilted back at a precarious angle. The girl was alert, waiting for a break in the steady monologue she'd apparently been listening to for some time. At last, she had an opening.

"Yes, Mrs. Manheim. I do have the information. Stockton Funeral Home emailed it over earlier."

She listened a few moments and interrupted. "No, that'll do it. I'll make sure Mr. Manheim's obituary is featured in our next edition. He's led a full life. You and the children and grandchildren must be very proud of him."

Pausing, she held the receiver to her ear, listening to a few more words from Mrs. Manheim. "I know you all miss him. We'll take care of everything. Don't worry. Goodbye." The girl hung up, trying to hide her relief at ending the one-sided conversation.

She bounced up like a coiled spring, and with grace and poise beyond her years, strode around the desk and extended her hand to Book.

Lenore made the introductions when the youth approached. "Nancy, this is Detective Booker. As you know, he joined the sheriff's office this week. Book, this is Nancy Drew Wallace."

Book's eyes flickered with insight he wasn't sure he should share. Nancy caught the look.

"You're right, Detective. My dad named me after the teen female detective, in the hope I'd grow up with wisdom and spunk."

Book nodded as though agreeing that she displayed those attributes.

"My older brother, George, called me 'Nan,' and a lot of my schoolmates copied him."

Intrigued, Book probed, "And who is George named after?"

"George Washington Carver, the trailblazing scientist who invented creative ways for peanuts and other crops to replace cotton as the foundation for farming in the South. Be careful not to ask my dad, 'What's in a name?' George won a scholarship to Yale last year to major in organic chemistry, following in Carver's footsteps. Dad's convinced I'll end up in England at Oxford or Cambridge studying medieval history or some such."

As if conjured by his daughter's words, Abner Wallace walked out of his office at the back of the long narrow room, cluttered with a printing press, endless stacks of paper, and other necessary tools of the trade. He looked the part of a prototypical country newspaperman—fortysomething, bespectacled, tall, and lanky, with a nap of salt and pepper running through his once-black hair.

Introductions complete, he said, "Come in. Let's talk about Ares Worldwide."

CHAPTER 35

Abner Wallace sat behind his desk—a larger and more battle-scarred version of the oak antique his daughter used in the outer office. His guests took the matching wooden chairs facing him. He grinned inwardly at Book's hesitancy to test the seemingly fragile—but actually quite sturdy—fan-back Windsor armchair.

Looking at Book over the top of his eyeglasses, Abner said, "I understand from Lenore you'd like to know about Ares Worldwide."

Book kept silent.

Abner cleared his throat. "You're wondering why a country editor decides to set about becoming an expert on military contracting." He eyed the detective again, pausing in hopes of a comment.

Book remained passive, waiting the newspaperman out.

Abner shrugged in resignation, hardly surprised verbal fencing with an expert interrogator was a losing proposition. "Let me explain the economics of country newspapers. There's no way to make money. Small newspapers are not getting hit as hard as big city dailies, but, with few exceptions, the owner is lucky to break even. The days of William Allen White and the *Emporia Gazette*, where an editor in rural Kansas can gain national renown, are over. The *Jefferson Weekly* is no exception."

Lenore said, "Then why do it?"

Leaning back precariously in his oak swivel chair, he laughed.

"There are days I ask myself that question. The bottom line is you have to love the newspaper business."

"So, how do you make ends meet?" she asked.

"Easy. You need satisfying avocations for cash flow, even if you own a country newspaper. In my case I'm a freelance writer, which, with a bit of luck and a lot of hard work, can be profitable. I focus on two topics. First is young adult literature, which is a booming industry. Nancy and I collaborate under the pen name Nancy Abner. We've developed quite a following with our blogs and reviews, and our readers credit us with an original point of view. From time to time, we get an article published in a magazine. No one suspects that half of our team is a teenager commenting on what teens like to read, and the other half is an old codger looking at today's writing from the perspective of yesterday's literature."

Comprehension flashed in Lenore's face. "The other topic, I assume, is military contracting."

"Right. I'm writing a book on the subject, a three-parter."

He raised one finger. "The first part highlights the growth of outsourcing in the military—how a fifth of the trillion dollars plus spent on wars in Iraq and Afghanistan early in the twenty-first century was accounted for by contractors providing a wide spectrum of services, unprecedented in any previous military conflict."

He raised a second finger. "The second part addresses the appropriate balance between what government officials—Defense, State, USAID, or other agencies—should do *versus* what should be outsourced. In the Middle East, for example, a few years ago we had over two hundred thousand military personnel and about the same number of contract personnel. That's a mix of American citizens, locals, and people from other countries."

He raised a third finger. "The third part focuses on the sordid issues of theft, fraud, bribery, rape, murder, and other crimes committed by contractors and their employees. The coverage also addresses the military and diplomatic downside of using contractors who have cost the US friends abroad, not just in the countries where the action takes place, but worldwide."

"What about Ares?" Book asked.

Abner sprung up from his desk, wired at the rare opportunity to hold forth about his favorite issue. "Do you want some coffee? I need caffeine this time of day."

They took a few moments to talk of lighter topics while coffee was served.

Taking a sip of the hot brew, Abner gave a satisfied sigh, and settled back in his chair, cup cradled in both hands.

"What got me interested in the topic was having a military contractor in my backyard. At first, I had no idea what a huge presence Ares Worldwide was in the contractor community. And they've grown year by year. In Iraq and Afghanistan, the US began to transition from military to civilian control in 2010–11. In reality, the nature of the contract activity—what gets done for what taxpayers shell out—didn't change that much. A huge money-making opportunity fell into the laps of Ares and other military contractors. The Department of State took over a lot of operations from the Pentagon. Ares mounted an aggressive marketing effort. The Bronsons cleaned up, despite the military withdrawal from Afghanistan."

"I had no idea about the scope of my family's activities," Lenore said.

Abner gave Lenore a compassionate look and continued. "In addition to their new responsibilities with State, the Bronsons manage the full gamut of outsourced operations, centered in the Middle East, but worldwide, as their name asserts. Security for DOD, State, and CIA personnel and operations is a big-ticket item everywhere. Contractors do everything overseas from military scut work—literally taking out the garbage—to guarding truck convoys and piloting drones over Yemen and other sites."

Emotion heating up, Abner rose out of his chair and began pacing.

"Several of Ares's contractors or, to be more accurate, mercenaries—and I call them that, because that's what they are—had been accused of murdering or raping civilians in Iraq and Afghanistan. Murder posed a particular problem because the applicability of US law is a murky area."

Book said, "I've seen a lot about mercenaries in the media. I just hadn't put it together with Ares. How do the Bronsons manage all this from a rural county in Virginia?"

Abner grimaced. "You have to give them credit. They control Jefferson County. Their base is safe. They're two hours from DC, with easy access to the Pentagon, State, and the Congress. The 'farm,' on the outskirts of Jefferson County, is the headquarters of their operational command and control. From here, they can direct and monitor activities throughout the globe. They have a staff who are in supervisory and observational contact with each of their projects."

Book said, "I've seen the outskirts of the Farm."

Abner continued. "Ares is the primary contractor responsible for training the Middle Eastern military to take over when the US military phases out. They also play a major role in support for Ukraine in the war against Russia. North Carolina is where the training is done. Routine negotiation and management of contracts is done out of a midrise at Tysons, Virginia."

"How have you learned all this about Ares, Abner?" Lenore asked.

"Research on the internet gets easier every day. A world of information is out there if you know where to look. A network of folks are unhappy with the government's trend toward excessive reliance on military contractors. We share information and swap tips about what's going on."

"But how can you find out what takes place at the Farm?" Lenore asked. "Jeb and Robert Lee work hard to keep that place bottled up."

"Well, I have an advantage in access to the Farm, which I'll explain. The Farm is a closed community and operates much like a regular military post in an isolated area. Those who work there, live there. There are office buildings, homes, even an elementary school. All the infrastructure you'd find in a small town is available, and quite modern: eating places, recreation, pharmacy and health care, stores, a chapel. The employees work hard, but they're given frequent vacations and a lot of time off with their families so they can get away to areas, such as DC, New York, and Florida. They're well paid, comparable to what they'd make overseas, and they're willing to put up with the inconvenience of being isolated at the Farm."

Book said, "If the Farm is isolated and self-contained, how'd you find out what's going on inside the fenced enclosure?"

Abner grinned. "Therein lies my advantage. Some jobs have to be done in any community, such as trash collection, cleaning homes and offices, delivery of supplies. No way elite Ares personnel are going to take on these jobs. A lot of the workers are people from my part of town. They see things. They tell me. A few of them even do a little snooping, including filming what goes on. People who work in a 'secure' area are the same everywhere. They get complacent and careless."

CHAPTER 36

Marlene Booker decided to stop for a must-have cup of coffee in Leesburg, Virginia, gratified the drive from McLean in the luxurious Mercedes had gone well so far, except for the inevitable bottleneck around Tysons. The GPS navigation system projected she was running on time, sixty minutes away from her scheduled ten o'clock meeting with Book.

She took comfort in knowing Jonathan and Rebecca were each staying with close friends during the time she was away in Jefferson County.

Yesterday, when briefing her new boss on her future plans, a lawyer's instinct cautioned her not to mention her upcoming tour of Jefferson County. Acting on the principle that it's better to beg forgiveness than to ask permission, once she returned would be time enough to fill in Senator Green on anything of note that transpired.

Once she picked up her to-go cup of coffee, she reconsidered. A bit of advance warning might be prudent. While cruising in the Benz, the stately redhead took advantage of the hands-free Bluetooth technology to call the senator.

"Mags, this is Marlene. I need to speak with Thaddeus." She felt comfortable with the easy relationship she'd developed with the senator's entourage, most of all Margaret McTavish, his ubiquitous legislative assistant, at her desk even on a Saturday morning.

The senator's sonorous voice resonated in the spacious sedan equipped with Bang & Olufsen speakers. "Marlene, a pleasure to hear from you this morning."

"I'm en route to the country to spend the weekend with Book. This is his first week as detective in the Jefferson County sheriff's office."

"Enjoy your weekend." Only a trained listener could detect the note of caution in the mellifluous cadence. Marlene was aware of the adverse publicity surrounding the Georgetown killing of Scooter Thomas and Book's subsequent resignation from the DC police had been the only discordant note in the senator selecting her to lead the investigation of military contracting.

"Thanks." Lawyer's instinct kicked in again, reinforcing the sensitivity of alerting Green about a possible visit to the Bronsons.

"There is one thing I should mention about the trip. Jeb Bronson, the CEO of Ares Worldwide, lives in Jefferson County. He was Book's commanding officer when they served in Afghanistan, and he's a friend of the family. Good manners demand we stop by to say hello. But it occurred to me you would want to be aware of the contact in the light of Ares's prominent role in our investigation."

The senator hesitated a beat too long before responding. "Jeb Bronson's dad Robert Lee is an old friend of mine. He was a strong supporter of my election. Please give him my regards."

The brief pause clued Marlene, ratifying her decision to low-key mention the visit but reveal nothing of her plans for dealing with the Bronsons.

CHAPTER 37

As Marlene cruised into the heart of Jefferson County, she thought, *What a beautiful morning.* Wispy pink clouds billowed across the surface of a pale blue sky. A mélange of red and purple blooming azalea bushes decorated the nineteenth century courthouse. *Small town America. Gotta love it.*

Noting she was ten minutes ahead of the GPS schedule, she cast a mocking glance at the navigation system, proud she'd won the imaginary race. In her peripheral vision, on the far side of Courthouse Square, she spotted the sheriff's office, where the scheduled rendezvous with her husband was to take place.

Her good humor quickly evaporated when she spied Book holding the elbow of a statuesque blond as he helped her into a blue Jaguar. The tony ride was parked in front of a small building with a sign that proclaimed it the offices of the *Jefferson Weekly*. Marlene pulled out of traffic and hit the brakes, drawing a glare and a middle finger gesture from the bearded driver of a battered Chevy pickup truck.

Angry thoughts competing with confusion roiled in Marlene's brain. *What the hell is Book up to? He's been gone a week, and already he's running around with a wealthy bimbo who looks like Uma Thurman.*

Fantasies she'd had during the drive about how the weekend might go were obliterated. In outraged wife mode, she was determined to get to the bottom of her husband's dallying with the local gentry.

Belatedly aware of her precarious location, she eased into an open parking space and turned off the Mercedes. Uma Thurman pulled into traffic and sped away.

Book strolled across the square in the direction of the sheriff's office. To her annoyance, the son of a bitch was whistling.

Once her husband entered the multistory red brick building, she jumped out of the sedan, slammed the door, and beeped the remote locks. Striding rapidly toward the sheriff's office, she repeated the familiar mantra she'd often resorted to in past times of stress. *Calm down. Calm down.*

All lawyers believe in two maxims—never take a knife to a gunfight, and never go into a confrontation with your mad showing.

Marlene demurely entered the sheriff's offices, determined to play the role of the proper wife coming to spend a weekend with her husband and to meet his new colleagues. She had no idea how Book had described the state of their marriage or the circumstances causing him to be working two hours from his family. But she was determined her words and actions would give them no clues. The good wife betrayed no surprise at the numbers of the sheriff's staff who *just happened* to be working on a Saturday morning.

Shirley stepped forward to welcome her and made the rounds, introducing all the deputies present, starting with "Book's partner Carmen."

Another irritated thought slammed Marlene's consciousness: *How many gorgeous women has he hooked up with in one week?*

Shirley said, "Book's in with Sheriff Garrett."

Marlene socialized with ease and could sense from the reaction of Shirley, Carmen, and others that her husband had already been accepted as an integral member of this "cop family." She asked the usual questions an outsider would ask about Jefferson County and responded to the usual interest in her family, whipping out her cell phone with pictures of Rebecca and Jonathan engaged in soccer, dance, and other activities.

When the wall clock registered ten o'clock, she saw Book—noted for an uncanny time sense—glance at his watch and look up from his conversation with Garrett. When his eyes met Marlene's, he jumped up and hurried out to embrace his wife.

After shaking hands with the sheriff and chatting for a few minutes, Marlene signaled she was ready to leave. She and Book made their excuses and headed outside. She decided to wait till they got to his new living arrangement to confront her husband about his rendezvous with the fetching blond.

CHAPTER 38

Marlene followed Book into the mansion, indifferent to the splendid artwork in the spacious tiled foyer. The anger she'd kept hidden during the visit to the sheriff's office, and while following Book on the drive over unfamiliar country roads, exploded as he turned to welcome her into his new living quarters.

Her open right hand lashed out, almost of its own volition, and slammed into Book's left cheek. Countless thousands of hours slicing through pool, lake, river, and ocean waters had built powerful arm and shoulder muscles. The slap impacted without warning.

Book staggered from the force of the blow. Athletic reflexes and a keen sense of balance enabled him to avoid being knocked to the ground. He stared in amazement as Marlene, in full Teutonic Goddess mode, was about to unleash another thunderbolt with her left hand.

"Stop. What the hell's going on? What'd I do?" Both hands were raised in a gesture, half surrender and half defensive.

Breathing in gasps, she tried to regain control. *Calm down. Calm down.*

This was not the icy cool way she'd intended this to go. She'd never struck her husband. Book, trained to kill with bare hands, had never hit her. Even during virulent arguments, they'd respected each other. She agonized, *What am I doing?*

"I NEED . . ." Realizing she was shouting, she stopped talking and took a deep breath. *Calm down. Calm down.*

Marlene turned and walked back outside. She stood for a moment taking a fresh breath of the country air and looked at—but barely seeing—the peaceful scenery. The Blue Ridge mountains in the distance painted a portrait of redbud trees, greens, and browns framed by a clear azure sky. In time, the soothing view helped her gain control and slow her pounding heart. A bit calmer, she reentered the residence.

Book stood transfixed, waiting for his wife's next move.

In a measured tone, she said, "I need you to tell me about the blond in the blue Jaguar."

Enlightened, Book didn't know whether to explode with laughter or anger.

"The blond's Lenore Bronson, Jeb's sister. The family's a mess. For whatever reason, she hates her father and brother. I got to know her quite by accident when I stopped for a beer at a bar just outside the Jefferson County line. Some bozo knifed her. I took her to the local hospital for treatment. After she was released, I drove her home to Bronson Stables."

He didn't have to be much of a detective to register Marlene's disdain at his stopping for a beer or the raised eyebrows at "getting to know" Lenore.

Undaunted, he continued. "When Carmen and I investigated the murder at Bronson Stables, Lenore agreed to help. Her theory, which fits with what little we know, focuses on ways Ares Worldwide may be implicated. Bear Lansky, whom we've identified as our prime suspect, is a mercenary. He was the main liaison between Ares and the Bronsons. He's disappeared on a flight to Qatar. He supposedly left before the murder, although faking the flight records would be child's play for Jeb."

Book was gratified to note his wife's body language was starting to ease at the last piece of news.

"How does that explain the two of you at Courthouse Square at nine fifty this morning?" The icy lawyer was back in control.

"Lenore's friend, Abner Wallace, editor of the *Jefferson Weekly*, is something of an expert on military contracting, in general, and Ares, in particular. She set up a meeting this morning at eight o'clock so Abner could brief me. We were just finishing when you saw us on the sidewalk. There's nothing going on between Lenore and me."

"What about Carmen?" she asked.

"Carmen? What the hell does she have to do with this? She's my partner, for God's sake. You've never questioned my relationships with any of the female cops I worked with in the past. What's gotten into you? Carmen's just a kid."

"She looks like a sexy, healthy, attractive, mature woman to me. When you describe her as a kid, you're either blind or hiding something."

Losing his temper, Book said, "Enough. I've taken enough undeserved crap today to last a lifetime. Either cut it out or get in the Mercedes and drive back to McLean. I've been dying of loneliness from a week away from you. I can't take any more. You and your damned 'trial separation.'"

He turned on his heel and stalked through the mansion, ending up standing on the expanse of patio surrounding the shimmering pool. Holding his breath, he awaited the dreaded sound of the car engine firing up.

Instead of the sounds of Marlene departing, Book heard footsteps behind him. He grew conscious of his wife's presence at his back. Arms slipped around his chest. Her head nestled between his shoulder blades. Neither of them spoke.

"I've been dying of loneliness, too," she said. Feeling his muscles tense, she gripped harder. "Don't turn around. I'm embarrassed. I'm acting like an ass. In sixteen years of marriage, you've never given me cause to doubt your fidelity. Seeing you on the sidewalk with Lenore is no justification for acting like a jealous schoolgirl. Carmen obviously likes and respects you—just as Shirley and Pat do. Nothing other than my own demons could lead me to believe there's anything with your partner other than collegiality."

Book spun around and pulled his wife into a strong embrace, coals of passion warming.

She returned the embrace. To lighten the mood, she said, "I like what you've done to the place. Do all members of the sheriff's staff live in palaces?"

He chuckled, sensing they'd gotten past one of the low points in a severely tested marriage. He told her the story of Shirley's referral to her erstwhile off-and-on high school boyfriend, Homer Smedley, which had led to the once-in-a-lifetime house-sitting windfall.

Pointing to the outdoor pool, he said, "Sorry, I should have told you to bring a swimsuit."

Marlene looked at him with a lascivious grin, slipped off her herringbone jacket and dropped it on a poolside chair. The cashmere sweater followed. She bent over and removed boots, socks, and slacks. Bra and panties joined the pile.

Getting into the spirit of the striptease, Book began pulling off his clothes.

Marlene's svelte figure dove into the water and took off to the far side of the pool. He was a half-step behind her, but there was no way his best swim strokes could hope to keep up with her championship fleetness.

They floated and raced in the pool for a leisurely interlude. A final race ended, as usual, with Marlene far ahead. Just shy of the poolside target, she reversed position in the water and embraced her husband. She locked powerful legs around his waist. He embraced her and they kissed. They exited the pool, and he pulled her onto his lap in one of the comfortable lounge chairs. The first explosion of passion sated, the pace of lovemaking slowed but persisted as the sun swept across the sky.

They dozed. When Marlene awakened, she said, "I'm starved."

CHAPTER 39

Robert Lee Bronson sat stiffly in the plush leather desk chair, his signature Cohiba cigar clamped between his teeth, bracing for the inevitable confrontation with his son.

Jeb slammed through the study door. Wasting no time with preliminaries, he stalked up to the desk, pointed an accusing finger at his father, and demanded, "What's this I hear about you flying a combat team up from North Carolina?"

"You heard right. The team arrives at the Farm within the hour." The old man still had some hard bark on him. Jeb's anger didn't cause him to flinch.

"Why'd you order that? We'd agreed it was *my* job to direct Ares. I can't have you interfering in the chain of command."

"Sit down. And don't raise your voice to me. Never forget who's in charge. You've been slow to realize the threat Booker poses. I decided it was high time to act. Past time. If we're not careful, we'll be playing catch-up."

"Nothing's changed, old man. I won't tolerate your interference."

"Everything's changed. You'll do as you're told."

"What are you talking about? What's changed?"

"This morning, Book and your sister spent two hours at the *Jefferson Weekly* getting briefed on military contracting, highlighting Ares as the 'bad boy' of the outsourcing world. You'll recall, we'd suspected Abner Wallace was spying on the Farm. The guy Bear Lansky killed out by the stable was hired to bug Wallace's office."

Jeb's face showed his amazement at what had transpired that midnight at the stables.

"I've just finished listening to a recording of Abner Wallace briefing your favorite detective about our company and our supposed transgressions. Turns out the local newspaperman has a whole tribe of spies—including cleaning ladies, deliverymen, and garbage collectors—documenting what goes on at the Farm. God knows what all he's been able to find out."

"That's it? The local editor's a snoop? Big surprise."

"No. That's not '*it*.' Not by a long shot. Book's wife took a job with the Senate Armed Services Committee. She's lead investigator for their probe of military contracting. She arrived this morning in the first step of her snooping campaign, and she plans to visit us over the weekend."

Jeb recoiled at an even more devastating surprise.

Robert Lee said, "I got a phone call from Senator Green this morning. He thinks of me as a friend and campaign supporter. His idea of a courteous quid pro quo is to alert me to the activities of his staff. The poor fool's so honest he seems to think all his supporters are equally straightforward."

Unwilling to let his complaint rest, Jeb said, "You should have worked through me rather than ordering the team."

Robert Lee slammed his hand down on the desk. "Dammit boy. Our survival's at stake. Don't you realize we've gone beyond the boundaries of playing games with the system? Marlene Booker has a reputation as a 'take no prisoners' lawyer. Green, whatever his faults for being too trusting of his supporters, is a real ballbuster of a politician. Pat Garrett's off the reservation and backing Book. Everything's going to come unraveled unless we act, and act now."

"So be it. But, for the record, I'm still not happy about how you handled this. Where do we go from here?"

Robert Lee relaxed at signs his son was prepared to back off. He outlined an aggressive strategy, beginning with Jeb taking the lead during the upcoming visit with Marlene and Book.

CHAPTER 40

The following afternoon, when Jeb Bronson welcomed her at the door, Marlene gave a perfunctory handshake and walked into the foyer like she owned the place. Book followed her, acknowledging his former CO with a minimum of warmth. The signals were clear. This meeting was to be all business. No way the Bookers were cutting the Bronsons any slack.

"We'll meet in Robert Lee's study," Jeb said, guiding them through the mansion's maze of rooms.

Ever the Southern gentleman, the elder Bronson stood and greeted Marlene and Book with surface courtesy. The formality rang hollow in light of the unstated, but understood, purpose of the confrontation—getting the goods on Ares Worldwide.

Once seated, drinks were offered and declined. Marlene opened the discussion, "Let me get right to the point. Senator Thaddeus Green has designated me the lead investigator of an inquiry of the Armed Services Committee into military contracting. When I say military contracting, I should make it clear we're including, in addition to the Department of Defense, related outsourcing by civilian agencies, such as the Department of State. The scope of the investigation centers on the Middle East but has the potential to range around the globe at our discretion."

Robert Lee said, "When you say, 'at our discretion,' is it fair to interpret that to mean 'at *your* discretion?'"

"The senator asked me to play a lead role. However, staff serve at the pleasure of the Congress. In the final analysis, the senators call the shots."

Everyone in the room knew that in Washington, staff did the paperwork and the senators, often as not, followed their lead.

Marlene was certain Robert Lee and Jeb were receiving the heavy-handed message she was transmitting—leaving little doubt they would need to contend with her at every juncture.

With stilted correctness, Jeb said, "How can we assist your investigation?"

"I came down this weekend to visit Book, and this seemed an ideal opportunity to meet with both of you. While I'm here, I'd also like to tour the facility in Jefferson County you call the Farm."

"I regret to say that's impossible," said Jeb. "I explained to Book in another connection, the Farm is a secret military installation, so visitors are not permitted."

Robert Lee interrupted. "However, if a bipartisan Congressional delegation were to request a tour, I'm sure we could persuade our DOD sponsors to agree."

When hell freezes over, she thought, recognizing the ploy as a bald-faced attempt to trump her power play with one of their own.

"I'll give Senator Green a call to discuss your offer," she responded. *You boys want to play hardball. I'll show you how it's done.* "You understand how these investigations work. While the staff operates behind-the-scenes, the senators prefer to hold hearings where key witnesses are called to testify—under oath and before TV cameras. In light of the major role Ares Worldwide plays on this issue, I'm sure you will both be called to testify quite soon, Jeb in his capacity as the current CEO and Robert Lee as a former CEO."

She looked Robert Lee in the eye and registered the thinly concealed venom as he returned her gaze. Despite having dealt with powerful, and often vicious, corporate leaders throughout her career, she fought to conceal a shiver at the old man's animosity.

The objective of a warning shot across the bow had been achieved, message given and received—although Marlene wasn't quite sure how to interpret the message Robert Lee and Jeb had given her.

Once in the Mercedes and headed down the drive past the stable, Book said, "If looks could kill, Robert Lee would have struck you dead on the spot."

CHAPTER 41

"Alpha One calling Alpha Three. Stay with your vehicle. Alpha Two and I are in position. The coast is clear. Proceeding with plan."

"This is Alpha Three. Roger."

Alpha Three, also known as Pedro Rodriguez, the driver of the black Ford Expedition, was waiting nearby for the team to complete the mission.

Alpha One, a.k.a. Dave Richards, gave a thumbs-up to Alpha Two, Larry Wade. There was no reason to use the speaker in his headset. He had an unobstructed view of Larry, illuminated by the feeble light at the rear of the building housing *Jefferson Weekly*. The duo wore dark blue jogging outfits, the top concealing the utility belt containing their weapons and tools.

Eager to commence the break in, Dave moved to the rear door of the newspaper facility. He'd delighted in regaling his buddy Larry with his experiences as a burglar in his native Harlem, which Larry couldn't appreciate having grown up in rural Ohio. He'd bragged about the ability to breach any locked door in less than sixty seconds. Tonight, he was as good as his word. The old-fashioned Yale lock proved to be no match for his skills. In thirty-five seconds, Dave hauled open the battered wooden door.

Dave pulled a paint canister from his utility belt and began spraying a message on the chipped red brick wall next to the wooden door: BURN NIGGER BURN. The spin was in place. Proof whatever happened tonight was racist in origin—pointing the finger at Jefferson County's past—and not attributable to other motives.

The two intruders crept into a storage area behind the press room. Dave froze when he heard a sound in the main press area, holding up a finger to alert Larry.

The building was supposed to be empty. Dave's orders didn't spell out what to do if someone were present.

Jeb Bronson had made clear the importance of the mission. Without further hesitation, Dave pressed ahead. The organization was not kind to those who fucked up. Whoever was in the next room fell into the category of collateral damage.

He moved forward to the adjoining door, opened it, and peered in. A tall, slim Black man was facing away, leaning over a workbench. The mercenary crept behind his prey and struck a vicious blow to the back of the neck, easing the unconscious victim to the floor. A kick to the temple assured he'd stay out cold.

Dave glanced around and confirmed Larry followed him into the room, providing the expected backup, not that he believed backup would be needed against a civilian target.

The premises secure, he gestured for Larry to go outside to retrieve the accelerant, a five-gallon container of gasoline they'd brought. Jeb had assured him there'd be plenty of paper around to feed a roaring fire.

Before torching the building, Dave took one last look at the unconscious victim lying in the center of the target area. *Sorry buddy. Shit happens.*

Making a fuse out of twisted newsprint, he set the *Jefferson Weekly* offices ablaze.

The arsonists rushed out the back of the building and ran to their escape vehicle two blocks away. With Pedro at the wheel, they sped away in the Expedition. The blaring siren of fire engines could be heard racing toward the inferno on Courthouse Square.

Pedro piloted the SUV through the deserted countryside, headed for their second destination of the night.

"Ten minutes to target," he said.

Dave illuminated the watch dial on his left wrist. Midnight. Right on schedule.

CHAPTER 42

Dave relaxed as Pedro cut the power. Lights in and around the Jensen's mansion blinked out. The residence was isolated, with the nearest dwelling more than a half mile away, its lights barely visible in the distance.

Dave thought, *I love it when a plan comes together,* echoing the mantra of the *A-Team,* his favorite TV show.

Checking out the garage, Dave confirmed the Mercedes and Sequoia were inside. The targets were there. He headed for the rear of the mansion.

Dave was confident Pedro and Larry would be breaching the front door just about now.

Jeb Bronson had cautioned the team members about Book and described in detail his exploits in warfare. The three combat veterans were skeptical their victim could be that dangerous. After leaving Jeb's briefing, they'd lampooned Book's most publicized exploit as a detective—gunning down an unarmed teenager in a dark alley.

Dave expected his team would have the advantage of surprise. The plan was to catch their targets in bed.

Dave walked through an azalea garden leading to an Olympic-sized pool, surrounded by a tiled patio. He gaped in titillated fascination when he glimpsed a woman drop her towel on the chair and stride nude toward the water. He recognized her from Jeb's briefing as the hit team's principal target Marlene Booker.

He heard Marlene yell, "I'm going back in the water for a few laps."

The reply rang loud and clear.

"Okay. I'll be right back. Gotta check the circuit board and see if I can fix the lights."

Shaking off his reverie at Marlene's nude silhouette, Dave began running toward the swimmer, knowing the movement would catch her eye, but gambling fright and the ferocity of the attack would cause her to freeze. He drew his KA-BAR fighting knife from its sheath. He fantasized plunging the seven-inch blade into her naked torso. The plan was to stab both victims, simulating a break-in and robbery gone bad.

"BOOK, ARMED INTRUDERS," Marlene screamed.

Damn the bitch. Far from freezing, as he expected, she ran for the ladder leading up to the high dive. Dave knew the scream would alert her husband, who was God-knows-where looking for the circuit board.

On reflection, he relaxed, confident his primary target was trapped on the high dive or in the pool.

"Don't run, baby," he yelled. "Stick around. You and I can have some fun." The fantasy of raping the bitch before knifing her increased his excitement.

When she reached the top of the ladder and stepped onto the diving board, she looked back.

He thought, *Fuck me. She's not a bit afraid. It's like she's inviting me to follow her.*

He shrugged off the disquieting notion. The different reactions of those on the brink of death never failed to amaze the assassin. Some were terrified and in a state of total collapse; others seemed to welcome the impending death. No one, in his experience, faced death with the grim defiance of this bitch lawyer. He looked forward to watching the fear transform her face, just before he plunged the knife in her chest.

Gripping the KA-BAR in his right hand, Dave began to climb the ladder. When his head cleared the level of the diving board, he was surprised to find her standing on the end, facing him.

He'd expected his target to dive in, seeking to escape. Since his youth, he'd been a strong swimmer. He was confident of his ability to trap her in the pool.

Trap. Stab. Kill.

Once atop the ladder, the assassin pulled himself onto the diving board and began to move toward his prey. Halfway across the board, he was startled to see her leap forward, driving her shoulder into his knees. Disoriented, his arms windmilled as he flew through the air and landed on the surface of the pool in a stinging belly flop. Air was driven out by the impact. He clutched the KA-BAR desperately.

In a reflex, he inhaled, drawing water into his lungs. He panicked, taking in more water with each choking gasp.

Dave felt the target grasp the back of his jogging top. Each time he twisted to strike her or squirm away, the bitch maneuvered his body, staying out of reach. *She's the lifeguard from hell. Trying to drown me.*

Terrified of a watery grave, he struggled to swim to the surface. No matter how hard he stroked, he couldn't move upward. He released the KA-BAR to exert full force in the fight for the life-giving air above the all-encompassing liquid. In desperation, he inhaled water.

His Special Forces instructor had impressed on trainees the necessity to get to the surface at once if liquid gets in your lungs. Dave resisted the natural tendency to cough up the water or swallow it, knowing that would cause him to inhale still more water involuntarily. He realized he was fighting instinctive behavior but was powerless to stop.

"Drowning is quick and silent." The instructor's words echoed in his brain. "Rapid body movement uses up oxygen faster, speeding up system shutdown."

No shit, Sherlock, he thought, just before falling unconscious.

* * *

Marlene felt the attacker's body go limp. From her lifeguard experiences during several summers at Santa Monica beach, she knew drowning victims could display a remarkable capacity to recover. She wasn't prepared to take his demise for granted.

Keeping a strong grasp on her attacker's jogging top, she swam to the surface. Greedy gasps of air replenished her waning energy. When in training as a competitive swimmer, she could hold her breath over two minutes, longer than she'd just been submerged. She realized it was different when fighting for your life.

Each time natural buoyancy brought the body up, she pushed her attacker's shoulders down to keep the dying man's face submerged. After a brief interval, she concluded the issue was no longer in doubt.

The intruder's dead. I killed him.

She groped in his utility belt for the holster she'd felt earlier when the two were struggling. With a tug, the pistol came free—a Glock—the type of weapon Book had insisted she spend hours at the range learning to shoot. She remembered her husband's constant references to the pistol's reliability even after being submerged in water for a long period of time.

She thrust the intruder's body away with a shudder. She resolved not to lose it. *This is no time for regrets. Book's in danger.*

A few quick strokes brought her to the edge of the pool. Using powerful shoulder muscles, she climbed out and raced toward the mansion, hoping she'd arrive in time to help Book.

CHAPTER 43

Book resisted the impulse to rush to his wife's aid, knowing Marlene could take care of herself in the pool.

Naked and unarmed, he debated his alternatives for self-defense. Clothes and weapons had been left in the upstairs bedroom, when Book and Marlene returned for another bout of swimming and lovemaking at the pool. The bedroom—accessible by the stairway off the foyer—was not an option.

He had no doubt the intruders were Jeb's mercenaries—ex-Special Forces—with the same training and experience he'd had while in the military. He reasoned they killed the power and guessed they would be wearing night vision goggles.

Having explored the layout of the dwelling, he was familiar with the route to the kitchen. On his way there, a plan to deal with the attackers began to crystallize. Little of the moonlight filtered into that part of the house. Bare-ass naked, he made his way, with a minimum of groping, along walls and through doorways.

Once in the kitchen, his first move was to locate the knife rack. A ten-inch chef's knife and a large boning knife were selected by touch. He knew from his earlier inspection they were quality German knives with heavy, razor-sharp blades.

His second move was to the commercial-type gas range, which could be operated even with the power turned off. He checked the pilot light to ensure it was on. He located matches in an adjoining cabinet drawer, just in case. A roll of Bounty paper towels provided a ready source of combustible material. He tore off towels and began wadding them up, piling the tinder on top of the stove. All he needed was a source of flammable alcohol.

Checking out the mansion his first day, he'd noticed the Jensens kept a generous supply of Cognac brandy in a nearby pantry. He used the alcohol-laden liquid to saturate the paper towels. The range was now a bonfire waiting to be torched with the switch of a gas burner.

Hovering by the stove, Book detected the quiet shuffle of approaching steps. He couldn't make out shapes in the inky darkness, indicating to him the intruders would also be blind without night vision goggles, which had been designed to collect and magnify ambient light.

Timing was everything. A delicate balance between being patient until the attackers drew close but acting before they could use their weapons. Knives would assure a level playing field, depending on how many attackers came at him. If they chose the option of guns, the situation could get hairy.

One of the attackers brushed against the array of pots and other utensils hanging from the ceiling rack over the island in the center of the kitchen, making a discernible rattle.

Without hesitating, Book set fire to the pyre piled on the stovetop. The blaze flared with a blinding explosion of light. Two intruders were caught in the glare, causing the men to scream with pain. The unexpected illumination was magnified many times by the NVG optics. Book minimized the glare by squinting as the blaze flared on the stove.

His plan worked.

Temporarily blinded, the intruders tore off their headgear and threw them on the floor.

Book leaped across the room to strike at their moment of maximum vulnerability. The intruders were brandishing KA-BAR fighting knives, rather than the pistols he was sure they also carried.

Stabbing the larger of the two men in the throat with the ten-inch chef's knife, he followed up by driving the boning knife into the area midway between the ribs in an attempt to pierce heart or lungs. He believed it was a killing blow. In any event, the big man was down.

Book yanked out the boning knife and turned to the second attacker, surprised to see his opponent retreat a few steps.

The second attacker was out of reach of a knife thrust, and, worse yet, he was drawing a pistol.

The pistol was aimed at Book's torso.

I'm already dead, he thought, as he sprang forward in a desperate move to reach his attacker before he fired.

A naked Marlene materialized, running into the room, brandishing a Glock. Her pale body was visible in the diminishing glow from the stovetop. She fired three rounds into the intruder's back.

The attacker staggered, fell to the tile, and didn't move.

"You're alive," she said, grabbing her husband's extended arms.

"Thanks to you. When he pulled his pistol, I was sure I'd bought the farm. What happened outside?"

"Just one intruder. Don't worry. He's dead."

CHAPTER 44

Book verified both intruders in the kitchen were dead and confiscated their Glocks. Marlene still held the pistol she'd taken from the corpse in the pool.

He cautioned her to wait in the kitchen while he did a quick reconnaissance of the downstairs and grounds to confirm all attackers were accounted for.

Satisfied the mansion was clear, he returned to the kitchen and lifted the receiver to check the house phones to see if they were working. No surprise. The phone lines had been cut.

"Better head upstairs and get dressed. I'll call Pat Garrett on my cell and fill him in."

When the sheriff picked up, Book said, "Pat, we've been attacked at the Jensen place. Marlene and I are unharmed. Three mercenaries are dead."

"Thank God you're okay. I've been trying to call you. Yours is the second crime scene tonight. The offices of the *Jefferson Weekly* were torched around midnight. The fire chief says it was arson, with gasoline used as an accelerant. Firefighters found a body in the debris."

Shocked by the news of the arson attack, Book kept silent, listening to the sheriff.

"I've talked with Abner Wallace. He and his daughter are both safe. They're headed to the sheriff's office where we can protect them. You and Marlene should get over here ASAP."

• • •

Pat stood in his outer office, which was the epicenter of a maelstrom of activity. Shirley arrived from her nearby apartment and was manning communications, calling in deputies from their homes and passing out assignments. Even George and Sam had shown up and were trying to look busy.

When Pat spied Book and Marlene rushing through the building's outer door, he waved them into his inner office. Eyeballing the Bookers, Pat was relieved to see they looked unharmed. He knew from experience no one survived a home invasion, even after killing intruders, and came away without at least some psychological damage.

"Fill me in," he said.

Before they could respond, Pat spotted Abner Wallace and Nancy hurrying into the office. He held up a finger to Book and Marlene and hastened out to meet the newcomers.

"Are you both okay?" he asked.

An angry Abner pointed across Courthouse Square to where the newspaper offices were still smoldering. "What happened? Was anyone found inside?"

"The firefighters got there too late," Pat said. "They found a body. Whoever it was burned to death."

Nancy gasped. "Uncle Ptolemy." Tears began flowing down her cheeks.

"My brother," Abner said. "Those bastards killed him."

Having little doubt who the newspaperman identified by the label, "those bastards," Pat asked anyway. "Who do you mean?"

"Jeb and Robert Lee Bronson. They must suspect I've been feeding Detective Booker compromising information about Ares Worldwide. They figured torching the premises of the *Jefferson Weekly* would intimidate me. They wouldn't have known my brother was there, not that it would have stopped them. Ptolemy sometimes came by at night to print flyers for his church."

Pat recalled driving past the Baptist church a few miles out in the country. He often thought of stopping by to say hello to the minister, but never yielded to the impulse. Even today, the Black community stayed separate, partly through their own preference, partly through White avoidance. Abner and Nancy were notable exceptions, always at the center of daily life in the community. The sheriff felt guilty about his oversight, even though it wouldn't make any difference to Ptolemy now.

"We don't know who did this. But I promise you we'll find out."

Abner said, "You don't for a minute believe the bullshit painted on the back of the building to make the arson look like a hate crime, do you Sheriff?"

Pat shook his head. "No, I don't. But we need to follow the evidence. I hope you'll keep your feelings about the Bronsons to yourself until we investigate."

"Who's going to do the investigating?" Abner asked.

"I already called in the FBI. They should be here in an hour or two. Also, I'm going to follow this case."

"What about Detective Booker?"

"You'll find this out soon enough, so I might as well tell you. Book and his wife Marlene were attacked tonight, a short time after your place was firebombed. They're both unharmed and are waiting in my office to brief me. Shirley will get you settled in the interrogation room where I'd like you to wait till I've had a chance to hear their story."

Pat rejoined Book and Marlene. Shirley plied the trio with soft drinks and potato chips. About to resume questioning, he spotted Carmen running into the building. He waved her to come to his office.

"There's no doubt these guys were experienced Special Forces," Book said. "KA-BAR knives, Glocks, NVG, and communications were off-the-shelf military equipment."

After Book's briefing about the attack, Marlene summarized what happened by the pool, explaining how she turned her lifeguard training on its head to drown one of the attackers. She added how she took the attacker's Glock to rush to Book's rescue.

Pat's cell phone rang, interrupting the report of the home invasion. He listened for a few minutes. "Good work. Stake out the Jensen place until the FBI arrives."

He turned to the others. "The deputies report finding three dead intruders. One drowned in the pool. Two killed in the kitchen—one knifed and the other shot in the back. What they found jibes with what you've reported. Driving to the crime scene, the deputies identified a black Ford Expedition parked a couple hundred yards up the road. The model is the same as the one Mary Connolly believed was used by Bear Lansky."

"That clinches it," Book said.

"It doesn't clinch anything." Pat pointed at the Bookers. "You and Abner Wallace have tried and convicted Jeb and his dad. We need evidence. My guess is we'll have a hard time making a direct connection between the Bronsons and either of these incidents."

Cutting off Book's protest before it could be voiced, Pat raised his hand in a halt gesture. "You know damn well you can't be part of this investigation. What happened at the Jensen place is an officer-involved killing. Our first step is to clear you and Marlene of any wrongdoing."

Ignoring the flare of anger on Book's face, he turned to Carmen. "You're in charge of the Bronson Stables murder investigation. You'll also be the liaison with the FBI. I'm going to ask the Feds to take the lead on both of tonight's crimes—the arson killing and the home invasion. My hunch is they'll agree. There're ample grounds for federal involvement. The arsonists might have thought they were clever, trying to make the firebombing look like a hate crime. But that's an open door to the Fibbies. If military equipment was used in assaulting you, that's also a federal crime. Hell, Marlene, your central role in the Senate inquiry is probably grounds for the FBI getting involved—damned if I know how things work in Washington." He could tell from her expression that his guess was right on the money.

Book leaned forward, a scowl starting to form. Pat could see he was disposed to argue, to protest being left out of the investigations. Marlene reached a hand and squeezed her husband's arm, a clear signal to go along with the sheriff's position.

Carmen sat still, stunned at the turn of events that put her in a central role of investigating a major crime spree. She had no clue what was involved in liaising with the FBI but concluded she would soon find out.

CHAPTER 45

Speeding from the site of the *Jefferson Weekly* firebombing, Carmen headed toward the Jensen place where Book and Marlene had been attacked. Her goal was to familiarize herself with both crime scenes before the arrival of the FBI special agents.

She'd learned nothing of consequence from interrogating Nancy and Abner. The teenager was in shock over the loss of her favorite uncle. Abner vented his rage, claiming the Bronsons were the alleged perpetrators, but offered no supporting evidence.

She thought, *What the hell does being a liaison with the FBI involve?*

Her fourteen weeks of training at the state police academy in Richmond had touched only peripherally on the Feds. She recalled Sergeant Trenton's lectures on FBI jurisdiction over bank robberies. The sergeant seemed to show off while recounting details about the sixty banks robbed in Virginia during the first six months of the previous year, taking a perverse pride in proclaiming how the rate of the sometimes-violent robberies doubled in comparison with prior years. Like cops everywhere, the Virginia State Police focused on crimes on the rise.

Her hope for the day was that Jefferson County's issues would turn out to be as simple and straightforward as a bank heist.

Having no wish to be the victim of friendly fire, Carmen called ahead when she neared the Jensen place to alert the two deputies guarding the residence. She assumed showing up in the middle of the night unannounced could run the risk of provoking a violent reaction from nervous cops who were babysitting three corpses.

Upon arrival, she spotted Ronald Sargent walking out the front door. Maglites swapped flashes as they beamed them in each other's faces. Although the power company had been alerted, the electricity at the property was still out.

She strained to adopt a neutral expression at the sight of Ron, a medium tall, well-built blond with a buzz cut and sparkling blue eyes. His face sported a wicked grin.

"Well, if it isn't our favorite detective. Come to solve the crime and show us hayseeds how it's done?"

The taunt was familiar behavior from Sargent. The deputy had graduated in the Virginia State Police Academy cohort just before Carmen. He was hired by Garrett on the strength of finishing third in his class. He never bothered to hide his jealousy over Carmen finishing first in her group. She'd overheard office gossip that his resentment was compounded when she was assigned to work with Book—a job he coveted.

"Hi, Ron. Sheriff Garrett assigned me to be liaison with the FBI. He's asked the Feds to take the lead in investigating this home invasion." Calling the sheriff by his formal title rather than "Pat," the usual practice in the office, betrayed her determination to assert her authority.

"Is Billy Cooper here with you?" she asked. The sheriff's office, though small, was blessed (or cursed) with two Billys—one Black, one White—making for considerable confusion. Cooper was Ron's best buddy.

"No . . . Deputy Williams is. He's standing guard over the bodies in the kitchen."

Carmen grinned. Billy Williams was her closest friend on the force. Ron made no secret of his dislike for him.

Billy Williams was a local sports hero who'd left Jefferson County to take a sworn officer's job with the higher-paying Fairfax County Police Department. As a result of his duty in Fairfax, Williams was the best trained and most experienced of the deputies.

Pat had persuaded him to take a position closer to home. At the time, there was a local sweetheart who was part of the attraction, but the two had split up soon after his return home. Billy and Carmen represented the sum total of the diversity the sheriff had achieved to date—one Black man, with Carmen counting double as Hispanic and female.

Billy and Carmen had enjoyed a brief fling soon after she arrived in Jefferson County, but they broke it off. He confided he was uneasy because they were perceived as the Odd Couple among the hitherto all-White, all-male deputies. But the two had remained friends. They got together at least once a week for lunch or dinner at the Jefferson Café.

"Come around back," Ron said.

They walked around the side of the dwelling, passing the garage on the way to the patio. The full moon had crept from behind errant clouds. In the distant woods, an owl hooted—"Who-o-o-o, who-o-o-o."

"Voilà." Ron pointed to the corpse lying on the tiles by the side of the pool. "When Billy and I fished him out of the water, he was stone cold dead."

Since she knew Ron was counting on her adverse reaction to the sight of the cadaver, she braced herself to avoid displaying any outward sign. Apart from an involuntary gasp, she succeeded.

Carmen crouched by the body and pulled on forensic gloves, even though she had no intention of touching anything. She'd leave that to the FBI's forensics investigators.

The victim's headgear was lying nearby. "Where are his Glock and his KA-BAR fighting knife?" she asked.

"No sign of Glocks or any other pistols, although all three men have empty holsters. The two dead guys in the kitchen have wicked looking knives beside them. This one here"—he nudged the body with his boot—"has a scabbard, but it's empty."

She walked to the edge of the pool. She already knew the guns were accounted for but saw no need to share that information with Ron. Book and his wife had brought the three intruders' Glocks with them, as well as Book's Glock and SIG, and handed them over to the sheriff.

Carmen remembered Marlene explaining how she drowned her assailant in the nine-foot deep end near the high dive. She pointed to the diving area. "Apparently Marlene won Olympic medals in swimming. She told Pat and me how she grabbed her assailant's sweatshirt and maneuvered to keep him from stabbing or striking her, holding him underwater until he drowned. Watched him throw away the KA-BAR so he could stroke harder to reach the surface, not that it did him any good."

Carmen climbed the ladder and walked to the end of the diving board. To minimize reflection, she pointed her Maglite straight down toward the bottom of the pool. The glint of metal from the knife shone dimly. The weapon was visible at the bottom of the pool directly under the high dive board. She climbed down and walked over to Ron.

"The perp's knife is in the pool just under the high dive. Needs to be in the notes you share with the FBI."

Ron bristled. "Who are you to give me orders?"

"Just do it, Ron. The sheriff sent you and Billy out here to secure the scene. Your job is to write this up so we can brief the Fibbies."

He pulled out the notebook and began scribbling. His expression hinted he'd find a way to get back at her for this minor indignity.

"I'm heading into the kitchen," she said.

Ron hurried ahead. Carmen was content to follow, giving the antsy deputy the illusion of playing the lead role.

Billy Williams met them at the entrance to the kitchen. He gave Carmen a welcoming smile, and, with a nod, acknowledged

Ron. "Shirley tells me you're the liaison with the FBI. Here's what I figure happened."

Billy flashed his Maglite on the night vision goggles. "Book told me he was Special Forces in Afghanistan. He'd have anticipated the perps would come in with NVG once they killed the lights. To ambush them, he arranged a bonfire on this gas stovetop." He shone his Maglite on the range with the pile of ash on top.

"Bounty towels soaked with brandy would have flared up instantly, blinding the attackers. Too much light is painful to anyone wearing the goggles, enabling Book to catch the big intruder off guard and stab him in the throat and chest with kitchen knives."

To bring his point home, Billy shone the Maglite on the corpse with the protruding kitchen knife.

He continued. "Then, Book miscalculated or got unlucky. The second guy stepped back out of reach of a knife thrust. The perp must have recovered some of his vision. My guess is he threw down his KA-BAR and drew his pistol. Someone shot him in the back, probably Book's wife, who must have taken the weapon from the intruder in the pool. All three holsters were empty, so the Bookers undoubtedly took the pistols to the sheriff's office."

"Bullshit," Ron said. "Did they teach you in Fairfax how to make up these fairy tales? It's obvious Book shot that guy in the back. I looked up our hotshot detective on Google. He got fired from the Washington PD for gunning down some teenager in a dark alley. That's why he came here. He's a backshooter pure and simple."

"Knock it off, Ron," Carmen said. "Billy's reconstruction jibes with what Book and his wife told Pat. Marlene took the Glock from her attacker after she drowned him in the pool. She ran in the kitchen and shot the intruder who was aiming to kill her husband. All the killings were self-defense. I checked Book's Glock and SIG myself. Neither were fired recently. The Fibbies will be responsible for sorting this out. Ron, your version doesn't jibe with the physical evidence. Billy's does."

CHAPTER 46

Sheriff Pat Garrett sat behind his desk, disappointed there wasn't time for a quiet chaw of tobacco before the arrival of the reinforcements from Washington. He was impressed by the FBI's response to his call. A half hour after his first contact requesting help, he'd received a confirmation call from the Bureau.

FBI special agents from both the Violent Crimes and Civil Rights Divisions were en route from headquarters, testimony to the political sensitivity of the issues raised by the complex crimes in Jefferson County. In keeping with the FBI's practice of relying on their nationwide network of field offices, the Richmond Division was sending both investigative and forensic teams.

The sheriff summoned Carmen to his office to ensure she was present when the FBI showed up. The Feds needed to see her seated at his right hand. Pat was determined to get across the idea, rookie or not, she would play the lead role as his *alter ego* in the investigations.

Carmen rushed through the outer door, waved to Shirley, and braked to a halt long enough to fill a mug with black coffee before hurrying into Pat's office.

"The FBI will be here soon," Pat said. "They're sending troops from DC and Richmond, giving our situation the highest priority. Before they arrive, brief me on what you found out at the Jensen place."

She took a seat across from Pat's desk and leaned forward. "According to my read, events at the scene unfolded just the way

Book and Marlene reported. Billy Williams did a reconstruction of the home invasion, virtually identical to the story told by the Bookers. On the other hand, Ron's theory is Book shot one of the intruders in the back. But his version of events doesn't jibe with the physical evidence."

Carmen paused, causing Pat to wonder if she would voice her all-too-apparent conviction Ron's "theory" was based on jealousy of his colleagues rather than any actual evidence. The sheriff gave her credit for restraint in biting back the comment.

"The FBI will question everyone, take forensics, and draw their own conclusions. Just brief them on how you see it. Ron and Billy are free to call it as they see it."

Shirley poked her head into the office. "The Feds just pulled up outside."

A man and woman strode through the office, displaying none of the hesitation visitors—even other law enforcement—customarily showed. Even though the time was four hours past midnight, their erect bearing and confident manner broadcast they came to take charge.

A massive Black man, six-four and over 250 pounds, looking like he was auditioning as a linebacker for the Washington Commanders football team, led the pair. Quiet, intense eyes beamed from a face that, in contrast, had a gentle, sad, and almost poetic look.

Most women would have been dwarfed behind the behemoth. Not this one. Athletic elegance glided across the scarred wooden floors. A pallor of tiredness shone through tanned cheekbones. Despite the hour, alert brown eyes photographed her surroundings—Pat fantasized he could hear the *click click* of the camera as each image registered in her brain. Auburn hair framed a commanding face. To some, it may have seemed ordinary, but to Pat, it was the most beautiful face he'd ever seen. Her stylish black wool pantsuit was both professional and flattering.

The pair flipped open their FBI creds, and the large man made the introductions. "Special Agents Lyle Manning and Dominique Legrand. I'm from the Civil Rights Division, here to decipher your report of a *possible* hate crime, *possibly* masking something else. Dom's from the Violent Crimes Division, responding to your report of a home invasion, *possibly* confounded with a Senate investigation of military contracting, *possibly* also related to a local murder a week or so ago."

Lyle looked up from his notepad and said, "You ever have any *simple* crimes in Jefferson County, Sheriff Garrett? Say, somebody stealing chickens from their neighbors?"

"Call me Pat. We're pretty informal out here in the boondocks." He didn't rise to the gentle gibes. "The past couple of weeks, things have gotten a little more interesting. I'd like Deputy Garcia . . . Carmen . . . to brief you on what's been happening."

Carmen began with the murder at Bronson Stables, relating Mary Connolly's early morning report of the killing, and spelling out the possible involvement of Bear Lansky. She explained how Ares Worldwide reported that Lansky had flown to the Middle East. While the official record of the flight indicated it occurred *before* the sheriff's office identified him as a person of interest and obtained a warrant for his arrest, she shared her suspicion Lansky didn't leave until *after* the crime was committed on Thursday. She described Mary's belief she'd seen Lansky at Courthouse Square at the time he was supposedly headed out of the country.

She highlighted Book's arrival to take over as county detective.

Dom interrupted. "Why isn't Detective Booker here?"

Pat said, "Because he and his wife Marlene were the ones attacked in tonight's home invasion. They killed the three assailants in self-defense." He made a sign for the deputy to continue.

Carmen said, "The attack on the Bookers occurred at the Jensen place—a mansion with an Olympic-size pool—about ten minutes out in the country. Book is house-sitting while the owners are traveling abroad."

"What's the significance of the pool?" Dom asked.

"Marlene drowned one of the attackers in the pool. Book killed a second attacker with a kitchen knife before she arrived in the kitchen. She'd retrieved a Glock from the intruder she drowned and used it to shoot a third attacker who was about to gun down her husband."

Dom raised her eyebrows. "I'm anxious to question those two. You did say, when you called in, Pat, that the perps appeared to be former Special Forces, maybe mercenaries working for Ares Worldwide."

"Yes."

Dom said, "I assume it's no coincidence Marlene Booker is a lawyer who heads up a Congressional investigation of military contracting. I understand the headquarters for Ares Worldwide is located in Jefferson County."

"You did a lot of homework in the wee hours," Pat said.

Dom grinned. "Amazing what you can learn sitting in an SUV for two hours with a laptop computer."

CHAPTER 47

It had been a long night. And the wee hours had stretched almost to dawn when Richmond's FBI contingent arrived.

"Sheriff, I'm Special Agent Todd Davenport." Medium tall, big-boned, fair-haired, and blue-eyed, wearing a gray light-wool suit, the new arrival flipped open his creds as though he and Pat Garrett were the only law enforcement officials in the room. He avoided eye contact with Lyle and Dom.

Uh-oh, a country boy with something to prove, Pat thought, struggling with fatigue.

"Have a seat, Todd. We go by first names around here. I'm Pat Garrett." He pointed around the room, introducing each person in turn. "Lyle Manning and Dominique . . . she likes to be called Dom . . . Legrand, your colleagues from the Civil Rights and Violent Crimes Divisions. And Deputy Carmen Garcia. Carmen will be my primary liaison with the FBI."

Turning to Dom, he said, "How would you like Todd to assign his troops?" He was not dismayed at the newcomer's flare of annoyance at the not-so-subtle way he made clear his expectation FBI headquarters was in charge.

Dom picked up the ball and ran with it. "How you deploy your investigative and forensic teams is up to you, Todd. We have two crime scenes to cover tonight—a home invasion and an arson at the local newspaper. Tomorrow, in daylight, a third area will be included. A murder is believed to have occurred, a few days ago, outside a place called Bronson Stables. These three crimes may or may not be connected. The sheriff's persuaded they are. We're keeping an open mind."

Todd nodded, stiff posture signaling discomfort with his role.

"Lyle will stay with your team at the arson site on the other side of Courthouse Square where the body of a middle-aged Black man was found around midnight."

"Understood," Todd said.

"I'd like you to accompany Carmen and me to a second crime scene, which appears to be a home invasion. The bodies of the three intruders are still on site. Two deputies are protecting the scene. Carmen can brief you concerning recent developments and the sheriff's theory of possible connections among these seemingly random crimes. Will that work for you?"

Pat noted the tough female special agent left no doubt she was giving orders and expected them to be obeyed, despite phrasing her directives as a request for agreement.

"Give me a couple of minutes to split up my teams and I'll be ready to roll," Todd said. If there was any lingering resentment, the man from Richmond hid it well.

Pat ruminated as the investigators filed out of his office. In a typical case, the infighting was between Feds and locals. The sheriff was gratified that this time the Feds were the ones who were squaring off to fight among themselves—central office vs. field office.

He leaned back in his chair, propped his feet on the desk, and reached for a chaw of tobacco to help him think about all that had happened that night.

CHAPTER 48

Book awakened with a start and seized the SIG SAUER resting on the nearby table. He sat upright in bed. The sensation of great peril galvanized his movements. The pistol was loaded and ready to fire, the trigger's cocking mechanism serving in lieu of a safety. Eyes tracking, his aim followed the room's perimeter.

No intruder.

Marlene stirred beside him, reached over, and began stroking her husband's back. Book relaxed, realizing last night's near-death experience had replayed in his subconscious during a deep, if all-too-brief, sleep.

The pendulum of his thoughts swung from life-threatening peril to life-affirming sex—nothing excites the libido like facing death and coming away unscathed.

He laid the pistol on the well-trampled rug and rolled over to respond to the romantic overture of the comely redhead who was sharing his bed for the first time in too many days.

In the aftermath of lovemaking, cuddled in his arms, she said, "I'm going home. I need to brief the senator about what's happened. Amid the turmoil of an FBI investigation, there's nothing to be accomplished here."

He stared into her emerald-green eyes, careful not to fracture the fragile truce they'd forged. The wisest course of action was to sidestep her comment about leaving.

"I'm committed to staying. Even though I can't be party to the FBI investigation, Pat and Carmen will keep me up to speed on key developments. We have to find out if any of these crimes can be linked to Jeb and Robert Lee Bronson."

Knowing how quickly the volcano containing his wife's emotions could erupt, he waited for the explosion.

Affecting indifference, she shrugged her shoulders. "I have a job to do in Washington. I can't let concern about whether or not Ares Worldwide is implicated in these developments in Jefferson County interfere with the broader inquiry into military contracting worldwide."

Book showed his relief at Marlene's attitude.

She said, "For today, screw the big picture. I'm starved. Where can we get a good breakfast?"

"Just a short stroll across Courthouse Square."

With the Jensen place sealed off with crime tape, they'd had no choice but to stay at his old room at the Silverado Motel, located a couple of blocks from the courthouse.

"The Jefferson Café is close by, and the food is excellent. The café's the hub of gossip in town. We'll find out more about what's going on than the FBI will learn examining the crime scenes."

CHAPTER 49

Strolling into the Jefferson Café with Marlene on his arm, Book was pleased to see his usual table in the corner by the back wall was available.

"Good morning, Book." Alice hurried over, menu in hand, to greet the couple.

"This must be your beautiful lawyer wife I've heard so much about. Welcome to the Jefferson Café, darlin'. Your hubby's been just over a week, and he's already one of the county's favorite residents. Did he tell you how he saved Annabel Lee's life?"

Noting his wife's surprise at the effusive greeting, he grinned. Such a welcome was unlikely at restaurants in Northern Virginia, and unthinkable in downtown Washington.

After Alice bustled away, Marlene asked, a hint of acid in her tone, "Who the hell is Annabel Lee?"

"Don't start. Annabel Lee is the waitress heading here to take our order."

Annabel Lee's words gushed faster than the coffee she was pouring. "Judge Newsome told his sister, Mary Alice, who told my friend, Mabel, who told me that the Clanton trial may not occur for two months or more. I can't stand to wait that long. What'll I do?"

Book reassured the waitress the delay in the trial date was routine and not a cause for concern, knowing the real reason for the delay was payback time for a years-old feud between the judge and Pa Clanton.

Mollified, and oblivious to having ignored the newcomer, Annabel Lee took their orders and hurried into the kitchen.

"Last night, you noticed the bruises on my back and shoulder," Book said. "Axe handles swung by the Clanton brothers at Annabel Lee's house were the cause of those injuries."

He briefed Marlene on the clash with the Clantons, playing up Pat's spectacular shooting that saved the day, and downplaying his own foolishness in failing to call for backup. The link between the trap sprung at Annabel Lee's and the confrontation at the Old Virginny Bar and Billiards was glossed over.

Realizing her latest flare-up of jealousy was once more proven unfounded, Marlene shifted the focus of her anger.

"You've been in the area less than two weeks." She began ticking off points on her fingers. "One, you've been cut in a knife fight in a bar, where you never should have been in the first place. Two, you've been attacked and badly injured by Pa Clanton and his three sons. Three, we narrowly missed being massacred by three mercenaries in a home invasion. Four, we are under sentence of death by Jeb and Robert Lee. Five . . . well, I can't think of a five . . . but I'm sure there must be one. Let's get out of this godforsaken county and go back home."

• • •

Carmen made a beeline to the table where Book and Marlene appeared to be in the throes of a heated argument.

"Am I interrupting?" Carmen asked, in the tone new arrivals always assume when they know damn well they're unwelcome.

"Please join us, Carmen," Book said, half-rising. "We're anxious to hear what the FBI is up to."

Book looks like he's gotten a reprieve from a death sentence, Carmen thought, while she verbalized, "I feel like I haven't eaten in a week. Give me a moment to order."

Ignoring the menu Annabel Lee was offering, she ordered the

works—pancakes, eggs, bacon, and orange juice. Grasping the mug of coffee the waitress sat down, she took a generous swig.

When the food arrived, talking between mouthfuls, Carmen continued to brief Book and Marlene. She described the composition of the FBI teams from Washington and Richmond, spelling out the tension between headquarters and the field. Once she was sure Book got the message, she let it drop.

"I have no idea what new information, if any, Lyle may have discovered at the arson scene. Dom and Todd were close-mouthed about their findings at the Jensen place. But I came away convinced their investigation was consistent with events you two reported. Your story about the home invasion also jibes with what I observed at the scene. The one piece of new information the FBI picked up concerns the black Expedition the three mercenaries drove. There's no doubt it came from the Farm."

Anticipating Book's enthusiasm at the news, she held up a cautioning hand. "The authorities at Ares Worldwide reported the Ford SUV stolen last night. But, *get this*, they reported it to the state police. By the time word reached Jefferson County, it was too late for us to act. The Bronsons are covered whether the crimes succeed or fail."

CHAPTER 50

After Carmen left, Book and Marlene walked back to the privacy of the motel. As they entered the room, she said, "I'm serious about you quitting this job and going home. You're in danger here, and you're putting our family in danger. Besides, we miss you. Rebecca and Jonathan are worried about us splitting up."

Book kept silent.

"I'm lonely. I didn't realize how lonely until I felt your arms around me in the pool. I missed you. Despite the danger, I've enjoyed being with you more in the past twenty-four hours than in the past twelve months." She reached out to grab his hand as though to drag him back to McLean.

"Neither of us can go until the FBI clears us," he said.

"That's a lame excuse," she said, releasing his hand. "Once they've interviewed us, they'll let us go. Face it. Lyle and Dom aren't going to hang around here. They'll talk to us, also the Bronsons, and head back to DC. The detailed forensics and investigating will be left to the Richmond field office. We'll be more available to Lyle and Dom in Fairfax County than we are in Jefferson County."

Book frowned, walked across the room, and sat at his desk, half facing away from his wife.

"I've made a commitment to Pat. I can't abandon him in the middle of a crisis. Carmen's bright and competent, but she's inexperienced. Billy Williams, who trained in Fairfax, is the only other deputy worth a damn."

"You're saying the sheriff and his crew are more important to you than the twins and me. Even if it means putting us in jeopardy."

Book heaved an exasperated sigh. "Dammit! I'm *not* saying that. Our family is the most important thing in my life. The trial separation was *your* idea, or I wouldn't have come here in the first place. This is more than just a job. Pat knew my history. He took a gamble in spite of it. I gave him my word; told him he could count on me."

"So, this mess we're in is *my* fault." She felt her face flame scarlet with anger.

"No. It's nobody's fault—except the Bronsons. But it's happened. We can't just wish it away. Even when you go back to work on the Hill, the Bronsons will consider you an ongoing threat. They know you have the power to showcase Ares Worldwide during a Senate hearing. Jeb and Robert Lee fear the investigation could unearth crimes they've committed. Their Pentagon contacts can't insulate them from Congress."

"Then come back and protect me. Protect Jonathan and Rebecca."

"The threat doesn't work that way. We're more at risk together than apart. Look what happened at the Jensen place. We both could have been murdered. If anything happens to you or the kids, anything at all—even if it looks like an accident—Jeb knows I'll kill him. I won't need proof, and I won't wait for the cops."

"Mad Dog Booker," she said, tears running down her face.

"I've done some hard things in the past. Jeb knows better than most how far I'm willing to go. Nothing would stop me. No mercy. No fear of consequences. Staying here will keep our family safe."

He walked over and wiped her cheeks with his thumbs. Her body trembled and she tried to back away. He held her closer, and she finally relaxed against him, only half-believing his assurances about the extent to which fear of retaliation would keep her safe from the Bronsons.

"If you're right," she said, pushing him away, "they'll come after you. Just as soon as the FBI pulls out. The Bronsons have a whole army of mercs at their disposal. All you have is a small rural sheriff's office to back you up."

Distraught, she let her arms fall to her sides.

"If you stay in Jefferson County, they'll kill you."

CHAPTER 51

Tapping her coffee cup with her spoon, Dominique Legrand got everyone's attention. Weary faces turned in her direction. The room grew quiet.

Eight people were seated around a mahogany table large enough for a dozen or more on the second floor of the courthouse. Coffee, tea, soft drinks, and pastry were laid out on a credenza, courtesy of the Jefferson Café.

"I'm Special Agent Dom Legrand. I'd like to thank Commonwealth Attorney Bartholomew Suffolk for arranging for us to meet at the courthouse." She waved at the head of the county's legal staff, equivalent to a DA in urban jurisdictions.

"His administrative assistant, Barbara Halloran, will take notes if there are no objections." Cold eyes scanned the room, confirming everyone's acquiescence.

She noted each attendee as she spoke, going around the room in turn. "We have Sheriff Pat Garrett and Deputy Carmen Garcia, who represent local law enforcement. The Virginia State Police are represented by Colonel Virgil Haywood. Thus far, his office has not been involved in the investigation, but in view of the nature of the crimes committed and suspected, we thought it important to keep the state apprised of developments."

The colonel nodded his head in appreciation at being included. Dom gave him an appraising look.

He was a stocky, barrel-chested, fiftysomething man who appeared vain about staying in shape. Hair cut military short, clean shaven, boots spit-shined, and knife-edged creases in pants and shirt. At first glance, his appearance posed the question whether he was the real deal or a martinet. A closer look at the intensity in his steel gray eyes testified the lawman was no one to trifle with.

Dom continued around the table with her introductions. She went into detail about the roles of each member of the FBI team.

Bodies rustled nervously during her remarks. She raised a hand to still the murmur from the attendees.

"I have one more player to add to the group. Detective Andrew Booker joined the sheriff's office around the time these crimes unfolded. He was not involved in last Saturday night's investigation because he and his wife Marlene were the ones attacked in the home invasion. The two of them killed the three intruders. We've checked them out, and the FBI is satisfied they acted in self-defense. In no way are they considered persons of interest. I would like to include Detective Booker in this briefing if there's no objection."

No objection noted, she turned to Carmen. "Deputy Garcia, would you ask Detective Booker to join us."

Book entered the room and took the seat the sheriff indicated.

She asked Sheriff Garrett to relate his reason for contacting the FBI, treating him with punctilious professionalism.

Pat ticked off events, beginning with the suspected murder at Bronson Stables. He briefly described the arson killing in the workroom of the *Jefferson Weekly* and the apparent home invasion. He then cited the theory shared by Abner Wallace and Detective Booker that the crimes were linked with Ares Worldwide orchestrating the conspiracy.

Dom watched as Book's face grew more tense at Pat's understated way of describing events. She approved as the detective passed on the opportunity to comment.

Carmen also passed.

"Thank you, Sheriff," Dom said. "Now, I'd like Special Agent Lyle Manning to fill us in on the firebombing."

Lyle pushed back from the table and stood, looming over the group, an effect Dom knew he cultivated. "You all pretty much know what happened at the offices of the *Jefferson Weekly* around midnight Saturday. I'd like to point out one new piece of information. To put things in perspective, you need to know the newspaper's owner and editor Abner Wallace informed the FBI about a briefing on Ares Worldwide he gave to Detective Booker and Lenore Bronson earlier this week. Ms. Bronson's brother and father run the military contract; however, she is not involved with the company. It appears the corporate headquarters is in Jefferson County."

Glancing at Dom, he said, "An intriguing piece of equipment was found in Abner Wallace's office—a sophisticated bugging device. The device records everything that's said, including background noise. The recording is rebroadcast to a nearby receiving station and can either be monitored at the station or rebroadcast to a listener in a remote location. Technicians find it difficult to trace, and it's almost impossible to trace after being damaged by smoke and fire. I'm not optimistic we'll track down those responsible for the bugging."

Colonel Haywood said, "Was any information recovered from the device?"

Lyle shook his head. "No. I'm wrestling with two questions. Is this a hate crime in a civil rights context, reprehensible, but unconnected to any of the other crimes? Or is this part of a larger conspiracy? We've examined the available evidence to determine whether there's a conclusive answer to either question."

Lyle hunched his massive shoulders, as if the weight of competing hypotheses was too much to bear. He reached down and took a huge swig of coffee. Mind and spirit rebooted, he resumed.

"Someone wrote 'BURN NIGGER BURN' on the back wall of the newspaper office as a not-so-subtle effort to paint this as a hate crime. On the surface, Ptolemy Wallace's murder would appear to add substance to this theory. So would the fact that his brother, the owner of the establishment, is Black. If you go back far enough, Jefferson County's history of race relations is pretty rocky."

He paused and looked at each person around the room. Dom sensed the participants were awaiting the final act of this drama.

"I'm not persuaded by any of this. The graffito could be nothing more than clumsy misdirection designed to lead us away from the real motive behind the arson. Moreover, Ptolemy Wallace came at odd times to use the equipment to make copies for his church. Even his brother was unaware he would be there. No way the killers could have known. His death was a tragic circumstance—collateral damage, which adds no weight to the speculation of whether or not this was a hate crime."

Lyle lowered his voice to add to the drama, causing his listeners to lean forward in their chairs.

"This brings us to the issue of ownership of the newspaper, the scene of the crime. In most civil rights situations, this would be persuasive. But Abner Wallace makes a good case for his crusade to gather evidence against military contracting, in general, and Ares Worldwide, in particular, offers an alternative motive. He argues discovery of the listening device in his office confirms a conspiracy of the Bronsons being out to get him."

He raised his voice to hammer home the conclusion to his remarks.

"What it comes down to is a lack of hard evidence. My best professional *guess*"—he paused—"is this is *not* a hate crime. Unless new evidence turns up, I don't plan to investigate it as such."

He sat down. The chair creaked ominously but tolerated his bulk.

Dom spoke. "Special Agent Todd Davenport will wrap up our presentation. Next, we'll open it up for questions and discussion."

Todd stayed seated—six-four Lyle was a tough act to follow. "You're aware of the facts of the home invasion. Three mercenaries attacked Booker and his wife shortly after midnight. It may or may not be a coincidence this happened minutes after the arson. The attack was an assassination attempt in the guise of a home invasion and robbery gone bad. The Bookers turned the tables on the mercs and killed all three. The perps have been identified as former employees of Ares Worldwide. The men each carried a Glock, a KA-BAR knife, night vision goggles, and communications gear—all military issue. They drove a black Expedition, which, the previous evening, the local Ares facility reported stolen to the state police."

Colonel Haywood interrupted. "We informed Jefferson County of the Expedition's theft as soon as we heard of it. But it was too late."

Todd continued. "The spokesman for Ares in North Carolina said the MO was similar to home invasions reported near their facility. In one case, the residents were knifed to death. He speculated it could be the same perps, a fact no one has been able to verify. Whether or not the home invasion attack on the Bookers at the Jensen place is related to other crimes is unconfirmed at this time."

Sheriff Garrett spoke up. "What can you tell us about the suspected killing at Bronson Stables?"

Todd said, "We can't confirm a struggle or knifing occurred outside the stable. Although the scenario the sheriff outlined for us is plausible, there's no actual evidence. 'Suspicious dirt' and the absence of a shovel, as discovered by Fix Magruder, who's in charge of the stable, could be explained any number of ways. We've been unable to find the body of a murder victim. Hazy descriptions of eyewitnesses at the Jefferson Café and the Silverado Motel suggest there may have been an unknown visitor in town who used a false name when he stayed at the motel the Wednesday night before the alleged incident. In a nutshell, we've come up empty. However, this incident warrants further investigation."

Dom opened the meeting for questions and discussions. Apart from belaboring a few points already covered, nothing of interest was said. She thanked everyone and wrapped up.

As Pat moved toward the door, Dom caught his sleeve.

"Pat, hold on a minute? I have something I'd like to discuss."

He stared into her brown eyes, holding her gaze a moment too long. "I can do better. How 'bout you come to my house? I'll cook a light supper. We can talk there. Maybe drink some wine."

She shook her head. "I'll take you up on dinner, but you can forget the wine. Then I need to get back to work."

CHAPTER 52

Sitting next to Dominique Legrand on the drive home, Pat Garrett fought to control overpowering emotions. Out of the corner of his eye he could see her glancing at him.

Even though she must be exhausted, she was taking in the surroundings: the barn, garage, outbuildings, and nearby fields of his sixty-acre farm. He felt the need to explain to her that the farthermost three-quarters of the spread was farmed by a neighbor.

Clutching the steering wheel until his knuckles turned white, the normally nerveless sheriff, who'd faced down Pa Clanton and his boys without blinking, was scared. Dom was the first date—if this was a date—he'd brought to his home since his wife died.

As he turned into the long, rock driveway leading to the house, Dom reached over and pulled his right hand from its rigid two o'clock position and held it gently but firmly.

At that moment, he relaxed, thinking, *maybe it'll be all right.*

Jake and Boomer met them at the door. Dom dropped to one knee and, while stroking their thick chocolate coats, talked to them in a low voice for several minutes.

"You have a way with dogs."

"I grew up on a farm in Iowa and told them some adventures I shared with my black Labs. They seemed to relate to the stories. Such beautiful, well-behaved dogs. You must be an excellent trainer."

Pat let the compliment pass without commenting on the vet

who'd been his lover until her death nearly a year ago. The vet was the trainer who deserved the credit.

Guiding her to a leather club chair in front of the fireplace, he decided not to take the time to build a fire. Neither spoke. She was too tired. He was too excited.

The Labs plunked down on either side of Dom's chair. Jake nuzzled her left leg until she acknowledged his presence by scratching behind his ears.

Rummaging in the pantry, Pat found a bottle of Cabernet Sauvignon he'd picked up on a tour of a winery near Middleburg, Virginia, opened it, and half-filled a large wine glass.

A grateful look rewarded his efforts. She took a generous hit on the wine.

"Relax here. I'll fix us a light dinner. Give me ten minutes."

In the kitchen, he fired up a grill pan and slapped on a sirloin steak. He figured it was big enough to share. His usual practice was to eat half and save the rest for a sandwich the next day. Ready-to-cook biscuits went into the oven, which he didn't bother to preheat. He heaped chopped Gala apples and seedless grapes into the fruit bowl, to which he added handfuls of English walnuts and a tad of mayonnaise.

He decided to set up the well-worn wooden farm table in the kitchen, rejecting the dining room table as pretentious. He vetoed the idea of lighting candles. He was trying to strike a balance of informality so Dom would feel at home. He was anxious for her not to think of this as a seduction . . . even if it turned out to be just that.

When the meal was ready, he went into the next room to invite her to join him. The empty wine glass was sitting on the small side table next to the bottle. She'd taken a couple more hits of the Cabernet.

Curled up in the chair, Dom was sound asleep. The Labs were sprawled beside her.

CHAPTER 53

Awakening the next morning, Dom stretched luxuriously. The week's tiredness had dissipated. Refreshed, she lay in bed a few moments, cataloging her memory of the previous evening. She had a clear recollection of relaxing in the comfortable chair before the cold fireplace, accompanied by the Labs, and enjoying the wine. Even the small amount she drank was far too much.

She knew she'd fallen asleep in the chair. *How'd I get in bed?*

Dressed in a borrowed Virginia Tech sweatshirt long enough to cover her rear, Dom explored the farmhouse, wending her way toward the kitchen, where she found Pat pouring coffee into a large mug marked "Sheriff."

They exchanged an awkward "Good morning."

She opened the refrigerator, impressed by its contents, which surpassed the meager fare in her kitchen.

"I'm going to make you an omelet," she said, watching as he passed her the uneaten biscuits from last night's dinner.

"Keep the biscuits," he said. "Eight seconds in the microwave, and they'll be just fine. I'm an expert at handling leftovers."

Focusing on the omelet pan, she added a bit of oil and butter. When the pan reached the optimum temperature, she poured in four whipped eggs. After a minute, shaved sharp cheddar cheese was folded into the egg pocket. With a flourish, she slid an appetizing omelet onto Pat's plate.

He poured Dom a mug of coffee and sat at the farm table, waiting while she finished preparing her own omelet.

"On the drive from DC, I checked you out on the internet. Virginia Tech master's degree in agricultural economics, war hero, came home to tend the farm when your parents took ill, stayed to run for sheriff after they died, married and widowed, and many-time award winner at Cowboy Action Shooting. Quite a résumé."

She smiled at Pat's embarrassed reaction and continued. "I called a fellow agent, Al Tucker, a guy who competes in those NRA tournaments, to ask about you. When he got over being pissed at a three a.m. call, he raved about your shooting skills. I remember his exact words: 'Pat Garrett's the most dangerous man in the world with a handgun. Some people can draw and fire faster, measured in hundredths of a second. But no one can draw and shoot with more accuracy than Pat.'"

Noting that the fulsome praise made him uncomfortable, she waited to gauge his reaction. "What did Al mean?"

"What he said is pretty much true. He's a good judge, since he's won many awards—more than me. Like a lot of athletes, I was born with fast reaction time. Thousands of hours of practice at the range have honed muscle memory, so drawing and shooting are as natural as breathing and walking."

Dom listened intently.

"As far as accuracy is concerned, my shooting is a freak of nature. There's a trick—unconscious—of coordinating mind, eye, and hand, so I aim automatically, without appearing to aim, not using the sights on the gun. The best trick shot artists have the knack."

Her response was a nod to confirm she was interested.

He went on. "Having trained at Quantico, you know the preferred technique is to draw, aim, and shoot, all in one fluid motion. The goal is to group your shots on target in a pattern about the size of a small pie plate. If you put two or three shots in the perp's center body mass, he goes down—today's high-powered ammunition guarantees that.

I can do better. On a good day, I can draw and shoot faster than all but a handful of people in the world, most of whom are military or law enforcement. Here's the kicker. I can hit a particular button on the bad guy's shirt, seemingly without aiming. I do aim, but in my own unique fashion."

"Show me," she said.

"Glad to." He rooted around in a closet and found an old pair of his deceased wife's boots. "Put these on."

He placed a Colt Python .357 revolver with a six-inch barrel in a Western holster and his everyday-carry Glock 17 in its duty holster in the back seat of the Police Interceptor. He included several boxes of ammunition, a few paper targets, and a wooden box with shooting accessories. They drove to a remote section of his farm and stopped near a high dirt embankment.

Dom marveled at the layout, which was unlike any outdoor range she'd ever seen. Taking a second look, she realized the embankment was in two parts, set at a right angle. The range area formed a rectangle, with two sides closed, two sides open. The arrangement offered the dual advantages of safety and flexibility. The shooter had the option of firing up close or at a considerable distance. Two massive wooden walls were set front and center before each part of the embankment. Walking toward the walls, she realized they were made up of railroad ties, eight feet tall and stacked three deep.

Taking two life-size standard silhouette targets, Pat stapled one on each wall, placed about the height of an average man. The middle of the target revealed the outline of a head and torso. Two fluorescent red circles, each the size of a quarter, were pasted dead center on the torso and on the head. A small bull's-eye was printed in each corner of the target.

Out of the wooden box, he retrieved ear protection and shooting goggles. Dom put on her set and watched as Pat did the same.

He strapped on the duty holster and seated the Glock, loaded and ready to fire. He walked to a spot twenty-five feet from each target.

With blinding speed, Pat drew and fired six times at the target to his immediate front, whirled to his left and fired six more times. The shots sounded like two bursts of an automatic weapon, rather than individual shots from a semi-automatic pistol.

He holstered the gun and beckoned her to come forward. "Let's take a look."

She walked to the first target. The red dots in the head and torso were neatly punctured. In a similar fashion, the bull's-eyes at the four corners were perforated. "Damn, that's some shooting."

They moved to the other target. "Oh, my god," she said, part amazement, part admiration. The second target displayed six neat holes identical to the first target.

"Let's see what you can do with the six-shooter," she said, with a half-mocking, half-expectant tone.

He strapped on the Colt in the Western rig. A speed loader was tucked in the belt.

Facing the first target, he drew with what she imagined to be even greater speed than with the Glock. Six loud reports, muted by the ear protection, rang out. Reloading, he began firing at the target to his left.

Not waiting to be invited, she ran forward to examine the first target. At first glance, she couldn't believe her eyes. Could he have missed the target?

Blinking and taking a second look, she realized what had happened. Each of the original holes was somewhat enlarged. Pat aimed for the spots where the Glock's bullets had penetrated in his first volley.

"Holy shit! You *are* the most dangerous man in the world." She strolled over to examine the second target. No surprise. Each of the six original holes had been drilled a bit larger.

"Let me give it a try."

He unbuckled the Western holster, walked over to Dom, and buckled it around her small waist. He loaded the Colt.

She strolled to the identical spot where he stood and faced the first target. Knees bent, the bottom of the holster hung just below her buttocks.

In a lightning move, she drew the revolver with her right hand. Reached over with her left to brace the frame while it swung up in a smooth arc. Aligned the sights with the target, eyes focused on the front sight. Squeezed the trigger smoothly and fired six rapid shots. Holstering the empty weapon, she completed the combat shooter's cycle.

"Let's check how you did," he said.

Together, they walked toward the target. Six holes were visible in a tight group around and in the fluorescent red circle, dead center on the torso.

Nodding approval, he said, "Experts claim the goal of combat shooting is to place two or three shots inside a circle the size of a small pie plate. Your group would fit inside a coffee mug. That's damn fine shooting. The bad guy's dead for sure."

CHAPTER 54

Dominique turned to Pat and said, "Lyle and I have to leave before lunch. He just texted me that there's been another killing of a Black male protestor in Charlottesville. Todd may be joining us there. White supremacists are reportedly involved."

His disappointment was somewhat tempered by her expressed interest in finding ways to continue their relationship, bridging the two hours from the nation's capital to Jefferson County.

After she left, he got back to reality and met with Bartholomew Suffolk to try to persuade the commonwealth attorney to support a continuing investigation of Jeb and Robert Lee Bronson.

Suffolk was unyielding in his opposition to any moves against the family responsible for him gaining his position in the first place. "If you can persuade Judge Newsome to support us, I'll investigate," he said. "Otherwise, no dice."

When pigs fly, Pat thought. The meeting did nothing to change his dim opinion of Suffolk, whom he regarded as a puppet and, along with the county judge, part of Robert Lee's Punch and Judy act.

Getting an unequivocal "no" out of the courthouse encounter had taken longer than expected. He was fifteen minutes late for the one o'clock meeting he'd scheduled. This flew in the face of his firm rule that everyone, the sheriff included, would show up on time for all scheduled events.

Under the threat of black thunderclouds, he stalked across

Courthouse Square. He looked up at the second floor where the Clantons were ensconced in the jail.

In a down moment, the sheriff thought, *My one accomplishment this year is putting away those sorry bastards.*

After seeing Dominique enter his office, he'd decided chewing tobacco was a nasty habit and had quit cold turkey. His temper wasn't improved by symptoms of nicotine withdrawal. Calm nerves were frayed. His temperament, composed most of the time, was on the verge of boiling over.

Barging through the outside door, he stormed toward his office. A cheery "Good morning," from Shirley was ignored. He felt a twinge of guilt at the hurt expression on her face and chastised himself. *Get ahold of yourself, you cantankerous SOB; she hasn't done anything.*

Andrew Booker, Carmen Garcia, and Billy Williams looked up when he entered the room. They averted their eyes upon noticing the expression on Pat's face, which mirrored the weather forecast.

"Let's get started," he said. "We're late." Left unstated in the accusatory tone was the all-too-obvious reason for the delay. "I wanted to brief you on the status of our investigation. The FBI teams are leaving. Lyle Manning and Dom Legrand are heading to Charlottesville, where a Black man has been killed in a possible racial incident.

"The bottom line is the FBI turned up nothing new. After cleaning up a few loose ends, Todd Davenport and his team will be returning to Richmond later today. Colonel Haywood made it clear he sees no basis for involving the state police. Unless we discover something locally, these crimes will go unsolved. We're a bit handicapped since Book can't be involved in the home invasion inquiry because it's an officer-involved killing."

Staring at Book, Pat added, "Take the lead in the arson and murder at Abner Wallace's building. You'll also be responsible for the Bronson Stables suspected murder, including following up on the arrest warrant for Bear Lansky." He shook his head at how illogical the law could sometimes be. "None of that makes any sense, of course, since we assume a common conspiracy ties those cases together with the home invasion where you and Marlene killed the three mercenaries."

Noticing Billy Williams fidgeting in his chair, he said, "Billy, you're needed on the investigating team. We can use your experience across the board. Also, you can backstop Carmen in those areas that are off limits to Book."

Book spoke up, "You met with Attorney Suffolk earlier today. Will he support the investigation?"

Pat hesitated, deciding his staff deserved a candid answer about the impact of local politics on their jobs. "No. We can expect zero backing from the commonwealth attorney or the county judge. Jeb Bronson chairs the board of supervisors. It's anybody's guess how much rope he'll give me to pursue these cases before he fires me. He'd do it tomorrow if he didn't expect a backlash from the voters. He may be reluctant to take any steps that might stir up the Feds or the Virginia State Police."

Carmen gave a grim chuckle. "Sounds like what some call a Mexican standoff."

The clumsy joke was almost enough to shake the sheriff out of his bad humor. He attempted a grin, which didn't make it to his eyes. "In spite of everything, we need to do our jobs."

"You can count on us," Billy said.

"One more thing," Carmen said, clearing her throat and looking uncomfortable. "If the investigation is entering a new phase..."

Pat thought, *She means "dying down."*

"... I'd like to take a few days personal leave. Maybe some leave could be advanced, if I haven't been here long enough to earn the days off."

"Of course. I'll have Shirley arrange it. You and Book work with the Richmond feds to tie up what needs to be done, and you can plan on leaving at the end of the week."

After the meeting ended and the attendees dispersed, He

continued to follow Carmen with his eyes as she walked over to talk with Shirley.

Pat knew Carmen had come into a fortune from her stepmother's trust. He wondered whether inherited wealth was going to her head. *Is she planning to quit law enforcement?*

CHAPTER 55

Robert Lee Bronson puffed on a Cohiba cigar. He eased back in his black executive chair, assuming an air of command as his son entered the room. "What's the status of the warrant for Bear Lansky?"

Jeb said, "The sheriff is having no luck. He's seeking the good offices of the military to force our hand. Our lawyers are putting up a smoke screen to block any attempt to bring Lansky back from the Middle East. Fortunately, the Pentagon has little interest in a murder investigation when no corpse has turned up. The FBI dropped their inquiry—another point in our favor."

"Stalling is a great short-run tactic," Robert Lee said. "But, in time, the system will force us to give him up." The old man knocked off the ash of his cigar to underscore the point.

"No matter what happens," Jeb said, "Lansky is never again setting foot on American soil."

"Do you mean what I think you mean?"

Jeb said, "I know you always liked the big guy, but it would be a disaster if Garrett brought Bear back to testify."

"Agreed," Robert Lee said. "But when the chips are down, how will you prevent it?"

"The Middle East is a dangerous place. My crystal ball foretells a fatal accident in Lansky's future. His Humvee runs off a cliff. An IED explodes. He's a victim of terrorists or friendly fire by some of the troops he's there to train. A million ways to die."

The old man eyed his son. "Without leaving our fingerprints on the incident?"

"We've done it before. Lansky's not our first embarrassment."

Robert Lee said, "Our most serious problem right now is Marlene Booker. My source in Senator Green's office tells me she's taking an aggressive approach to the investigation of military contracting. Ares Worldwide could be in her crosshairs. I want her stopped."

Rising from his chair, Jeb began to pace around the study. "Easier said than done."

"Why? Threaten her. Kill her if you must. Kidnap one or both of her kids and use them to make her back off. Entrap her in a sex scandal. Everybody in Washington is screwing somebody they shouldn't. She and Book are separated. A beauty like her—the media would eat it up."

"Are you smoking a cigar or something stronger?" Jeb said. "None of those gambits will work. Sex is a great temptation for those who are susceptible, which she's not. I can tell you how Book will retaliate if we try kidnapping her children or killing her."

"How?"

Jeb made a chopping motion with his hand. "At the first hint of a threat to his wife or kids, Book will react in just one way. He'll kill us. No mercy. No bullshit about the rule of law. You have to know the man. What made Book so deadly in combat was that he obeyed one imperative—defeat the enemy, whatever it takes."

The elder Bronson blustered. "But you were his commanding officer. He followed your orders."

"He followed orders because I was smart enough to give orders I knew he'd obey. Sometimes, with a bit of reverse psychology, I pretended to push him one way when he was damned and determined to go another. In the end, when I let his instincts win, we both won. He had the best battlefield sense of any soldier I ever met. We don't want him coming after us."

"Call up some of the troops from North Carolina," Robert Lee said. "What can one man do against an army?"

Jeb's disagreement was apparent. "Pat Garrett would join forces with Book. The situation has gone too far to assume violence is the answer. Besides, armed conflict will bring back the FBI. This time, they'd have plenty of evidence pointing our way."

"You may be right, son. Give me time to think."

Robert Lee ambled over to the window and looked out at the lake. He watched, but was indifferent to, the antics of a great blue heron. After a few minutes, he returned to his high-back chair.

"The answer is to kill Book first. Then decide how to handle Marlene."

CHAPTER 56

WHITE SULPHUR SPRINGS, WEST VIRGINIA

Carmen began the first phase of her time off with a phone call to her dad. They agreed to meet at the Greenbrier on Sunday so they could discuss the scenario for what he was bound to regard as a crazy plan.

Scheduling their meeting at the Greenbrier had the symbolic value of bringing father and daughter back to the historic resort where Katherine had treated them to a memorable family vacation. Despite mixed feelings about her stepmom, the stay had been one of the highlights of her teens.

Carmen drove her piece-of-shit green Honda with care, praying it would make the final stage of the car's last voyage with her at the helm.

The valet who took her keys to park the aging Honda made little effort to conceal his contempt at the pathetic state of the vehicle. She took a perverse satisfaction at his reaction and looked forward to upgrading to the top-of-the-line Range Rover she'd ordered from a dealer in Tysons.

Strolling around the well-kept gardens at the resort, Jose and his daughter reminisced about their last visit and shared remembrances of Katherine. Carmen related how, during the lunch at the Boar's

Head Inn, she'd realized she *liked* her stepmom, regretting the awareness came less than an hour before a sniper's bullet struck on the campus of UVA.

During a far-too-filling lunch, she told him about the time in high school when she'd found Katherine's diary and scrapbook containing memorabilia documenting how they'd met, fell in love, and married. Carmen confessed to feeling guilty as she'd searched through the mementos recording the timeline of a parental storybook romance. But she'd been unable to get herself to put the personal items away and had read them thoroughly.

"Dad, it didn't really register with me at the time, but now I've been thinking about that mine collapse and how you and Katherine met. I think there's more to what happened."

Carmen explained some of the illuminating entries from Katherine's scrapbook that had come to mind the last several days: news headlines, clippings, and editorials documenting the cave-in of a local coal mine, Old Grady Two, which had trapped a dozen miners several years earlier. Coverage questioned safety procedures of the mine's owner, Consolidated Mining and Energy, Inc. As hours slipped into days, the media had focused on the plight of the trapped miners and speculated whether they would be found alive.

News reports featured the arrival of a group representing the company that had come to observe rescue operations and, in the words of CEO Roger Carruthers, "to ensure safety procedures are adequate." Katherine's image had been showcased on the front page of the local paper. Descriptions of her role had left it unclear whether she'd represented management or, as later clarified, was providing oversight from a concerned board of directors.

After five suspenseful days, the miners had been saved, having experienced severe hardships, including hypothermia, hunger, and thirst, although injuries from the cave-in itself were limited to a few broken bones and sprains.

The community had celebrated the dramatic rescue. National

media coverage had been intense, with half the stories praising the successful rescue and half questioning the lack of safeguards that had put the workers in jeopardy in the first place.

Three of the victims of the cave-in, however, had not prepared to settle for reassurances given by the CEO that they would be compensated for their suffering and the agony of their families. After several hours of steady drinking at the Starlight Bar, they'd decided to seek revenge against the company. In their alcohol-addled brains, they'd zeroed in on Katherine as the visible symbol of management's culpability. They decided to kidnap her and demand three million dollars ransom. Under cover of night, they waylaid her in her motel and hid her in an old barn owned by a cousin of one of the miners.

The search for the captive had been showcased in the media for two days. The company agreed to pay the ransom, but the kidnappers decided to double their demands. With six million dollars, they would each end up with two million, more than enough to last them a lifetime. The money-obsessed miners insisted the ransom be handed over before they would her.

While negotiations were underway, Sheriff Jose Garcia had located the run-down farm where Katherine was being held. The local paper reported that, in an armed confrontation, he'd faced down the kidnappers. The malefactors wanted no part of a shootout with a decorated war hero. In the end, no one had been hurt. After the men sobered up, they'd decided to surrender.

The sheriff later testified on behalf of the kidnappers, citing the mental stress caused by the ordeal of the cave-in and urging the court to be lenient. At trial, they were found guilty, but the presiding judge let them off with a suspended sentence. A few weeks later, the press headline read, "Hero Sheriff to Wed Kidnapped Lawyer."

Neglecting to mention the steamier details Carmen had read in Katherine's scrapbook and diary about her romance with Jose, Carmen explained her theory about the final chapter in her stepmom's life: "Dad, I think responsibility for Katherine's assassination must lie with the leadership of Consolidated Mining and Energy." She spelled out a plan to verify her suspicions.

Jose protested, arguing she had zero evidence to support the far-fetched hypothesis. Worse yet, if she *were* proven correct, the course of action outlined could prove suicidal.

She was unmoved. "This is something I owe Katherine. I was too pigheaded to appreciate her at the time. Now I realize what a good mom she was to me."

Jose said, "If anything happens to you, I couldn't forgive myself for letting you do this."

"This is my choice, Dad. You need to respect it and support me. Katherine would approve."

When they parted late Sunday afternoon, he hugged her longer than usual. Remembering her dad as a stoic man who showed little emotion, she was surprised to see tears dampening his cheeks.

CHAPTER 57

TYSONS, VIRGINIA

Waking refreshed despite a scant six hours of sleep, Carmen reflected on her discussion with her dad. His concern on her behalf was understandable. Notwithstanding his misgivings, she was convinced her plan was the best way to wreak vengeance on Katherine's killers. She intended to enjoy her brief stay in the luxurious suite she'd booked at the Ritz-Carlton Hotel, located less than a mile from where she'd be in meetings for much of the week. She showered, dressed, and headed to the restaurant to have breakfast with her one and only ally in this risky undertaking.

Seated at a table in the center of the dining room—looking gorgeous and impeccably dressed, as always—was Matilda Fleming Stevenson, nicknamed "Tiger Tilly." Blond tresses were showcased in an elegant French twist. An oval face was dominated by piercing blue eyes and an arrogant mouth, which was softened by a rare smile.

Tiger Tilly earned her nickname and a reputation for ferocious play as a fullback, and principal scorer, on UVA's soccer team. Carmen's nickname, "Cheetah Carmen," had been granted in recognition of the incredible speed at which she could maneuver a soccer ball down the field, often resulting in the winning goal for the Cavaliers, sometimes by a last-second pass to Tiger. The young women were the stars who'd accounted for three straight winning seasons during their stay at the university. Not personally close during their college years, they'd stayed in touch out of a sense of camaraderie.

The two could not be more different in background, temperament, and lifestyle. Carmen was Hispanic, from the poorest county in Virginia, and had perceived herself as poor—up until the shock of inheriting Katherine's wealth. She was proud of her underdog status. Despite a starring role in soccer and a respectable showing on the basketball court, her self-image was that of a serious student, not a jock, and she avoided the University of Virginia's vibrant social and political circles like the plague.

Tilly hailed from aristocratic Richmond, Virginia's state capital. She hovered near the epicenter of the social and political scenes on campus, being elected class president and chair of too many activities for Carmen to remember. Without visible effort, she'd attained stardom. Her father was a state senator, one of a proud line of Stevensons who'd combined wealth and political influence.

Tilly made no secret of her political ambitions. She'd outlined to Carmen her career path over a beer during one of their rare get-togethers at a student hangout: governor, US senator, perhaps even president. To that end, she chose to enter the law school at the University of Virginia rather than accept offers of admission from Yale and Harvard.

"Staying local is the way to build a support network and, over time, a constituency," she'd said, confiding her grand strategy for political success.

After hearing of her former teammate's good fortune through that mysterious network that operates among the wealthy, Tilly had called Carmen, urging her to capitalize on her stepmom's riches and the political connections of the Stevenson branch of the family tree. But the advice fell on deaf ears.

When Carmen telephoned her sister alumna to request help, hinting at the broad outlines of her plan to seek revenge for her stepmom's assassination, Tilly had jumped at the chance to get involved. Perhaps she hoped for a future political ally or campaign contributor. Or maybe the challenge of turning "cinder girl" into Cinderella appealed to her ego.

When reunited at the breakfast table, Tilly hugged Carmen, and she responded in kind. Carmen thought, *Perhaps there's more genuine affection and mutual respect than I realized.*

After a few minutes of catching up on the past few months in their divergent lives, Tilly got down to cases. "Let me see if I understand what you're planning. You believe Katherine's killing was orchestrated by the leadership of Consolidated Mining and Energy. During the year your dad managed the trust you inherited he chose to sign over proxy voting control of your stepmom's stock to management. His arrangement didn't pose a threat to their balance of power or the firm's strategy, as you hypothesize Katherine's actions had. Am I on track so far?"

Carmen was impressed Tilly had extrapolated from the little she'd been told to hit on the essence of the issue. She nodded.

"You intend to carry on where Katherine left off, starting at tomorrow's annual general board meeting. With thirty-five percent of the stock, you stand a good chance of controlling the board. If your reading of management's policy direction is accurate, you could be a major obstacle to their goals. Your intent is to block them. If you force their hand, they'll have no alternative but to eliminate you. Have I grasped the main points of your situation?"

"Yes," Carmen said, confirmed in her conviction that Tilly's social facade concealed a brain with amazing analytical horsepower.

"Well, I assume you haven't enlisted me as a bodyguard in this suicide mission. How else can I help?"

Carmen smiled at the bodyguard reference, musing, *if she chose such a role, the Tiger would acquit herself quite well.*

"It's essential that I be credible to those board members. When they look at me, they'll see a twenty-five-year-old Hispanic woman, with limited job experience, from a rural county—in other words, an unqualified hayseed. It's not enough to say, 'Hey, I inherited a hundred million dollars last week and I own one-third of the stock, follow me.'"

Both women laughed at the absurdity of the situation. As humor subsided, Tilly waved a hand as though to clear the air for a fresh perspective.

"Reality is determined by perception," Tilly said. "When you look like a wealthy, mature, influential woman, and conduct yourself that way, you'll be viewed as such by the board. Purchasing a top-of-the-line Range Rover was a good start. The word will get around you're driving a hundred-thousand-dollar car. You're staying in a penthouse suite at the Ritz-Carlton. Way to go. I'll bet my ass most board members are staying here or down the road at the Hyatt. Make sure you drop a subtle mention of the penthouse."

Carmen nodded at how quickly Tilly had picked up on the method behind her extravagant madness.

"Clothes, accessories, and how you carry yourself are what's important. You're athletic and graceful, a definite plus. You're attractive. We'll get you in the hotel salon and tone up your blah hairdo. Also a manicure—make those fingers forget they ever shoveled manure. Then we're off to Neiman-Marcus and Saks in the mall adjacent to the hotel to shop for a new wardrobe."

Tilly guided Carmen through a mind-blowing shopping trip. The nouveau riche young woman purchased two business suits—one blue wool with subtle pink stripes by Yves Saint Laurent and a second gray silk by Dolce & Gabbana. They selected a Michael Kors Pleat Front Dress in an arresting lime color and additional outfits to round out her wardrobe. An array of high-fashion shoes and handbags from Manolo Blahnik, Salvatore Ferragamo, and other designers complemented the outfits.

The design expert at first balked at her protégé's insistence the handbags accommodate a 9 mm "Baby Glock", but at last bowed to the reality of the need for self-defense.

A side trip to Tiffany & Co. across Route 7 led to the purchase of matching necklaces, earrings, and rings. Tilly emphasized the crucial role of the optimal watch, leading Carmen toward the counter where a dazzling array of timepieces was on display.

"Most of the members of the board are going to be men. Rich old farts. What fat old rich guys like to brag about is their watch." Holding her arm out as though showcasing a watch while mimicking a stereotypical board member, she said, "'It costs more, it's fancier, it has more gadgets.' Like guns are to some men, watches are to wealthy guys—they're driven by penis envy. 'Mine's bigger than yours.'"

Waving off Carmen's skeptical look, she added, "Your watch has to be more elegant and equally or more expensive. A Patek Philippe. It's best in class. Their dicks will shrivel when they get a load of your timepiece."

Although Carmen was growing jaded at the astronomical prices she paid during a day of high-end shopping, the notion of shelling out over thirty thousand dollars for a white gold watch studded with diamonds freaked her out. But in the final analysis, the overwhelmed shopper bowed to Tilly's insistence and enthusiasm.

They took time off from shopping for clothes and jewelry for Carmen to show Tilly her Range Rover.

"I selected this car because, at a hundred thousand dollars, it's pricey without looking showy. On the road, it offers a comfortable ride. The Range Rover has the power of an eight-cylinder engine with over five hundred horsepower, giving the SUV amazing pickup. Off road—which it will be a lot in Jefferson County—it's one of the toughest and most versatile vehicles ever manufactured. Everything comes standard in the Supercharged model. The one modification I insisted on was removing the rear seats to install a gun safe."

Carmen opened the gun safe to reveal two 9 mm Glock 17 pistols, numerous ammunition clips loaded with hollow-point rounds, a combat shotgun, a sniper rifle, and a Kevlar vest. Tilly's eyes widened as she examined the arsenal. She reached over and, with reverence, touched each of the weapons.

The day ended with a fashion show in Carmen's suite. Tilly applauded while Carmen pranced around the room showing off the day's purchases. Her mission accomplished, Tiger Tilly departed.

Carmen gave a shiver of anticipation at the next day's confrontation.

I'm ready to tackle whatever Consolidated Mining and Energy has to offer.

CHAPTER 58

JEFFERSON COUNTY, VIRGINIA

Once the FBI wrapped up their forensic investigation at the Jensen place and removed the yellow crime scene tape, Book moved back into the mansion, thankful to say goodbye to the Silverado Motel. He tossed the few belongings he'd brought to the motel into the Sequoia and made the short drive to his home away from home. But he could take no comfort from the luxurious accommodations. His thoughts lingered on the romantic moments shared there with Marlene. He redoubled his running and exercise regimen to cope with mounting sexual frustration.

Carmen had only been gone a few days, and already he missed his partner's input on the investigation. *What's Carmen up to?*

Book consulted Lenore, but she had little to add. One piece of information she did share landed like a bombshell.

"When you interviewed me at the house I intimated when I knew you better I'd share the root cause of my life getting fucked up. A single incident changed me forever. My brother Jeb came home from college one weekend to join the family in celebrating my fourteenth birthday. That night, after the birthday party, Jeb went out with friends and got roaring drunk, something he didn't do too often. He came to my room sometime past midnight. After a clumsy attempt at seduction, he raped me. Daddy refused to believe my account of what happened. Or pretended he didn't. The next day, Jeb came to me and, in tears, pleaded for forgiveness. I told the son of a bitch he could await forgiveness until hell freezes over."

Book was astonished to hear this tale of family incest.

"I was exiled to my Aunt Rosemary in Richmond. Lucky for me, my aunt was more forward looking in her thinking than I'd given her credit for. When she discovered I was pregnant with Jeb's child, she arranged for me to have an abortion."

Lenore raised her arms in frustration.

"I hate my brother for raping me and Daddy for his denial of what happened."

"Why did you come back home to live?"

"Because it's home. After extensive travel abroad, I discovered there was no other place in the world I wanted to live. Jeb, Daddy, and I have an unspoken truce. The past is never mentioned. We coexist. But we don't live together."

CHAPTER 59

Returning to the mansion following another unproductive day of detective work, Book saw a FedEx truck pulling out of the long driveway.

"Are you Mr. Booker?" the driver asked, when the two vehicles stopped side by side.

Acknowledging he was, Book signed for a FedEx envelope. He continued up the driveway, parked by the front door, and entered the residence, keeping the envelope tucked under his arm. He walked into the kitchen, now restored to good order thanks to the cleaning crew organized by Shirley's real estate friend, Homer Smedley. He opened the refrigerator, popped open a can of Coke, walked out by the pool, and settled into a lounge chair.

When he ripped open the envelope, a cascade of pictures spilled onto his lap. He stared, transfixed, at the first one. The figure in the picture was Franco Moretti.

Son of a bitch—Mr. FBI's Most Wanted.

Spotting Moretti's image triggered a flare of anger that blurred Book's vision and caused his hands to shake. He dropped the photos onto the tiled patio. Never before had he experienced such all-consuming hatred. Not toward the worst of the criminals he'd confronted in DC. Not even toward his enemies during wartime in the Middle East. In those instances, his dominant motivation had been professionalism. He was doing a job and, if the bad guys had to go down, so be it.

With Moretti, it was personal. The man was a monster, pure and simple. In addition to Lou and others for whose deaths he'd been responsible, Moretti had maliciously wrecked Book's life and threw his family into chaos. The urge to retaliate turned Book's stomach fluid to acid.

Sorting through the photos now spread out on the lounge chair, he realized each of them included Moretti, sometimes featured in the foreground, sometimes in the background.

Few observers would have connected the person in the photos to the world's most sought-after. But to Book, there was no mistaking the likeness.

After he regained his composure, he began examining the photos with care, comparing the various shots of Moretti with the description engraved on his brain. The aftermath of extreme plastic surgery was obvious—especially around the eyes, ears, nose, and chin. Hair, once ebony black, was now a rusty brown, with gray flecks at the temples. The fugitive had lost at least twenty pounds. Once stocky, bordering on obese, he now looked fit—a killer physique reflecting the killer in his soul.

Book thought, *Who would guess the person in the photos was the same individual who is wanted for a multibillion-dollar theft and the brutal murders of four people—his wife, a business partner, a woman during a carjacking, and a toddler left to die in the wilds of West Virginia.* Book added Lou Bernstein and Scooter Thomas to the list of victims. He held the fugitive accountable for arranging his partner's ambush in Moretti's residence and the teenager's death in the alley in Georgetown.

Identity confirmed, Book turned his attention to other puzzles: *Where was Moretti when the pictures were taken? And who sent the envelope to Jefferson County?*

He decided to address these questions in reverse order. Taking care to hold the FedEx delivery by the edges to avoid adding more of his fingerprints, he examined the envelope. At a glance, it was obvious the information identifying the sender was bogus.

Jack Dough was the name given.

John Doe—the universal designation of an unknown person. *At least the son of a bitch has a cop's sense of humor.*

He recognized the location in Southeast Washington as a nonexistent address and had no doubt the phone number, despite its 202 area code, would turn out to be inoperative.

Leaning back in the chair, he contemplated the best way to tackle the problem. He pulled out his cell phone and dialed.

"AJ, do you know who this is?"

The line was silent for several heartbeats. He could visualize Alexandra Jacquard, one of his closest friends in the MPD's Consolidated Forensic Laboratory, staring at the phone, deciding how to react to the unexpected call. She would have flagged the ring on her caller ID and known at a glance it was an unfamiliar number. Book had upgraded to an iPhone in the months since he'd last called AJ. His opening remark would have alerted her to the caller's desire to remain anonymous even though she would recognize his voice.

"Yes."

"Good. I need a favor."

"Can't talk now. Call me tonight at eight." She recited a DC number, beginning with a 202 area code, and hung up.

Rather than being disappointed by the abrupt dismissal, Book was encouraged. The conversation was classic AJ behavior indicating she intended to help but wanted no trail leading back to her. Above all, no electronic footprints her straitlaced boss could track. Brook Smithey (unkindly called BS by all of his subordinates whenever he was out of earshot) had been a pain in AJ's ass ever since he'd been promoted from the lab spot next to hers.

● ● ●

At eight sharp, AJ picked up the phone on the first ring.

"Hi, Book. Did you call just because you miss me?"

Alexandra and Book had nearly had a fling a few years back when Marlene was away on a business trip to London. While still a member of the elite SWAT team, Book had ended a confrontation with a hostage-taker by shooting the man just before he pulled the trigger to kill his abused wife and their ten-year-old daughter.

Decompressing at a cop bar after the action, Book drank too much and had been on the verge of succumbing to AJ's sexual overtures. She, for one, was anxious to cross the invisible line from friends to lovers. They'd ended up in the bedroom at her condo. He called a halt to the flirtation on the brink of passing the point of no return.

He knew AJ gave herself high marks for showing class in restoring their relationship, first on a professional basis, and eventually as friends. Whatever she felt in her heart, she'd said she respected Book for remaining faithful to his wife, even though she never got over being pissed at the abrupt end to their evening.

Book ignored her jocular question.

"I've a tough, possibly insoluble, forensic problem. I can't think of anyone else who can help me."

Clearly annoyed at the clumsy attempt to challenge her professional pride, she snapped, "Tell me what's going on."

"I have new info on Franco Moretti."

"Oh hell, not again."

"I'm afraid so. I received a FedEx envelope today. Full of pictures of Moretti in various backgrounds, in what appears to be a European city. The sender's info is phony. I'd like you to examine the pictures and envelope and see if you can identify the source. It would also be helpful if you could come up with something that pinpoints the locale and gives a rough time frame for the photos, but I have another source of help for that information."

"Book, you're on thin ice. The Department warned you to stay away from the Moretti investigation. Some of those sons of bitches in Internal Affairs would welcome an excuse to reopen your case and put a nail in your coffin. The FBI won't appreciate your interference.

Moretti has nothing to do with your job—whatever the fuck it is—in Bubba County. BACK OFF!"

Alexandra cursed herself under her breath for getting so emotional. *It's a bitch when you care about someone.*

The phone line was quiet for a moment. She knew he was giving her time to allow her emotions to subside, a tried and true tactic she recognized. But it worked. She heaved a noisy and obvious sigh.

"Go ahead. I've got a grip."

"Moretti ruined my life. Now these pictures provide a clue. It's time to track down the bastard and ruin his. Once I've finished, I'll turn him over to the FBI. The sons of bitches in DC can eat crow."

"I must be crazy for getting involved." She paused a beat. "Here's what you do. Make a copy of the photos. Put the originals in a big slider bag. Put the FedEx envelope and the slider bag with the originals in a FedEx box. Ship them to me overnight. I'll give you my friend's address and contact you as soon as I know something."

CHAPTER 60

JEFFERSON COUNTY, VIRGINIA

With a satisfied expression, Book hung up the phone. AJ, his favorite forensic scientist, had reacted just as he expected. The puzzle of who'd sent the mysterious FedEx envelope was on the road to being solved.

The focus of his attention shifted to the remaining puzzle: where was Moretti when the pictures were taken?

Europe was his best guess. His notion of what Europe looked like was based on TV programs and several movies his wife had coerced him mainly because it was a prelude to foreplay with Marlene.

Rudolph Van Hollen, one of Book's closest friends, was his first choice to solve this riddle. Rudy was a travel editor at the *Washington Post* and an expert on Europe. He did frequent TV gigs focused on tourism in the US and abroad. Born in Frankfurt, Germany, offspring of an Army major and his German bride, the travel guru spoke fluent German, French, Italian, Spanish, and who knows how many other languages.

Rudy and Book had become friends while attending high school in Bethesda, Maryland and had continued to socialize when both took jobs in neighboring DC.

Rudy's teenage son Warren became addicted to narcotics, started dealing, and was targeted by the mob. Book had rescued the boy and put away the drug dealers who threatened his life. The crisis had cemented the friendship between the two men.

"If you ever need help with anything, anything at all, you just have to ask," Rudy had pledged.

It was payback time. Book picked up the phone and called his friend. At the conclusion of the call, he dispatched a set of the photos.

CHAPTER 61

TYSONS, VIRGINIA

Carmen's suite at the Ritz-Carlton showcased numerous mirrors. She checked out the view in each as she tried on the various outfits Tilly had helped her select. She settled on the Dolce & Gabbana gray silk suit and blouse, Ferragamo shoes and handbag, and a matching emerald necklace and ring.

She wondered whether a white gold and diamond watch would go with emerald jewelry. Then, the humor of Cinderella second-guessing the Fairy Godmother's fashion sense struck her. She couldn't help laughing out loud.

After the brief spasm of mirth abated, she finished getting dressed and headed down to Valet Parking. She was a bit surprised the pricey Range Rover hadn't been stolen or vandalized.

During the short drive to Consolidated Mining and Energy's headquarters, a moment of panic set in. She was taking on one of the country's biggest corporations, convinced the leadership had arranged for Katherine's killing. If she was wrong, she'd be a target of front page ridicule. If she was right, she'd be painting a target on her back.

The crisis of confidence caused her to lose control of the SUV. The vehicle lurched part way into the lane on her right. Horns blared from morning commuters headed toward DC. She jerked the wheel and pulled back into her lane. Realizing she had to turn right at the next intersection, she again lurched into the right lane, cutting off a red Prius. Horns blared again from pissed off motorists. She resisted the temptation to give the other drivers the finger, guiltily aware she was the one responsible for the spasm of road rage.

Arriving at Consolidated Mining and Energy, Carmen's resolve stiffened. She knew she had to do this—for Katherine.

She remembered Tilly's advice about premeeting activities: "No one with any sense tries to eat at these breakfast buffet sessions." In preparation, Carmen had eaten a fulsome room service breakfast before leaving the Ritz-Carlton.

She strolled over to the coffee bar. Heeding her mentor's warning to avoid the juggling act chinaware required, she passed up the delicate cup and saucer. She filled a take-away cup with black coffee and took a sip of the piping hot brew. The delicious taste of the coffee made her wish she could take the coffee maker with her when she returned to Jefferson County.

"I see you've been to these meetings before."

Surprised by the voice behind her, she spun around, almost spilling the java. Her eyes locked on a man looking down on her with a smile on his face. She stepped back to get a better view. Broad shoulders tapering to a slim waist outlined a powerful frame that did justice to a charcoal wool suit. A dark blue button-down shirt framed a bold red tie decorated with tiny gold tennis rackets.

"You startled me."

"Sorry. I was impressed with how well you know the routine of handling this morning buffet extravaganza. Eat nothing and avoid filling your hands with dishes you want to discard as soon as you realize there's no way to juggle everything."

She laughed, put at ease by his casual manner—correction, *flirtatious* manner.

Her instinct to respond in kind was put on hold by remembering her reason for being here. If she was going to smoke out whoever killed Katherine, she needed to marshal support to take over the board and challenge management. Flirting with the first cool guy she met was no way to start the day.

"The truth is this is my first time. I just joined the board."

"I know. You were written up in the handouts for the meeting. Is it true you're a police officer in Jefferson County?"

"Deputy sheriff," she corrected automatically. "Are you on the board? I don't recall seeing your name in the materials I received." Deciding a little flattery, bordering on flirtation, wouldn't hurt, she added, "I'm sure I would have remembered."

"My mom's a board member. She's been in an assisted living facility for a couple of years. I attend to exercise her proxy." He extended his hand. "Russ Boudreau."

"You must play a lot of tennis," she said, mindful of the tie's pattern and reacting to his viselike grip and the calluses on his hand. She felt an immediate attraction and rewarded him with a smile.

"Guilty as charged. I was on Yale's tennis team. I try to play at least once a week. Maybe you could join me sometime." The invitation was punctuated by an engaging grin.

"Soccer is more my speed. I wouldn't know what to do on a tennis court."

She imagined Tiger Tilly whispering, *Be careful, Cheetah. If he beams that sexy look at you one more time, you'll be in bed with him in your suite. Stay focused on your game plan.*

CHAPTER 62

Carmen couldn't decide if Russ Boudreau was flirting with her or taking advantage of their joint presence at the breakfast buffet to pump her for information. *Well, two can play Twenty Questions.*

She took him by the arm and led him to a far corner of the room where floor-to-ceiling windows looked out onto a magnificent inner garden. The sight was so unexpected in the midst of hyperurban Tysons, she almost lost her train of thought.

Catching herself, she said, "Russ, let me tell you my game plan for the board meeting. I realize I'm new and don't know the ropes..." She held up a hand to forestall his predictable reassurances. "Hear me out."

He nodded.

"My intention is to take control of the board in memory of my stepmom, Katherine Harriman Garcia, who was moving toward a takeover when she was struck down by an unknown assassin more than a year ago." In point of fact, Carmen had no firm knowledge of Katherine's intent, but the assertion fit the raison d'etre behind her stepmom's murder.

"Hold on a minute," Russ said, looking perturbed. "How'd you know Katherine was maneuvering to take over the board? Just a trusted few were aware of her plans."

It's true. Carmen fought for self-control to subdue her elation. Her theory of the motive for Katherine's killing was proving out.

She leaned close to her breakfast companion and whispered,

"When we had lunch at the Boar's Head Inn in Charlottesville the day she was killed, she told me of the intrigue in the company and her plans to act. If she were successful marshaling enough votes, she intended to move key policies in a very different direction."

Tilly's caution echoed in her subconscious. *"Be careful not to go overboard making up this shit."*

CHAPTER 63

Carmen prepared to greet Brent Johanson and Roger Carruthers as they approached the window corner where she and Russ were huddled in earnest conversation. She now knew, or thought she knew, either Chairman Johanson or CEO Carruthers—in all likelihood, both of them—were implicated in Katherine's murder. She struggled to maintain a "cop face" and reveal nothing of what she was thinking and feeling.

"Good morning, Ms. Garcia," Johanson said, His mellifluous voice, with just a touch of country, matched a persona suitable to any Washington politician. She noted the fine tailoring on his brown plaid wool suit barely masked a gut that swelled against a tooled western belt with an ornate silver buckle. He stood eye to eye with the stalwart woman, a height achieved by virtue of high heels on ebony black cowboy boots.

"Please call me Carmen, sir," she replied, matching the vigor of his handshake with forced enthusiasm of her own.

"*Sir!*" Carruthers guffawed.

"Carmen, everybody calls this old coot 'Colorado' from the days he did real work back in the mines of his home state. Now he just rides herd on the biggest corporation in the mining business. If it weren't for ExxonMobil and the state-owned oil companies, we'd be the largest energy corporation in the world. Let go of that young lady's hand, Colorado, so I can shake it. I'm—"

"Roger Carruthers, CEO of Consolidated Mining and Energy," Carmen said, in an effort to break the rhythm of the duo's comedy routine.

"Right you are. Call me Rog, Carmen." He paused. "I have a problem with where you parked your Range Rover."

She thought, *What the . . .*, but kept silent.

"That's some sweet buggy. Give me your car keys and I'll have it moved to the VIP parking section."

Opening her purse with care so as not to reveal the Baby Glock, she withdrew the key fob and placed it in the CEO's outstretched hand.

He held up the keys, and a young man in a green blazer and tan slacks materialized out of nowhere and retrieved them. The errand runner disappeared as quickly as he'd appeared.

She thought, *If they're trying to impress me, they're succeeding.*

She noticed Russ take a step back, leaving her cocooned between the two suits. A couple dozen people had wandered in since she and Russ arrived and were casting covert glances toward her at the center of the meeting's power grouping.

A photographer slipping through the crowd, camera poised, caught her eye. Carruthers moved to her left, bracketing her between the two corporate leaders. His midnight blue double breasted suit typecast the CEO as the "strictly business" member of the pair, with the chairman representing the "good ole boy" constituency.

Carmen assumed her one-third stock ownership had her auditioning for the "prominent stockholder who's just joined the board."

Johanson said, "We're mighty pleased you could attend this meeting. Katherine was a great asset to the board, and we miss her. Please accept our condolences."

Never one whose strong suit was hypocrisy, she bit the inside of her mouth to keep from reacting in accordance with her instincts. Looking her most angelic, she replied in a voice that dripped Southeast Virginia honey, "Thank you for your heartfelt sympathy.

I know no one could take Katherine's place, but I'll do my best to contribute in ways to make her proud."

Russ stepped forward to rejoin the group. "I'd be happy to brief you on the issues and previous actions of the board."

Carmen said, "Thank you." She felt more comfortable with Russ than with the corporation's power duo.

"You're in good hands with Russ," the chairman said. "We'll arrange for Russ to sit next to Carmen at the main table so they can compare notes." His affect communicated the objective of the moment had been achieved.

"You two have some refreshments."

He glanced at Carruthers. "Russ can start by taking Carmen around and introducing her to the other board members."

A panorama of new faces paraded past. Her last encounter before the breakfast buffet ended was with a mountain of a woman wearing a bright red evening gown, with a face flushed the same color.

In a confrontational tone, the Lady in Red asked, "What are you going to do about the policies of this company that threaten people's lives with pollution, global warming, and annihilation?"

CHAPTER 64

WASHINGTON, DC

Book pushed the ornate buzzer outside the front door of Rudolph Van Hollen's brick Tudor style home on Foxhall Road in Northwest Washington. Reluctant to endure the two-hour drive to the city, he'd nevertheless respected his friend's reasons for refusing to discuss Franco Moretti's whereabouts over the telephone.

Rudy opened the door and threw up his hands in disgust. "You son of a bitch. Don't you know it's a federal offense to conceal the whereabouts of one of the FBI's Most Wanted?" He continued talking while he walked back through the foyer. "Of course, you know. You're a goddamned officer of the law."

He looked over his shoulder at Book who remained frozen in the doorway, mouth agape. "Well, don't stand there like a doormat. Get in the house before any neighbors or cruising patrol cars see you."

In an effort to get his irate buddy to calm down, Book said, "It might not be a bad idea to lower your voice. You don't want Moira or the kids to get wind of what we're discussing."

"You let me take care of my family. Besides, everybody's at the high school watching Warren play baseball. He's the starting pitcher and the team's MVP. I should be there instead of babysitting you and risking a prison term."

Book followed Rudy into the study and slumped into a wooden Georgetown captain's chair across from the travel guru's desk. "Should I slink out of the house now or wait till you beat on me some more?"

"Okay. Okay. I get the message. I agreed to help, without reservations. If you asked me to sail across the Atlantic in a leaky boat, I'd say 'When do we cast off?' ... At least give me the satisfaction of bitching about this god-awful situation."

"Bitch all you want. But tell me what you found out."

Rudy shrugged in resignation and walked to the bookcase lining the rear wall of the study. He pulled out a copy of Plato's *Republic* located in the right corner of the top shelf, reached into the recess, and pressed a virtually invisible switch. A section of the bookcase swung out, revealing a wall safe. He manipulated the combination, withdrew a large manila envelope, and dumped the Moretti photos on the desk.

Picking up a photo at random, Rudy held it up as though it were a trophy, unable to conceal professional pride at his detective work.

"The photos paint a clear and unambiguous picture—Moretti is in Geneva, Switzerland. My bet is he's staying at the Four Seasons Hotel on Quai des Bergues in Geneva, or at least he was when the photos were taken."

Book was impressed with his friend's ingenuity, even though that was precisely why he'd sought Rudy's help.

"The hotel is on Lake Geneva, just in front of Pont du Mont-Blanc. On a clear day, you can see the mountain, Mont Blanc, from the bridge."

"You sure?" Book asked, his throat dry.

"Oh, yeah. I've been there. I've stayed at the Four Seasons. I've walked on the bridge. sailed Lake Geneva—even climbed the Alps, including Mont Blanc. Whoever took these photos wanted you to find Moretti, which adds credence to the likelihood he's still there. All the scenes were photographed in Geneva. The city's quite distinctive—even if it lacks a world-famous landmark like the Eiffel Tower or Big Ben."

"Why Geneva? I would have expected any international fugitive with money to head for one of the countries without an extradition treaty with the US. There are several dozen candidates in the Middle East, Africa, Asia . . . even Russia."

"There's money and then there's MONEY." Rudy spread his arms wide apart to convey the notion of a huge fortune. "You told me Moretti stole billions and hid at least several hundred million dollars abroad. Swiss banks are a favorite refuge of illicit fortunes. With a nest egg of such magnitude, he could afford a pick of fraudulent identities and travel documents. Some of the world's renowned plastic surgeons practice in Switzerland. From these snapshots, it's obvious our fugitive hired the best."

Rudy moved from his desk to join Book in a matched pair of Stressless chairs across the room.

"Geneva is an international enclave dating back generations. Countless thousands of foreigners, including delegates representing governments worldwide, are based in the city or come to attend meetings. The UN, the World Health Organization, and the International Red Cross are among hundreds of groups—official and private—represented in Geneva. After New York City, Geneva is the most cosmopolitan city in the world as far as international organizations and businesses of all types are concerned. No one who looks even a bit like Moretti would seem out of place as a meeting attendee, tourist, or resident."

Interrupting the travelogue, Book said, "When were these snapshots taken?"

"The pictures are recent, perhaps during the past month. You can see buds on the trees and blooms on the bushes in the gardens. No question it's spring."

"What are the odds he's still hiding out there?"

"Your guess is as good as mine. I'm a travel writer, not a fortune teller. Moreover, we can't tell from these photos whether he suspects someone is following him and filming his movements."

Rudy grinned wickedly. "Here's a wild thought. Have you considered the possibility Moretti is aware of who is shadowing him and is colluding with the photographer? Remember how he set you up in Georgetown. He let you see him, and then he sandbagged you, setting you up to shoot that kid."

"Are you suggesting Moretti has set a trap, luring me to Geneva to have me killed."

"Thereby getting rid of his main adversary."

"Risky. Why wouldn't I inform the FBI?"

"Do you plan to notify the Feds?"

"Of course not. I'm going to track down the son of a bitch on my own. Once I have him in hand, I'll call the FBI—in Washington rather than at the American Embassy in Bern. I know just which special agents I'd like to see get the headlines for bringing him back to the States to face justice." He had a quick and satisfying image of Dominique Legrand and Lyle Manning accompanying Moretti on a one-way flight to Dulles International Airport.

"*You* know you're not going to notify the Feds right away. *I* predicted that's how you'd react. Of course, *Moretti* hasn't known you for thirty years like I have, but maybe he's smart enough to anticipate what you'd do."

Book reflected there'd be hell to pay when Marlene figured out he was walking away from a death threat in Virginia only to walk into a death trap in Switzerland.

CHAPTER 65

After leaving Rudy's house, Book drove to a block on Connecticut Avenue, three miles north of the White House. He entered the conservatively decorated foyer of an impressive stone apartment building and spoke to the security guard seated behind a broad marble counter. "Apartment 43, please. I'm expected. The name's Booker."

The guard consulted the list on his computer and pointed to the elevator. "Fourth floor, turn right. I'll call to say you're on the way up."

AJ was eagerly waiting for him in the open doorway, barefoot, wearing jeans and a blue pullover. She stepped forward, rose on tippy-toes, and kissed him.

Her enthusiasm prompted Book to break off the kiss. But he continued to hold her, not quite sure where to put his hands.

"I'm glad you called to say you were in DC and wanted to come over. I felt bad about all the shit I gave you on the phone the other day. I get it you want to go after Moretti. Count on me to support you in every way possible."

He nodded thanks, holding her at arm's length, but letting go as she started to move forward for another kiss.

"Just so we're clear, Alexandra, I'm coming to you as a friend and expert forensic scientist. I'm not in the market for a lover."

Looking contrite, she stepped aside and waved him into the apartment. "I hear you. But you're the one who should be 'clear.' I'm still in love with you, and, if the opportunity arises, I'll have you in my bed."

Until then, I'll be good. Would you like coffee or something stronger?"

"Coffee would be great. I'm on the wagon."

He took a seat at the table in the small kitchen and watched her manipulate the fancy automatic espresso machine.

Struggling with the mechanism, she said, "You'd think for seven hundred dollars, Suzuki would have gotten a coffee maker that could produce a simple cup of java. Voilà. This is the gizmo I'm supposed to push."

"Where's Suzuki?" Suzuki Nakasone was AJ's best friend. A flight attendant for Japan Airlines, she was often on travel.

"She's on vacation in Tokyo for a couple of weeks visiting family and catching up with old friends. She likes me to stay here when she's away. I enjoy the change. Luxury accommodations. Although sometimes her fancy gadgets are a bit much. Especially this damn espresso machine. You'd think it would have a button that says, 'simple cup of coffee.'"

The logistics completed, Book briefed AJ on what he'd learned from Rudy. He asked, "Were you able to find anything about who sent me the envelope with pictures of Moretti?"

"Yes and no."

"What the hell does that mean?"

"There was trace evidence of cigar ash on the envelope and on some of the photos. Not enough to identify the brand. My guess is someone was smoking a cigar near where the FedEx envelope was assembled."

"That's it?"

"Pretty much. There are lots of fingerprints on the outside of the envelope, but none on the photos themselves. I did identify a couple of yours. I'll continue checking, but I don't expect to turn up anything other than a few FedEx employees. Whoever did this was careful. They could anticipate you would have the evidence examined. There are indications they wore surgical gloves when handling the photos and envelope."

Book mused, speaking more to himself than to AJ, "My suspect is a cigar smoker. Someone who, for whatever reason, wants me to find Moretti."

AJ shook her head. "Close, but no cigar, if you'll pardon the pun. We know someone who smokes was in the room where the FedEx envelope was filled with photos, but that doesn't mean he's the same person who did the deed. We know one more thing that's crucial."

"What's that?"

"We know the sender has an accomplice who spent at least several days in Geneva snapping photos of Moretti. Organization and advanced planning is evident. If Moretti himself isn't the one setting you up, perhaps it's a confederate who knew he was in Geneva."

CHAPTER 66

TYSONS, VIRGINIA

Carmen sat through six hours of board meetings, punctuated by an hour and a half lunch. She agonized, *Will these meetings never end?* Way too much food. And the schedule called for a dinner from seven to nine. She resolved to skip it.

Even with Russ Boudreau's coaching, following the proceedings was giving her a headache. She did succeed, however, in identifying a few mavericks on the board. Members who opposed management's position on several key points, like the Lady in Red who'd accosted Carmen during the breakfast buffet.

She'd forgotten how tiring it could be to sit in a chair all day and breathed a profound sigh of relief when the last session ended.

Russ apparently felt the same way, "Thank God that's over. Tomorrow should be more interesting."

"How so?"

"The main issue for this board meeting—mineral rights—is scheduled in the morning."

"What's the story on mineral rights?"

"Would you like to go somewhere and have a drink? I'll tell you all about it," he said.

"How about coming up to my suite at the Ritz-Carlton, where

we can have that drink, and get a light supper sent in. Just the idea of sitting through tonight's scheduled feast with the board exhausts me. You can tell me everything I always wanted to know about mineral rights but was afraid to ask."

By issuing the invitation, Carmen knew she was playing with fire. She imagined she could hear Tilly whispering, *What are you doing, girl? You know nothing about this guy. You invite him over just because he's handsome and sexy as hell. For all you know, he's working for the dark side.*

Russ gave a whistle as he entered Carmen's suite. "Pretty fancy digs for a deputy sheriff in a rural county. Fancy penthouse suite, hundred-thousand-dollar SUV, jewelry with a Tiffany look . . . yet you seem as wholesome as mom's apple pie. Who is Carmen Garcia and what is she up to?"

"Just what you see, Russ—a country girl from Virginia who came into a fortune and is trying to learn how to navigate in the big city. Just because I've kicked the manure off my boots doesn't mean I've forgotten how it smells."

"Picturing you wading through manure is difficult to imagine."

"Been there, done that."

As they sat together on the couch, he pulled her close and leaned forward to kiss her.

Her body responded almost without her giving her movements conscious thought. The months without sex had taken a toll on her self-control. Edging over, she met him halfway. One kiss led to another, and she could feel his eagerness pressing against her as they embraced.

His right hand cupped her breast. In the absence of a protest, he eased the gray silk Dolce & Gabbana suit jacket from her broad shoulders and let it fall to the floor. The small buttons on her blouse were soon under attack.

When the phone on the desk rang, she said, "Sorry, gotta take this call."

Moving to extricate herself from Russ's passionate embrace, she was startled to be gripped tighter.

"Forget the phone."

"You're not listening to me." She shoved Russ away, using a move she'd learned at the Virginia State Police Academy.

The romantic mood shattered, she picked up her blouse, walked to the desk, and answered the phone.

"Hold on a moment, Tiger, my houseguest is just leaving."

CHAPTER 67

Carmen tried to focus her thoughts on the next day's meeting, pondering whether mineral rights could be the focus of management's strategy and her key to seize control of the board.

The mineral rights issue had been covered in prelaw courses at UVA. In late-night Google research, she'd updated her knowledge base. Basically, a mining company would buy the right to search for and excavate specified minerals beneath the surface of the landowner's property—coal, oil, gas, or other minerals. Theoretically, the surface, to the extent it was destroyed, would be restored to its original condition. In a best-case scenario, the landowner could make a lot of money without interfering with surface use of the property. There were no limits to the horror stories in worst-case scenarios.

Without question, Consolidated Mining and Energy's main target was uranium mining. Company management was seeking to acquire uranium mines and mineral rights offering access to Uranium-235 and U-238. Recent innovations in exploration techniques suggested there were large untapped sources of uranium in Virginia, the Western United States, and Canada. One-fifth of uranium mined worldwide came from Canada. Recent information indicated US production was due for a major increase.

Rumor suggested there was growing support in Congress for legislation to expand funding for nuclear power, the principal use for uranium. This was plausible given the rising domestic interest in nuclear power to counter global warming. The US was already the principal producer. A nasty corollary rumor was whispered concerning Brent Johanson and Roger Carruthers bribing legislators to support such a law.

From her internet research, Carmen was aware there were major nuclear power facilities at North Anna in Louisa County in central Virginia, just off Interstate 95, and Surry in Surry County, near Norfolk and the Hampton Roads metropolitan area. Nuclear power accounted for 15 percent of Virginia's total electric generating capacity. In the US as a whole, there were 104 nuclear power plants, accounting for 20 percent of the country's electrical capacity, and a half dozen more were on the drawing boards. This was the first resurgence of nuclear power since the 1979 disaster at Three Mile Island had terrified the nation with fears of a nuclear meltdown.

Pouring yet another cup of black coffee, once delicious but beginning to taste bitter, she struggled to decide what position to take at the morning meeting. Was the national interest served by expanding nuclear power? If so, what were the odds Johanson and Carruthers were on the right side? Was her prejudice against them warping her judgment? Was Consolidated Mining and Energy's management team trying to bribe legislators?

Was uranium the issue that had led to Katherine's killing?

Doubts plagued Carmen. *Am I in over my head?*

CHAPTER 68

GENEVA, SWITZERLAND

The United flight from Dulles International Airport to Geneva arrived on schedule at seven thirty Wednesday morning. Book shook off the effects of the six hour time change.

Even though he felt naked without his Glock and SIG SAUER, hiding a pistol in his luggage would have been too risky. No local law enforcement officer in the United States had authorization to bring a handgun into Switzerland. The backup gambit had been to put his Emerson Commander combat knife inside a shaving kit before he checked his suitcase. Retrieving the suitcase, he cleared customs without incident, and left Geneva International Airport, locally called Cointrin Airport. Knowing the airport was located on the border between France and Switzerland, he looked around for the exit toward Geneva.

Expecting to be met, he eyeballed the horde of vehicles outside the airport entrance for an awaiting vehicle or a familiar face. Nothing.

"Book."

Someone was calling his name, but he failed to spot the caller. Scanning the tangled traffic, he saw an arm waving from a black four-door sedan. A Volkswagen Jetta was at the end of the taxi line, trying without success to ease through to the curb.

Realizing there was no way to be heard over the cacophony of blaring horns, yelling drivers, and the terminal loudspeaker announcing flights, he made a gesture with palm raised indicating to the Jetta driver he should stop and stay in place. Book worked his way through the crowd and climbed into the car.

When he closed the door, the vehicle sped off. "Buckle up," Curt, the driver, said, keeping his attention focused on the maze of cars blocking the route. Book was a bit unnerved at the number of near misses, but Curt seemed to have collision avoidance radar that kept them safe.

Curt Hartmann and Book had been friends since their days serving together in Afghanistan. A bull of a man, Curt's huge bulk made Book's six foot two appear tiny. Over beers, they'd often argued who suffered more near-death experiences in combat, and who deserved the most credit for saving the other guy's life.

Now stationed in Stuttgart, Germany, Curt was assigned to the US Army's Africa Command. At Book's request, he'd driven his personal car the five hours from Stuttgart to Geneva, bringing weapons and other special gear.

"Head for the Four Seasons?" Curt asked.

"Not yet. We have reservations at the Hotel de la Paix, located on the Quai du Mont-Blanc facing Lake Geneva, just a short distance from the Four Seasons. Based there, we can keep an eye on Moretti with minimal risk of him spotting us."

"Have you decided where we'll take him?"

"Best to finalize our plan once we've located Moretti."

"Piece of cake," Curt replied. "All we have to do, in the middle of a major Swiss city, is subdue an infamous fugitive who's responsible for several killings, drug him, slip him into my Jetta, smuggle him across the border, drive to a safe haven not yet identified, contact the FBI, and hold our fugitive until turning him over to whoever's going to extradite him to the US."

The two men had discussed the pros and cons of seizing

Moretti and holding him in Switzerland, but they were worried about the reaction of the Swiss authorities. France and Germany were regarded as safer bets. Book believed the FBI would have better access in either of those countries, in all likelihood enlisting the cooperation of Interpol.

In France, the National Police had a reputation for being tough on international criminals. The German situation was somewhat more complicated. Police responsibility was vested in each state. There was no national police force, memories of police excesses under the Nazis having ruled that out. Instead, they had the GSG9, created in the aftermath of the incident during the 1972 Summer Olympic Games in Munich when Black September Palestinian terrorists kidnapped and murdered Israeli athletes. The GSG9 operated much as a national police unit, but their responsibilities were limited to counterterrorism. There was no assurance they would be able or willing to deal with Moretti's situation.

Curt argued for Germany, on the grounds of his fluency in the language, which he'd learned from his paternal grandmother while growing up in a German enclave in Minnesota. Book leaned toward France.

Book said, "You make a good case for heading to Germany, since neither of us speaks French. It's hard to tell how much of a problem that might pose as we try to account for apprehending an American fugitive without official authorization. On the other hand, the French border is just the other side of the airport. There's a lot to be said for getting the hell out of Dodge ASAP."

"On board any way you want to play it. I owe you, bro."

"We owe each other," Book replied.

Driving toward downtown Geneva in companionable silence, they passed the main train station, the Gare de Cornavin, which marked the city center, only a few blocks from their hotel.

They drove into the parking structure, collected their hand luggage, and checked into a small suite.

Once in their room, Book asked, "What weapons did you bring?"

"See for yourself," Curt said, opening the suitcase and removing the clothes folded on top.

"You haven't gotten over your love affair with the Beretta."

"Yeah, but it's a nine-millimeter so our ammunition will be compatible. I got you a SIG P226, with a fifteen-round magazine. We each have shoulder holsters and plenty of spare magazines."

Book examined the illegal items concealed in the suitcase. When he was satisfied, he put each on the bed. "We have enough firepower to fight and win a small war. But that's not why we're here. These weapons are essential for self-defense. But, if we resort to gunplay, our mission has already failed."

He held up a case containing a hypodermic syringe and needle, with several bottles labeled insulin, leaving a standard commercial insulin kit in place.

"This hypo is our most valuable weapon. With it, we can subdue Moretti and keep him comatose for hours at a time. Nobody questions insulin. Being in a diabetic coma would explain why our passenger is unconscious."

CHAPTER 69

TYSONS, VIRGINIA

Carmen was one of the first to arrive at the breakfast buffet Wednesday morning. Russ Boudreau had yet to show his face.

Early in the morning, after nearly a sleepless night, she'd decided on a strategy to deal with the company's campaign to expand their holdings of uranium.

She made a beeline for the Lady in Red, who'd accosted her the previous morning. Today, her fellow early arrival was wearing green, but the dress was much the same style of pseudoevening gown as the red outfit from the previous day. The agitator blinked with surprise and some apprehension at Carmen's approach. She was clearly comfortable confronting others but seemed fearful of being confronted herself.

The newly minted board member read the nervousness in the veteran's eyes. "I need an ally at this board meeting. I'm asking for your help."

The woman's jaw fell open at the remark. Despite a well-deserved reputation as a firebrand agitator, she seemed flummoxed at the request to be part of a team working *for* someone's cause.

"W-what do you have in mind?" she stammered.

Carmen replied, "Yesterday, you asked what *I* was going to do about this company's dangerous policies. Today, I have an answer."

The Lady in Green stared at her.

"My plan is to mobilize enough allies to block any initiative by management related to the acquisition of uranium, either through buying mining companies in the US or Canada or obtaining mineral rights. Also, to impede any lobbying efforts related to uranium or nuclear power. Even though I control one-third of the stock, I can't accomplish this without reliable allies. I'm asking you to help."

"Why me?"

"I'm convinced you support the issues I support."

The firebrand, whom Carmen learned was Bernice Kimball of Roanoke, Virginia, said, "Of course I do."

"And I'm sure you know where everyone on the board stands on all the major issues."

"That's true."

Carmen continued, "Would you like to hear a theory why no one asks you to support them?"

A pensive Bernice nodded.

"The answer's simple. You're perceived as always attacking everybody. No one thinks of you as being *pro* any issue. All they see is you being *anti* the issues supported by the other side."

Bernice protested. "But I do support a lot of worthy causes."

"Sure you do. Here's your chance to show the other board members where you stand on uranium and nuclear power. Help me enlist the support of members who think as we do."

She took Bernice's arm and the two walked over by the windows overlooking the garden. She explained how her strategy would unfold during the course of the meeting, based on her study of the day's agenda.

Bernice's eyes gleamed with excitement at the prospect of helping block management's initiatives. "I'll take you around to meet with board members who lean toward our position. If everyone goes along, we can command a majority."

Carmen stared at the entrance and frowned as Russ walked into the dining room. The look froze as she realized he was having an intense conversation with the CEO and the chairman of the board. Carruthers and Johanson appeared to be giving him instructions.

CHAPTER 70

GENEVA, SWITZERLAND

The Viper picked up the phone on the third ring. "Yes."

"It's me."

"You have some information for me."

"Yeah. Booker arrived on the morning United flight from Dulles. He was met at Cointrin Airport by some big dude in a black Volkswagen Jetta. Honest to god, that guy must weigh over three hundred pounds. They drove to the Hotel de la Paix. Booker and the big dude carried heavy suitcases into the hotel. The dude could have brought weapons in the Jetta."

"Anything else?"

"Nah. My instructions were to meet Booker's plane, follow him, and report to you. Mission accomplished."

"Right. Now, here's what you do. Leave Geneva by the fastest means possible. Never return to Switzerland. If you do, you're a dead man. Got it?"

Silence on the phone spoke volumes. The Viper hung up the receiver, sat back in the easy chair by the window overlooking Lake Geneva, and poured a whiskey. The irritating caller was already forgotten.

He weighed plans to trap Booker and his sidekick, dismissing scenarios at the Four Seasons or the Hotel de la Paix, concluding the best strategy was to capitalize on Moretti's penchant for evening rendezvous with high-priced escorts—evenings that ended with the deaths of the unfortunate prostitutes.

FBI warnings that Moretti was "armed and dangerous" were dismissed out of hand—the Viper would hardly consider someone "dangerous" who had only killed four people, including two women and a small child. But now the Viper found these new murders in Geneva impressive indeed. The deaths painted a picture of a remorseless, stone-cold killer, who would act without hesitation or fear of consequences. *A man very much like myself.*

The Viper finished sipping his whiskey and smiled at having solved the puzzle of how to set a trap for Booker.

CHAPTER 71

TYSONS, VIRGINIA

Carmen glanced around the boardroom at the allies she'd enlisted during the buffet breakfast. Somewhat to her surprise, with Bernice Kimball's help they'd unearthed a sizable group of stockholders opposed to the direction Consolidated Mining and Energy was headed.

Chairman Johanson was going through his trademark aw-shucks routine of paper shuffling before calling the meeting to order. His plaid wool suit was a shade of green that reminded Carmen of the piece-of-shit Honda Civic she'd given a decent burial upon acquiring the Range Rover.

She'd managed to avoid Russ during the premeeting interval and now stared hard at him as he settled into the seat beside her.

"Why are you avoiding me?" Russ asked.

"You seem to be chummy with Johanson and Carruthers." Her tone was accusatory.

"So what?" His body language signaled he was on the defensive. "They lead this company. It's important to stay on their good side."

"Does staying on their good side mean they give you your instructions for the day?"

"What do you mean?"

"Cut the bullshit, Russ. Were you told to try and stop me from recruiting allies before the board meeting?"

"No, of course not. We were just chatting."

"Don't fence with me." She could feel the warmth as her face flared pink with anger.

"Are you going to support us in our attempt to block their efforts to acquire uranium and to force them to stop lobbying Congress about nuclear power plants?"

"Just because I tried to sleep with you doesn't mean I have to vote with you."

"Yes or no, Russ."

"It'll have to be no. Nuclear power is the future of energy in this country and the world. Uranium is essential for nuclear reactors. I can't support you and live with my conscience."

"Your conscience can go screw itself. You've sold out."

Carmen huddled outside the meeting room with Bernice and the other allied board members who made up a formidable coalition in opposition to management. There was broad agreement they'd gained ground in some battles, but the war was to be won or lost the next day. Carruthers succeeded, with Johanson's help, in fending off the best efforts of the mavericks to derail plans for uranium and nuclear power.

Carmen rebuffed repeated attempts by Russ to initiate a conversation. Nothing would induce her to talk with him or to entertain an apology for his sexual aggressiveness the previous evening.

She thought, *Tilly was right about that weasel. He is working for the dark side.*

By the end of the day, Carmen was exhausted. The tension of trying to keep pace with the machinations of management wore her out. Nevertheless, satisfied with the day's accomplishments, she took the elevator to the garage area, walked over to the VIP section, and climbed into her Range Rover. She drove toward the Ritz-Carlton, taking care to stay in the proper lane to avoid sparking another outbreak of road rage.

• • •

Opening the door to Suite 2409, Carmen yawned from weariness left over from the meeting. She was still fuming at how Russ had fucked her over, even if she'd rebuffed his attempt to fuck her by force. He'd done his best to manipulate her to swallow the management line during the board meeting. She felt dirty and wanted a shower, perhaps a good soak in the whirlpool.

She took a few steps into the room, stopped cold, inhaled deeply, and exhaled slowly.

Her senses dialed danger. Something wasn't right.

The odor of stale tobacco smoke permeated the air. *No, not smoke.* She recognized the stench of the habitual smoker prone to impregnate clothes and rooms. This morning, when she left, the suite smelled fragrant from the floral arrangement her dad had sent. Tonight, the stench was like standing in a pool hall next to a dedicated smoker who can't wait till his next fix.

Carmen cautiously walked over to the desk by the window and quietly set down the small library of papers accumulated during two days of meetings. She set the Salvatore Ferragamo handbag beside the papers, opened it, and drew out the Baby Glock. In accordance with her custom, the weapon was loaded and ready to fire.

She cleared the suite, starting by entering the open door of the smaller bedroom. The door of the bathroom was ajar. No one was in the bathroom, the closet, or under the bed. The smaller area of the suite was safe.

A quick perusal of the living room confirmed there were no problems. On to the master bedroom. The door was open, and the room was clear. The closet was also clear, as was the area under the bed.

The bathroom loomed as a potential source of threat.

On previous days, she remembered, housekeeping had left the bathroom door open. Today, it was closed. No way she was going to open that door.

Glancing at the Baby Glock, she muttered sotto voce, "Need more firepower."

Tiptoeing on the plush carpet, she crept to the desk, holstered the pistol in her handbag, hung the bag on her shoulder, and left the suite. Deliberating whether to call 911, she decided first to confirm the nature of the threat.

Like other cops, she was reluctant to be accused of crying wolf.

In the parking garage, she opened the back door of the Range Rover, unlocked the gun safe, and lifted out the combat shotgun, together with a box of double-ought buckshot. Once the weapon was loaded, racked, and ready to fire, she engaged the safety. Not having brought handcuffs, she tucked a few plastic restraints in the handbag. Eyeing the Kevlar vest, she hesitated, retrieved it, and locked the gun safe. Verifying the coast was clear in the garage, the well-armed deputy headed back to Suite 2409, carrying the shotgun and body armor wrapped inside a small blanket kept in the SUV for that purpose.

Back in the master bedroom, Carmen knelt behind the foot of the bed, faced the bathroom, and aimed the shotgun. She clicked off the safety. Preparations complete.

The suite was tomblike quiet. She took care to make no noise. No sound emanated from the bathroom.

Breaking the silence in an authoritative cop voice, she said, "You there, inside the bathroom, listen up. I'm a cop. I've got a combat shotgun loaded with double-ought buckshot. The gun's aimed at the bathroom door. If the door moves before you hear me say 'come out,' I'll fire and keep firing until you're dead. I've called 911."

The last statement was a lie. She had no intention of alerting the authorities until an actual threat was confirmed. No way would a Jefferson County deputy sheriff become the butt of a joke bound to be repeated over and over in Fairfax County Police Department district stations.

"When you're ready to come out, yell 'ready.' Then wait till I tell you it's okay."

The deathly quiet became quieter still. She caught herself holding her breath and remembered to breathe normally, as she'd been taught to do in a combat shooting situation.

One minute passed. Two minutes. Muffled whispering was audible behind the door.

She thought, *Bingo*. Someone *was* in there. Better to have called 911. Too late for second-guessing.

"We're ready to come out. Don't shoot."

"How many of you are there?" Carmen fought to keep the relief from echoing in her voice.

"Two."

"Do exactly as I say, and you may live through the night. Open the door no more than six inches. Drop your weapons through the crack in the door—guns, knives, and anything else you may be armed with. If I find any hidden weapons on you, I'll shoot to kill. Once you've sent out your weapons, close the door again and wait for further instructions."

In a few moments, the door opened the prescribed distance. Two H&K pistols equipped with suppressors slid to the floor. The door closed.

Keeping the shotgun pointed at the bathroom, Carmen eased to the wall near the pistols, staying out of direct line of sight of the door, and took the weapons. She slid them under the bed on the far side of the room and resumed her position, sheltered at the foot of the bed.

"Listen up. Clasp your fingers together on top of your head. Get down on your knees. Line up one behind the other. The man in front can open the door slowly, then clasp your hands back on top of your head. Walk on your knees out of the bathroom into the bedroom. Stop and wait for me to tell you what's next."

Without incident, the deputy herded the two would-be hitmen into the suite's living room, where she ordered them to lie face down. She traded the shotgun for the Baby Glock to make it easier to manipulate the flex-cuffs. After her attackers were secured, she dialed 911.

"This is Carmen Garcia. I'm a deputy sheriff from Jefferson County. My boss is Sheriff Pat Garrett. I'm in Suite 2409 at the Ritz-Carlton Hotel in Tysons. Send backup."

After confirming her call was being taken seriously, she continued.

"I'm holding a shotgun on two men who came to my suite with the intent to kill me. Please inform any cops sent here that an armed police officer from another jurisdiction is holding two would-be murderers at gunpoint."

CHAPTER 72

GENEVA, SWITZERLAND

Curt Hartmann answered the ringing phone in the third floor suite at the Hotel de la Paix, listened a few moments, and hung up the receiver.

He turned to Book, who was just entering the sitting room after taking a nap to recover from jet lag.

"The concierge called to say a woman left an envelope for you at the desk. I'll pick it up." Curt pulled on a jacket to mask the shoulder holster containing the Beretta.

His sleepy-eyed suite-mate held up a hand.

"Hold on a minute. No one knows we're here. How can we be getting messages?"

"There's no such thing as confidentiality at a European hotel," Curt said. "We registered under our real names. Had to show our passports. Anyone who's so inclined could track us down once they know we're in Geneva. We're counting on Moretti not knowing. Otherwise, there's no hope of catching him by surprise."

"Roger that. Learn what you can about the messenger."

Curt returned, holding a small white envelope, which he handed to Book.

"What'd you find out?"

"The concierge had never seen the woman before. He didn't get her name. She said, 'Make sure Mr. Booker gets this envelope.'"

Book checked out the envelope. He examined the seal. Held the fancy envelope up to the light. Smelled it. Tapped it on the desk. Satisfied there was no danger, he tore open the flap and looked inside. He found a single piece of fine white paper with a handwritten note.

He read aloud:

"Cher Book,

> You don't know me, but I know a great deal about you. You're searching for Franco Moretti—or Herbert Bonar Baldwin, as he calls himself in Geneva. I can deliver him to you. I'm a lady of the night, or, as a policeman like yourself might say, a call girl. Perhaps I should clarify that I am a *high-end call girl*. I earn more than 4,960 Swiss francs for providing an evening of companionship, entertainment, and, if I like the client, sexual pleasure. That amounts to approximately $5,000 in US currency. Modestly, I would describe it as a bargain, but who am I to say.
>
> The price for Monsieur Moretti is $50,000. I understand you may not have that much on you in cash, but I'll take a check—a certified check. I know you're an honorable man. And I'm sure, as a husband and police officer, you would not want to explain why you gave a call girl—even a high-end call girl—a check in that amount. The banks are open, so you should have no difficulty making the necessary arrangements.
>
> Leave the check, made out to Emmanuelle Bourgeois, in an envelope with the concierge. He's taken a fancy to me, so he's as trustworthy as that breed ever is. I'll pick up the check at four o'clock. If everything is satisfactory, I'll return one hour later and leave you an envelope containing all the information you need to apprehend the FBI's Most Wanted fugitive.
>
> Affectueusement,
> Emmanuelle

"I'll be damned." Curt sat down on the couch, hands raised in the air in a theatrical manner. "What are you going to do?"

"Give her the money, of course. What choice do we have? If we don't pay her, she could tip off Moretti we're in Geneva looking for him. Why didn't she try him first? He could outbid us without breaking a sweat."

"She's afraid of him," Curt said. "He's wanted for four brutal killings. You're a cop. Whatever else happens, you're no threat to her life."

One minute after five, the two men headed for the elevator and descended to the *rez-de-chaussée*, the ground level on which the concierge desk was located. Book went to the concierge and confirmed Emmanuelle had left another envelope. Curt rushed out the front door and spied a figure walking in the direction of Lake Geneva.

"Should I tail her?" he yelled.

"No. Let her go." Book added in a quiet voice. "She planned this with care. Left nothing to chance. We need to follow her playbook and see where it leads. My guess is she's sincere about giving us Moretti. We don't need her for anything at this point. Besides, if we confront her, we'll be forced to deal with the Swiss police. The mission is to capture our fugitive and get him out of the country without involving the authorities."

"Ten-four," Curt said. "Let's go back to the room and check out the envelope."

CHAPTER 73

TYSONS VIRGINIA

In the wee hours of Thursday morning, Detective Bernard (call me "Bernie") Eisenhower informed Carmen Garcia she was free to return to her hotel. Twice he'd made her repeat her version of events that occurred at the Ritz-Carlton in Suite 2409, even though there'd never been a moment when she thought he doubted the tale she recounted. The ritual irritated her, even though she recognized it as a tried and true interrogation technique.

The Fairfax police confiscated her combat shotgun, double-ought ammunition, Kevlar vest, and Baby Glock, along with the two H&Ks the would-be assassins brought with them. After the assassins' fingerprints were confirmed on both weapons, on the suppressors, and on the ammunition they'd loaded before setting out on their mission, she witnessed Bernie's attitude harden toward the pair.

After several hours of going through the motions of a police investigation, Bernie said, "We've arrested Cornelius McKinley, a.k.a. Butch McKinley, and Archibald Everett Douglass, a.k.a. Razor Douglass, on attempted murder charges. Their records show they've been up to their ears in crime, right up to the time they served in the military. They failed to clean up their act while in uniform. Both were dishonorably discharged because of misdeeds in Afghanistan."

Once Carmen's story was validated, Bernie allowed her to call

Sheriff Garrett. She assured her boss she was fine. There was no violence, just the threat of violence. Pat offered to drive to Tysons. Touched by the sentiment from the normally undemonstrative, old-fashioned lawman, she rubbed her hand across her eyes so none of the local cops would think she was crying. Stretching the truth a bit, she assured Pat she was in no danger.

When she was leaving, Detective Eisenhower confided to Carmen, "Butch and Razor are scum of the worst sort. You were lucky to get the drop on them."

In response to her raised eyebrows, Bernie amended his statement. "Well, maybe not lucky, it was damn fine police work."

By the time she got back to the Ritz-Carlton, the adrenaline rush was starting to wear off, replaced by a mind-numbing tiredness. She staggered into the bedroom, set the alarm for three hours sleep, and collapsed, fully clothed, onto the bed.

The clanging wake-up call startled her. In a panic, she groped for the Baby Glock before remembering it had been confiscated by the Fairfax police.

Despite being exhausted by the night's ordeal, she swung by the Range Rover to replace the Baby Glock with her service pistol. The threat in her suite was sufficient warning her life was in danger. She dismissed the possibility that her trouble at the hotel was triggered by the Bronsons, believing it was because her actions echoed those of her stepmom Katherine and triggered retaliation by Carruthers and Johansen.

● ● ●

Carmen was starved when she arrived at the breakfast buffet. She'd awakened too late to have room service. Ignoring Tilly's advice, both hands were now full. She devoured a plate piled with scrambled eggs, muffins, and fruit. She polished off her second cup of coffee and was eager for a refill.

No one in Carmen's group of supporters seemed aware her attention had been distracted. Spurred on by Bernice Kimball's excitement, they were enthused about the previous day's successful attempt to block the moves of Chairman Johanson and CEO Carruthers to advance the company's involvement with uranium and nuclear power.

Once her hunger pains were assuaged, Carmen tuned in to the conversation. The breakfast interlude proved useful for caucusing with like-minded board members who'd been corralled by Bernice—the Lady in Red (or Green)—who today wore the same type of dress, but this time in a pale blue.

Realizing the group was getting a bit carried away, Carmen sought to infuse a dose of reality.

"Yesterday went better than expected, but today is when we win or lose on the big issues. Any suggestions about how to proceed?"

The group grew quiet. Looks were exchanged, but no one was prepared to volunteer any ideas.

A man who had not yet spoken cleared his throat. He was half a head shorter than the smallest woman in the group, dressed in a midnight blue blazer and dark gray slacks. His button-down white shirt sported a bow tie with bold red polka dots. Glasses with Clark Kent black frames looked incongruous perched above a too-small nose.

"I'm Walter Maynard, professor of economics at George Mason University. I don't own a lot of stock like many of you, but I've been on the board three years so have some notion of how things work. I also happen to know quite a lot about economics as it relates to uranium and nuclear power."

Keying to his audience's attentiveness, Maynard's voice grew stronger and more assertive. "May I suggest we've been on the wrong track trying to confront management head on. Carruthers and Johanson have been at this a long time. They rose to leadership positions because they have the know-how to win. Rather than try to block them, we should try a little finesse. You understand I'm from academia. We prefer finesse over confrontation."

Intrigued, Carmen probed, "What do you have in mind?"

The professor continued, now in full lecturing mode. "A study. The time-honored way to block an initiative without appearing to is to call for a study. Carruthers and Johanson have been asserting uranium mining and nuclear power are the way to go for the company. We've protested. But no one on either side of the issue has offered any tangible facts. I propose we challenge them to support their position with hard evidence. Conduct a study. Analyze the dollars and cents involved if the company were to pursue their initiatives, projecting costs and earnings over the short run and the long run. We might even suggest the study consider the impact of such an approach on the national economy."

"Sounds like such a gambit could work," Carmen said. "Everyone on our side of the issue should support us. And a lot of folks who are on the fence or leaning toward management's side might be induced to come around. Actually, I would feel better about it myself, because these are issues about which I have little background."

"I could go along," Bernice agreed.

Despite the best efforts of the CEO and the chairman to derail the study, Professor Maynard's suggestion prevailed. The board kicked the can down the road. Carmen heaved a sigh of relief, having won the day.

As she gathered up her papers and prepared to leave, Carruthers came over to her. "You must be very proud of yourself. Your first board meeting and you managed to lead a rump caucus blocking our best efforts to move the company into the future."

"I did what I thought was right. Just as my stepmom Katherine Harriman Garcia did what she thought was right when she served on the board."

Carruthers face grew dark. "Unfortunately, Katherine came to a tragic end in Charlottesville. I understand you had a close call last night at your hotel suite."

"How'd you hear about that? It happened so late I don't believe it made the morning news."

"Russ told me. Johanson and I asked him to look after you in hopes he would persuade you to our point of view."

"Well, he worked hard 'looking after' me. But I don't see how he could have heard what happened in my hotel suite."

"Carmen, you need to be aware we will *always* hear about developments involving anyone who plays a key role affecting Consolidated Mining and Energy."

"That sounds like a threat."

"Colorado and I work hard protecting the company. *Whatever it takes.*"

CHAPTER 74

GENEVA, SWITZERLAND

Emmanuelle Bourgeois stood in front of the Salle du Grand Casino, a half hour early for her eight o'clock rendezvous with Baldwin in the guise of Moretti's Geneva identity. She had been told not to be late, but she was certain her client for the evening would not expect a high-end call girl to be *this* early.

After a nervous wait, Moretti appeared on time and strolled toward her. His pace quickened at the sight of his date. She held out her hand as he approached. He ignored the gesture, clasped her around the shoulders, and drew her close. He sought to kiss her on the lips, but she turned her face away, and he had to settle for a peck on the cheek.

Experience had taught her *never let the client take control*.

Rather than appearing upset, he inclined his head at her rebuff. "Let's go to my home. It's near here."

"I thought you were staying at the Four Seasons."

"I enjoy the convenience of a five-star hotel. But I find a private home provides the proper setting for a pleasant evening."

"My goal for the evening is to ensure *your* pleasure," She said. *Maybe I'm pushing it a bit too far.*

It was essential to maintain a certain distance—not "hard to get," but short of "promiscuous."

The walk to his home was enjoyable and, as he promised, short. A balmy breeze off the lake cooled the air. The smell of blooming flowers reminded her why she loved Geneva in the spring.

He played the part of the perfect gentleman, with an arm primly circling her waist, chastely caressing her Yves Saint Laurent filmy silk dress. He would risk no further rebuff.

He stopped on the sidewalk and once again pulled her close. Expecting another attempted kiss, she deliberated whether to yield this time. His grip tightened and her arm began to hurt, but it would be a mistake to show pain or, worse yet, fear.

When he forced her onto the steps in front of the building, she opened her mouth to scream. A claw-like hand seized her throat. She was unable to breathe, let alone call for help. He released the hand choking her and reached into his pocket for the door key. She gasped for air, and tried to cry out, but the only sound was a strangled squawk.

Emmanuelle, an athlete as a youth, worked out for an hour every day and was strong. But there was no way to break free of his iron grip. She kicked him in the shins. In retaliation, he struck her viciously in the face. Jamming her body against the wall with his hip, he got a hand free to open the door. He shoved her inside. Despite her efforts to flee, she stumbled and fell to the floor, moaning, certain he planned to kill her.

• • •

The moment Moretti turned to close and lock the front door, he was attacked by two men—one big, the other huge—who seemed to appear out of nowhere. Each attacker seized one of his arms, and they slammed him against the wall. The big man kicked the door shut while the giant struck him in the solar plexus. The blow felt like a hammer wielded by the Norse god Thor. Air rushed from his lungs. Fear filled him as he experienced near suffocation.

He heard, "Don't hit him in the face. We need him to look presentable."

His arms were twisted behind his back and flex-cuffs were used to bind his wrists. Plastic restraints secured his ankles.

Regaining his breath, he opened his mouth to scream. Duct tape forced his lips closed and was wrapped around the back of his neck.

"Careful, we don't want him to choke." The big man was speaking, cautioning the giant not to do anything that could prove fatal.

Moretti recognized the voice. Booker, his worst nightmare.

• • •

Emmanuelle rose to her knees in the foyer. She stood, swayed, and staggered toward the bound prisoner. She towered above Moretti, pointing an accusing finger. "KILL HIM."

"You don't mean that," the detective said. "You were terrified. He hurt you. But that's the end of it. Now it's time for you to leave and forget this ever happened."

"You have no idea what terrified means." She sobbed and stuttered as tears streamed down her cheeks. "The bastard was going to torture . . . and then murder me. I'll never forget the horrific gleam in his eyes. I thought I'd seen evil before . . . now I've seen the devil himself."

CHAPTER 75

The Viper entered through the patio doors at Moretti's town house an hour before anyone was expected to show up. He hid in the dining room, waiting for Moretti to bring another prostitute home. As he expected, Book and Curt attacked Moretti as soon as the fugitive dragged the call girl through the front door.

The assassin thought, *Exactly the way I would have planned the assault.* He crept through the house toward the foyer, handgun at the ready. Reading meaning into every sound, he heard Emmanuelle's rescue and departure.

The Viper leaped through the double doors leading to the foyer, expecting to startle his targets into immobility. He got a quick glimpse of the two men standing over the fugitive's trussed figure. The handgun swung to align the sights with his priority target, Book's torso. The second the pistol discharged, the sight picture revealed the wall, but no victim.

The reaction time of the men was astonishing. They separated, each headed across the large foyer at an oblique angle. The Viper noted their intent to bracket him—one hurtling to his right, the other his left—making it impossible to keep both in range at the same time. Moreover, they could target him with impunity, without any danger of hitting one another by mistake. A brilliant maneuver, and one they must have practiced countless times.

Rather than follow up on his missed shot at Book, the Viper turned his weapon on the giant who had drawn his weapon and was prepared to fire. The adversaries fired simultaneously. Both men were hit.

The assassin realized he was wounded, seriously, but not fatally. His bullet had struck home, but in all likelihood inflicted no more than a flesh wound on Curt. It was time to finish his assignment and kill Book. He dropped to one knee and trained the weapon on his primary target.

Not enough time.

The bullet penetrating his side caused him to groan in pain, something the Viper had never experienced in his career. *I give pain; I don't receive it.*

The unmistakable rhythm of a Swiss police siren penetrated the residence. If arrested, the best the assassin could expect would be life in prison. Time to escape, before his adversaries finished killing him or the Geneva police arrived.

Limping through the patio doors, he cursed Emmanuelle, who must have alerted the police.

● ● ●

Book and his partner emptied their weapons at the attempted assassin's retreating figure. Curt was in no shape to pursue, and the detective was not about to leave him.

"Who the hell was that?" Curt said.

"Doesn't matter now. What's important is to get the hell out of here before the police come in. Are you okay?"

"The bastard shot me in the thigh. I don't think it hit an artery or a bone. Painful, but not severe. I may need some assistance to walk, so I'm no help carrying Moretti."

Book said, "We'll leave him and beat a quick exit. The Geneva police will take Moretti in for questioning. I'll contact the FBI, and they'll alert the Swiss to his Most Wanted status. Let the Feds sort out the extradition issues."

He draped one of Curt's arms over his shoulder and supported his friend. The pair stumbled out of the residence and onto the sidewalk, heading for the side street where they'd left the Jetta.

Just before they cleared the corner, a white Toyota screeched to a halt as two Geneva police officers leaped out and ran up the brick steps into Moretti's residence. Book began to relax when he heard commands screamed in French, the common language of the authorities in that part of Switzerland. He rejoiced at the thought Moretti would be in custody. Hopefully for the rest of his life.

Returning to their suite at the Hotel de la Paix, he assisted a dazed Curt in getting undressed and into the shower to clean up.

"Your wound doesn't look too bad. I've seen you with worse."

"Yeah, but then I had an honest-to-god medic to look after me. Now all I've got is your sorry ass."

The wounded man staggered, and Book helped him out of the shower, tending to the leg wound with the bandages from the suitcase, packed with something for every contingency.

Once he muscled the giant into bed, he asked, "What can I get you?"

"I'd like a double Scotch on the rocks. But I'll settle for a pitcher of ice water. Set it on the bedside table and go make that call to the FBI. You can't be sure how long the Swiss cops will hold Moretti."

Book used his international satellite phone to dial the number Dominique Legrand had given him to her direct line at FBI Headquarters. The call connected and he was gratified, but not surprised, to discover she was working at her desk. After all, the time was about four o'clock in the afternoon in Washington, DC. She could look forward to a long night.

"Dom, this is Book, calling from Geneva, Switzerland. I've tracked down Franco Moretti—in this country, he calls himself Herbert Bonar Baldwin. The Geneva police picked him up, but that's a long, complicated story, and I'd prefer to tell it to you over a beer . . . or maybe a cup of coffee . . . after I get back to the States. I don't plan to stick around, because my involvement has been sort of . . ." He groped for a word. ". . . unofficial."

After listening a few moments to the FBI special agent's hurried but cogent questions, none of which he wanted to answer, he cut her off.

"Never mind that for now. Call the Geneva police immediately. Alert them about Moretti being on the Most Wanted list. Make sure they hold him until you get here. At least, I hope you'll come. This'll make a great collar on your record."

He listened briefly as Dom began a spiel he interpreted as designed to prolong the phone conversation.

"If you're having this call traced, don't bother. By the time anyone gets here, I'll be long gone."

He hung up and dragged a reluctant Curt out of bed.

"Sorry, fellow. We have to hit the road while we still can. From here, we're heading across the border into France. There are no border formalities to slow us down, so we'll be out of Switzerland in less than thirty minutes. From France, we'll head for Germany. My plan is to travel to Stuttgart and your family. They'll look after you better than I could."

CHAPTER 76

TYSONS, VIRGINIA

"What possessed you to pick those two clowns to kill Carmen Garcia?" Brent Johanson snarled at Roger Carruthers. "Even their nicknames are a clue to their incompetence. A twenty-five-year-old rookie deputy sheriff captured them, a female for god's sake. The Fairfax police are grilling the pair at this moment. I hope to hell they can't identify you."

Carruthers adopted an air of unconcern. "No clues lead to me or—more importantly, and to address your real worry—to you. I never met them in person. Contact was by phone. Payment was in cash, delivered by a go-between. The word on the street was they were the best hitmen available on short notice. Remember, you insisted Carmen be killed to prevent her from attending the last day of the board meeting. When you want it bad, you get it bad. Murphy's Law hasn't been repealed. 'Anything that can go wrong, will go wrong.'" If he could have thought of another cliché that applied, he'd have piled it on.

"The damage is done," the CEO said. "We should have used Hunter. He was successful with Katherine in Charlottesville."

Johanson said, "You know damn well your friend Hunter

is shooting big game in the Canadian Rockies. He's out in the wilderness with his Nakota Sioux guide as we speak, freezing his ass off tracking down moose or black bear. He's not scheduled to fly back from Calgary for another week. We can recruit him to hit Carmen, but not until after she's returned to Jefferson County. She'll be even harder to kill on her own turf, but Hunter is more than up to the challenge. He's in luck, since Garcia's guardian angel, Booker, is away on some mysterious trip."

The chairman added. "The sheriff down there, Pat Garrett, is reputed to be a tough old bastard. He's some sort of wizard with a handgun. Wins a lot of trophies in Cowboy Action Shooting competitions. One year, Garrett won the NRA Bianchi Cup Championship. You better warn Hunter to watch out for him."

"Hunter doesn't believe *anyone* could pose a threat to him. Any suggestion of vulnerability would be resented, with unpredictable consequences. You know him better than I do, since he's one of your Colorado buddies."

Johansen laughed. "Yeah. Y*ou* talk with him, because *I* don't want to get within a country mile of the son of a bitch."

Carruthers said, "Right after Hunter gets back in town, we'll point him toward killing Garcia."

"The killing has to occur at least a couple of weeks before our August meeting," Johansen said. "Carmen must be stopped before her damned *study* is scheduled to be voted on by the board."

CHAPTER 77

JEFFERSON COUNTY, VIRGINIA

Pat Garrett gave Jose Garcia a call and briefed him on the little he knew of Carmen's attempted assassination. Semis, pickups, and sedans moved to the slow lane as Jose set a speed record driving from the tip of Southeast Virginia to Jefferson County. Flying over Interstate 81, lights and sirens all the way, Jose didn't even slow down on the final approach to Courthouse Square.

Ill at ease, the two sheriffs were waiting in Pat's office for Carmen to arrive. The crusty veterans, who'd shared danger with equanimity, were on their third cup of coffee. Sweat soaked the underarms of their khaki shirts.

• • •

Carmen attempted a quick hello to Shirley, but the demonstrative woman hugged her for several moments before letting go.

"Your dad's in with Pat. The sheriffs will demand to know the whole story. You might as well spell it out, because there'll be no stopping them until they learn how much danger you're in."

The men sprang to their feet as the door swung open. Carmen held up both hands.

"Hold on. I wasn't hurt. I'll tell you in detail what's going on. But first, sit back and relax. You both look ready to charge a pride of lions and rip into them barehanded."

Her remarks broke the tension. The men laughed.

"Come here, pumpkin," her dad said, holding out his arms. Carmen let herself be swallowed in the comforting embrace.

Pat held out his arms and she experienced a bone-crushing hug.

Overcome with sentiment, she said, "Here's the lowdown." Narrating the flow of events at her Ritz-Carlton suite took several minutes. She paused for breath.

"I now know both Brent Johanson, the chairman of the board of Consolidated Mining and Energy, and Roger Carruthers, the CEO, were behind Katherine's assassination at UVA."

Noticing their faces light up in a flare of anger, she wagged her finger in mild reproof.

"Not *know* the way a prosecutor knows and is convinced she can prove it in court, but *know for a moral certainty*, the way a cop knows. Johanson and Carruthers also orchestrated the attack on me by Butch and Razor. But there's no chance the Fairfax police will turn up evidence connecting anyone in Consolidated to the crime."

"What's their motive?" Pat asked.

Carmen sat in the chair, next to her dad, facing Pat's desk.

"The motive was the impeding vote the next day on top management's plan to expand company activities related to uranium and nuclear power. The attempted hit was a desperation move to take me out of play. Thanks to my thirty-five percent of the stock, and with the help of a few maverick stockholders, our coalition stood a good chance of voting to block management's strategy. Our group succeeded in postponing events for three months while a study is conducted. At the August meeting, the board will vote, this time for keeps."

Her voice grew softer. "Between now and August, Johanson and Carruthers will stage another assassination attempt."

Hatred blazed in the faces of the two men. A fortuneteller's crystal ball wasn't required to read their thoughts. Ben Franklin's adage came to mind, "An ounce of prevention . . ."

Carmen held up her hand as though directing traffic. "No. We're law enforcement. The emphasis is on *law*. We're not going to kill them. Besides, others are involved. The sniper's still out there. Why they didn't use him—assuming it's a him—for the attack at the Ritz-Carlton is beyond me. But there's no doubt he'll be their candidate, sometime this summer. Our next step is to set a trap."

"Hmmm, a real brain teaser," Pat said ironically. "How to prevent a skilled sniper, with at least one successful assassination on his scorecard, from targeting a deputy sheriff who's out and about every day in a rural county? And to boot, how to capture a guy who's going to be shooting from a hundred yards to half a mile or more away?"

Jose added, "And our assassin could show up anytime between now and the August meeting."

Carmen shook her head, choking out a laugh. "Okay. You guys have had your fun. Now let's put our heads together and stop the assassin before I get killed. Then we'll find a way to link Johanson and Carruthers to Katherine's murder and the attempt on my life at the Ritz-Carlton."

CHAPTER 78

THROUGH FRANCE TO GERMANY

Book had a blurred memory of the drive from Geneva. He and Curt Hartmann had crossed from Geneva into France without incident, but, once over the border, problems cascaded. The five-hour trip had taken eight hours, with frequent timeouts to care for Curt's wounded leg.

The giant had stoically endured the pain from the shooting. But, as they drove through Besançon, France, Curt went into shock, experiencing sweating, rapid breathing, and nausea. His heart rate registered over 170 beats per minute. Book feared seeking medical attention in France would invite disaster.

Book's knowledge of battlefield first aid was thorough and well-practiced. He wagered he could keep Curt's shock under control. Checking the leg wound, he confirmed bleeding had stopped. He maneuvered his half-conscious buddy into the rear seat and placed him on his back with his legs elevated. Body temperature seemed okay. Every thirty minutes, he pulled off the road, squirmed into the rear seat, and checked to assure the shock was not getting worse.

They drove into the foothills of the Black Forest to the spa in Baden-Baden, Germany. Book considered stopping there to seek medical attention, but he decided Curt's strong constitution showed signs of fighting off the shock. No more nausea. Heart rate moderating. Little sweating. Bleeding stopped. Book pushed ahead to Stuttgart.

By the time they reached the outskirts of Stuttgart, Curt claimed he was recovering. He insisted on arriving home in the front seat of the Jetta. He gave directions to the small cottage off base where the Hartmann family lived.

"Our housing allowance doesn't cover the high cost of German utilities. But we enjoy living near downtown. There's good bus transportation to the base school where Gretchen and Ralph attend. Dorothea is taking graduate studies in German literature at the University of Stuttgart. She drags us all over the country to experience cultural events. You'd never believe my wife grew up on a farm in rural Minnesota."

Book helped Curt limp through the front door. On spotting them, Dorothea unleashed a barnyard vocabulary aimed at her husband's "so-called friend."

"How did you let this happen? He told me he was going to Geneva to help you and said there was no danger."

Dorothea turned on her spouse, ready to throw wide open the spigot of blame, when she saw him falter and almost fall in an attempt to sit in an easy chair.

"Oh my god, darling. Are you all right? What happened to you?"

Curt tried to explain why a shot in the thigh was neither life-threatening nor grounds to head immediately to the base hospital. She wasn't buying his story. Husband and wife argued. After much shouting, a compromise was reached in which Curt promised to seek proper treatment "off the books" from a base doctor who owed him a favor.

During the furor, Book kept quiet, moved to the far corner of the living room, and sat in an uncomfortable antique wooden chair. Once he felt confident his friend's condition had stabilized and he would be well cared for, Book prepared to say farewell.

Having forgotten her earlier curses and accusations, Dorothea kissed him on the cheek and insisted he should return for a visit as soon as possible.

"If we move Gretchen's bed into Ralph's room, that will give us a spare guest bedroom. Plan on staying awhile. There's so much to see in this part of Germany."

Out of his wife's view, Curt rolled his eyes, tuned in to how little tourism would appeal to the beleaguered detective.

The two children came in from playing to welcome their dad. Gretchen, a shy six-year-old with golden locks—who strikingly resembled her mother—showed off her doll and gave the visitor a warm goodbye hug. Ralph, at ten already determined to play the part of a young man, offered his hand, which Book solemnly shook.

With a sigh of relief, Book took the train from Stuttgart to Frankfurt am Main International Airport, and, from there, boarded United's flight to Dulles.

The plane was late, the trip from Frankfurt taking over nine hours. After 9 p.m., United Flight 933 finally touched down at Dulles International Airport. Book was exhausted, not having slept on the plane. In fact, he couldn't remember when he'd last gotten any rest.

● ● ●

Special Agent Lyle Manning waited at Dulles International Airport in one of the private interrogation rooms overlooking the US citizen section of immigration where incoming passengers lined up to have their passports validated. Today, the lines were short.

He confirmed Book was on the incoming flight from Frankfurt. In fact, the FBI office in the American Embassy in Bern had filled in the blanks on the detective's itinerary since he departed the States a scant four days earlier—flew from Washington Dulles International Airport, arrived Geneva, checked into Hotel de la Paix with a male companion, somehow got from Geneva to Stuttgart, took the train from Stuttgart to Frankfurt, and flew back to Dulles.

Lyle couldn't guess what the traveler was up to in Geneva. He assumed he'd have a better idea once he heard from Dom.

He was at the airport on a mission from Dominique Legrand, quasi-official in nature. She'd called after arriving in Geneva and outlined the role he was being asked to play. He'd agreed, not without misgivings.

Andrew Booker moved to the front of the line and showed his passport to the stern-faced official who gave him a perfunctory, "Welcome back to the United States." While giving the formal greeting, he buzzed the room where Lyle was waiting.

The alert was unnecessary. Lyle was already heading out of the interrogation room to greet Book. He steered the newcomer back to the privacy of the room.

"Dom sent me to meet you."

Lyle could tell from Book's reaction he'd expected to be met on arrival.

"She made the call you suggested to Geneva and alerted the police to Moretti's Most Wanted identity. They held him awaiting her arrival. Searching his home, they found two large freezers in the cellar. Five female cadavers were inside. The young woman who called the authorities was lucky to escape with the few injuries she reported."

"Did they find out who she was?" Book asked, more interested in Emmanuelle's fate than in Moretti's victims.

"No. Dom said she left without volunteering any information. When the Geneva police tried to call back, there was no answer from her cell phone. She removed the battery, perhaps destroyed the phone. These days everyone seems to be catching on to how cops trace cell phones. Do you have any information you'd care to share about the mystery woman?"

"No."

"Hmmm." Lyle looked thoughtful.

He was certain Book knew a great deal about the witness but was unwilling to stipulate. He decided to let it slide.

"How'd you figure out Moretti was in Switzerland?"

Book briefed Lyle on the arrival of the FedEx envelope with the incriminating photos of the fugitive in various locales in Geneva. Without going into detail about how he got the information, he noted the presence of cigar ash residue in the envelope. He related how a "friend" had helped him interrupt Moretti in the process of assaulting a young woman in the foyer of the fugitive's home, subdue him, and leave him trussed like a Thanksgiving turkey for the Swiss police.

Lyle said, "Dom is following up with the Geneva authorities to explore extradition. The American Embassy is supporting her. You'll be relieved to know she decided to treat you as a confidential informant," he said.

"What does that mean in practice?" Book asked.

"So far as Geneva police know, there's no record of you being at Moretti's home. There's no evidence to indicate who bound the fugitive's wrists and ankles with plastic restraints. The Geneva police failed to find identifiable prints in the residence, apart from those of Moretti and the females in the cellar. Information is missing documenting the presence of your 'friend' Curt Hartmann at the Hotel de la Paix. No attempt will be made to check the DNA of the blood found in the foyer; the police simply reported blood from a gunshot wound. If it's not yours, my guess would be it came from Hartmann, or maybe from the third intruder who was shooting at you guys."

"In short, you won't be involved in the case. As far as the record shows, you weren't present. You won't have to testify, either in Switzerland or the US. For official purposes, you're a ghost."

Book's expression tried for impassive, but Lyle noted the relief.

CHAPTER 79

MCLEAN, VIRGINIA

Marlene Booker glanced at the clock on her desk. A quarter after ten, time to wrap it up. She'd been working since dinner—pizza once again. Rebecca and Jonathan were happy with pizza, she had no complaints, and it went from freezer to oven to table in less than fifteen minutes.

She leaned over to answer the phone, her pulse quickening. Caller ID signaled Book was on the line.

Where the hell has he been?

"Hello." She tried and failed to keep the chill from her voice.

Her husband's unexplained absence stretched her patience to the breaking point. He hadn't touched base in five days. Her repeated phone calls to the mansion and the sheriff's office in Jefferson County had yielded no information and were becoming embarrassing.

"Marlene? Your voice sounds strange. Are you all right?"

"Am *I* all right? You disappear for a week without telling me where you're going. There's no way to get in touch with you. I don't hear from you. What I know for sure is, the last time we were together, we agreed the Bronsons would try to kill you. And you've got the nerve to ask how *I'm* doing?"

"Look. I'm sorry. You've every reason to be upset. I'm at Dulles, heading home in a taxi. Everything's fine. I've got some good news to share."

"Hurry." She sat in her maroon executive chair with tears running down her cheeks, thinking. *Damn him, if I didn't still love him, a divorce would be easy.*

● ● ●

On the way home, Book rehearsed a speech in the taxi in an attempt to diffuse Marlene's anger.

He jumped out of the taxi and rushed through into the foyer. After checking to ensure the lock was secure and the security system armed, he hustled to Marlene's study. She sat behind the desk, fists and jaw clenched as if ready for a fight.

Hand raised in a conciliatory gesture, he said, "You're mad. Before you say anything, let me tell you what's going on."

"I'm listening," she said, in a tone that offered the condemned man a hearty meal before execution.

He tried to remember the speech he'd rehearsed. Nothing came to mind. *To hell with eloquence, start talking and pray she'll listen.*

"I've been in Geneva. Some information sent to me indicated Moretti was hiding in Switzerland. Curt Hartmann met me and together we put down the bastard. Geneva police have him in custody. Dominique Legrand flew to Switzerland to arrange extradition. Lyle Manning met me on my return to Dulles and told me Dom is treating me as a confidential informant, meaning I'm off the hook for whatever coloring outside the lines may have been done in Europe. The Moretti affair is behind us."

Her face remained impassive.

After several moments, she sighed and waved her hands in dismissal.

"You don't understand. I never doubted your version of the Georgetown killing. I supported you unconditionally during the administrative hearing and throughout the trial. The problem with the Moretti incident was always your reaction. It destroyed your life and the life we had as a family. You retreated to your new job as a detective in a rural sheriff's office two hours away. There was no place in that life for me or for Rebecca and Jonathan."

When he held up a hand, trying to explain, she ignored him.

"The issue has never been Moretti. The son of a bitch can rot in hell, spend the rest of his life in prison, or drink cocktails on a beach in Tahiti. I couldn't care less. How can you think risking your neck and Curt's to have him arrested would please me? You tracking down Moretti in Geneva shows how tone deaf you are to what matters to our marriage and our family's future."

Book's shoulders slumped. The fatigue he'd been fighting during the trip came crashing down. He opened his mouth to speak, but words refused to come.

I've lost her. Nothing else matters.

Defeat had never felt so final. Not after his arrest. Not during the administrative hearing or the trial. Not even while getting drunk in Georgetown.

He walked out of the study, headed for the bar in the rec room, took down a glass, opened a bottle of Maker's Mark bourbon, and poured himself three fingers of the Kentucky whiskey. The liquor, made for sipping, was downed in two gulps. The unfamiliar taste caused him to flinch. Another three fingers were poured and gulped. The second glassful went down easier. By the third hefty serving of bourbon, his shoulders were shaking. His face was wet from crying.

● ● ●

Marlene came into the room when he tipped the glass for the third time. She was stunned at the sight of her husband crying and tumbling so hard off the wagon.

Maybe I came on too strong. I've never seen Book fall apart like this.

She racked her brain, the glib lawyer at a loss for words.

"Book, you can't drink. You promised Pat Garrett you'd lay off the booze."

Off balance and snarling, he turned on her. "Why should *you* give a damn what I told Pat? Why should *I* give a damn?" He waved the glass like a baton, looking at it as though bewildered to find it empty.

"You were pretty damn clear you didn't respect my choice in trying to get my professional life back on track in Jefferson County. Or place any value on loyalty to Garrett when he needs my backing to stand up to the Bronsons. You say I don't know what matters to our marriage and family. Well, you've shown you don't believe I bring anything to the marriage. Bourbon's all a man can depend on in this world."

A bit wobbly on his feet, he turned back to the bar. He reached for the bottle of Maker's Mark, but his hand trembled so hard the bottle fell over on its side. Whiskey splashed on the bar. He snatched the bottle and held it triumphantly in the air. Three fingers of liquor were poured, some spilling over the side of the glass. As he gulped the latest helping, he began choking and coughing.

"Goddammit." He clutched the bottle and hurled it against the wall where it shattered, spraying the contents over a red leather sofa. He staggered and almost fell.

Marlene rushed to his side and steadied him.

"Don't touch me."

She touched her fingers to his lips.

"Shhh. Don't say anything. We've both said too much tonight. Come with me."

Staggering, he numbly followed her lead as she guided him up the stairs to their bedroom. Undressing her drunken husband was a challenge, but she prevailed. She eased his naked body into the bed, pulled a sheet and light blanket up to his neck, and stood for several minutes staring at his prone form.

Realizing she still loved him despite everything, she stripped off her clothes, climbed under the covers, and snuggled close.

CHAPTER 80

JEFFERSON COUNTY, VIRGINIA

Lenore Bronson stood outside her father's study, eavesdropping on a shouting match between Jeb and Robert Lee. She couldn't believe what she was hearing.

Jeb was talking in a loud, sarcastic tone. "You were so damned confident the Viper would ambush Book in Geneva. I've known Book for ten years. He's one of the deadliest and most elusive of the Special Forces soldiers I served with. He's the personification of 'hard to kill.' But you bragged about your 'foolproof' plan to lure him to Geneva as a target for assassination."

Her brother's heavy footfalls echoed through the door as he paced the study, clunking on the hickory parquet flooring, muted when he crossed the Persian rug.

"Book's turned the tables on us. The Viper escaped. Book vanished before the Swiss police arrived. Moretti's in custody. The FBI bitch Dominique Legrand is in Geneva negotiating the fugitive's extradition. What happens if she brings Moretti back and he testifies against us?"

"Moretti isn't aware we set Booker on his heels," Robert Lee said. "He knows nothing of the private eye who followed him, taking pictures. There's no way he could find out we sent those pictures to Booker, pointing him toward Geneva. Unless the police call the deception to his attention—and they're clueless—he won't learn about the Viper's trap. We should never have gotten into business with Moretti and made ourselves vulnerable to Booker's investigation. Moreover, if Moretti were to expose our role in setting up the detective in Georgetown, he'd implicate himself in the murder of a Black junkie."

"Julian Thomas was the teenager's name," Jeb said. "Scooter. The DC police will remember him, even if you don't. What implicates Moretti, implicates us. Besides, he may try to trade his information for a lighter sentence."

Robert Lee scoffed. "Who's going to reduce the sentence for a Most Wanted poster boy who murdered four people, including two women and a toddler? To say nothing of the women he murdered in Geneva."

• • •

Lenore saw movement out of the corner of her eye. Adams was watching her, a curious expression on his face.

He'll tell Robert Lee I was eavesdropping outside the study door.

Standing up straight and trying to appear nonchalant, she strolled toward the rear of the mansion. Adams's burly figure followed. She's always been afraid of Adams's hulking form. Now her fear was intensified. She broke into a run, racing toward her living quarters. Adams sped up, but, with his limp, there was no way he could keep pace.

Once in the bedroom, gasping for breath, she locked the door. She moved into the adjoining boudoir and crossed the room to a cherrywood gun cabinet.

Lenore was known locally as a "gun nut." She enjoyed target shooting as well as hunting in season. Rifles, shotguns, revolvers, and pistols of various models were displayed inside the glass front of the cabinet. The glass door was never locked. The drawer at the bottom containing ammunition for each of the weapons was secured. Lenore lifted the top of a two-part planter containing a Shamrock in bloom. The key to the gun cabinet drawer was hidden between the top and bottom halves of the planter.

Nervous about what Adams was up to, she ran to the bedroom door and listened. Hearing nothing, she rushed back to arm herself.

Like many country girls, she'd learned to hunt with a rifle and shotgun at a young age. As an adult, she honed her expertise with handguns. Lenore took pride in being an excellent shot with all types of weapons. She unlocked the ammunition drawer and took out a box of double-ought buckshot, spilling the shotgun shells onto her desk. Another box of shotgun slugs, containing heavy lead projectiles, was dumped next to the double-ought.

She opened the boxes and rammed five shells into a Remington 1100 autoloader, alternating slugs and buckshot. The Remington, her favorite shotgun, was not designed to be used in this fashion. But both the double-ought and the slugs would be deadly in close quarter combat inside the mansion. She put spare shells in the left pocket of her navy-blue cardigan sweater. Once armed, she calmed down.

Examining the array of handguns, she selected a Glock 19, removed the magazine, filled it with 9 mm cartridges, and rammed the magazine home in the pistol's grip. Racking the slide, she inserted a round into the chamber. She loaded two spare magazines and placed both in the empty sweater pocket. She took a holster from the drawer in the bottom of the display case and slid it onto the belt holding up her jeans. With the Glock in the holster, both her hands were free to work the shotgun.

She hurried to the desk and picked up the phone to call 911. No dial tone.

The bastards cut the line.

Quiet movements in the hall outside the bedroom door caught her attention.

They're coming.

Slipping from the boudoir into the bedroom, she knelt in the corner with the entry to her left. Kneeling, her target silhouette was minimized.

All her potential assailants were right-handed. Anyone coming through the door, unless they came part way into the room, would have to lean in to shoot in her direction. A handgun would be difficult for the shooter; a rifle or shotgun would leave him even more exposed.

The doorknob rattled. "Lenore, open the door. It's Jeb. Adams told me you were upset. He tried to approach to find out the problem, but you ran away. Open up, so we can discuss whatever's bothering you."

She kept quiet to give no clue to her location.

"Lenore, Father's worried about you. Adams and I will have to break down the door if you don't open it. We're doing this for your own good."

She snorted. *Like it was for my own good when you raped me on my fourteenth birthday in this very room.*

Fingers holding the shotgun tensed. She forced herself to relax and to breathe normally.

After a few moments, a quiet murmur of voices signaled the forthcoming action.

The door shuddered from the impact of outside forces.

The frame began to splinter. One more smash and a jagged opening appeared in the center of the door. She saw a hand reach in, unlatch the bolt, and feel for the key in the lock. The door swung open on damaged hinges. No one came through.

"Lenore, the door's open. We want you to come out now. No one's going to hurt you."

She ignored her brother's appeal, recognizing the ploy to draw her into the hall where they could deal with her.

Without further warning, Adams charged into the room, his limp barely impeding his rapid movements. Head bent, his body was almost at a ninety degree angle. He looked left and sent four shots into the left quadrant of the room on the wall opposite where Lenore knelt. She was not on that side, or one of the bullets would have struck her.

She hesitated a half-second, then fired.

The force of the blow from the lead shotgun slug struck Adams's right shoulder. He landed on the bed face down. He didn't move.

Lenore focused on the empty door frame. Jeb leaped through, firing to the right quadrant of the room where she was kneeling. The first shot missed, too high. The second round struck her. She screamed as she fired, aiming at her brother's upper body.

Most of the full load of eight lead pellets impacted her target. Jeb's face was filleted like a fish. Pieces of bone and brain matter flew across the room. Throat and chest were bathed in scarlet. She knew Jeb had died instantly, but she felt numb.

No regrets. No satisfaction.

Her side flashed with pain. She glanced down at a bloody palm clutching the bullet wound. Memory of the loss of blood from the knife wound at the Old Virginny flashed a warning to drive to the hospital immediately.

The left pocket on her sweater was ripped apart. Both magazines fell to the carpet. One was dented. The shot that had injured her was a ricochet. She realized Jeb's bullet hit a magazine and was deflected from her midsection to the less lethal flesh above her left hip.

Although movement pained her, she had to flee if she hoped to survive. She drew the Glock from her holster and glanced at Adams sprawled on the bedspread. She moved to finish him off.

She planned to sneak out past wherever her father was lying in wait. He would have his favorite weapon—a .270 Winchester—and be lurking in some dark corner in the event she evaded her brother and Adams. Robert Lee abhorred handguns and shotguns, but he cherished his bolt-action deer rifle. He could use the Winchester to bring her down, with no more emotion than he would devote to killing a wild animal.

Staggering, she hobbled toward the bed. Adams's shoulder was shattered, and his body was still. His right eye was visible, but she couldn't tell if he was watching her.

The shock from the wound in her side was starting to make her dizzy. Her hand holding the Glock was shaking. She moved closer to the bed to guarantee a kill shot.

Without warning, Adams's leg kicked out, knocking her off balance. The pistol discharged into the ceiling. Lenore fell to the floor. The monster leaped on her, crushing the air from her lungs. She tried to aim the weapon at his head, but he seized her wrist and gave it a twist. The Glock flew across the room.

One hand clutched her throat and squeezed.

Powerless to resist, her larynx was crushed, cutting off the airway to her lungs. She tried to scream, but no sound came out. She knew suffocation would quickly lead to death and she almost welcomed the end to suffering.

Adams held her throat and lifted her face until killer and victim were eye to eye. He stopped choking her. The monster stroked her golden hair. With one hand on her head twisting her hair, he began rocking her back and forth. The rhythm grew faster and more violent. The pain was excruciating. No neck could withstand such pressure.

After a few moments, she felt nothing.

CHAPTER 81

MCLEAN, VIRGINIA

Book awoke to the aroma of coffee and looked up to see Marlene holding a steaming mug out to him. Disoriented, he realized his wife was smiling. The friendly expression puzzled him. He struggled to sit up in bed. A hammering pain shot through his head.

He recognized the telltale symptoms of a hangover, a sensation he hadn't experienced in many months.

"Pancakes are in the kitchen. I laid out your pajamas and robe on the chair. Hurry down. Rebecca and Jonathan are waiting to see you."

He lay back on the pillow, mystified, but strangely pleased. Admiring the sway of his wife's hips as she left the room, he took a swig of coffee. Despite burning his mouth, the brew hit the spot.

He stood up to go to the bathroom and caught himself as he stumbled. His head ached even more when he was upright. A doozy of a hangover.

In the shower, he turned the water temperature to scalding hot. His body began to respond, and he eased the setting from red to blue. For the final splash, he shivered under an icy stream. The regimen didn't cure the hangover, but he began to feel almost human. He toweled off, shaved, put on pajamas and robe, and headed downstairs.

"Dad, you're back!" The twins gave a welcoming shout as he

came into the room. He eyed Marlene, certain the greeting was well coached. Still, the sentiment brought a grin to his face. He reached for each of the teenagers and hugged them, a glint of moisture in his eyes. The answering hugs made his heart beat faster. *Maybe I haven't lost my family after all.*

Sunday pancake breakfasts were once a family ritual, designed long ago by Marlene to ensure there was at least one occasion each week when the family members' busy schedules would intersect. After he'd gone into the blue funk in response to the killing in Georgetown, he'd stopped coming to breakfast—Sunday or any other day.

The twins bombarded their dad with tales of what was happening in their lives. A far cry from the rare days in recent months when he'd thought to inquire how things were going and was met with a teenage all-purpose "fine."

Earnest efforts were made to explain the mysteries of soccer, a sport he still failed to understand, even in the past when he'd attended their games. Jonathan lectured, "I'm a forward, Dad. My main job is to score goals. In our last game, I scored two. That's the best I've ever done."

Not to be upstaged, Rebecca chimed in on her dad's tutoring about soccer.

"I'm a midfielder—on my team we're called 'mids.' My job is to stop the other team from scoring. I'm the best at stealing the ball and passing it to the forward so they have a chance to score." She cast a nervous eye toward her mom, half expecting a caution about bragging, but all she noticed was a proud look.

The family banter went on until the prodigious supply of bacon and pancakes—an assortment of buttermilk, blueberry, and pecan— was exhausted. At last, having fulfilled the mission assigned by Mom, the twins said their goodbyes and took off to parts unknown.

Once they were alone, Marlene said, "Let's go into the rec room. We need to talk."

Sitting on one cushion of the leather sofa, she held her husband's hand while he perched on the other cushion. She placed two fingers on his lips. "Just listen."

She sighed. "I love you. This 'trial separation' was a mistake. Damn the day I proposed it. We need to work our way through whatever has cursed us these past months. I'm willing to do whatever it takes."

With an embarrassed laugh, she realized her fingers were still on his lips and took them away.

Book cleared his throat. "I don't know what to say. I love you. The trial separation never made sense to me. But you wanted it, and I was desperate to do anything to please you. The happiest I've been in a year was when you came to me on the pool patio. I began to hope again for the first time in . . . forever. Last night, I lost hope, certain you no longer loved me. Why should you? I've made your life hell. I've made Jonathan and Rebecca's lives hell. How can you ever forgive me?"

"There's nothing to forgive. We experienced a tragedy, and we let it harm our family . . . our marriage. The worst is behind us. We're going to get past this."

"I still have commitments in Jefferson County. I can't abandon Pat."

"You're honor bound to stay and help Garrett deal with the Bronsons. With you there, Garrett will prevail. There's light at the end of the tunnel, and it's not an oncoming train." Neither of them laughed at the feeble joke. "Jefferson County is two hours away," she said, in a desperate attempt to rationalize the situation. "Some people commute longer distances to their jobs in DC."

"Commuting isn't an option for a detective."

"Of course not. But I can come down more often, maybe for long weekends. You can travel home at times. We'll make it work. Once this crisis with Ares Worldwide is over for both of us—me with the Senate committee and you with the Bronsons—are you willing to consider leaving the sheriff's office and finding a job in the Washington area?"

"Yes . . . yes . . . yes. There are lots of things I can do around here."

From his expression, Marlene could tell he couldn't think of one, despite an air of dogged determination. But she knew it was true. Book was a man of multiple talents, and there was always demand in both public and private sectors for a military veteran with a detective's experience and her husband's relentless drive.

CHAPTER 82

GENEVA, SWITZERLAND

The concrete bed was the prominent feature in the spartan cell at Champ-Dollon prison. Franco Moretti lay on the hard surface. Discomfort was a bit moderated by the skimpy mattress and blanket provided. The toilet was useful, but didn't serve to light up the room. The dimensions of the cell were restricted, measuring two by three and a half meters. He stared at the concrete desk, feeling no desire to write, even if he were provided the implements.

Who would he write? He'd killed his wife and the partner who was his best friend when he caught them in bed together. His parents were dead. No children or siblings. He was a pariah in his own country. People in Switzerland knew nothing of him, except for those in Geneva's law enforcement community who were working hard to ensure he served life in prison.

His cell opened. A prison guard stood at attention by the steel door. "Monsieur Moretti, your lawyer wishes to see you."

He felt nothing but contempt for Ulrich Simon—despite his reputation as the best criminal lawyer in Switzerland— but welcomed any respite from the boredom of spending twenty-three hours out of every twenty-four in his cell. He jumped to his feet and followed the guard down the winding corridors to the interview room.

Simon sat waiting for his wealthy client. "Monsieur Moretti, you are looking well today. I trust *tout va bien*."

One of the more annoying habits of his attorney was to sprinkle English conversation with snippets of French which, even when he understood them, never failed to irritate him.

"What progress have you made in getting me out of this hellhole?"

"None. You will be incarcerated in Champ-Dollon until your trial. If you are found guilty, the likelihood is you will spend the rest of your life here."

Moretti stared at the attorney, whose pudgy build and foppish airs reminded him of Hercule Poirot, Agatha Christie's renowned detective.

If only he possessed Poirot's famous "little grey cells."

"You told me Champ-Dollon was the most crowded prison in Switzerland, so why would they keep me here? Conditions are intolerable. I'm stuck in isolation and allowed outside my miserable cell for only an hour a day."

"You must understand the mentality of the public prosecutor and the judges in Geneva," Simon said. "They hate foreigners. Geneva and other cities in Western Switzerland have more foreign criminals cross the border than any other part of the country. The authorities put you in the same category with other foreigners, even though your murders are far more flamboyant."

"Mr. Simon, it is gross malpractice for my lawyer to refer to 'my murders.' I've not been convicted. Your job is to demonstrate why *no* murders allegedly committed have anything to do with me."

"*Bien sur.* My apologies."

"To return to my question, why keep me here if Champ-Dollon is overcrowded?"

"Prison overcrowding is a chronic problem in Switzerland, most of all in Geneva. A modern prison, La Brenaz, opened in 2008. The goal was to transfer prisoners to ameliorate conditions. The judges seized on the opening to sentence even more foreigners. Now, La Brenaz is crowded and Champ-Dollon is still operating at twice its planned capacity. You can understand why odds are you'll remain here."

"Damn you Simon, you talk like I'm already convicted. What the hell kind of a lawyer are you?"

"*Excusez moi*. The key to my success as a criminal lawyer is that I avoid the temptation to bullshit my client. 'Bullshit' is the applicable word, *n'est-ce pas*?"

The lawyer stared at the ceiling as though consulting his mental dictionary.

"You're at high risk of being convicted. The public prosecutor is aware of your FBI record. The Geneva police found bodies of five young women in freezers in your basement. DNA from your sperm was in the vagina of each of the victims. Investigators have documented you purchased one of the freezers and supervised its delivery to the basement one month prior to your incarceration. On the night of your arrest, a young woman called to claim you had only that night abused her physically and sexually. There's a preponderance of proof against you."

Moretti glared at his attorney, momentarily speechless.

"To counter such a mountain of evidence, you have given me *rien*. Nothing. In spite of that, you would be pleased if I pretended an acquittal is expected. Now is the time you should ask yourself not what kind of a lawyer *I am*, but what kind of a defendant *are you*?"

"All right, you've made your point. I'm paying you a fortune. What have you done to earn your fee?"

"*Voilà*! Now you have asked the right question. Dominique Legrand, an FBI Special Agent, wishes to discuss your extradition to the United States. I recommend you listen with great care to what she has to say."

Moretti sat back and weighed the pros and cons of extradition. He hesitated. *Would I be better off in prison in Geneva, as miserable as the prospect is, or returning home to face justice in the United States?*

"When am I scheduled to meet with her?"

"Right now. She's waiting."

The convict sighed. "Bring her in. But you stay."

Simon moved to the door to alert the guard.

• • •

Dom entered the room and paused. She studied the prisoner. After a moment, she walked forward and accepted his handshake.

"Has your lawyer told you why I'm here?"

"Yes. He says you want to persuade me to opt for extradition."

"More right than wrong. My intent is to lay out the facts and let you decide. Little persuasion should be needed. Monsieur Simon has informed you what will happen if you decide to throw yourself on the mercy of the courts in Geneva."

"My lawyer believes the authorities have a strong case against me."

"Public prosecutor Jean Louis Boucher is convinced you will be convicted. I'm sure you are aware of the hard evidence against you." Dom chuckled. "Do you know the meaning of the French name, Boucher?"

Moretti looked at Simon for an answer. "Butcher."

Dom nodded sagely. "*Exactement.* The prosecutor is a 'butcher' and proud of the title. He's one of the leading proponents of changing the laws to permit capital punishment."

She took her time, taking the seat at the table facing Moretti.

"But don't worry. The Swiss are reluctant to condemn prisoners to life in prison without parole. However, there's an exception for people convicted of heinous crimes. The murders committed on the five women found in freezers in your basement fit the exception like a glove. The worst you have to fear is life in prison, and, most probably, that is your future."

Moretti snorted. "If you expect to scare me with the threat of life in a Swiss prison, you'll have to do better than that. If I return to the States, I could face a prolonged trial, many years in prison, followed by execution."

"You're right. But there's less certainty of conviction. You'd have a home field advantage you lack here."

"If I were to sweeten the pot, how would my chances look back home?" he asked.

"Sweeten it?" Dom raised her eyebrows.

"Suppose I could point you to those who committed other murders in the US and abroad, and who defrauded the US government out of billions? Might that persuade the Justice Department to take the death penalty off the table?"

She temporized, realizing he might see through her ploy. "The Feds are not alone in being after your scalp. Murder is still subject to state and local jurisdiction."

His triumphant grin signaled he saw an opening to exploit. "The attorney general can be persuasive with other levels of government if he chooses."

"How do I know you're not blowing smoke?"

"You know about the incident in Georgetown involving Detective Andrew Booker. In fact, I read in the *International Herald Tribune* you were on the scene in Jefferson County, Virginia during another incident involving Book."

"Yes, I'm familiar with those incidents." She was growing uncomfortable with the direction Moretti was taking.

"Suppose I told you the Georgetown killing of Scooter Thomas happened exactly the way Book testified? Suppose I could further prove there was a conspiracy to set up the detective?"

"You would have had to be part of any such conspiracy."

He waved his hand as though to dismiss such a small issue. "Speaking hypothetically, if I were a part, I would know the other parties."

"Assuming I can sell your story in Washington, who were those other parties? I need facts you can back up or I'm not about to raise the issue with the attorney general."

"Jeb and Robert Lee Bronson instigated the plot."

"What was their motive?" she asked.

Moretti said, "Ares Worldwide held several subcontracts with my Force Support Corporation. Numerous crimes, including bribery and murder, were committed under that contractual relationship. The Bronsons were concerned Book might stumble across evidence leading back to them if he continued to investigate me. The setup in Georgetown was designed to take him off the playing field."

She thought, *Everything fits*. Moretti's scenario explains why the Bronsons were behind the attempt of the three mercenaries to stage the home invasion at the Jensen mansion to kill Book and Marlene in Jefferson County.

"Mr. Moretti, I believe the Justice Department may have some interest in your story. Does this mean you're prepared to go along with extradition?"

"Agent Legrand, if you spent twenty-three hours out of twenty-four in my cell for a few days, you'd be happy to sell your soul to the devil."

CHAPTER 83

JEFFERSON COUNTY, VIRGINIA

"Pat, Dr. Warshawski's on Line One," Shirley Ralston said.

"Sheriff Garrett here," he said, picking up the receiver.

"Pat, you need to come to the hospital. Robert Lee Bronson brought Adams in; his shoulder's blown to hell by a shotgun slug. He almost bled out, past the point of no return. A near thing, but he'll live."

The sheriff sat back in his swivel desk chair and stared into space.

"Pat, you still there?" The physician's voice held a note of alarm.

"Yeah. What does Robert Lee say happened?"

"The old man claims he was cleaning his shotgun. The old story, 'he didn't know the gun was loaded.' Supposedly, the shotgun accidentally discharged, striking Adams. Could it have happened that way?"

The sheriff's fundamental skepticism at any report of an "accidental" shooting was magnified by the recollection of a hunting trip with the elder Bronson when he raved on about his disdain of shotguns and handguns. "Not a chance. No matter how Adams got shot, it didn't happen by accident." Pat cleared his throat. "I'm on my way."

Heading out the door, he said to Shirley, "I'm going to the hospital. Adams has been severely wounded. Contact Billy Williams and Carmen and tell them to meet me there . . . no, not there." He paused a moment to consider possible scenarios.

"Tell them to go to Bronson Stables and stake out the main house. Inform them Adams was shot. The scene may be dangerous."

"What kind of danger?" she asked.

"Dammit, Shirley, if I knew, I'd spell it out. Get them to Bronson Stables on the double. I'll join them later. Alert Ron Sargent to meet me at the hospital."

Although the effects of nicotine withdrawal were mitigated, Pat still experienced a residual grouchiness. Each time he aimed his ire at his administrative assistant, her hurt feelings ignited guilt like an overactive ulcer.

Fired by impatience to get to the hospital, he sped out of Courthouse Square. In his peripheral vision, he noticed a woman swerve her Platinum Toyota Tundra to get out of his way. Her pickup ended up on the sidewalk in front of the Shenandoah Café. In the rearview mirror, he spied Alice racing out the café's front door to see what had caused the ruckus.

The sheriff's cruiser skidded to a stop in front of the emergency room. He hurried inside.

A nurse standing by the emergency entrance pointed the way. "Sheriff, go through those double doors, Room 104. Dr. Warshawski's in the recovery room with Mr. Adams."

Approaching the recovery room, Pat noticed Robert Lee at the end of the corridor whispering into a cell phone. In the room, two nurses hovered over Adams. Pat smiled at Isabel, who had assisted in the operating room when he'd undergone an emergency appendectomy a few years earlier. Dr. Warshawski was checking the bedside monitor above the bed and making a notation on a chart.

Addressing the physician, Pat asked, "How's Adams?"

"A fifty-fifty chance of survival, which is better odds than when he checked into the emergency room. We can thank Robert Lee for getting him here so fast."

The sheriff wondered, *Can we thank Robert Lee for shooting him?* Walking up to the elder Bronson, he said, "Tell me what happened."

Robert Lee sank onto the only available chair in the recovery room. "I've already given the details to Dr. Warshawski. The nurse," indicating Isabel, "made me fill out a report of the shooting."

"Tell me in your own words."

Sighing, he mumbled in a low monotone, "Sitting at my desk, I was starting to clean the shotgun. My habit is to unload any weapon before cleaning, but I screwed up. Adams came in to tell me something, causing me to look up from the shotgun. Somehow, the weapon discharged. The slug struck him in the shoulder. I applied first aid to stop the bleeding and drove him here as fast as possible. A tragic accident."

Pat refrained from verbalizing the story was a crock of shit and asked, "Who else was at the house when this happened?"

Startled by the unexpected question, Robert Lee stayed silent for a moment too long.

"No one. Lenore drove the Jaguar to Richmond to visit her aunt. Jeb went out to the Farm to meet with a group who came in from North Carolina last night. The chef gets Monday off, so she was away visiting relatives in West Virginia. The cleaning crew come in on Tuesday. The house was empty except for Adams and me."

Realizing the story was a complete fabrication, the sheriff stood, weighing the implications.

Ron Sargent rushed into the recovery room.

Pat turned. "Ron, place Mr. Bronson under arrest for attempted murder. Confiscate his phone. Cuff him. Escort him to the jail."

Pat had no idea if Bronson was guilty of attempted murder or any infraction, except lying while talking, but he wanted the old man on ice for now.

He walked into the corridor and flicked on his cell phone, hoping he wasn't too late to stop whatever the elder Bronson had set in motion at Bronson Stables.

CHAPTER 84

Carmen was on high alert watching the Bronson mansion. When Billy Williams drove through the front gate, she waved to indicate he should pull in next to her Range Rover. Finally, she answered her phone, which had been vibrating for a while.

"Carmen, are you at Bronson Stables?" Caller ID confirmed the sheriff was on the line.

"Yes, Pat. Billy and I just arrived. We're parked behind the stable, which blocks the view of our vehicles from the main house."

"What's happening?"

"There are two black Ford Expeditions in the driveway. My guess is they're from Ares Worldwide. A blond woman exited the front door. Looks like Lenore. No . . . Lenore's height and weight and a similar hairdo, but, at a closer look, she's not Lenore Bronson. Wait . . . she climbed into Lenore's Jaguar. The car's heading this way. What'll we do?"

"Stop the Jaguar and park it out of sight. Lock her in the rear of Billy's cruiser."

Focused on instructions from the sheriff, Carmen lost sight of what was happening outside the main house. Billy poked her shoulder to attract attention. She spied three men carrying black body bags. Two men were sharing the weight of one cadaver pouch. The third man had a body bag slung over his shoulder. Both bags were dumped in the rear of the same Expedition. None of the men looked in the direction of the departing Jaguar.

Carmen said, "Hold on, Pat."

She turned to Billy. "Stop that Jaguar. Force the driver to pull behind the stable and park next to us. Lock her in the rear of your cruiser."

"What's going on?" Billy asked.

"Do it."

He shrugged and ran off.

Getting back to the phone, she grimaced at the sound of the sheriff cursing.

"Goddammit, Carmen, what the hell's going on."

"Sorry, Pat. Billy's detaining the woman. Three men carried two body bags out of the house and dumped them in the back of one of the Expeditions. Hold on . . ."

In response to the latest request to hold, she could hear the sheriff swearing and threatening severe repercussions if he was put on hold one more time. Her attention was captured by activity at the front of the mansion. One of the men was using a spray can to paint a message on the stone wall to the right of the black walnut double doors. She squinted and spelled the words to herself, "B-U-R-N N-I-G-G-E-R . . ." in the middle was a word difficult to decode. The final word she knew was "BURN."

Damn. She decoded the message: BURN NIGGER-LOVER BURN.

"Pat—" Her words were drowned out by a torrent of swearing coming through her receiver.

"Sheriff, shut the fuck up." She surprised herself by shouting into the phone. Even more surprising was the answering quiet.

"Listen, Pat. Two of the men are getting ready to carry five-gallon cans into the residence. The third man is painting a sign about burning the place. Get the fire department out here. And bring as many deputies as you can to back us up."

Calm now, the sheriff said, "They're trying to destroy the evidence of two killings. You've got to stop them. I'll be there with backup as fast as possible. Try shooting to pin them down."

"Ten-four." Carmen hung up.

She pulled the Glock and fired in the general direction of the three men at the front door. There was little expectation of hitting anything, but the shots should distract them from the planned arson.

She fired off three more rounds.

Billy ran back from the cruiser, his face a mask of confusion. "What the hell are you doing?"

"Pat said shoot to pin them down. We have to stop them from torching the place. Keep firing while I get my sniper rifle."

She removed the sniper rifle, scope, and ammunition from the gun safe in the Range Rover. Donning the Kevlar vest, she congratulated herself on having replaced the items confiscated by the Fairfax police after the incident at the Ritz-Carlton.

Moving cautiously toward Billy, she asked, "Do you want the shotgun?"

Without pausing from aimed fire, he nodded. He knelt by the stable, bracing his body against the nearest corner for support.

Billy's shots were not close to any of the targets, but they kicked up dust and were doing the job of keeping the men pinned down behind the black vehicles. At odd intervals, one of the intruders would poke his head up and shoot back. The return fire was equally wide of the mark.

With an almost gleeful expression when she placed the combat shotgun and ammunition by his knee, Billy said, "This is a real by-god shootout."

Remembering from her earlier visits to the stable that there were several sandbags next to the tack room, she went inside and carried out two, one at a time, cradling her rifle in her left arm. Handing one sandbag to Billy, she placed the other on the ground, sprawled prone, and set the rifle on top of the second sandbag.

Following her dad's guidance, Carmen had grown up being meticulous about keeping her weapons cleaned and sighted in. There was no doubt the bullets would hit where she aimed.

The slight wind posed little problem to good marksmanship. The range was no more than 250 yards. She sighted, waiting for the man who was most active in returning fire to move from cover. When he did, she took aim, held her breath, breathed out a bit, and gradually squeezed the trigger. Not intending to fire, she wanted to see how much time he would give her when he emerged from the protective vehicle.

Not enough. She'd have to cut corners on the shooting sequence.

Twice more, the sniper firing sequence was repeated, without the final touch to send the bullet spiraling through the barrel of the weapon. Once she had the rhythm right, the final squeeze on the trigger did its job. The bullet found its mark.

"You got him," Billy exulted.

"Only a flesh wound. He'll be less anxious to show his face and shoot back at us. Our goal is to pin them down, not kill them."

"Now they know we have a rifle; they'll either hunker down or jump in their vehicles and try to escape."

Billy's second hunch was proven correct. In a few seconds, three men mounted the Expedition loaded with the body bags and started the ignition.

Anticipating their attempt to flee, Carmen began shooting at the tires. The front and rear tires nearest the deputies were shredded. She continued firing to disable the engine and smiled when the SUV came to a halt.

Abandoning the first vehicle, the trio climbed into the other Expedition. The second SUV was masked by the disabled Ford, making it a poor target. They elected to drive out the way they drove in, probably having no idea there was a back exit from Bronson Stables. The Expedition followed the road in the line of fire leading toward the stable. Realizing the dilemma, the driver swung the SUV in a wide curve and headed for the white horse fence circling the property.

By now they were in shotgun range, a little over one hundred yards away, and Billy commenced firing, sending lead slugs slamming into the SUV. Carmen kept aiming the rifle at the tires, shredding the one in front, sending the vehicle into a skid. The driver managed to regain control.

Determined not to allow them to escape, she began targeting the men inside, blowing out the front windshield, causing the driver to crouch down out of sight. He couldn't see to drive, but he denied Carmen a target. The SUV was still over sixty yards from the nearest section of fence. A steep ditch between the fence and the road was now visible. The Expedition slowed and came to a stop. No one got out.

Carmen turned to her partner. "Get on the loudspeaker in your cruiser and tell them to throw their weapons away from the vehicle. Tell them to climb out with their hands on their heads and kneel on our side of the Expedition. Make sure they know if they try anything, I'll shoot to kill."

The handguns were hurled from the SUV's windows. One, two, three—that was it, unless they were carrying concealed backup guns.

The three men kneeled in the dirt, staring toward the deputies who were about to arrest them.

"Why are you shooting at us?" the apparent leader of the trio spoke up as the deputies drew close. "We didn't do nothing."

Slightly built, he was shorter than his companions, one of whom was a tall and heavy behemoth, the other a lanky beanpole.

"You call carrying two body bags nothing? And you were about to torch the mansion."

The short man had one hand on his head, as directed. The other was pressed to his bleeding shoulder. "Mr. Bronson authorized us to remove the bodies of his son and daughter. They were dead. We were doing what we were told."

"Did he also tell you to burn the place down?" Billy asked.

"We weren't gonna burn nothing," the behemoth shouted. "You got no right to arrest us."

"You're kidding, right? Cuff 'em Billy."

CHAPTER 85

Driving into Courthouse Square, Book recognized the FBI vehicles from Richmond. By staying home Monday, he missed the excitement at Bronson Stables.

On reflection, he didn't regret the decision to prolong the reconciliation with Marlene, who'd also taken off Monday. They enjoyed time together in ways not experienced in over a year.

Shirley beamed when Book walked through the door. She jerked her thumb in the direction of Garrett's office. "He's expecting you."

Pat wasted no time bringing Book up to speed on developments.

"We were in a shit storm without an umbrella. I called the FBI Richmond field office and asked for help. Todd Davenport immediately responded by bringing his investigators and forensics teams. The Feds are swarming all over Jefferson County. They've even invaded the sanctity of the Farm."

He paused. "Sorry to tell you this, but Lenore Bronson's dead. I know you two were friends. Best we've been able to reconstruct the crime scene, Jeb Bronson and Adams broke into her bedroom suite. She killed her brother with a buckshot blast to the head. Wounded Adams in the shoulder, but he managed to kill her by breaking her neck."

"Lenore shared with me some background about problems she had with her family," Book said, shaking his head sadly. "I guess things got out of hand. Damn shame she was killed."

Pat continued the recital of events stemming from the incident at Bronson Stables. "Robert Lee drove Adams to the hospital, where Althea Warshawski operated and saved his life. The old man told some cock-and-bull story about how he shot Adams by 'accident.' Figuring we'd sort out the charges later, we arrested him for attempted murder. When I finished listening to Robert Lee's far-fetched lies about what happened, I dispatched Carmen and Billy Williams to Bronson Stables. They arrested four employees of Ares Worldwide. One was a woman named Veronica Kenney."

Book said, "Damn. I take off one day and the county falls apart."

"Kenney admitted Robert Lee told her to drive Lenore's Jaguar to Richmond and buy gas at a station near Virginia Commonwealth University using an Exxon credit card Lenore kept in the car. The Lenore look-alike was instructed to leave the Jag in a nearby shopping center with the car unlocked and the keys inside—an open invitation to theft. Her movements would have supported Robert Lee's story about Lenore visiting her aunt in Richmond. The plan might have worked if we hadn't found Lenore's body in an Expedition in front of her home."

Book sighed and got up to pace. "Lenore was close to her Aunt Rosemary, with whom she lived during her teens after being raped by her brother on her fourteenth birthday."

Pat hesitated a moment. "I had no idea about the rape. That explains a lot about Bronson family dynamics. The call record in Robert Lee's cell phone confirmed he talked with Veronica a half hour before she was picked up trying to drive the Jag off the Bronson's property. That must have been when he gave her marching orders about how to pretend to be Lenore on a trip to visit Aunt Rosemary in Richmond."

"Anyone else arrested?" Book asked.

"Three guys were caught red-handed hauling body bags containing Jeb and Lenore's corpses out of the residence and putting them in the back of one of the two Expeditions. They'd made some crude efforts to sanitize the crime scene—collecting two handguns and moving Lenore's shotgun from her bedroom into the study. Robert Lee claimed the 'accidental' shooting of Adams occurred in the study. Which wouldn't explain how Lenore's prints, not his, were found on the shotgun."

Book shook his head, trying to follow the stream of events Pat was relating.

"To top it off, the perps were about to torch the Bronson place when Carmen and Billy scared them off. They spray painted, 'BURN NIGGER-LOVER BURN,' on the stone wall by the front door, to link the residential fire to the arson and killing at the *Jefferson Weekly*. I guess their hope was the FBI would label another arson a follow-up hate crime. One of the guys was winged in the shootout before being apprehended."

"Do you have cell phone links between Robert Lee and these guys?" Book asked.

"One of 'em, Frank Walcott. He claims old man Bronson—they call him "the General," even though he was never in the military—authorized them to remove the corpses. He denies any intent to torch the place. He also tried to fast-talk his way out of doctoring evidence at the crime scene."

Regretful at missing the latest action at Bronson Stables, Book said, "Sounds like Billy and Carmen got there in time. A few minutes later and the bodies would have disappeared, and the residence would have burned to the ground, eliminating the evidence incriminating Robert Lee."

CHAPTER 86

Lyle Manning was making great time on Route 7—fifteen minutes till arrival in Jefferson County—when his cell phone rang. Dominique Legrand was on the line.

"Hello, Dom. Are you still in Geneva?"

"Yes. And I expect to be here for a while. The Swiss judicial system is not thrilled to negotiate with foreigners, in general, and Americans, in particular. The good news is the public prosecutor Jean Louis Boucher is willing to forgo the opportunity to try Moretti for the five murders he's accused of committing in Geneva. Boucher told me he's sensitive to the adverse publicity the city will receive worldwide if Moretti's crimes are showcased in a public trial. Geneva's economy is dependent on tourists, and even more on the myriad international organizations and businesses that have made the city home for generations."

"I guess politicians are the same everywhere," Lyle said.

"In time, Boucher will finagle the details of the extradition. The Embassy is supportive. Even better, I'm told the White House is backing the extradition behind the scenes. It'll happen. I need to hang around for another week or so to ensure the wheels keep turning."

"There are worse assignments than being stuck in a city known as a tourist mecca," Lyle said, laughing.

"Yeah, yeah. See how much sympathy you get from me when you're pulling duty in Mississippi or Alabama on one of your civil rights cases. All joking aside, I need to keep you posted on what's going on with Moretti, who's volunteering information to get the Justice Department to take the death penalty off the table. Moretti says his company was a subcontractor and had numerous relationships with Ares Worldwide, some legal, some off the books—such as bribing foreign officials and murder. He profited to the tune of hundreds of millions of dollars. Closer to home, he conspired with Jeb and Robert Lee to set up Book in Georgetown. According to Moretti, the incident went down exactly as Book testified."

"I need to pull over to listen to this," Lyle said. "That's a motive for the Bronsons to order their mercenaries to assassinate Marlene and Book. Another motive is Marlene's role as lead investigator in the Senate investigation of military contracting. The arson and murder at *Jefferson Weekly* was a gambit to keep Abner Wallace from continuing to spy on Ares."

Dom said, "Moretti claims his testimony can tie Robert Lee to those crimes. If he can back it up, the Justice Department might go for a plea bargain and forgo the death penalty. I'll get back to you if I get any more headlines about Moretti."

During the remainder of his trip, Lyle mulled over what he'd learned from Dom. He entered Courthouse Square, pulled up to the sheriff's office, parked, and hurried in, anxious to share Dom's findings with Pat and Book.

"I'm glad I caught you both. I just got off the phone with Dominique Legrand." He secretly delighted in noticing Pat's eyes light up at the mention of the FBI special agent.

"According to Dom, Moretti, faced with the likelihood of a sentence of life without parole in a Swiss prison, opted for extradition. He's willing to take his chances with justice back home." Lyle proceeded to share highlights of the fugitive's testimony.

● ● ●

Listening to Lyle's presentation Book stood and paced the room. "Sheriff, I owe you big time for putting your trust in me when no one else would. Moretti's testimony is the final nail in Robert Lee's coffin. You don't need my help to finish the job of cleaning up Jefferson County. After I tidy up a few things, I'll be heading back to Northern Virginia."

Pat clasped Book's shoulder.

"I'm glad it worked out. You're a stand-up guy, Book. You deserved better than you got from the DC police after Georgetown. You have my support no matter what you decide to do. Before you go, however, I *do* need your help with a sticky problem."

The sheriff looked at Lyle. "Listen up. You may be interested."

Pat outlined Carmen's theory of Johanson and Carruthers' conspiracy to have a sniper assassinate her stepmom Katherine Harriman Garcia on the campus of the University of Virginia. He detailed the challenge of trying to prevent that same sniper from killing Carmen in Jefferson County between the present and the scheduled August board meeting.

CHAPTER 87

Hunter opened his laptop computer and reviewed an array of photographs snapped by the sleazy private eye who'd been hired by Roger Carruthers. The investigator was tailing Carmen Garcia and documenting her movements.

The digital file chronicled Carmen's travels around Jefferson County, with a focus on aerial and other views of Stephanie Wilkerson's hundred acres farm. The rural landscape was becoming as familiar to Hunter as the area around the Montana ranch where he'd grown up.

On the surface, Carmen's life seemed simple, starting with a familiar routine each morning—a horseback ride near dawn under the watchful eye of Mary Connolly. After her day's tour of duty, the rookie deputy retired to the garage apartment, where she continued to live, despite having inherited an unbelievable fortune on her twenty-fifth birthday.

The information provided to Hunter by the private eye indicated Carmen's workday movements as a sheriff's deputy were erratic and unpredictable. Her duties took her throughout Jefferson County. Hunter was beginning to recognize the most common destinations—Bronson Stables, the farm headquarters of Ares Worldwide, the mansion where Detective Booker was staying, the Jefferson Café, and to and from the sheriff's office on Courthouse Square.

Most of the locations were workable ambush sites for a skilled sniper like himself, apart from those around Courthouse Square. But the uncertainty of when the target might show up at any given place made planning virtually impossible.

Hunter told Carruthers that Jefferson County was not the sort of locale where strangers could expect to hang out without being noticed. In turn, he'd been warned Sheriff Garrett and his staff were not to be underestimated. Confident of his expertise, the assassin's reaction was to dismiss the warnings as an overreaction by his nervous Nellie employer.

The assassin began to focus on the first part of Carmen's day. Starting early, before her workday began, the one place where the eccentric hundred-million-dollar-heiress was certain to be found was Wilkerson's stable. According to the snoop, she followed an unvarying ritual. Around dawn, she guided a reddish-brown mare out of the stall, put on the bridle, threw a pad and Western saddle over the mare's back, tightened the cinch, and climbed into the saddle.

Mary Connolly—nicknamed Crazy Mary or Horsewoman Mary—supervised Carmen's riding lessons. Connolly had been a famous horsewoman when she was younger.

She appeared to be a stern but caring instructor, and Carmen's horsemanship was improving by leaps and bounds. The riding path from the stable to the woods was an open area, running several hundred yards. There was an excellent field of fire from several locations.

In Hunter's expert judgment, the site was ideal for an ambush—a predictable time and place to locate the victim. The only other people he would have to contend with were an old woman and a teenager who showed up to muck out the stable and care for the horses. There were several spots to use as blinds where he could hide while setting up a sniper shot.

He spent time reflecting on questions that framed the assassin's dilemma. Was Stephanie Wilkerson's farm the setting for an elaborate trap to catch him? Could Carmen Garcia, Pat Garrett, and Booker have figured out what Johanson and Carruthers have in mind for Katherine's stepdaughter? How could they know? Was the payoff balanced against the challenge worth the risk? Common sense told him the safe course would be to pull out now. But Hunter's ego was more powerful than his common sense.

When he first got into the assassination business, his mentor had confided the perennial cautionary tale about pilots, "There are old pilots, and there are bold pilots. But there are no old bold pilots."

The moral was clear. Be mindful of one's limits and never tempt fate by pushing beyond them.

Hunter shrugged resignedly. He'd never left an assignment unfinished, and he had no intention of starting now. The mind-boggling sum he was earning for this assassination weighed in favor of soldiering on in the face of risks. Ego demanded no less.

He turned on his cell phone. Made the call. When Carruthers answered, he said, "Tomorrow, July 4. Carmen has one more day on this earth."

CHAPTER 88

The twilight before sunrise cast an eerie glow through the woods. A balmy breeze rustled summer leaves. Small animals and birds amplified the quiet symphony.

The mild weather, even in the early morning coolness, ratified Hunter's choice of light cotton clothing—olive drab trousers and a long sleeve dark green shirt. Normal attire in the light of day and almost impossible to see in the fading darkness. The whites of his eyes were all that was visible in a swarthy face burned to a mahogany tan by countless hours outdoors.

He slipped along the path to the sniper blind he'd selected the day before, making no more noise than a shadow. From the blind, he would have an unobstructed view of the stable where Carmen was expected to begin her daily ride. The blind provided ample cover, making the shooter invisible to the target. His planned arrival time was a half hour before sunrise. He eyed his GPS running watch—5:19 a.m.

Right on schedule.

Drawing near, the impatience that seized him prior to each kill mushroomed—adrenaline pumping, pulse racing, breathing speeding up, mouth dry. He paused and forced his system to slow down, return to normal. Step-by-step, he practiced biofeedback to regain mastery of his corporal response, focusing on slowing his heart rate.

Mentally, he rehearsed the sniper sequence, mirroring actions of his body. Bracing to hold the weapon in an iron grip. Rifle butt pressing tight against his shoulder. Breathing controlled. Heart rate moderating. Index finger caressing the final trigger squeeze. The bullet speeding on its way.

The impact of the missile striking dead center between Carmen's breasts formed a virtual movie in his imagination. The crimson spurt as her heart gave a final gasp before it stopped pumping for all eternity. The quickening hardness in his groin gave him pause.

He struggled for total control. Conscious mind gained sway over innate savagery.

Drawing closer to the blind, he slowed his pace, pausing every few seconds to listen to the natural rhythm of the woods.

Something was wrong.

He froze. His predatory instincts were sending warning signals. Heightened consciousness filtered every sound and sensation.

The threat took human shape near the shooting blind.

A hazy form lurked in a patch of ground only twenty feet away. He waited, willing his vision to focus in the twilight. A Black man stood holding a pistol.

Carmen knew I was coming. THIS IS A TRAP.

For the moment, *how* she knew wasn't relevant. The imperative was to deal with his attackers.

Hunter was most deadly when facing danger.

Laying the sniper rifle quietly on the ground, he drew a razor-sharp Bowie knife from its sheath.

He crept toward the unsuspecting victim, whose head appeared fixated on the blind. Coming within the zone of attack, Hunter struck the hand holding the weapon and knocked the pistol to the ground. He seized his prey by his long hair, dragging him backward, prepared to slice the blade toward the throat to sever the carotid arteries on both sides of the Adam's apple. Suddenly, he felt a terrible pain in his right arm. The killing motion was aborted.

The stab wound shocked Hunter. Always the attacker, never the victim, the role reversal confused him.

The Bowie knife went flying before reaching the intended victim's neck.

Reacting instinctively, he pivoted and plunged his left hand like a lance into his opponent's solar plexus. The muffled GRUNT was proof the blow struck home.

Memory of the pistol in the holster at his side was overridden by the visceral need to best his adversaries with a blade. The Bowie knife glinted in the underbrush. He snatched it and slashed with one fluid motion. Clothing ripped, but he doubted he'd inflicted a mortal wound.

Two against one. I'll have to be quick. Kill silently. More cops will be coming.

He moved toward the first target, who was groping for the fallen pistol. With a swift kick, he knocked the Black defender away from the weapon. Following through, he plunged the knife into his opponent's side.

Pulling the weapon out, Hunter prepared to deliver a fatal stab. Without warning, a smashing blow struck the back of his neck. He staggered, trying to keep his balance, and moved a few steps away to buy time. His adversary followed and slashed his right shoulder.

Booker. The bastard knows as much about knife fighting as I do.

Hunter threw down the Bowie knife. His left hand groped for the pistol. Noise no longer mattered. He was in a battle for his life.

The handgun cleared the holster. He brought it to eye level. Prepared to fire. *Booker, you're a dead man.*

BAM BAM.

Two rounds struck Hunter's left shoulder. The pistol fell from limp fingers.

He stared in the direction of the third assailant. Pat Garrett stared back.

I lost to a rube sheriff, he thought and drifted into unconsciousness.

CHAPTER 89

The Jefferson County Hospital was humming like an overactive beehive, with staff buzzing about caring for the wounded. Book was feeling neglected. Dr. Warshawski had turned his care over to a resident while she focused on Deputy Williams and the assassin Hunter, both of whom were grievously wounded.

The resident, a solemn young woman whose ID read Ameera Nehru, confided she was from Mumbai, India. He recognized the metropolis as the historic city of Bombay from reporting of the 2008 massacre that killed and injured over 160 people. While she patched up the wound on his stomach, she kept reassuring him how lucky he was.

"Had the knife penetrated deeply into your abdomen, your liver could have been punctured."

The detective would have been more inclined to shrug off the impact of the Bowie knife, which had ripped open two inches on his stomach, as a minor incident, if Nehru didn't persist in describing the dire effects of stab wounds, not only on the liver, but on kidney, spleen, and intestines. Memories of stab wounds he'd inflicted intruded. He struggled to push them out of his mind.

After she finished suturing him, Nehru paused to admire her handiwork. "That should hold you. The sutures can be removed in a couple of weeks. Come back here if it's convenient. Otherwise, any competent physician can do the job. Needless to say, you should avoid strenuous exercise until the wound is completely healed."

She laughed, somewhat out of character for one so serious. "Follow doctor's orders. Don't get in any more knife fights."

Book wandered into the hall in search of the sheriff. He spied Ron Sargent seated in front of one of the recovery rooms reading an old issue of *People* magazine with Scarlett Johansson, featured in her latest movie, on the cover.

"Where's Pat?"

"Down the hall in Billy's room. Billy just came out of surgery. He's going to pull through.

"The doc's still in with that SOB Hunter. I'm standing guard once he's sent to the recovery room."

The detective headed down the hall toward Billy Williams's room. The sheriff was standing in the room staring at the empty bed. The patient hadn't yet arrived. Pat turned when he heard the door squeak open.

"How you doin', Book?"

"According to the resident who patched me up, better than I have any right to be. If I ever go to medical school, I've got a head start. She gave me three credit hours on serious wounds in the abdomen. My stomach will hurt for weeks thinking about it."

"I hear you. Speaking of 'might have been,' we were damn lucky we didn't lose both you and Billy. I've been second-guessing my plans for our trap to catch Hunter."

"Don't go there. When I was in Afghanistan, I knew a Jewish officer. He used to quote the Yiddish proverb: 'Man plans, and God laughs.' The saying was to remind us that when combat begins, the best laid plans fall apart. The main thing is we caught the bastard and Carmen didn't get killed."

They heard the squeak. Carmen was standing in the doorway.

"Damn straight I didn't get killed. Before you intercepted Hunter, Mary Connolly and I were beginning to wonder what to do next. Mary was calm through it all. The bigger the crisis, the better she performs."

The sheriff cleared his throat. He looked at Carmen.

"We'd have been in real trouble if you hadn't gotten the idea of using the Wellerton Agency to investigate Johanson and Carruthers. Hunter had no idea his conversations with them were recorded. According to Commonwealth Attorney Suffolk and Judge Newsome, we may even be able to use some of that material in court."

"Those two have certainly changed their tune," she said.

Pat shrugged. "Rural county politics. Robert Lee was the king. They know he's been dethroned. The power equation shifted in my direction. Odds are, I could be elected chair of the board of supervisors in the next election."

"Go for it," she said.

"That'll be the day," Pat snorted, sounding like John Wayne in an old western.

Jose Garcia and Lyle Manning walked into the room. Carmen hugged her dad.

Lyle asked the sheriff, "What would you have done if we hadn't located Hunter in the dark?"

"I don't know. We played the odds. We did everything we could to make Stephanie's farm the logical *place* for a sniper to attempt a hit on Carmen. Around dawn, when she has her riding lesson, was the logical *time*. There was little doubt Hunter would reach the same conclusion."

Lyle nodded agreement.

"There were four locations an experienced sniper could be expected to stake out. One of us was at each spot. Book was the floater. We knew *when* he was coming, and we knew *where*. The hitch was, when Book saw him in the semidarkness and alerted me, he'd already gotten too close to Billy. As luck would have it, we were able to stop him before things got out of hand."

Lyle said, "This has been a helluva year. We brought down Moretti, the Bronsons, and Hunter. The stage is set to bring down Johanson and Carruthers. It doesn't get any better than this."

CHAPTER 90

CHARLOTTESVILLE, VIRGINIA

With some trepidation, Carmen Garcia walked into the Boar's Head Inn. This was her first trip to Charlottesville since she'd graduated from the University of Virginia. Her first time back at the famous restaurant, which had been the setting for the final meal with her stepmom.

Tiger Tilly was seated at a table in the center of the dining room. A blond ponytail hanging almost to her waist contrasted with a black silk see-through Dolce & Gabbana sleeveless dress. Black undergarments showed enough of the attractive underlying figure to pique a viewer's interest. Carmen had no trouble identifying the ensemble, which was one she considered during the life-changing shopping trip at Tysons. In the end, the dress was rejected because Tilly ruled it "too racy for the image you're trying to cultivate."

Carmen gave a mental shrug. *Too racy for me maybe, not for her. I have to take the Tiger for what she is, since there's zero likelihood she's going to change.*

The young women beamed smiles when they embraced.

"Isn't this where you and Katherine ate before she was shot?"

"Yes. In a way, our lunch today is in honor of her memory. After Katherine was murdered, I decided to forgo law school and become a cop. Now, I've decided to leave the Sheriff's Office and enter law school this fall. The dean told me UVA's willing to agree to enrollment on the strength of my earlier acceptance."

With a quizzical expression, Tilly said, "And you want my advice about . . .?" She brightened, blue eyes flashing comprehension. "You've decided on a career in *politics*!"

"Of course. And who better than you to outline a plan to help me reach my goal?"

"You don't need any help from me, girl. You paid your dues in taking down Consolidated Mining and Energy. Once you've learned to fake sincerity as a 'woman of the world' and a mover and shaker of high finance, politics should be a piece of cake."

"I'm serious," Carmen said. "You've given a lot of thought to how UVA can be your springboard for future political success in Virginia, and maybe beyond. I'm open to hearing how I might do the same."

During the luncheon, they discussed Tilly's ideas about what courses Carmen should take in law school, what outside activities to participate in, summer jobs at prestigious law firms, and career moves after graduation."

In conclusion, Tilly said, "If we put your looks, brains, and money, together with my connections, we'll be an unbeatable political team."

Carmen left the restaurant and reflected on Tilly's advice.

Maybe I will join forces and run with her.

She smiled. *Or maybe I'll run* against *her.*

CHAPTER 91

MCLEAN, VIRGINIA

Rebecca Booker jumped out of the pearl beige Mercedes GL-550, waved to her soccer teammates, and ran up the flagstone steps of her McLean home. She turned to watch the spacious SUV speed off toward the late Friday afternoon sun. The teenager inserted a key, pushed open the double oak doors, and started inside.

She flinched when an attacker seized her neck from behind in a vicious chokehold. He forced her forward and kicked the door closed. He maneuvered her toward the wall displaying the keypad for the security system.

Her body went rigid with a combination of panic and resistance upon hearing a male voice growl, "Enter the password."

The chokehold tightened, cutting off the life-giving flow of oxygen to lungs and brain. Struggling to escape, every movement brought increased suffering. Dizziness impeded reasoning.

Terror coalesced in one thought, *Am I about to be killed?*

She gasped for breath when the chokehold eased.

The implacable voice repeated the phrase, "Enter the password."

Her fingers groped toward the keypad. Slowly and painstakingly, she entered the numbers for the security sequence.

After her attacker released the chokehold, her legs were so shaky she almost fell. The intruder helped her stand.

"See how much easier life gets when you do what you're told. Before we walk to your room, I'm securing these restraints so you aren't tempted to try anything foolish."

He pulled her arms behind her back and applied flex-cuffs. Having seen the devices demonstrated by her dad, she knew flex-cuffs couldn't be broken but must be cut off.

Ankle restraints were slipped over sneakers. Pushed ahead toward the stairs, she was able to crab forward in a shuffle, but there was no way to run. Escape was impossible.

Step-by-step, she labored upward toward the second floor where the bedrooms were located.

Am I about to be raped?

Rebecca was learning the classic lesson of captives everywhere—uncertainty heightens fear. There was no hope screams for help would be heard beyond the confines of the three acre lot where the Booker's luxury home was situated.

The closer they got to her bedroom, the more she hesitated. A stubborn streak kicked in. Stopping in her tracks, she refused to move forward.

"We have a choice, you and me. You can proceed to the bedroom and climb onto the bed. Or I will choke you until you do."

His quiet voice, speaking the unspeakable, was more frightening than if he shouted.

Trembling with fear, she tried to crawl onto the bed, but her body rebelled. He hoisted her the rest of the way. Sprawled on the bedspread, Rebecca inched away from her captor.

Fascinated, like observing a spider spin its web, she watched him set his backpack on the end of the bed, open it, and remove a long coil of slim climbing rope. He pulled a wicked looking stiletto dagger out of a sheath concealed inside his shirt, cut through the flex-cuffs, sliced off four lengths of the rope, and secured her arms and legs to each of the four bedposts. Rebecca knew there was no way to break climbing rope without a knife or other tools.

Terror peaked when her captor pulled out a roll of air conditioning tape, ripped off a piece, and moved it near her mouth.

"Please. Don't gag me. I promise not to scream. Besides, our house is isolated, and no one would hear me even if I yelled."

Her protests were ignored. The tape was plastered over her mouth and behind her neck. She could breathe through her nose, but her lips were frozen in place.

CHAPTER 92

"I'm home. Rebecca—you back yet?"

Reaching for the keypad on the wall, Jonathan Booker was struck from behind. Dazed, he slumped to the floor. Not quite unconscious, he heard a strange voice talking quietly, almost reassuringly.

"I'll enter the password for you. We wouldn't want to be interrupted by security, would we?"

Someone was pulling on his arms, stretching them behind his back. He could feel wrists being constrained. Ankles were ensnared in a similar fashion. He kicked out, but feet met empty air. Like kicking a phantom.

"Who are you?"

The phantom said, "You're in no position to ask questions."

Now alert, Jonathan tucked his knees and launched a powerful two-legged kick in the face of his captor. Taken by surprise, the intruder was bowled over onto his back.

Dazed, but quick to recover, the attacker stared at the youth, who was thrashing around on the tile floor of the foyer trying to get into position for a follow-up kick. Without hesitating, he struck a powerful blow to the teenager's crotch, ending the struggle in a heartbeat.

Jonathan's body contorted in pain. He groaned, choked, and felt the urge to throw up. No matter how hard he tried, there was no way his hands could move around his body and cradle his testicles, a perennial, if futile, effort of men to relieve the anguish.

"Any more attempts at aggression and I can promise you even greater pain."

The teenager moaned.

The intruder forced Jonathan to his upstairs room and secured him to the bed.

CHAPTER 93

Just after seven o'clock, Marlene Booker guided the BMW Coupe into the center space next to the Mercedes Sedan. She glanced over her right shoulder at the vacant space for the Toyota Sequoia and her face lit up, thinking of her husband.

She thought, *Book's rural detective's stint is over at last. He'll be returning to McLean tomorrow morning.*

She mentally ticked off her reasons to feel pleased. Her husband had escaped unscathed (*well, almost*) from perilous situations after confronting Hunter and other killers. He was coming home, a full-time husband and father.

Later this weekend, she expected a telephone call from Geneva. Dominique Legrand had promised to fill her in on the latest developments in Franco Moretti's negotiations with the Department of Justice to strike a better deal by further implicating the Bronsons in the conspiracy to set up Book.

Her husband was out of the woods on the Georgetown incident and finished with Jefferson County. She planned to devote this weekend to family.

I'll ask Rebecca and Jonathan what we should all do together.

She walked through the breezeway linking the garage and the rec room and stepped into hell.

"I'm home!" she called out. "How about we order Chinese?"

Marlene screamed with pain when a hard object smashed into her left leg below the knee. She knew from a childhood experience that her tibia was broken. Falling to the floor, she prayed to whatever saints looked after athletes, *Let it be only a simple fracture.*

The man standing over her held a baseball bat in his right hand, a stiletto in the left.

Through the pain, the bitter awareness of being the victim of another home invasion penetrated her consciousness. *Assassins?*

"Who are you? Where are my children? If you've harmed them, I'll—"

The intruder put down his weapons and clapped. "What a performance. I was right to disable you the moment you came into the house. I'd heard about you killing two Special Forces mercs—drowning one in the pool and shooting the other. But until seeing you in action tonight, I didn't believe the story. You're *formidable*."

Marlene couldn't resist sneaking a look at her broken leg. No compound fracture. The extreme hurt was there, but she was determined to ignore it. She focused on her attacker, who lapsed into French.

"Are you from France?"

His expression revealed she'd scored a point.

"*Bien sur.* Spunky and clever too. Even suffering from a broken leg, you guess I'm from France. Can you guess who I am?"

Memory flashed on her husband's account of the unknown shooter who'd intervened in Geneva when Book and Curt were taking down Moretti. She surmised he'd come to exact revenge for his foiled attack.

Mocking her terror, he laughed. "Some call me the Viper." He brandished the stiletto. "Behold, my fang."

She looked up, unable to resist pleading. "My children?"

"Your son and daughter are in their rooms."

Seeing her face contort, he held up a hand. "Unharmed. At present. Do as I say, and they'll survive. Take me to the master bedroom. Your husband returns tomorrow morning. You and I have time to plan his welcome home party."

CHAPTER 94

Saturday morning Book thought about stopping for a quick cup of coffee before finishing the last hour of the drive home. He even toyed with the idea of buying a pie to take home from his favorite bakery on the outskirts of town. But he decided to press on, anxious to return to a normal life with Marlene, Rebecca, and Jonathan.

What was I thinking, taking a job two hours away?

Contemplating the bleak future if the trial separation had led to divorce brought on a cold sweat. He gave silent thanks at having dodged a matrimonial IED.

Overall, he was content with the way things turned out. Moretti was in FBI custody and would soon be on his way back to the US. The fugitive's testimony would be the final push down the chute to prison for Robert Lee Bronson.

He was relieved at the prospect of being exonerated for the killing of Scooter in Georgetown. But it would be a long time, if ever, before he forgave his colleagues in the Metropolitan Police Department for throwing him to the wolves.

A team effort had saved Carmen and captured Hunter. He'd honored his commitment to Pat Garrett. Above all, Marlene stuck by him when the situation was critical.

Punching the gas, he watched the speedometer creep past eighty and began rehearsing stories in the event police in Loudoun or Fairfax County stopped him.

• • •

Bored by the silence, sitting in the bedroom watching Marlene lying bound and muzzled on the bed, the Viper peeled the tape from her mouth, placed her in a cozy blue velvet bedroom chair, and secured her hands in front with flex-cuffs. Believing a broken leg neutralized her as a threat, he left her ankles unbound.

Placing a bottle of water within reach, he handed her three Aleve tablets taken from the medicine cabinet. "Swallow these. The pills won't kill the pain, but they'll take the edge off."

"Why the improved treatment?" she asked.

"You make a better listener this way, and I'm in a talking mood."

"What shall we talk about?"

"My life. I'd like to share some stories."

"Why should I care?"

"My stories will prove truth is indeed stranger than fiction."

"Sounds as though you're a legend in your own mind."

"Don't forget, you're my prisoner. Sarcasm can be fatal, even wrapped in a cliché made famous by Dirty Harry."

"Sorry. I'm all ears." Marlene thought of Scheherazade. *If she could keep the Persian king from killing her for a thousand and one nights by telling stories, maybe I can stay alive one more day by listening.*

The Viper began with the story of his first killing. His father was a French soldier who fought in Algeria until the country won independence in 1962. Cruelty was common after such gruesome wartime experiences. He beat his young wife to keep in practice, and, by the time Henri (the Viper's birth name) was ten, he took a strap to the youngster at the slightest provocation. When Henri reached fourteen, he saw his father hitting his mother in the kitchen of the houseboat on which they lived. The youth, already as strong as most men, seized a frying pan and began striking his father in the head. His mother helped him dump the molester in the Seine and told the police her husband had deserted them.

A life of petty crime led Henri to be promoted to an enforcer, moving step-by-step up the criminal ladder, at length becoming a professional killer—a position he considered the top rung. His reputation grew, and he was able to command a fabulous sum for each hit. Prominent figures in many countries—politicians, businessmen, wealthy husbands whose wives came to despise them or covet their fortunes—all fell victim.

His trademark was execution with a stiletto. He relished telling Marlene how he used the Seine to dispose of the bodies of reporters from *Le Monde* and *Le Figaro* who mocked him as "the Viper."

Marlene couldn't resist asking, "Did you ever kill a woman?"

"In 1996, I murdered Louisa Kingsolver."

"The cereal heiress found drowned in her pool in Greenwich, Connecticut?"

The Viper smiled at the recollection. "Relatives paid handsomely to have her executed so they could inherit. They contacted me through—"

The story was interrupted by the ringing of the phone on her bedroom desk. The Viper looked at caller ID and saw the call originated in Geneva. He set the device on speaker so he could hear the conversation, carried the receiver to Marlene, and cautioned her with a stern look.

"Hello Dom, I've been expecting your call. Do you have anything that will help our Senate investigation?"

"Moretti's been a gold mine of information since he decided to negotiate for extradition. You'll be interested in the ways Ares Worldwide subcontracted with Afghan firms, who in turn contracted with Moretti's corporation to get the actual work done. Many bribes changed hands in the process. Other crimes, including murder, were committed. I'll send you an email with the details. If your investigators follow up, it'll save the prosecutors in Justice a lot of steps."

"We'll follow up. Are you getting any time off to enjoy Geneva?"

"I went for a short walk around lunchtime. This is a beautiful city. I intend to plan a trip here if I ever get a vacation in this lifetime. How are *you* doing? Is Book home yet?"

"We're fine. Book will be home anytime now, anxious for his favorite pancake breakfast. We usually have pancakes Sunday morning, but in celebration, we're moving the breakfast up to Saturday. Of course, he'll miss his daily helping of grits at the Jefferson Café."

"Grits?" There was a brief silence on the phone. Dom cleared her throat. "For myself, I never saw the romance in grits or understood how they got so popular in the South. Give me pancakes every time. I'll call again when there's fresh news."

The Viper tore the phone from her hand, strode to the desk, and slammed down the receiver.

"What's this about 'grits?'"

Marlene gave him a look of dewy-eyed innocence. "What do you mean?"

"What the hell are grits, anyway? Are they sort of like farina?"

"Grits are a popular Southern breakfast cereal, made from ground corn. Farina is made from wheat. Why this interest in American breakfasts?"

"I'm curious why you and Dom went from talking business to discussing food. It doesn't feel right. What are you trying to pull?"

"Maybe it's a woman thing. You wouldn't understand. Food is a central focus in our lives. Moreover, all of Book's colleagues know he's crazy about Sunday morning pancakes. In our marriage, pancake breakfasts are the main occasions we can get together with Jonathan and Rebecca as a family. He missed that in Jefferson County. But grits were important to him. Trust me on this."

Marlene knew he could detect the truth behind her words. *But his face says he knows I'm lying.*

The Viper shrugged in frustration.

CHAPTER 95

GENEVA, SWITZERLAND

Dominique Legrand scratched her right ear, contemplating Marlene's reference to "grits." She recalled Pat Garrett regaling her with the tale of how the waitress Annabel Lee had flagged danger by alluding to Book supposedly ordering grits for breakfast on the day the Clantons had set a trap at her home.

Dom dialed Lyle Manning. "Lyle, Book's wife is in danger. I don't know the specifics. I talked with Marlene at her home, and she used code language to alert me to a menace of some kind. Someone was obviously monitoring our call, and she was afraid to be explicit."

"What do you suggest?"

"Call Book and warn him. He's en route home, probably somewhere on Route 7 headed east toward Tysons. Also, alert the FBI Hostage Rescue Team. HRT can helicopter from Quantico to the CIA helipad, which is less than a mile from Booker's McLean house. They can be on site in a half hour."

"I'm on it."

CHAPTER 96

MCLEAN, VIRGINIA

Lyle phoned Book and summarized the conversation with Dom, conveying Marlene's coded alert.

Book said, "I've crossed the county line from Loudoun into Fairfax on Route 7. If I speed as fast as possible, I can be at my house in twenty minutes. I'll be there before HRT. No way I'm waiting for backup. Tell HRT to form a perimeter and wait for my signal. If they don't hear from me by ten o'clock, they should assume I'm dead and follow protocol."

Lyle knew there was no point in arguing. Book was determined to rush to his family's rescue. "Understood. I'll call Fairfax police and have patrol cars rendezvous with you on Route 7. They can clear the road and give you lights and siren. The convoy will help you avoid Saturday traffic. I'll brief HRT to expect an armed homeowner who's law enforcement and former SWAT."

"Warn Fairfax to kill the siren when they get near my house."

Book pressed the accelerator to the floor. He had no idea how fast the Sequoia could go. He'd heard the vehicle's top speed was over 115 mph. For fun, he'd raced up to 100 while cruising around Jefferson County. He was going to push the SUV to its limits.

In less than two minutes, a Fairfax County cruiser swung onto the highway, coming from the direction of Reston. Starting behind him, the cruiser pulled ahead. When he passed, the driver waved for Book to follow. The cop kept a consistent 100 yards ahead, pacing the Sequoia's best speed. Through the rear view mirror, another cruiser was visible, trailing by about 100 yards.

Contrary to Book's expectations, the cop steered the most direct route, cutting through the crowded intersection at Tysons and swinging north on Route 123. He was even more amazed to find police cruisers blocking major intersections along the way.

The detective wondered how the hell Lyle had gotten the troops organized so fast.

Once the parade of vehicles drew closer to the CIA, the sirens cut off. Before the entrance to the Booker property, the lead cruiser pulled over and signaled the Sequoia to stop.

The officer said, "I understand your family may be threatened by one or more intruders. HRT is en route, arrival ten minutes. I'm told you won't wait. Do you want us to go with you?"

"No. It's my home territory. The enemy's an unknown. Best I go alone." He held up his cell phone. "If I need help, I'll call."

Noting Book's weapon, the cop said, "You're armed, but I've got a Kevlar vest in the trunk. I suggest you wear it."

"No thanks. Maneuverability is more important than protection."

Waving his hand, Book ran down the driveway. "No time to talk."

He raced to the house, circling to the rear patio. An inconspicuous fire escape leading to an attic window was masked by shrubbery. He climbed, careful to make as little noise as possible. Crouching before the window, he reached behind a chimney on the roof, manipulated a keypad to turn off the security system, climbed through the window, and entered an attic storage area.

Feeling dampness on his shirt, he was startled to see blood, and realized the bandage applied to his stomach wound by Dr. Nehru was leaking. Her caution to avoid "any more knife fights" seemed oddly prophetic.

He crept down to the second floor, passed Jonathan's room, and spied his son tied to the bed. Slipping inside. he eased the door closed. Pulling the combat knife from his jeans, he cut the rope and flex-cuffs, leaving it to the youngster to pull off the tape.

"Are you hurt?" he asked in a whisper.

Jonathan ignored the question. Rubbing his wrists and ankles to restore circulation, he briefed his dad on the situation.

"I think there's only one intruder who bound both Becca and me. Becca's in her room. I think she's okay. I saw a gun under the intruder's shirt, and he's armed with a knife, like the paper cutter in your study. He took a baseball bat from my closet. I'm pretty sure he hit Mom with it because she screamed when she entered the house last night. I could hear them talking in the master bedroom but couldn't make out what they were saying."

Book handed Jonathan his knife. "Cut your sister loose. Sneak down the back stairs. Go out the patio doors. I've disabled the security system. Run to the end of the driveway. Two Fairfax cops are waiting there. The FBI's Hostage Rescue Team should be standing by. Tell HRT to enter through the patio. Brief them on the layout of the second floor. I'm going to confront the intruder in the master bedroom. By the time HRT gets here, I'll have rescued Mom. If not, they'll know what to do."

"Dad . . ." Emotions stored up over past months threatened to spill out.

"I know . . . there'll be time for that. Your job now is to save Rebecca and alert HRT. Hurry."

● ● ●

He drew the SIG SAUER and moved down the hall in a combat stance. At the door to the master bedroom, he paused to listen. To his surprise, the intruder was describing what sounded like an assassination.

Marlene interrupted with a question, apparently feigning interest in the story. "You'd been to Geneva before?"

Book instantly knew the intruder's identity and why he'd come. His intent was to massacre everyone in the house.

Rage clouded Book's vision.

No mercy. I'll kill him.

Book stepped over the threshold, aiming dead center at the intruder's chest.

• • •

The moment the Viper glimpsed movement in the doorway, he grabbed the Glock positioned on the desk and dove behind the blue chair on which his captor was seated. He heard the gun discharge and felt the bullet strike his outer thigh. The wound was painful, but not disabling. The imperative was to stop Book's assault. He leveled the Glock at Marlene's head.

"Throw down the gun or I'll shoot." Fingers seized auburn hair and locked her body to his.

Book had no target. The assassin's figure was masked by his wife. He weighed the risks of discarding the SIG versus keeping it pointed in the direction of the intruder. The .357 revolver nestled in a paddle holster in the small of his back provided insurance if he were to give up the pistol.

Before Book could decide, Marlene altered the dynamics.

She stretched her bound hands over her head and seized the Viper's wrist, forcing the Glock toward the ceiling. Ignoring excruciating pain in tibia and scalp, she pivoted her body, thrusting forward with her one good leg, pulling her assailant against her back as she spiraled toward the floor. The Viper's gun discharged, harmlessly, except for a shattered bedroom window.

Book placed two rounds in the assailant's shoulder. The gun flew across the room.

With his good arm, the Viper reached under his shirt and drew the stiletto from its sheath, threatening to plunge it into Marlene's torso. The elbow exploded with the bullet's impact. The knife fell and lay forgotten. The assailant bellowed from the pain of his wounds.

Walking toward the two entwined figures on the bedroom floor, Book pointed the SIG at the forehead of the intruder who had brutalized his wife, captured his children, and threatened his life. He prepared to fire.

Marlene shouted, "No."

She struggled to sit up. "You can't jeopardize our future to kill this son of a bitch. He's finished. Let the authorities clean up the mess."

Book hesitated. He heard Marlene's words, but his finger tightened on the trigger. After several moments, he holstered the SIG, collected the Glock and stiletto, hurled them out of reach, and bent down to embrace his wife.

Her voice choking, she asked, "The twins?"

"Jonathan and Rebecca are safe. They're outside with the Fairfax cops. By now, the FBI's Hostage Rescue Team has arrived. The good guys are in charge. Your talk with Dom did the trick. She alerted Lyle, and the rest, as they say, is history."

CHAPTER 97

GEORGETOWN, WASHINGTON, DC

Two months later, Book, Marlene, Pat Garrett, Dominique Legrand, Carmen, and her dad Jose sat at a round table in the private room in the rear of the 1789 restaurant.

Marlene said, "How fitting our special dinner should take place in the restaurant where Book and I went to celebrate our anniversary before Moretti disrupted our lives."

Raising her champagne glass, Dom said, "Let's toast a bright future." She gave a warm look to Pat, thankful their relationship was growing as time passed.

Accompanied by a murmur of good wishes, six hands were raised in a good will salute.

Earlier, Marlene had observed the waiter discreetly filling Book's flute with sparkling cider when pouring everyone else at the table a flute of Dom Pérignon champagne.

"Where do things stand with the Viper?" Jose asked.

"I have an update," Book said. "Once he gets out of the hospital, police in several countries are standing in line to try him for assassination, among other crimes. Fairfax police arrested the Viper, and the commonwealth attorney intends to prosecute for attempted murder."

Pat took a sip of champagne. "Robert Lee is going to court in Jefferson County. Judge Newsome and Commonwealth Attorney Suffolk are competing to see who can put the most distance between their past and future to show voters they're no longer beholden to Robert Lee. The big news, which I haven't had a chance to share with any of you, is we found the body of the man Bear Lansky killed at Bronson Stables. The corpse was hidden in a mining cave not far from the Farm. His name is Emil Lloyd. He was the one Lansky had hired to bug Abner Wallace's office to find out how much Abner knew about Ares Worldwide. Once the Pentagon learned there was a corpse, the brass stopped dragging their feet about bringing Bear back to the States to stand trial."

Dom said, "The Justice Department is working up a case to prosecute crimes related to Ares Worldwide, focusing on the conspiracy between the Bronsons and Moretti. Once our favorite fugitive started talking in Geneva, he couldn't stop."

Pointing at Book, she added, "He gave us chapter and verse about how you were set up in the alley near this restaurant. Two mercenaries kidnapped Scooter, drugged him, shot over your head with a revolver to draw return fire on the teenager, and helped Moretti escape out the rear of the alley. The Bronsons knew where the fugitive was hiding in Geneva. In fact, they arranged everything in Switzerland: plastic surgery, bank transfers, and buying the town house where Moretti lured the women he murdered. Robert Lee and Jeb used Moretti as bait to lure you to Geneva for the Viper to kill."

Carmen said, "Pat briefed me on the aftermath of the assassination plot at Stephanie Wilkerson's farm. Jefferson County has Hunter cold for my attempted murder, stabbing Billy Williams, and slashing Book in the abdomen. Thanks to Wellerton's recordings of conversations Hunter had with Johanson and Carruthers, Dom confirmed the Justice Department is investigating the corporate leaders of Consolidated Mining and Energy for the murder of my stepmom at UVA."

Book said, "A year ago, Georgetown was the scene of the worst night of my life. Tonight, Marlene and I have a lot to celebrate and friends to share the occasion."

ACKNOWLEDGMENTS

This is the third book Becky Hilliker has edited for me, and she has added immeasurable value to each one. It takes a team to produce a book, and the editor plays a pivotal role on the team.

I would like to thank John Koehler and the other members of his capable team for their role in publishing this book under considerable time pressure. Their work on *SETUP* met the high standard they set on *THE GENERAL'S BRIEFCASE* and *MOTIVE FOR MURDER*.

Danielle Koehler deserves special mention for her contribution in creating the book cover and in innumerable other ways. She also designed the author's website (raycollinsauthor.com).

Most of all, I am thankful for the support of my wife Betty Ann and our children, Jim, Ann, Nori, and Susan. Betty Ann has never spared criticism when my writing wandered too far off the path as well as offering innumerable suggestions to improve the story. Nori has made major contributions in many facets of book production. Jim, Ann, and Susan have been a much-needed cheering section.

www.ingramcontent.com/pod-product-compliance
Lightning Source LLC
LaVergne TN
LVHW041742060526
838201LV00046B/886